Cramoisy reached  took her hand reassuringly.

'Don't distress yourself, child. Listen to me. You were singing a fragment of Amaru's opera.'

'B-but you said it was burned. How could I have –'

Cramoisy raised his hand to stroke her cheek.

'You are your mother's daughter. You have inherited her talents, her gifts. You will need guidance in how to use them . . .'

'You mean – I heard the music in the Illustre's mind?' Orial could not begin to make sense of the revelation.

'It's a kind of music telepathy. That's how your mother once described it to me. You will need to develop great mental discipline if you are to use it effectively.'

'And you want *me* to transcribe the Illustre's thoughts?'

'He needs you, Orial. You could be the one to save him from his own despair.'

. . . Orial looked down at the table; her own hands, slender and unscathed, rested on the embroidered cloth.

Not my hands. But his . . .

She looked up.

'When can I meet the Illustre?'

Songspinners

Sarah Ash

MILLENNIUM

Orion Paperbacks
A Millennium Book
First published in Great Britain by Millennium in 1996
This paperback edition published in 1997 by Orion Books Ltd,
Orion House, 5 Upper St Martin's Lane, London WC2H 9EA

A CIP catalogue record for this book
is available from the British Library.

ISBN: 0 75280 582 7

Printed and bound in Great Britain by
Clays Ltd, St Ives plc

For Eve and Louis, my parents

ACKNOWLEDGEMENTS

My grateful thanks to:

Caroline Oakley, my editor, for her patience, insight and expertise
Alison Sinclair for long-distance writerly encouragement and commiserations

Steve Jeffery and Vikki Lee-France – for cheering me up

David Pringle: the Lifhendil first appeared in my short story 'Airs from Another Planet' in *Interzone*

And Michael, Tom and Chris

NOTE ON OPERA AND
OPERA SINGERS IN BEL'ESSTAR

The female roles in opera were always taken by castrati as women were forbidden to appear upon the stage (as in Rome in the seventeenth century). One or two castrati devoted their careers to the portrayal of female roles, thus acquiring the title of 'Diva'.

PROLOGUE

AT IRIDIAL'S SHRINE

Shadows flicker on the painted walls of the shrine. Shadow-petals from the slow-burning lotos candle, perfuming the vaults with its somnolent fumes, essence of summer water-meadows, sun-warmed shallows.

The girl sets the lotos candle down on a ledge.

Petals of rose-white light warm the dank darkness.

Meadows of painted primavera flowers embroider the walls, a constellation of star-daisies, marigolds, nodding windflowers, white and gold and azure blue.

The girl balances the cithara against her shoulder, picks up the quill plectrum . . . then lets fly a quiver of darting notes, sweet enough to charm the slumbering spirits of the dead from their sleep.

The lotos flame flickers.

The notes falter.

'Mother . . .?'

Her soft voice barely stirs the enfolding silence, the dusty, timeless silence of the vault.

The flame burns brighter.

The girl lifts one hand to shield her eyes.

Fire licks at the painted walls, flames burst into flower, smoke curls into the air.

The girl begins to cough on the acrid fumes.

Flames all around her, crackling, roaring. Beams come crashing to the floor. Sparks sting her skin.

'Mother! Help me!'

She stretches out her hands blindly into the blaze, trying to fumble her way through the searing heat.

The cithara drops to the floor.

'Ai – my hands, my hands!'

White fire flickers from her clawing fingers, the bones broken sticks of charcoal against the dazzle. The skin is blistering, flaking away in flecks of flame, weeping fiery liquid.

Her mouth twists wide open in a smoke-choked scream of agony.

'Aiii . . .'

The air trembles, shifts, re-settles.

No smoke. No flames. No fire. Only the eternal silence of the vaults,

1

the Undercity of the Dead.

The girl slides to the dusty floor, gasping.

Slowly, shakily, she examines her hands, finger by finger, palm by palm.

They are undamaged, the pale skin smooth and whole.

CHAPTER 1

Morning mists swathed the spa city of Sulien, mingling with the steam rising from the hot baths and pump rooms.

At this early hour, Orial thought, shivering as she dressed herself, the city seemed like a shadow of itself, the soft rose-tint of its ancient stones dulled to damp grey by the miasmic fogs. Only when the sun had dried the mists would the warm colour of the carven stone begin to emerge and the rose-stone city appear from the fog like the enchanted City of Khitezh in the legends. And by that time she would be occupied with Papa's patients in the Mineral Water Sanatorium, too busy to witness the moment of transformation she had so loved to watch on her way to the Academie for Young Ladies. But schooldays were over, she was eighteen now and her father's assistant, working with him in the worthiest of all employments: healing the sick.

The Sanatorium treated a wide variety of patients and complaints, ranging from gout-swollen toes to the many forms of rheumatism. A culvert and elaborate system of pipes drew water from the central source of the hot springs to supply the treatment baths and sprays. Patients attended for an hour or so a day; only the serious cases stayed within the Sanatorium whilst most others took lodgings nearby.

A fragrant aroma of brewing qaffë wafted from the dining room as Orial came hurrying down the stairs. Her father was already seated at the breakfast table, a cup of qaffë (black) in one hand, a pen in the other, annotating the day's schedule. Orial leaned down to kiss his cheek and sat herself opposite him, surreptitiously adjusting the slipping straps of her clean starched pinafore. Try as she might, she could not achieve the neat appearance of the other nurses in the Sanatorium; a stray lock of hair, a wayward strap, a loose button, all usually contrived to work against her. And Dr Jerame Magelonne was insistent that all his staff should be immaculately turned out.

Freshly baked buns, yellow and fragrant with saffron, steamed in the basket; she split one and spread it liberally with butter, watching the butter melt into the warm dough before taking a bite. The fun was in wondering when your teeth would crunch into the knob of sticky loaf sugar hidden in the golden centre of the bun. She watched her father reach for a bun, split it, butter it, eat it – and all without once looking up from his *Sulien Chronicle*. A smile began to twitch at the corners of her lips. How did he manage it?

'Singular,' Dr Magelonne muttered. 'Very singular.'

'What is so very singular, Papa?' Orial rose and refilled his cup with qaffë, then leaned over his shoulder to scan the columns of black print.

'This wave of piety sweeping through our neighbours in Allegonde, both the capital and the court. We shall not see Prince Ilsevir in Sulien this season; it says he has been miraculously cured by praying to the Blessed Mhir – and in consequence, has abandoned his life of pleasure to devote himself to matters of the spirit.

'Apparently he has ordered all the opera houses and theatres to be shut down. Not before time, in my opinion. Opera's a mindless, vacuous entertainment, fit only for those stupid enough to part with their money.'

'Opera,' Orial echoed wistfully.

'And wholly unsuitable for young girls of an impressionable nature!' Dr Magelonne said sharply. Orial retreated, nodding resignedly. This was an argument she would never win – and she had learned long ago not to pursue it with her father.

It was well known in the Sanatorium why Dr Magelonne vehemently resented any mention of music. When Orial's mother Iridial died, he had forbidden the playing of any music in the house. Orial understood. He had worshipped Iridial, who had lived and breathed music. Her death had almost destroyed him. The very sound of music would surely provoke memories too painful to be endured, so not one note was to be heard in the Sanatorium and there were no music lessons for Orial. Indeed, at her father's express wish, she had been given different tasks to occupy her at the Academie for Young Ladies whilst the other pupils received instruction in musical accomplishments. Yet whilst Orial dutifully plied her embroidery needle or dabbed at a water colour, she'd often caught strains rising from the music room below. And, oh, how she'd yearned to join in that distant sweet harmony . . .

'At least we are a more phlegmatic people than our hot-headed neighbours.' Dr Magelonne drank down the last of his qaffë and neatly folded the newspaper. 'There is always some kind of ferment seething in Bel'Esstar. Let us trust they do not try to bring their religious fervour over the mountains.'

'So what is to be done today?' Orial asked, returning the conversation to more neutral ground.

'The usual rheumatic complaints . . . neuralgia . . . and a stubborn case of gout. Nothing out of the ordinary, my dear.' Dr Magelonne sighed. 'We have to accept that the days of Sulien's glory have passed. When I was a boy, the Prince's father regularly crossed the borders to take the waters and all his court came too. But Ilsevir's interests lie elsewhere. He doesn't wish to while away his days in a fading spa resort.'

'Poor Papa. Longing for a complex and challenging case . . . and obliged to pass your days curing fat gouty old gentlemen!'

'Who all believe a couple of glasses of spa water a day will cure them. At least it gives me time to work on my treatise,' he said abstractedly.

A bell jangled in the courtyard. Orial jumped up. The first patient of the day had arrived.

'My cap. I've forgotten my cap.' She went hurrying up the stairs to find the starched white cap and, standing in front of the mirror, attempted to pin it on straight.

It was three days now since Orial had experienced the vision of flames, and since then she had not returned to the Undercity. It was the first time she could remember feeling reluctant to go back. Most days she contrived to slip away unnoticed from the Sanatorium to her mother's shrine for an hour or so. Only there could she practise the art which she had taught herself. The art which she loved above all other. The art forbidden to her.

Music.

So far she had contrived to keep her obsession secret. But of late she had begun to fear her fingers would betray her. She would find herself unconsciously tapping out the latest melody she had composed on the wall of the laundry room as she stood in the queue to collect warm towels. Or nimbly running figurations up and down the treatment slab as she waited to help peel away the hot mud packs from a patient. She could not stop. The music simply flowed from her as naturally as water flowed from the hot springs. It had become as much a part of her life as breathing. Concealing it from Papa was becoming more and more difficult. And she hated to have to resort to deception.

Up here in the cool Sulien daylight it was easy to rationalise what had happened. A dream. A waking dream. She must have become drowsy, practising down there in the dark, she must have nodded off for a few moments – and dreamed the fire, the flames, the searing pain.

It was foolish to stay away for fear of a vivid dream.

Towards four o'clock Dr Magelonne came out of his office with a letter in his hand. She saw her opportunity.

'Shall I take that to the post for you, Papa?'

'Thank you, my dear. I wouldn't normally wish to remove you from your duties at the Sanatorium but this is important . . .'

As long as she was back by the time the Sanatorium closed its doors to day patients at five, he would not worry. And she could post the letter in a matter of a few minutes.

Orial tied her cape ribbons about her throat, seized the letter and almost danced out of the Sanatorium courtyard into the street.

Free!

*

A stranger could lose his way under Sulien – and never see the light of day again. But Orial had been coming to the Undercity alone since she was a child. The underground labyrinth that the ancient city's builders, the Lifhendil, had constructed held no terrors for her. She had studied the plans of the labyrinth in the Museum and had discovered her own secret ways in the dark.

Few people ventured below ground now, only the ingenieurs who maintained the vast subterranean reservoirs, the Priests and Priestesses of Elesstar who officiated at funeral rites, and the bereaved who, like herself, came to light candles at the memorial shrines. Only once a year was the Undercity filled with people – and that was the Day of the Dead.

As a child, Orial had never feared the dark. To her, the Undercity was a place of hidden wonders. She did not believe the stories of blood-sucking ghouls who haunted the shrines, looking for live victims. She had seen the occasional brown rat in her explorations . . . and that was all.

She had come to love the ancient wall-paintings that decorated the Undercity. She had spent hours gazing at the flaking colours applied by long-dead artists of the Lifhendil until she felt she knew the people pictured there almost as well as those in her everyday life above. She had even given them names, characters: this tall, dark-skinned young man, with fishing spear and tuft-eared hunting cat slinking at his heels, was Black Heron the Hunter; these two laughing girls, arms interlaced, were Ylda and Nanda, the best of best friends (Orial had always longed for a close companion of her own age but Papa had never encouraged it). The Lotos Princess, her favourite, sat singing and playing a gilded cithara to a rapt audience. The painter had depicted the irises of her eyes with exquisite attention to detail: even with the fading of the centuries, it was still possible to see in the splash of lamp-light the tiny brush-strokes of rose-pink, purple and gold flecking the blue.

Rainbow eyes.

Orial passed the Princess and her entourage and entered the vaulted hall of the Reservoir of Blue Dragonflies.

Tall fluted columns rose out of the deep waters to support the roof, each column carved with lotos leaves. And every wall was covered with a frieze of water-meadows and rushes.

The Lifhendil sense of perspective and scale was a little skewed here, Orial thought, for the sapphire-winged dragonflies that darted across the water-meadows were painted the same size as the slender men and women who were pointing to them. The Lifhendil had portrayed themselves as tall, elegant, slim-waisted. Men and women alike wore their hair long, bound back in elaborate fillets and ribboned braids. The coloured gauzes that draped their bodies were as vivid as the jewel-colours of the dragonflies: sky-azure, crimson-garnet, grass-green emerald.

As Orial passed by her fingers drifted over the inscriptions that bordered the friezes. The people who inhabited Sulien nowadays had no way of translating the unknown language of the Lifhendil. The names of the dead were lost. The purpose of the Undercity was unknown. Ancient artefacts were unearthed from time to time in back gardens or foundation trenches when new houses were being built – but nothing had yet been found to shed any light on the practices or beliefs of the city's builders.

Orial skirted past the Lotos Chamber and slipped through the Hall of Green Ninufars. All was dark – and all was still, not even the black waters of the funerary reservoir stirred. No ingenieurs were dredging the surface of the waters today, no Priests preparing for a funeral . . .

The sudden low murmur of voices took her by surprise. She crept on – and saw a gleam of light.

Light in Iridial's shrine. Lantern-light.

She shrank close against the wall, wondering who could be in her mother's shrine, fearing tomb robbers, necromantists.

The lantern-light cast distorted shadows. *Flapping of torn wings, rotted cerecloths* . . . In sudden panic, Orial dropped her own lantern.

A figure materialised in the doorway, frozen, as if listening.

No. It could not be. The dead do not return. And yet . . .

'Who's there?' The voice was light as a woman's, sibilant with fear – yet the stance and costume were those of a full-grown man whose hair was dyed a startling crimson. This was no ghost. Orial snatched up the lantern and made straight for the doorway.

And the stranger saw her.

'*Iridial!*' The whispered name went echoing up into the dark vaults, faint as the drift of incense smoke. 'But they said you were –'

'N-no.' Orial shook her head. Her heart was beating too fast. 'I am called Orial. Her daughter.'

'Iridial's daughter? But – I thought –' The stranger was still staring at her.

'Who are you?' Orial asked, recovering her self-possession. 'And what are you doing down here?'

'So like her,' murmured the stranger.

Orial felt a shiver, chill as melting snow, trickle down her spine. No one had ever mistaken her for her mother before.

'Who are you?' she repeated. She had the oddest sensation that the stranger was blocking the entrance to the shrine so that she should not see what lay beyond. And suddenly she wanted to see, to know what he was trying to conceal.

'Orial Magelonne,' said the man in his curiously light voice. 'Daughter of Jerame Magelonne. Does your father still work in the Sanatorium?'

'He runs the Sanatorium.'

'Praise be,' said the man. 'Because –'

A groan, low and ragged, issued from the shadows of the shrine behind him. Orial froze.

'What was that?' she whispered, and tried to look over the man's shoulder. 'Who's in there? Who are you hiding?'

The stranger shifted, trying to block Orial's view. He placed his hands, heavy with ornate jewelled rings, on her shoulders.

'Can I trust you, Orial?'

'Trust me?' She stared up into his eyes suspiciously. But all she saw there was weariness and desperation.

'Cra. . .mois. . .y. . .' It was a man's voice, faint and racked with pain.

'You can trust me, I swear it. On my mother's name,' Orial said swiftly. 'Now tell me what's wrong.'

The stranger beckoned her into the painted chamber.

Another man lay in the corner of the shrine, half-propped against the wall. His head lolled forward, face covered by his dishevelled hair.

'He needs urgent medical attention.'

'But why did you not bring him to the Sanatorium? Why down here?'

'It's a long story.' The stranger knelt down beside the man, dabbing rather ineffectually at his forehead with a handkerchief. 'We had to be sure.'

Orial knelt on the other side; the man's breathing was shallow and she could see sweat glistening on his pale, stubbled face. His body seemed to exude a sour odour – the stale fearsweat overlaid with another, more pungent, smell. The smell of charred flesh . . .

'Sure – of what?'

'Is it safe, Cramoisy?' the man whispered.

'Safe from the officers of the Commanderie?' asked the stranger he had called Cramoisy.

'The Commanderie?' Orial repeated, not understanding.

'We are refugees from Bel'Esstar. Artists persecuted by Girim nel Ghislain's regime. Surely you have heard of Girim nel Ghislain?'

Orial shook her head.

'My father read me an article about Prince Ilsevir's conversion, but I have never heard of this Girim nel Ghislain before.'

'There! I told you!' Cramoisy said to the man. 'Now are you satisfied? We're safe.'

'Safe . . .' he repeated, and his head slumped back against the wall.

'He's wounded?' Orial ventured. She was swiftly calculating how she could bring help – and not betray her secret. Someone was bound to ask what she was doing down here when she had been sent to post a letter.

Cramoisy nodded.

'Badly wounded?'

'This is no ordinary man, Orial Magelonne. He needs the very best medical care available.'

'But what is wrong with him?'

Cramoisy drew back the cloak which he had draped over the man's body. The sickly odour of burned flesh grew stronger. Orial stared.

'His *hands*?'

Makeshift bandages swathed the man's hands. Even in the flickering light Orial could see that the white gauze was stained where some fluid had leaked through, clear and yellow as varnish.

'The Commanderie torched the Opera House,' Cramoisy said. 'His scores were inside. He insisted on going back in to try to rescue them. We tried to hold him back –'

'A fire,' she repeated softly, hardly hearing what Cramoisy was saying. She looked from her own hands to the clumsy bandages.

White fire flickers from her clawing fingers, the bones broken sticks of charcoal against the flamedazzle . . .

Coincidence . . . or premonition?

Cramoisy reached out and clutched hold of her; Orial felt the jewels in his rings bruising her arms.

'Do you think your father can help him? I'll pay anything he asks. Anything. It's just – if he loses his hands – he's a musician, Orial. A composer.'

A composer. A real composer.

'My father hates music. Even the mention of it,' she said.

'But if he's a physician, he'll have taken an oath – an oath to treat the sick, the wounded. No matter who they are, what they have done.'

Orial considered. Her father's voice, coldly accusing, resonated in her mind.

'Musicians. How could you disobey me, your own father. Orial? After all my warnings?'

'Orial, I beg you . . .' Cramoisy's eyes had filled with tears.

Orial looked again at the man with the burned hands. The pale face drifting between unconsciousness and waking was young, she saw now, he could not be so many years older than she. And for a moment she felt the anguish of his situation as acutely as if it were her own. Young, gifted, with all the promise of his life to come, blighted by an act of crazy, selfless bravery.

'Wait here,' she said, starting to her feet. 'I'll go and fetch help.'

'Well, where is this new patient?' Dr Magelonne demanded, coming out of his office. 'I hope our visitors from Bel'Esstar realise that I do not normally treat outside Sanatorium hours.'

'They've taken him to your consulting room, Doctor,' said Sister Crespine crisply.

9

Orial hovered apprehensively in the shadows as her father strode down the corridor. Spring was late this year in Sulien and the staff were still obliged to light the lamps by five in the afternoon. As Dr Magelonne reached the doors to the consulting room, Orial saw Cramoisy rise from the chair where he had been waiting.

Dr Magelonne stopped abruptly.

'What are you doing here?' he said in a low, tight voice. 'You know you are not welcome, Cramoisy Jordelayne.'

'I come not for myself,' the man said, drawing himself up to his full height, 'but for my friend Amaru Khassian. Please help him, Jerame.'

'I won't have you near my daughter. I won't have you corrupting her. God knows what malign trick of fate has brought you two together –'

'I came here because I could think of no one else who could help. No one else with the expertise.'

'I don't want to hear your blandishments.'

'I can pay,' Cramoisy said with chilly hauteur, 'if that is what is concerning you.'

Dr Magelonne looked at him without speaking.

He's going to refuse, Orial thought, anguished. *He's going to send them away.*

'You'd better wait here,' Dr Magelonne said. He opened the door to his consulting room and shut it smartly behind him before Cramoisy could follow.

Orial saw him surreptitiously dab at his eyes with his kerchief. She ventured out of the shadows and approached.

'You are shivering, sieur. You must be cold and hungry after so difficult a journey. Can I offer you a dish of tea?'

Cramoisy nodded.

'That's most kind of you. But – are you not afraid that I might corrupt you, child?'

'Please take no notice of my father. He doesn't mean to be so abrupt.'

The patients' parlour was deserted but coals still glowed in the grate. Orial hurried down to the kitchens and ordered a tray of tea with sponge fingers and seed cake.

By the firelight, she poured the tea into the delicate porcelain bowls.

'Sugar? Lemon? Do try Cook's sponge fingers . . . they are excellent dipped into the tea.'

Cramoisy cupped the bowl in his fingers and raised it shakily to his lips, sipping at the hot liquid.

'Have you lodgings for tonight?'

'I must wait to hear how Amar is first.'

Amar. Orial could still hardly believe it.

'Is he really Amaru Khassian? The composer of the opera *Firildys*? *The Cassalian Canticles*?'

'The very same.' Cramoisy reached for a sponge finger.

'And you are –' The light, musical voice, the smooth, hairless cheeks . . . Orial was sure now that she was in the presence of one of the fabled castrato opera singers of Allegonde.

'His Firildys.' Dark eyes met hers conspiratorially over the painted rim of the tea-bowl.

'*The* Jordelayne!' Orial clutched her hands together in excitement. 'The Diva! The toast of Bel'Esstar!'

'So my fame travels even over the mountains?' A slight smile flickered for a moment on the singer's lips.

'That was how you knew my mother.'

'Your mother, Orial, taught me everything I know. Without her I'd still be singing in the back row of the chorus. Your mother was – an inspiration.' Cramoisy reached for another sponge finger. 'You were only five when I last saw you. You don't remember me, do you?'

'I had no idea. I – I –' Orial tried to scry into the shadows of the past. Five years old. Just before everything had begun to fall apart – and her life was changed irrevocably.

'I was nineteen. At the start of my career. And I came all the way across the mountains to study with the greatest singer of the age: Iridial Magelonne. Do you know what they used to call her? The Sulien Nightingale. Her sudden fatal illness . . . so tragic. She had so much to live for.'

Cramoisy's eyes, warmed by the coals' glow, gazed into Orial's. 'So much to give.'

A thousand questions came bubbling up into Orial's mind. Here at last was someone who had known her mother. Someone who seemed not only prepared but eager to talk about her. Maybe Cramoisy could provide answers to some of the mysteries that shrouded Iridial's death. Mysteries that haunted Orial. She knew she had never been told the whole truth. She had a right to know what had really happened. She was hungry for information – and yet apprehensive of what Cramoisy might reveal. Was the past better left undisturbed?

She leaned forward and lifted the teapot.

'More tea?'

A turbulence of notes swirled about Khassian's brain with the violence of an autumn storm. Music so wild, so visceral, it shook him to the roots of his soul. Soon the page was spattered with a myriad black dots as he feverishly dipped his pen in the ink again and again

But as he scribbled on, desperate to capture the notes before they whirled away into the darkness, the black dots began to move on the page. He rubbed his eyes. Tiredness must be playing tricks with his sight. But no. The notes were milling around, a horde of tiny insects, crawling off the page on to his hands.

He tried to shake them off but still they came until his hands were covered in a coating of milling black insects. And the more violently he shook his hands, the tighter they seemed to cling.

He could feel the tug of tiny serrated mandibles, nibbling into his fingers, his palms, stripping away the flesh –

He was being devoured, eaten alive by his own creation.

In desperation he began to scrape his hands against the edge of the desk but only gobbets of raw flesh came away. He could see the white, bloodied bone beneath –

His mouth opened in a scream, a rasping scream of denial.

'Noooo!'

'Try to lie still, Illustre.'

Blinking in the lamplight, Khassian saw faces above him, faces he did not recognise. A man of middle years, his brown hair peppered with grey, was gazing thoughtfully down at him through gold-rimmed spectacles; a woman in a starched cap stood beside him.

'Who – are you?'

'My name is Jerame Magelonne.' The man's voice was quiet yet authoritative. 'You are in my Sanatorium in Sulien.'

The nurse was unwrapping Khassian's bandages, peeling away layer after stained layer. Beneath lay something claw-like, a raw, red mess of tissue oozing yellow liquid. A few charred flakes of skin still adhered to parts of the claw, others had stuck to the bandages and come away as the slow unravelling had gone on.

'Tsk, tsk!' Dr Magelonne clicked his tongue against his teeth in disapproval. 'Pus.'

'What – are you – doing?' Khassian said in a gasp.

'Lie back, Illustre.'

'What's happened to my hands? They shouldn't look like that.'

'Please lie back, Illustre.'

Sickened, Khassian sank back, fighting a sudden surge of nausea. He had always been squeamish, disgusted at the mere sight of blood, and hated himself for his weakness. 'What's gone wrong?'

'A little infection, that's all,' Dr Magelonne said briskly.

A little infection? The smell of the oozing flesh told Khassian that the physician was not being wholly honest with him.

'I'm going to drain the pus, Illustre. This may prove a little uncomfortable. Steel yourself.'

The doctor's probe sliced into his flesh. The pain of cold metal sang with a white and whining purity, honed steel drawn screeching across glass.

And then the cacophonous storm came whirling back and tipped Khassian into a howling vortex where all was chaos and darkness.

Orial sat gazing at her hands in the firelight. Slowly she raised them to the blaze until the flames lit the pale, flawless skin with fiery gold.

White fire flickers from her clawing fingers. The skin is blistering, flaking away in flecks of flame –

She shivered.

Not my hands, but his.

Amaru Khassian was a stranger from a foreign country. She had never seen him before in her life. And yet here in Sulien, at her mother's shrine, she had experienced his agony as the conflagration in distant Bel'Esstar seared his hands – as if it were her own.

What drew him here?

She saw again the pale face, the blank look of loss dulling the dark eyes that stared into hers.

What links us?

She gathered the tea-bowls on to the tray and set out towards the kitchen.

'The situation is grave, Diva.'

The door to her father's office stood open.

'Very grave. It is possible,' and Orial heard her father lower his voice as she went past, 'I may have to amputate.'

'Amptutate his hands!' The Diva's rich voice rang out, echoing the length of the corridor. 'But you can't! He's a composer – a keyboard player.'

Orial stopped, shocked.

'When did he sustain the injuries?'

'Three nights ago.'

'And how long have you been on the road?'

'We've been travelling since the night of the fire. Friends smuggled us out of Bel'Esstar in disguise.'

'If he'd seen a physician straightaway, then maybe there might have been some hope . . . But infection has set in. Wound fever. If it spreads, it will kill him.'

'And if we'd stayed to find a physician, he'd have been lynched for certain. Or burned alive for heresy. I believe that was their intent. Burn the Opera House – and all the heretics inside. Are you going to condemn him too, Doctor?'

'Of course I'll do all I can. Do allow me a certain professional pride, Diva.' Orial heard the stiffness in her father's voice; Cramoisy's words had stung him. 'I have the most advanced techniques at my disposal here in the Sanatorium. But there will be no miracles. The Illustre has suffered a very serious injury. Even if we can save his hands, I doubt that he will ever be able to play a musical instrument again.'

CHAPTER 2

He called me Iridial.

Orial stood at the oval looking-glass in her bedroom, gazing at her reflection by the soft lamplight. Her hair was still pinned up, confined beneath her starched nurse's cap. Slowly she drew out the pins and shook her hair free about her shoulders.

Do I really resemble her?

But her mother's hair had been fair, bright with the yellow-gold of early celandines. Her own hair was the golden-brown of velvet gaillardia petals – yet in the lamplight it glinted . . . was that what had made Cramoisy cry out? Or was there some other likeness, more subtle, of which she was unaware? Was it the way she moved, the way she held her head?

Orial sighed as she stared at her reflection. She could not remember. Try as she might to recall her mother clearly, her memories had faded to a few, bitter-sweet sensations. They were of a closeness, a warmth, never since recaptured; a voice, sweet and low, lulling her to sleep.

The portrait of Iridial that hung in her father's bedroom showed an ethereal young girl of delicate beauty, her hand resting against her cheek, gazing on some distant horizon. The colours of the portrait were muted, cloud colours glimpsed through a rainbow-haze of mist . . . Even her mother's eyes seemed touched with the iridescence of the rainbow: palest blue, striated with pink, amber, violet.

Rainbow eyes.

Orial had always thought it some fancy of the painter's. But now, as she unhooked the wire spectacles from her ears and peered more closely at her reflection, she saw for the first time that her own eyes were changing. The pale blue of the iris, paler than a dawn sky, was no longer the intense azure she had been born with. Were those streaks of rose radiating from the dark pupil in the centre? And gold? And darker violet?

'Just a few minutes, Diva. He's still very weak . . .'

'My poor, brave Amaru.'

'Cramoisy,' Khassian murmured as the singer bent over to kiss him. 'Are we . . . safe?' He shifted a little in the bed, wincing as the pain in his hands flared dully again, distant fires glimpsed through rolling smoke.

'Your hands. Do they hurt terribly? Dear, dear, you're feverish . . .'

The Diva dabbed at Khassian's forehead with a cologne-soaked hand-kerchief. The pungent scent nauseated Khassian.

'They've given me some kind of opiate to control the pain. I'm not always sure when I'm awake and when I'm dreaming.' His words sounded slurred, his tongue moved slowly, clumsily, in his mouth.

'I've brought a few little presents, *miu caru*, to distract you.'

Khassian blinked as the little room seemed to fill with hothouse flowers: scarlet trumpet-lilies, green-spotted orchids, bouquets and garlands which should have adorned the singer's dressing-room after the first night of the new opera.

'Cramoisy – you shouldn't have.'

'Nonsense. Nonsense.' He settled himself down beside the bed.

'The opera. It's gone, Cramoisy,' Khassian blurted out. 'Burned. Destroyed.' Damn it! He could feel tears welling in his sore eyes. He must not cry. Crying would not bring the opera back. Why this damnable weakness now, of all times, in front of Cramoisy?

'I know,' the castrato said softly. 'I know, Amaru.' His plump white hand reached out and rested gently on Khassian's arm. 'But there's time now, time to recover your strength.'

'Even the orchestral parts –'

'You mustn't upset yourself, *caru*. You must think beautiful thoughts to aid your recovery. Then, when you're better, we'll find a way to restore what's been lost.'

'All gone . . .' Khassian whispered.

Orial checked the schedules for the week ahead, scanning to see when she had been assigned to look after the composer Amaru Khassian.

Not once.

It was as if her father had deliberately left her out, restricting her work to the treatment baths and massage room – even the laundry. What did she fear? That if she were to tend Khassian she would be infected with his music, that it might seep on to her skin as she changed the dressings on his wounds? Or did she suspect Cramoisy – who spent a large part of every day at Khassian's bedside – of wanting to talk about Iridial with her?

'Why?' she whispered.

Her mother's death cast a long, chill shadow over her life. But she had learned long ago, with the stoicism of childhood, not to ask questions.

'*You must not distress your papa. You must not worry him . . .*'

The unanswered questions still haunted her. As if her mother's death had not been hard enough to bear, the silence surrounding it had made it worse. To this day, no one would talk about it. And, for want of the truth, Orial had begun to spin strange and morbid fantasies to fill the void. Sometimes she even convinced herself that Iridial had not died at all but had fallen in love with a stranger and run away with him.

And then she remembered the dismal funeral procession to the Undercity, the still, stiff form shrouded in white silk, the lapping of the deathdark waters, the slow, sad chanting of the mourners. She remembered casting white petals on to the waters. Papa on his knees at the edge of the reservoir, a sudden scuffle, people fighting to hold him, his voice raised, crying her name to the dark echoing vaults, as if calling could bring her back –

'Iridial! Iridial! Iridial!'

Fragments.

Fragments that did not make sense.

I will not be treated like a little child. I'm old enough to know for myself. I'm old enough to talk to whomsoever I please.

She took up the schedule and set off purposefully down the corridor towards her father's office. Hand raised to knock, she paused, hearing voices within.

She did not mean to eavesdrop. But she heard her name.

'I wish to apologise if I have seemed somewhat abrupt, Diva. It's just that I have the child's best interests at heart.'

'Child?' A smile coloured Cramoisy's voice. 'She's eighteen, Doctor. A young woman.'

'Orial knows nothing. And I want it to stay that way.'

'Don't you feel she has a right to know?'

'She is very precious to me, Diva. And I will do everything in my power to prevent any possible . . . recurrence. Do you understand me?'

Recurrence? Of what?

There was a silence. Orial drew away from the door, fearing she would be caught. But then she heard Cramoisy say, 'I'm not sure I do understand you, Doctor.'

'As soon as the Illustre Khassian is well enough to be moved, I want you to remove him from my Sanatorium. I would be grateful if you would make the necessary arrangements.'

The stillness of the Undercity wrapped about Orial like a dark shawl. At last she could be alone with her questions. But when she entered Iridial's shrine, she saw a sheath of ivory lilies strewn on the memorial plinth. Their rich scent perfumed the dank air, Orial could almost taste their perfume on her tongue. It was too early for lilies to be flowering in the fields; these expensive blooms were as rare as those adorning the Illustre's room in the Sanatorium. Cramoisy. He must have returned to the Undercity to pay his own tribute to the memory of his teacher.

Orial wandered around the shrine, unable to settle. Her secret place had been discovered, her privacy disturbed. After a while she reached behind the shrine plinth and lifted out the cithara from its hiding place, carefully unwrapping it.

The strings needed tuning ... but once Orial's fingers set to work the music flowed and the problems of the past few days receded. Receded for a little while ... for soon the thought insinuated its way into her mind that this strumming of her self-composed melodies was terribly amateur. There was so much she hungered to learn. The coming of Cramoisy Jordelayne and Amaru Khassian – real musicians – only served to remind her of her own limited training.

The cithara slipped into her lap, the strings' gilded reverberations slowly shimmered to silence.

'What should I do?' she said to the darkness. Her father's prohibition seemed so blindly, needlessly cruel. Had he any idea how much her secret pastime meant to her?

As Orial emerged from the Undercity by the upper gate into the late-afternoon light, she took a swift glance from side to side to check no one had seen her. The sun was dipping towards the west beyond the enfolding hills; clear light lit the winding streets, terraces and crescents below her, gilding the soft sandstone, warming it to a rosy pink. She shivered a little as she stood at the iron railings, breath caught in a moment out of time. She loved the ancient city. Its fashions might seem quaint to outsiders, its customs outmoded, even bizarre ... but she would not have exchanged it to live anywhere else – not even opulent Bel'Esstar.

'... two travellers ... foreigners ...?'

The distant voices penetrated her reverie. She looked around, wondering who was asking about foreigners. Few people were about; the more sprightly promenaders on the upper walks had already vanished, eager, no doubt, to attend the tea dance in the Assembly Rooms.

Further along the steep railings she saw that a tall man, plainly clad in a dark travelling cloak, had stopped the lamplighter who was lighting the upper links.

She came a little closer, planning to snatch a glimpse of the man's face as she passed by.

'Travellers come here every day. Strangers such as yourself, sieur,' the lamplighter was saying.

'One has red hair. Dyed to an unusual shade. Bright crimson.'

Crimson! Orial willed herself to keep walking. *Mustn't draw attention to myself.*

The lamplighter was shaking his head.

'Can't say as I remember, sieur.'

Who was he, this stranger? Orial risked a quick sideways glance and caught a brief impression of a stern face framed by long steel-grey hair. No other identifying features, no rings, no badge of office; dark clothes that betrayed nothing of the wearer's nationality or occupation.

17

Who is he? Suppose he stops me and asks me? I always blush when I lie. I would betray them –

In sudden confusion, she gathered up her skirts and began to run.

'And how are you feeling today, Illustre?'

Khassian could sense a distinct lack of warmth in the doctor's enquiry.

'You don't like me, do you, Dr Magelonne?'

'I'm a physician. I treat all my patients alike.' Dr Magelonne busied himself with snipping open the loose gauze dressings. 'Whether I find them sympathetic or not is irrelevant.'

Khassian winced as the last of the dressings was eased away. He had been enduring this unpleasant process now every two hours. He had endured it only because the stark reality of his situation was that, if he wished to save his hands, there was no alternative.

'Hm. This looks a little better than it did. A little cleaner.'

Khassian risked a glance, only to look away. The oozing mess of raw flesh and scar tissue in no way resembled anything that could be described as 'better' in his vocabulary.

'Tell me, Doctor. What – what is the prognosis?'

'When it comes to burns, I am not in the business of prognostication, Illustre. All I can offer you here is a programme of exercise for the joints and muscles if all has knitted back together satisfactorily. We provide the very best treatment here: hot mineral mud to ease muscles in spasm, exercise in and out of the warm spa waters. But I can in no way guarantee what the outcome may be.'

'I see,' Khassian said. In reality he did not see at all; his mind was a red, raging inferno. Somewhere beyond the terror of flames, he still screamed aloud, 'My hands, my hands!' as beams crashed down into the auditorium and clouds of smoke billowed up to choke him.

'And now I would like to ask *you* a question.'

Khassian gazed at the strange, claw-like appendages attached to his wrists where his hands used to be, slender hands, musician's hands, long-fingered and graceful . . .

'A question?' He tried to wrench his concentration back to their conversation.

'Did you know someone has been asking for you?' Dr Magelonne was washing his hands in a bowl, shaking the water off, meticulously drying each finger on a linen towel.

'Asking . . . for me? What manner of someone?'

'I'll be frank with you, Illustre. I have my other patients' wellbeing to consider as well as yours. If there is any likelihood of trouble –'

'Trouble? I don't quite follow . . .'

Dr Magelonne sat down in the button-backed chair at Khassian's bedside. Yet he did not relax, his whole body seemed tense.

'Look at it from my perspective, Illustre. Two fugitives arrive at my Sanatorium, on the run from a repressive regime in the country beyond our borders. They ask me to heal them, shelter them. Don't you think they owe me some kind of explanation if my generosity is likely to endanger my other patients?'

Khassian sighed and lay back on the pillows.

'Do you have papers, permissions, identification? How did you get past the border guards?'

'No papers . . . there was no time, Doctor. If friends had not smuggled us out, we would now be imprisoned, maybe even dead.'

'You will tell me, of course, that you committed no crime? That you are innocent of all charges?'

'My crime,' Khassian said, feeling a stir of anger, 'was to compose a work which dared to question the practices of the Commanderie. For this they labelled me a heretic. Have I burned down one of their shrines? Have I publicly defiled the holy texts? Have I tried to assassinate the Grand Maistre? Do you know what is really going on in Bel'Esstar, Doctor?'

Dr Magelonne shook his head. His eyes were still guarded, suspicious.

'Those who dare to speak out against the Commanderie are rounded up and taken away to be "converted". As a penance these converts are made to work from dawn to dusk on the building of a Fortress of Faith, the Stronghold. Girim nel Ghislain insists Mhir told him "in a vision" that this Stronghold would keep Bel'Esstar safe from the invading Enhirrans.'

Dr Magelonne's face showed no change of expression. 'And are the Enhirrans likely to invade?'

'Ever since the Commanderie took it upon themselves to "liberate" the birthplace of the Poet-prophet Mhir from the Enhirrans, Girim has been predicting a holy war.'

One eyebrow rose slightly. 'This is all . . . quite extraordinary.'

'You don't believe me?'

'The journals have mentioned something of this Girim nel Ghislain and his growing influence in Allegonde. But war with Enhirrë . . .' Dr Magelonne shook his head.

'He is a dangerous man. He has completely bewitched Prince Ilsevir.'

'Ah, the Prince. Isn't he your patron, Illustre?'

Prince Ilsevir. Khassian tried to hide the brief shadow of pain that flickered across his face. Ilsevir who had betrayed him. Ilsevir who had bestowed upon him the title of 'Illustre' and raised him to a position of privilege at court. Ilsevir who had been so much more than patron . . .

'*Was* my patron,' he said stiffly. 'Until his conversion. He insisted that I too should make a public affirmation of my belief. That I should publicly acknowledge that my opera was dissolute and recant my heresy. I could not do it.'

There was a silence in the room, a long, awkward silence. Dr

Magelonne seemed to be considering what Khassian had said, shuttling a roll of bandage to and fro between his fingers. Eventually he cleared his throat and said, 'Whilst I can sympathise with your predicament, Illustre, frankly I am still uneasy about your continuing to stay here. If these soldiers of the Commanderie –'

'Guerriors, they call themselves.'

'If these Guerriors are as fanatical as you make them out to be –'

'You want me to leave,' Khassian said quietly.

'I have my staff, my patients and my daughter to consider. It would be more appropriate for you to take lodgings in the city where I can visit you. I know of some very reasonably priced establishments . . . and I can put you in touch with a government official if you wish to make application for citizenship of Tourmalise.'

'And . . . my hands?'

'You want me to be utterly truthful with you, Illustre?'

Khassian swallowed. The doctor's tone had become even more detached than before.

'Tell me the truth.'

'I doubt you will ever regain the use of your hands. The nerves, the tendons, have been damaged beyond hope of repair. The playing of a musical instrument would be completely beyond you. I suspect you will even find it impossible to grip a pen or a conductor's baton.'

A chill mist seemed to envelop Khassian, numbing all his senses. Somewhere, far away beyond the frosthaze, he heard Dr Magelonne still speaking.

Beyond hope of repair . . .

Dr Magelonne, attended by two nurses, went from the hot mineral bath to the massage room, stopping only to wipe away the moisture which steamed up his spectacle lenses. He murmured a few words of encouragement to an elderly gout-sufferer, tested the mobility of an arthritic knee-joint, admonished a new patient for not restricting himself rigidly to the prescribed diet.

'A glass of mineral water on rising, another at midday and yet another at four. No alcohol – and definitely no spirits!'

But all the while, the stricken face of the young musician kept haunting him. It was as if he had read him a death sentence. Maybe he had been a little too harsh . . . but then, he believed it was better to tell the truth, no matter how painful. It might have been easier to come to terms with Iridial's condition if the experts could have given him any kind of realistic prognosis . . .

'Dr Magelonne.' The porter came padding down the corridor towards him. 'You have a visitor.'

'Now?' Dr Magelonne consulted his fob watch. Almost noon. He opened his diary, scanning the neatly written entries for the day. 'I'm not expecting anyone.'

'Said it was important. I've put him in the waiting room.'

Dr Magelonne opened the waiting-room door. A man was standing gazing out of the window, watching the rain trickle down the panes.

'I'm Jerame Magelonne. How can I help you?' he said formally.

The man turned around. He was tall, over a head taller than Magelonne. In the rain-washed light, his grey hair seemed touched with silver – yet his face was a young man's, burned dark by long exposure to a sunlight far fiercer than that which occasionally melted the rainmists of Sulien. Most astonishing was the blue of his eyes, a steely, penetrating blue, keen as a lance.

'My name's Korentan. Acir Korentan.' The stranger touched his right palm to his heart, an Allegondan greeting, Magelonne noted. 'I'm sorry to drag you away from your work, Dr Magelonne. I wondered if you could spare me five minutes or so . . .'

'Are you here on your own behalf,' Magelonne said, 'or someone else's?'

'Is there anywhere more private that we could talk?'

Magelonne opened the door to his office and ushered the stranger inside. Seated behind his desk he felt more in command of the situation.

'I won't waste your time, Doctor. I'm looking for a man called Amaru Khassian.'

'For what purpose?' Magelonne said carefully.

The steel-blue eyes did not waver.

'I wish to talk to him.'

Dr Magelonne assessed the stranger. His clothes were sombre; charcoal jacket, grey shirt, no adornments, all plainly cut to the point of austerity. A military cut. He wore them like a uniform. His whole bearing seemed to say 'soldier'. Or Guerrior of the Commanderie, thought Dr Magelonne, remembering what Khassian had told him.

'The Illustre Khassian is my patient. But he has been very ill. I cannot permit any visitors yet.'

A shadow clouded the peerless blue gaze. Annoyance at being thwarted . . . or a hint of concern? Magelonne could not be sure. He stared back at Acir Korentan, silently challenging him to gainsay him.

'I shall wait, then, until he is well enough to receive visitors. May I call again tomorrow?'

The lovage soup was cooling in its tureen, a skin beginning to form on the creamy green surface. Papa must have forgotten it was lunchtime. Again. Orial went hurrying along the corridor to her father's office – and stopped as she saw a man coming out of the study. The stranger. The stranger who had been asking questions about Cramoisy and Khassian.

She shrank into a doorway but he strode right past her, not even noticing she was there.

She watched him open the door into the courtyard, watched through the willow leaf-patterned glass as his shadow dwindled, disappearing beneath the archway. Only then did she realise she had been holding her breath.

Dr Magelonne was still sitting at his desk, eyes fixed on some distant point.

'Who was that?' Orial said.

'What?' He gave a little start. 'Oh . . . no one you need worry about.'

'I'm not a child, Papa,' she said sternly. 'He's from Allegonde, isn't he?'

Dr Magelonne nodded. He took out his handkerchief and began to polish the lenses of his spectacles, an activity he usually performed when he was troubled by something.

'Has he come to arrest the Illustre? You won't let him, will you? You'll protect him – and Cramoisy.'

'Listen, Orial.' Dr Magelonne stood up and drew her close to him. 'I don't want you to involve yourself in this matter. A good healer needs to cultivate a sense of detachment, hm?'

'But if they go back to Allegonde, they'll be arrested – tortured –'

'My dear, our business is to ensure that the Illustre receives the very best medical treatment we can provide. What becomes of him when he leaves the Sanatorium is *not* our concern.'

'But –' Orial began and then subsided. She knew it was no use arguing with Papa. She would have to employ more subtle means to maintain contact with the man who had known her mother: Cramoisy Jordelayne.

'Now what about lunch? I've worked up quite an appetite this morning.'

It only took a pasty and a mug of mulled ale to bribe the porter into telling her the address of the Diva's lodgings. But Orial would have not have had much trouble locating them; a street away, she could hear the sound of vocal exercises trilling out over the rooftops.

Cramoisy had taken lodgings on the first floor in one of the most exclusive of Sulien's crescents. The household was run by Mistress Permay who took great pride in gossiping about her aristocratic residents at the Assemblies. Mistress Permay looked at Orial with great suspicion when she asked to be taken to Cramoisy Jordelayne.

The apartment was reached by an elegant staircase of polished wood which curved upward from a marble-pillared hallway.

'Orial! My sweet!' Cramoisy pressed Orial to his bosom, kissing her cheeks, as if greeting a long-lost companion. 'You'll take tea with me? Splendid! Tea, Mistress Permay, if you please. Cream – and sugar.'

Mistress Permay gave a sniff and retreated.

'Does your father know you've come?' Cramoisy said in a conspiratorial whisper.

Orial shook her head. She wished the Diva had not mentioned her father.

'I can't stay long. He'll ask questions.'

'I won't breathe a word.'

Orial glanced shyly around her; taking in the gilded mirrors, the swagged brocade curtains, the elegant cushioned couches upholstered in delicate stripes of green, gold and ivory. Vases overflowed with spring flowers: pheasant's eye narcissus, vivid jonquils, muscari of a deep and tender blue.

'Diva –'

'Please. Call me Cramoisy.'

'Cramoisy. A man has been asking questions. About you. And Khassian.'

'Ah.' The Diva sat down, suddenly still.

'Someone must have followed you.'

All the animation had leaked from the Diva's face.

'But you mustn't be too concerned,' Orial ventured, trying to cheer him. 'Suliens don't like to talk to strangers – particularly nosy strangers.'

'What did he look like?'

'Tall. Long hair – grey – but he didn't seem old.'

Cramoisy shook his head distractedly.

'It could be anyone.'

'But what harm could they do to you here? You're beyond Allegonde's jurisdiction –'

The door opened and Mistress Permay reappeared, bearing a silver tray of tea. Cramoisy instantly reassumed his earlier vivacious manner.

'Tea! And some of your delicious petits fours, Mistress Permay. How thoughtful of you. I suppose it was only to be expected,' he said as he poured the tea. 'Girim won't let Khassian go. I wonder how many of the others managed to get away . . .'

'Tell me,' Orial said, 'about the Opera House. Before the fire.'

As Cramoisy talked, Orial saw the Opera House, alight with the glow of a myriad candlelamps, the sudden hush before the curtains opened, the surge of music from the orchestra hidden below the stage, the roar of the crowd as the Diva entered to sing his first aria . . .

The world of music in distant Bel'Esstar glittered like a dream-mirage. Entranced, Orial listened to Cramoisy's reminiscences and all the while she listened, she felt a terrible hunger.

'What do you feel when you first walk out on stage?'

'Fear. And elation. Such an intoxicating mix! It's like standing on a high, high cliff – and leaping off into the clouds, floating upwards on a current of music, almost touching the heavens –'

23

Arias, coloratura, cadenzas . . . Orial blinked as the unfamiliar terms rolled lightly off the Diva's tongue. He mentioned composers she had never heard of: Serafin, Capelian, Talfieri . . . She felt awed, humbled by her lack of knowledge. Her mother Iridial must have known it all – and more – at this age.

'Would you do something for me?' Orial, suddenly shy, could hardly enunciate her question. 'A favour?'

'Name it, child.' Cramoisy seemed in a generous mood.

'Would you sing for me?'

'But, yes. Yes of course I will sing for you.' The Diva rose to his feet and, clasping his hands, appeared to drift into a trance. 'Something simple, something requiring no accompaniment . . . Ah, I know. The little air Firildys sings when she is imprisoned: "Let me not die enslaved . . ." '

Cramoisy slowly walked away from Orial towards the door.

When he turned, she almost gasped aloud at the transformation. With one flick of the hand, Cramoisy pulled off his crimson perruque and dark red locks came tumbling down about his shoulders. His face, no longer animated, seemed pale and wan, his eyes dulled as they fixed on some distant point. He sank to his knees.

And as if from deep within the voice issued, low yet laden with longing. The melody gradually uncurled itself, a slow spiral yearning upwards yet never resolving . . .

Orial sat utterly still, transfixed. The music seemed to insinuate itself into her whole being; she was here, on the striped couch, and yet she was also, simultaneously, within the warp and weft that Cramoisy's voice was weaving. It had become the pattern of her breathing, the pulse of her blood . . .

Suddenly the air seemed to express all her lifetime's yearning to be one with the music, to live and breathe it as Cramoisy did. Suddenly everything she had done until this moment seemed meaningless – a fading shadow-world – and only the gold-spun threads of the music mattered.

And then it was over – and there was only emptiness.

'That was so . . . so beautiful.' To her horror Orial found her eyes had filled with tears; she was afraid Cramoisy would tease her for it. Her spectacles misted over; awkwardly she prised them off and tried to rub the thick pebble lenses on her apron to clean them.

'Look at me, Orial.'

Cramoisy's hand gently touched her chin, tipping her face up towards his. She tried to look away.

'You have your mother's eyes,' he said softly.

'Wh-what do you mean?' Orial swallowed back her tears.

'Has no one ever commented on them before? On their unique colours?'

'N-no.'

'And have you ever seen anyone else with such unusual eyes? Has no one ever spoken to you about them?'

'About my eyes?'

'I'm not trying to alarm you, child. Heavens, you've gone quite white! Here. Sit next to me.'

'You know something,' Orial said. 'That's why Papa didn't want me to talk to you. You know something about my mother.'

'I remember a great deal about your mother.' Cramoisy twisted his hair back and tucked it expertly beneath the perruque. 'But I don't want to antagonise your papa. Surely it is for him to answer any questions you may have about Iridial, not a virtual stranger?'

'Papa doesn't allow me to do anything!' Orial burst out bitterly. 'I'm not allowed to play music, to hear music. He won't have it in the house, not since Mama died.'

'So you have had no training, no lessons? No exposure to music?'

Orial stared down at her hands in her lap. Her secret. Could she trust Cramoisy?

'I – I have taught myself a few things.'

'Aha!' Cramoisy seemed genuinely interested and strangely unsurprised.

'I don't know if I am any good.'

'Let's give you a little test. The arioso I sang. I wonder if you can recall any of it?'

Orial focused her memory.

'Y-you must forgive my voice –'

Cramoisy merely made a graceful little gesture with one hand.

Orial cleared her throat. The green and ivory room receded, the ticking of the clock faded to silence. In her thin, clear voice she began to recall the poignant melody. The words escaped her . . . but the melody was as familiar to her as if she had known it all her life. After a while, aware that Cramoisy was staring at her, she stopped singing.

'Have you ever heard that melody before today?'

'Did I make a mistake?'

'You have an exceptional musical memory. Did you know that? Just like your mother. And –'

A whirring from the pendule clock on the mantelpiece interrupted Cramoisy as it began loudly to strike the hour. Orial started up.

'Five! I should have been back at the Sanatorium by now. And if Papa asks where I've been, I'll –'

She grabbed her cape and sped down the curved stairs.

'Thank you for the tea!' she called over her shoulder.

It was almost dark outside, a grey, misty Sulien twilight that dulled the roseate pink of the old stones to a sombre carnelian. The cobbles glistened with rain; one or two people hurried past, heads down beneath umbrellas. Orial stopped in the doorway to pull her hood up over her hair – and saw that someone was watching her. He drew back into the shadows of the doorway of the next house but not before Orial had recognised the tell-tale glint of watchful eyes, blue as polished steel.

CHAPTER 3

Khassian lay watching the raindrops slowly trickle down the unshuttered window panes. Beyond, a rainmist hid the distant green hillside from view. Did it always rain at this accursed spa? It had been raining since before dawn; he had lain awake listening to the drops pattering against the windows until the first wet light illumined his room.

Sleep eluded him. Whenever he drifted into a doze, images of flame and fire scored his dreams and he woke, sweating, terrified. There were other dreams too, drugged dreams, poppy-drowsed and darkly narcotic. Teetering on the edge of a black abyss, a stinking pit from whose smoke-wreathed deeps shrouded things crawled, clawing at him, threatening to pull him down into the depths.

Better to stay awake than to dream these terrors. Better to watch the dawn bring in yet another day.

I am twenty-five – and my life is over. All I have ever known, all I have lived for, is music. What use is a musician who cannot play? What use is a composer who cannot write down the music he composes?

He looked down at the burned ruin of his hands. He forced himself to try to move his right thumb, then the left. The new skin cracked and groaned. He bit his underlip until he tasted blood.

Nothing happened. He was willing the damn things to move – and the message was somehow not transmitting itself from mind to hand.

Fear. That was it. Fear of pain.

He must make himself endure the pain. It must be possible to make the mind triumph over the flesh, to learn to concentrate on the act of movement itself, not the sensation . . .

Exhausted by the effort, he slumped back, overcome by a sense of self-loathing. His physical frailty disgusted him. How could he be so weak-willed?

There was so much he still had to do. The opera. The burned opera. His most dearly cherished work. He had devoted a whole year of his life to the writing of *Elesstar*. It had become an obsession. It had not merely been a statement of his personal philosophy, it had become something of far greater import. It had become a plea for freedom, an anguished cry against the repression of personal liberties and the loss of free speech. It had been a single torch burning against the oncoming night.

And the forces of repression, they who proclaimed themselves to be the enlightened ones, had all but destroyed it and its creator together.

'Better they had destroyed me,' he whispered into the grey dawn. 'Better oblivion than this dragging life-in-death . . .'

It was all still there, in his mind. The score, the instrumental parts, the libretto, had burned to ashes along with the sets and costumes. But the phenomenal memory, legacy of the rigorous training his father had subjected him to from early childhood, retained every nuance, every note. Girim nel Ghislain might be congratulating himself that all trace of the heretical opera had been eradicated.

Girim was wrong.

There was some irony in that, at least, Khassian thought, a bitter smile twisting his lips. Somehow he would find a way to write it all down again. And, once it was written down, he would gather musicians, singers, to him here in Sulien . . . and there would be nothing the Grand Maistre and his Commanderie could do to silence his voice this time.

Another, more pressing, need had been nagging him for some while. He had tried to resist it but the urge to void a painfully full bladder had become inescapable.

Shamed, Khassian tried to reach for the bell on the table. Impossible to pick it up, let alone ring it! If no one came soon, he would wet the bed. Helpless as a doddering old man. His face burned with embarrassment at the thought. He leaned over the table and, after a few redundant attempts, caught hold of the bell handle in his teeth, shaking it from side to side.

In the distance he heard the sound of footsteps coming nearer. The bell dropped with a jangle to the floor as he lay back, exhausted by the effort.

When the nurse had departed with the noisome bedpan discreetly covered by a cloth, Khassian lay back and tried to forget the humiliation.

In the space of a few days, his life had shrunk to the confines of this room, his needs to the basic human necessities. He could do nothing for himself. He must be washed, shaved, dressed, fed like a baby. He, who had been the idol of the court at Bel'Esstar, was now reduced to this half-life –

'Illustre.'

Khassian looked around, startled. He had not heard the door open. And now a stranger stood in the room, a tall man, sombrely dressed.

'Who in hell's name are you?' Khassian stared at him through narrowed eyes.

'My name is Korentan,' said the stranger quietly. 'Captain Acir Korentan of the Commanderie.'

'So you've come to arrest me? Where's your warrant?'

'No warrant,' said Captain Korentan. He lifted his hands to show they were empty, as though yielding to an opponent in battle. 'And I come unarmed, as you see.'

'Get out.'

Captain Korentan stood his ground.

'I have nothing to say to you – or to any member of the Commanderie. Understand me? Nothing.'

The Captain sat down on the chair at Khassian's bedside. Khassian glared at him.

'At least listen to what I have to say, Illustre. The leader of our order, the Grand Maistre, is exceedingly distressed at what has –'

'Exceedingly distressed?' Khassian repeated, trying to hide the catch in his voice. Anger threatened to unman him, self-righteous anger that flared up, fiercer than the Opera House conflagration. 'Look, Captain Korentan. Look at my hands.'

Maybe he had hoped to see revulsion in the Captain's eyes, revulsion – and guilt. But the expression that momentarily softened the formal military mask was one of compassion.

'This should never have happened,' Korentan said.

Khassian heard the softer nuance in Korentan's voice but was so absorbed in his own anger that he ignored it.

'The Grand Maistre realises there is no way he can make adequate reparation to you.' Korentan instantly became formal again. 'He wishes at least to ensure that you have the very best medical treatment available.'

'And what's the catch?' Khassian said sneeringly.

'No catch.'

'Oh, come, Captain Korentan, do you think I'm that naive? What service must I then render in gratitude to the cause of the Commanderie?'

'No service, Illustre. We are a charitable order –'

'I don't need the Commanderie's charity,' Khassian said, almost spitting out each word in Korentan's face. 'Go back to your Grand Maistre and tell him he can keep his money. I want nothing from him.'

The Captain paused a moment as though about to speak – and then seemed to think better of it. He clicked his heels together, gave Khassian a curt bow and left the room.

In the kitchens, Cook was chopping vegetables and herbs for the lunchtime soup: leeks, waxy potatoes, spring parsley and chives.

'Morning, Demselle Orial,' Cook grunted, hardly glancing up from her work.

'Shall I help you?' Orial had been sent to restock the linen cupboard with clean towels from the laundry but if she was a few minutes delayed, no one would complain. And this was a good time to talk to Cook whilst no one else was around.

Cook shrugged and passed her a knife.

'Mind your fingers. It's sharp.'

'Cook . . .' Orial said, carefully shredding a leek into fronds of the palest green. 'What exactly did my mother die of?'

'She got sick,' Cook said bluntly. 'And there wasn't a cure for her sickness.'

'But what exactly *was* the sickness?'

Cook did not stop her work; if anything she seemed to chop rather more vigorously.

'I never knew the name for it. Doubtless your father did.'

'Cancer?' Orial said. 'Diabetes? Or was it some kind of contagion? Plague, cholera, smallpox?'

Cook slapped her knife down on the table.

'Heavens, child, why this sudden morbid fascination?'

'I'm not a child anymore,' Orial said defiantly. 'And I need to know. I deserve to know. Why won't anyone tell me the truth?'

Orial slammed her door shut and flung herself headlong on the bed.

Why would no one speak of it? Were the facts of her mother's death so horrible that they were trying to shield her from the truth?

Morbid fantasies invaded her mind, sickroom visions of decline and decay. These fever-tainted imaginings were beginning to distort her most cherished memories of her mother.

A loose tile in the bedroom fireplace concealed a hiding place where Orial had secreted her treasures since childhood. It was one treasure in particular which she sought now for comfort.

She drew out from the dusty crevice a slender volume wrapped in cloth. Opening the leatherbound book, she let her fingers stray over the yellowed title page, caressing the faded writing. The book's title, *A Treatise on Musical Notation with Divers Examples*, was underwritten in a graceful script 'Iridial Capelian'. This volume had escaped the bonfire Jerame Magelonne had made of all the musical scores the day after her mother's death, by virtue of its slenderness; it had slipped down behind the armoire where Cook had found it some weeks later and kept it hidden for Orial.

She had copied the exercises out, painstakingly ruling each stave line with care. She had set about the task of instructing herself in the finer points of musical theory with dedication, wrestling with the problems of ornamentation and transposition, trying to perfect her musical hand. She felt a closeness in working the theoretical exercises that her mother had once worked too; here a page was blotted with ink, there a passage was underscored with several lines and a question mark, where the young Iridial had laboured over its complexities. The image of her mother, hair in plaits, sucking her pen-top in concentration as she tried to work out how to complete a difficult exercise, always made Orial smile.

What possible harm could Papa have imagined would come to her through such dry, dull exercises? Did he fear her myopia might deteriorate? Certainly, as she moved the book closer to her eyes, the narrow stave-lines and tiny notes seemed harder to read than before. She held the spectacles up to the light and squinted through each lens in turn – but there was no trace of dirt.

I must be tired, that's all . . .

She unfolded her latest composition, smoothing the paper, and let her finger-tip move over the page, tracing the rise and fall of the melody. She could not but feel a swell of pleasure as she read through what she had written; it had taken a long while to translate the notes that flowed so easily on to the cithara into legible musical notation.

Her finger came to a halt over a passage where bars were crossed out, rewritten and crossed out again. She knew it was incorrect. She needed advice – musical advice of a kind that the *Treatise* could not give. She was so eager to learn, to improve her craft –

She shut the composition in the *Treatise* and sat with the closed book on her lap, lost in an impossible dream where Cramoisy swept her away to the Conservatoire as his protégé . . .

'How is my Amaru today?' Cramoisy leaned over to kiss Khassian's cheek, half-stifling him in a cloud of sweet perfume: orange blossom and syringa.

Khassian closed his eyes. He felt too weary, too soul-sick, to make the effort to talk.

'Shall I read to you from the *Sulien Chronicle*?'

He shook his head.

'Oh, my poor sweet. I know what's troubling you. It's your hands, isn't it? You're wondering to yourself what your future can possibly be . . . Now you mustn't fret.' Cramoisy stroked Khassian's cheek soothingly. 'I've had an inspiration. You need an amanuensis.'

Khassian opened his eyes.

'Dictate my music, note by note?'

'It's not a perfect solution, I realise that. But your faculties, thank the muse, are as acute as ever.'

To have to enunciate each note in turn, its pitch, precise time value, dynamic . . .

The act of composition had become as natural to Khassian as breathing. Long ago he had learned to weave and blend sounds upon the page, to translate the soundworld in his mind through the medium of pen and ink directly on to paper. The thought of trying to communicate his intentions through another appalled him. It would be like – like making love by proxy, giving instructions to a surrogate lover as to how to kiss, to caress, to arouse the object of his affections – whilst he watched, a helpless

31

voyeur. The image, at once obscene and absurd, repelled him.

'No.' He closed his eyes again. 'It's hopeless. I could never do that.'

'At least let's give it a try,' Cramoisy said coaxingly. 'We've known each other a long while, Amar. I know your music better than most people. And my musical hand was praised for its neatness at the Conservatoire . . .'

At last Khassian realised what the Diva was suggesting. *He* should transcribe the music: he, whose concentration barely lasted the length of an aria!

'Diva –' Khassian began.

'No, no, you mustn't try to dissuade me. It's a sacrifice I'm more than willing to make. A little less time in the coiffeur's, or with the tailor being fitted for new clothes, that's all it will mean. It's the least I can do for my oldest, dearest friend.'

It was, he had to allow, a noble offer. And Cramoisy, his Firildys, knew his vocal style more intimately than anyone else . . . anyone else in Sulien. But as to acting as an amanuensis, little more than musical secretary –

'Besides, the role of Elesstar was to be the greatest triumph of my career.' Cramoisy went gliding away across the room, one hand upraised in a theatrical gesture, the other clasped to his breast. 'The world must not be deprived of my definitive Elesstar because of a few canting fanatics.'

Khassian shook his head. The castrato's chatter was wearying him; he knew Cramoisy was only trying to distract him in his own inimitable light-headed way. But he didn't want distraction. Why didn't anyone understand? He wanted to be alone. Alone to mourn the loss of his life's work. Alone to mourn his spoiled dreams, his ruined future.

Orial could not rid her mind of Firildys's air. It wove itself into her dreams, it wound obsessively round and around her brain until she felt she would go crazy with the repetition. When she extinguished the lamp and lay down to sleep, her fingers began to itch to play it on the cithara . . . but to venture out alone on to the streets of Sulien in the middle of the night required more courage than she could muster.

She lay in the darkness, her thoughts constantly straying to Amaru Khassian lying in his plain Sanatorium bed two floors below. Could he really be the creator of that elusive, poignant melody? An aching envy racked her, that he should have been fortunate enough to be given all the opportunities to develop his gift whilst everything she had learned, she had been obliged to teach herself in secret.

At first light she rose. Going to the washbasin, she poured water in and splashed her face until the cold water made her shudder.

She sat desultorily dragging a brush through her hair, wincing as the bristles tugged at the snarls.

She could not blame her father for depriving her of a musical training. If anyone was to be blamed, it was long-dead Iridial. If she had not died, Dr Magelonne would not have banished all music from the house. If . . .

Orial threw the brush down on the floor. 'If, if, if. What's the use of wishing? Wishing won't bring her back.'

When she entered the morning room, she found her father reading the *Sulien Chronicle*.

'Listen to this, my dear.' He cleared his throat and began to read aloud:

'"DISASTROUS FIRE DESTROYS OPERA HOUSE.

'"Reports from Bel'Esstar, capital of Allegonde, tell of the destruction of the city's Opera House. The blaze is believed to have started in the green room during a rehearsal and spread rapidly to all areas of the theatre. All of the company escaped with their lives although there were several casualties, amongst them the Illustre Amaru Khassian. The Commanderie has paid for the Illustre to go to Sulien to recuperate."'

'Well! What are we to make of that?' He folded the paper and cast it down upon the breakfast table.

'The Diva told us the Commanderie torched the Opera House.' Orial picked up the pot to pour herself some qaffë.

'But can we believe him? He has a penchant for self-dramatisation. Perhaps he concocted this tale to elicit our sympathy . . .'

'And this version? Is it not equally likely to be propaganda put out by the Commanderie to cover their crime?' Orial said vehemently.

'You look a little pale, Orial. Have you been overtaxing yourself? And . . . I was probably mistaken . . . but I thought I heard you *singing* under your breath as you came down the stairs.'

'Singing?' Her hand shook, slopping her qaffë into the saucer. 'Surely not? It must have been Cook. She forgets sometimes.'

He took out his fob watch and checked the hour.

'I must go to take a look at our patients. See if they have passed a comfortable night. Take things easy this morning, my dear. I'll arrange for Sister Crespine to cover your first duty.'

Orial shakily poured the spilt qaffë back into her cup. A few stray drops spattered the *Sulien Chronicle*. As she mopped them up with her handkerchief, she stopped, seized with a sudden inspiration.

The *Chronicle*. Surely they kept records of all that happened in Sulien at their office? Iridial's death would not have passed unrecorded. Maybe there was some clue as to the cause of her mother's demise in the obituary column. And her father had just excused her the first duty of the day . . .

Dr Magelonne frowned down at the day's schedule.

He had not imagined it. Orial *had* been singing. In a low voice, soft and sweet, eerily reminiscent of Iridial's. And she had not even been aware – or so she claimed – that she was doing it!

It could only be the influence of the Allegondan creature. Orial had become rather secretive of late, disappearing on errands that should only take five minutes but took much longer. He could trace this behaviour to the night Cramoisy Jordelayne and his companion made their dramatic entry into the Sanatorium.

Well, it would all stop now. Khassian was out of danger. His bills had been settled. He could return for therapeutic treatment, if he so wished. Or – and Dr Magelonne lifted his pen and dipped it in the inkwell – he could be referred to another clinic on the other side of the city. Yes. That might be for the best . . .

'Dr Magelonne!'

The Diva swept into the office. Curse the man, was he psychic? The singer had dressed himself all in black: his chosen role for today, Magelonne guessed, was taken from tragic opera.

'I can pay Khassian's fees, Dr Magelonne.' He extended one hand and deposited a velvet purse upon the desk. 'No – don't ask me how I managed to raise the funds. I may regret the sale of my jet and diamond star, given to me by Prince Ilsevir himself . . . but we have to make sacrifices for our loved ones. It is all in the best interests of my poor Amaru.'

'Diva,' Dr Magelonne lifted the purse and held it out to him, 'the account has been settled.'

'What?' Surprise erased the tragic note from Cramoisy's voice.

'Captain Korentan paid the Illustre's fees last night. The Illustre is well enough to leave the Sanatorium. I have done all I can for him. Besides, it will be better for his morale to move into the city, where there are more diversions to keep his mind from morbid fantasies, from dwelling too much on what has befallen him.'

'He can leave?'

'Would you be so good as to arrange transport to your lodgings in the city? I will be needing the room for a new patient due to arrive later today.'

'You've done all you can? But he can't move his fingers! What are you saying, Doctor?'

'As his closest friend, you are going to have to be a support to the Illustre. Medically, the scars are healing. But the internal scars may never heal. He is crippled, Diva. If I were you, I would spend half that purse on hiring him a valet to attend to his personal needs. A discreet, quiet servant, who will not embarrass him by drawing attention to his disabilities.'

'La!' Cramoisy sat down in a flounce of black taffeta, as suddenly as if he had been pushed. He seemed utterly deflated. 'But – but what can I encourage him to do? His life has been dedicated to music.'

'He may in time become reconciled to teaching,' Dr Magelonne suggested, relieved that the Diva had not thrown a fit of artistic

34

temperament in his office. 'I am sure he has much to impart to pupils from his own experience.' His words sounded fatuous even to his own ears.

'But – you're not going to give up?'

'We can offer therapeutic treatment, but his hands are too badly damaged. It would take a miracle to restore them.'

Cramoisy gazed up at him, his eyes blank and stricken, and the doctor glimpsed for a moment the man behind the white mask of make-up.

'Do you really believe that Amaru Khassian can bear to continue living without the ability to make music?'

Khassian was dozing ... until he slowly became aware that someone was watching him. Someone whose blue-steel stare could pierce even through layers of sleep.

Acir Korentan.

'You are not welcome here, Captain,' Khassian said icily.

'I am aware of that.'

'Have you come to preach? My injuries a divine punishment for a dissolute life, the usual cant . . .'

'You've been badly hurt.' Korentan's voice was quiet. 'It takes time to let the wounds heal. And it takes a particular brand of courage to fight back when you've lost everything.'

More hurt than you have any capacity to imagine, Acir Korentan.

Khassian regarded the Guerrior through eyes burned dry with anger, an anger that still smouldered like an incurable fever. One foot tapped an obsessive tattoo. Yes, he had been hurt. And now he was seized with a vicious desire to strike back, to hurt those who had hurt him.

'And now you're going to tell me that if I have the courage to start out along the Path of Thorns, I'll find consolation for my injuries. You'll tell me about your moment of revelation, how your life was changed forever by one flash of insight. Look – spare me the sermons, Captain. Leave me to work through this by myself.'

'But you're not alone.'

'Don't waste your breath. I don't want to be consoled. Consolation's a meaningless concept.'

'Amar! Amar!' Cramoisy burst in, then stopped, seeing Acir Korentan there. 'Oh. It's you. The Commanderie agent.'

'My name is Korentan.' Acir bowed to the Diva. '*Captain* Acir Korentan.'

'I suppose you think us in your debt, Captain,' continued Cramoisy, not in the least put out. 'Is that why you're here? What do you want of us now?'

'You are in no way indebted to me or to the Commanderie, Diva.' Acir's manner at once became austerely remote. 'I merely acted on the request of the Grand Maistre.'

'What,' Khassian demanded from the bed, 'are you both talking about?'

'He,' Cramoisy stabbed his quizzing stick at Acir, 'has paid off your bill. Dr Magelonne wants you out.'

'And what does your Grand Maistre expect in return?' Khassian said, face immobile.

'Nothing but your full restoration to health, I assure you, Illustre,' Korentan said stiffly.

The offices of the *Sulien Chronicle* were in Angel Lane, housed in a crooked little building with its upper storeys timbered, overhanging the narrow street. A clerk was seated at a desk inside, a pencil stub stuck behind his ear, another in his hand as he busily annotated a handwritten sheet.

'Yes?' he said without even glancing up. From somewhere at the back Orial heard the whir of machinery from the printing presses. A tang of ink hung in the air, rich and darkly bitter.

'I wish to look at the *Chronicle* for the year '85.'

'Upstairs.' He gestured behind him to an ironwork spiral staircase which wound perilously upwards to a gallery above. Orial gathered her uniform skirts in one hand and climbed up slowly, step after narrow step.

The top gallery was lined from floor to ceiling with leatherbound copies of the *Chronicle*. Orial made her way along, craning her head to read the dates in the dim light. They appeared to be in chronological order.

At last she found the volume she had been searching for and hefted it out in a puff of dust. It was too heavy to hold, so she placed it open on the floor and knelt over it, leafing through yellowing page after yellowing page of old newsprint.

She could not have missed it. It was on the front page.

DEATH OF THE SULIEN NIGHTINGALE

It is with great sadness that we record here the untimely and tragic demise at the age of twenty-nine of Iridial Magelonne, renowned throughout all Tourmalise as the Sulien Nightingale. Her vocal artistry and sensitivity of interpretation were without parallel. Famed for her operatic career, she retired early from the stage on the birth of her daughter to devote herself to her family. However, she was soon persuaded back to the concert platform and her recitals in the Pump Room and Assembly Rooms in Sulien always drew large and admiring crowds.

Mourned by her pupils and admirers alike . . . etc, etc.

Orial scanned the columns in vain for any clues as to the cause of the 'untimely and tragic demise'.

The bland words in fading print intimately concerned her – and yet how curious it was to be reading about her own family, her beloved mother, as if of a stranger.

A later issue recorded details of the funeral procession to the Undercity: 'Crowds of mourners, many openly weeping, followed the singer's bier.'

Orial shivered; rubbing her arms, she found that her skin had prickled into goose pimples. Fragments of memory drifted through her mind, unconnected as gilded motes floating in a shaft of sunlight . . . and, just as swiftly, were gone.

Just five years old, she had witnessed scenes, experienced emotions, too terrible to understand.

'Not in front of the child . . .' 'Take her away, quick . . .' 'There's nothing you can do now, Jerame . . .'

It still did not make sense.

'All right, up there, demselle?' called the clerk below.

Orial blinked. His cheery voice jolted her back from the shroud-black corridor of her early childhood.

'Found what you were looking for?'

'Maybe . . .'

She was about to close the heavy cover when a name caught her eye. The official obituary column. The stark details set out in tiny, precise print:

'Iridial Magelonne (née Capelian), singer, in her thirtieth year. Cause of death: an ancient malady known as the Accidie.'

'What?' murmured Orial aloud.

'Beg pardon?' called the clerk.

The Accidie. It meant nothing to her. Orial lifted the heavy volume and replaced it on the shelf. *An ancient malady . . .*

She came slowly, carefully, down the spiral stair. At the bottom, she paused in front of the clerk's desk.

'Have you ever heard,' she said, 'of an illness called Accidie?'

He glanced up from his corrections, smiled and shrugged.

'Never heard of it.'

Orial stepped out into the lane. *The Accidie.* She had grown up in a Sanatorium, her father was a doctor, she had heard him and his colleagues use innumerable medical terms . . . and yet this one was unfamiliar to her. And why use an ancient term in a contemporary journal?

Dr Magelonne's study was lined from floor to ceiling with books of medicine and bound journals. Orial tiptoed inside, after first checking the corridor to make sure that no one had seen her come in. Her father was down in the treatment rooms, overseeing the first immersion of an elderly dowager crippled with rheumatism. Rheumatism was his speciality; he had written several papers on the subject and Orial was confident he would be busy for at least a quarter of an hour.

Dr Magelonne's obsession with order revealed itself in the meticulously organised shelves. Everything in its proper place, every shelf labelled: 'Anatomy', 'Rheums and Phthisis', 'Gout and its Treatments'.

Where to begin? An ancient malady might be found in an ancient tome . . . She pulled out the most decrepit volume she could see and started to check its yellowed pages.

'Orial!'

The book fell to the floor. Her father stood in the doorway.

'Sorry, Papa.' She dipped down and hastily retrieved the book, slotting it back in place, standing with her back to the shelf.

'Don't apologise. It's good to see you so interested in your work. When it comes to treating the frailties of the human body, one can never do too much research.' He came towards her. 'What were you looking up?'

'Oh – oh, nothing important.' Her hands were shaking; she hid them behind her back.

'You can always ask me. You know that, don't you?' He drew her to him, gazing earnestly into her eyes. 'I'm afraid I must seem somewhat preoccupied at present, Orial. My work takes up so much of my time. I want you to know that you can always come to me . . . and ask me anything.'

He kissed her on the forehead, his lips smooth and dry.

Anything, Papa . . . but the one thing I want to know.

CHAPTER 4

Acir Korentan strode past the elegant boutiques of Sulien on his way to the *poste restante*.

The trays in the baker's were piled high with elaborate confections of spun sugar, choux pastry and whipped cream – but where was the bread? Wholesome, honest bread, ballast for an empty stomach. True hunger could not be assuaged with such airy trifles.

Everywhere he looked, he saw triviality. The elaborately dressed wigs in the coiffeurs, the ambered scents drifting from the perfumiers, the qaffè houses in which so many seemed to idle away their days in gossip. Sulien was as hollow at the heart as one of the patissier's choux confections.

He was a simple soldier, accustomed to hardship and the ways of war. He had spent his years as a Guerrior fighting the Enhirrans to take back the birthplace of the Poet-Prophet Mhir. He could not understand the Sulien smalltalk about weather, who had won at lansquenet, who had danced the cotillion with whom at the Rooms last night . . . Had they no idea what was happening beyond the borders of Tourmalise? The world was turning upside down!

At the *poste restante*, he asked if any letters were awaiting him. One had arrived from Allegonde: he recognised the crimson rose-seal of the Commanderie. He signed for it and took it away to read in private.

It was drizzling again, a fine, cold mist that seemed to penetrate every pore. Acir Korentan shivered and turned up his collar. He could not get used to this dismal climate. After five long years campaigning in the red deserts of Enhirrë, he felt the damp in his bones.

Acir had been wounded on campaign. A scimitar slash across the shoulder in Enhirrë had left him babbling with wound fever for days; an arrow in the thigh at the siege of Ondhessar. Each time, thanks to the skill of the surgeons and his faith in Mhir, he had recovered with only a scar – and this cursed aching in damp weather – as evidence of his brush with death.

A thin, dark-burning smoke issued from behind the steamy windows of the shop opposite. He sniffed. The aroma of roasting qaffè beans was too potent to resist.

He pushed open the door of the qaffè shop and seated himself in an

obscure corner, close to the fire. The milky Tourmalise concept of qaffë
was insipidly weak compared to the strong, darkly aromatic drink he had
come to appreciate in Enhirrë. Maybe it was something in the roasting of
the beans . . . But the qaffë shop, with its dark-varnished wooden
booths, would offer privacy and warmth in which to read Girim's letter.

When the owner had brought him a steaming copper pot of hot qaffë,
he poured himself a cup and broke the seal.

'My dearest confrère . . .'

Dearest confrère. The words warmed Acir's heart. 'A diplomatic mission
of the utmost delicacy,' Girim had said, 'which is why I have confided in you,
Acir, as I can confide in no one else.'

'I am sorry to read that your efforts on behalf of our friend have so far
proved fruitless. Persevere, I beg you.'

Acir drank his qaffë, feeling his chill finger-tips slowly thawing. As he
placed the cup back on its saucer and reached for the pot to pour a second
cup, he was suddenly riven by the thought that this – even this – simple
action was beyond Amaru Khassian.

'For it is essential that our friend must come back to Bel'Esstar of his own
volition. Any attempt to use force is out of the question. We have no wish
to prejudice diplomatic relations with our neighbours in Tourmalise.
Neither do we want our friend to make himself a martyr to his cause.

'Nevertheless, I must remind you that if he remains resolute in his
heretical opinions, you may be obliged to resort to the other solution which
we discussed.'

The other solution.

Acir folded the letter, frowning, and slipped it into his breast pocket.

Never before had he doubted Girim's judgement. He had followed
Girim to the pitiless red deserts of Enhirrë, knowing that his cause – the
protection of the birthplace of the Poet-Prophet Mhir from the infidel –
was just.

But this seemed less than honourable. He was a Guerrior, a traveller on
the Path of Thorns. He was no assassin.

They had been walking in the Water Gardens of the Palace at Bel'Esstar
when Girim had turned to him. The memory was rippled with light, the
cloudy sky shot through with pale sunshafts, the silvered waters reflected
in the clear, intense grey of Girim's eyes.

'And if he establishes a core of revolutionaries in Sulien? One as
influential as Amaru Khassian could act as a magnet, drawing all the
dissidents to him. These are dangerous people, amoral, dissolute . . .
they could so easily wreck the work of the Commanderie. They could
destroy the dream for which we have laboured so long.'

'Is this man really so influential?' Acir could hear his own voice asking
above the trickling of the clear fountains.

'Believe me, dear confrère, he is. The Prince was utterly infatuated with him. He must publicly attest his loyalty to our cause – for if he does not, we risk plunging Allegonde into civil war.'

'But if he will not –'

Girim had stopped and gripped Acir by the arms, gazing into his eyes.

'Then he must not leave Sulien alive.'

'Kill him?'

'If he will not be converted, yes. As to how you kill him, that is up to you. You will have to make a professional judgement as to how and when – and you will have to be discreet. We don't want to make a martyr out of him.'

Girim's gaze pierced him to the heart; shafts of clear glass.

'Never forget, the future of the Commanderie rests with you, Acir.'

'Go away! We don't want your sort here! I'll call the Watch!'

Mistress Permay's voice, shrill with vexation, carried right up the stairs to Cramoisy's apartment where the Diva was pouring tea for Khassian.

'But I'm a friend of the Diva –'

'That voice,' Cramoisy said. 'Could it be –'

'Be off with you!'

Cramoisy set down the silver pot and hurried out on to the landing.

Khassian followed. He had reached the top of the stairs when he heard Cramoisy's astonished cry.

'Valentan!'

'You *know* this . . . person?' said Mistress Permay with a sniff.

'Know him! My dear Mistress Permay, this is Celestion Valentan, the celebrated tenor. Celestion, come in, come in. You look exhausted. However did you find us?'

Khassian saw Cramoisy helping a dark-cloaked man up the stairs, Mistress Permay fretting behind.

'It's all one to me, Sieur Jordelayne, but I'd rather those travel-stained clothes didn't come in contact with my striped brocades . . .'

'A fresh pot of tea would be much appreciated, Mistress Permay, I thank you.' Cramoisy said crisply.

Bloodshot eyes stared at Khassian from an emaciated, stained face darkened with several days' growth of beard.

'Amar?' Valentan said, reaching out towards him.

Khassian slowly raised his burned hands, palms upwards, as though to grasp the tenor's in greeting – and saw revulsion cloud the singer's face.

'Welcome,' Khassian said stiltedly.

'Tea!' Cramoisy commanded, steering Valentan into his apartments.

'The – the brocades,' he said, teetering on the edge of one of the striped and gilt couches.

'Fa to her precious brocades!' Cramoisy peeled the cloak off his shoulders and pushed him down on to the seat. 'Drink this tea.' He placed a bowl in Valentan's shaking hands and waited as he obediently gulped it down. 'More?'

Valentan nodded. A sharp tap at the door announced Mistress Permay's arrival with a second pot of tea; she put it down with a crack on the tray and, taking up the empty one, flounced off, not before glaring pointedly at Valentan.

'Her sand cakes are really quite palatable if you dip them in the tea.' Cramoisy demonstrated, pushing the little plate of shell-shaped spongecakes towards the singer. Khassian watched in growing amazement as Valentan wolfed his way through the whole plateful.

'Famished,' he said unapologetically between mouthfuls. 'Haven't eaten properly in days.'

'Then you'd better have these cress sandwiches too,' Cramoisy said, one eyebrow raised.

'Good,' Valentan said, nodding. 'Very good. I can't tell you how – how relieved I am to see the two of you alive.' There were tears in his eyes, tears spilling down his cheeks, leaving little pale runnels in the dirt. He seemed not to notice. 'Bel'Esstar's gone – gone crazy.'

'Tell us,' Khassian said.

Valentan wiped his cheeks with the back of his hand. 'I – I still can't believe I'm here. They arrested me. And the others. Singers, musicians, Poquelayne, Azare, Thanar . . . Rounded us up like common criminals. Put us up before some kind of tribunal.'

'For heaven's sake! On what charge?' Cramoisy sat down slowly, staring at him in disbelief.

' "Moral corruption." Girim nel Ghislain's term. It seems to cover whatsoever he wishes it to cover. A farce of a trial. We were all found guilty, all sentenced.'

'Sentenced – to what?' Khassian demanded.

'Oh, have you not heard of the Grand Maistre's humane methods of reforming the morally corrupt? I would have thought the Commanderie would have trumpeted their good works all over the whole continent by now.' Valentan's usually mellifluous voice was jagged with anger.

'We've heard nothing.'

'But you've heard of the Stronghold, Girim's Fortress of Faith? The place of worship to rival all others, centre of pilgrimage, erected to protect Mhir's shrine? How do you think Girim's building this mighty edifice, this hymn of praise in stone?'

Khassian shook his head.

'When I tell you that I and the others were sentenced to moral correction in the Sanctuary, you may begin to make a connection.'

'*You* have been building this Fortress?' Cramoisy said. 'But you're an artiste!'

'Not an artiste, Diva. A wretched sinner whose only chance of redemption has been to make a full public confession of my sins – and, like our patron Prince Ilsevir, to undergo conversion to the Thorny Path.'

'Oh!' Cramoisy said, shocked. 'How humiliating.'

'You must understand,' Valentan went on, his dulled eyes flaring at the memory, 'that I have been treated with the utmost compassion and mercy. In past times, we would have been burned at the stake or impaled for our refusal to be converted.'

'But this Fortress – it's being built by *prisoners*?'

'Forced labour. They call us the Sanctuarees. A Sanctuary . . . What image does that conjure up for you? A place of safety? A refuge? That's the image that Girim presents to Allegonde. His humane centre for the reformation of wrongdoers. *This* is the reality.' He tugged back his lank locks of hair, exposing his right ear. A thick metal tag perforated the lobe, bearing the number 329. 'Not Celestion Valentan any more. Just number 329.' The locks dropped back as he buried his face in his hands.

Khassian stared at him in redundant silence. Anger. Yes, he felt a kind of anger. But it was the anger of logic. The real fury was locked away deep inside him, a slow-burning fire frozen in a glacier. He could see the flame – but all he felt was cold, numbed by this recitation of suffering.

'I know what you need.' Cramoisy went to the stoppered crystal flask on the escritoire and poured a glass of the clear liqueur inside. 'Drink this. They call it pommerie here. It's an apple eau-de-vie.'

Valentan took a hesitant sip of the pommerie, grimaced, then nodded and took another.

'How did you manage to escape?'

'Me? Through the loyalty of the others. We made a pact. One of us should get away and somehow find help. We drew straws. I was the lucky one. They created a diversion . . . a stone unaccountably came loose from its straps as they were hauling it into place . . . I made a dive for the ditch and climbed up the boundary fence.'

'La! And did the Guerriors come after you?' Cramoisy cried.

'They shot at me!' Valentan lifted his cloak, showing a rent in the fabric. 'A bolt just missed my shoulder. Another grazed my cheek, see the mark? I was damned lucky it wasn't worse. The only advantage I had was my intimate knowledge of the backstreets of Bel'Esstar. These Guerriors have spent too long defending Allegonde overseas. I gave them the slip . . .'

'But how did you know to come here?' Khassian said. 'To Sulien?'

'It's no secret that you're in Sulien. Look.' Valentan fumbled in his mud-spattered jacket and brought out a folded newspaper, much crumpled. Cramoisy refilled Valentan's glass and shook out the newspaper to decipher the smudged print:

Following the disastrous fire at the Opera House, the *Diurnal* is distressed to have to report that Amaru Khassian, composer, was so upset at the loss of his scores that the balance of his mind was disturbed.

Girim nel Ghislain, Grand Maistre of the Commanderie, has generously paid out of his personal funds for the Illustre to seek treatment at the Asylum for the Insane at the well-known spa resort of Sulien in neighbouring Tourmalise. Accompanying the composer is gifted Diva, Cramoisy Jordelayne . . .

'Lies!' whispered Khassian. 'All lies.'

'I rather like the "gifted Diva" passage. You didn't let me finish.'

'And you believed this?' Khassian nodded towards the paper.

'In the chaos of the fire, no one saw what happened to you afterwards. We were all hefting buckets of water, running around like idiots. No one realised how badly hurt you were.'

'So you came to Sulien and asked for me at the Asylum?' Khassian said.

'They didn't seem too eager to receive visitors. But then, I don't suppose I looked too prepossessing like this.' Valentan ruefully indicated the straggly beard, the tattered clothes. 'But I wasn't going to give up. I hadn't come all this way over the mountains for nothing. I knocked at the door of every clinic, every sanatorium, in the city, until I was given this address.'

'But *insane*? You believed that I had gone insane?' Khassian got to his feet and began to pace. He was aware that Cramoisy was watching him apprehensively.

'It made sense. The shock of the fire –'

'Insane. That suits Girim's purpose so well.' Khassian could not stop pacing, could not contain the restlessness that Valentan's news had released. 'He can't arrest me here in Sulien – but he can discredit my work as the inane ramblings of a madman. Who else but a madman would write an opera as contentious as mine?'

'Amar –' Cramoisy was delicately wiping the newsprint from his finger-tips with a broderie handkerchief.

Khassian suddenly stopped by Valentan's chair and stared coldly down at him.

'How do I know that you're telling the truth, Valentan? How do I know that you're not another of Girim's agents, come to seek me out?'

'Amar!' Cramoisy exclaimed, one hand fluttering close to his rose-painted lips.

'*How* do I know?' Khassian repeated, ignoring him.

'You must excuse him, Celestion.' Cramoisy put his hands on

Khassian's shoulders. 'Can't this wait till tomorrow? Valentan needs sleep.'

'I have to know.'

'I can't prove anything to you,' Valentan said, his voice faint with weariness. 'All I can tell you is that to see you both here, alive, has given me hope again . . .'

Khassian still stared at his haggard face, the half-closed eyes, lids drooping with exhaustion. He wanted to believe him. But since the fire, he had become wary of everyone, even those he had once called his friends.

'We'll talk,' he said finally, 'in the morning.'

Acir Korentan sat up late into the night in his lodgings, reading his worn copy of the *Vineyard Verses* by the light of a single candle. Girim nel Ghislain had given him the book when he first joined the Commanderie and he had carried it with him ever since.

'*The Way is choked with thorns, yet bleeding, torn, I must go onwards into the darkness. I must bear the torch of Your word to set the hearts of the people aflame.*'

He scarcely needed the meagre light to see the words; he knew them by heart. When alone and shivering in the Enhirran desert night, he had repeated them again and again to comfort himself.

Oh, to relive those glorious days of the desert campaign when he had followed Girim's banner and fought to drive the infidel Enhirrans from the Poet-Prophet Mhir's birthplace! The Princes of Allegonde had neglected to garrison their distant desert citadel – and the holy place where the Prophet was born had fallen to the Enhirrans. The young Guerriors of the Commanderie fought a bloody and bitter campaign to relieve the citadel . . . and to the glory of Iel's name, had eventually driven the infidels out. Tears still stung Acir's eyes when he remembered singing Iel's praises with his confrères in the birthplace shrine; exhausted yet exultant from battle, they had raised their voices in a paean of praise.

He was a soldier, first and foremost. He had no skills as a negotiator. His eyes kept straying to Girim's latest letter.

'Stop this rebellion before it starts. If he will not come to us of his own volition, then you must take action of a different kind.'

Kill Amaru Khassian.

He took up his pen and began to write.

'Give me longer, just a little longer. These are delicate matters and take time –'

Begging words. Demeaning for a Guerrior to have to beg.

He slashed the words out and crushed the spoiled paper in his first.

He had no truck with assassination. He had always fought his adversaries face to face, blade to blade. He would not skulk in dark alleys, stalking his victim like a thief.

Why was Girim in such a hurry? Two or three escaped musicians did not constitute a revolution. So far as Acir could tell, the castrato was only interested in furthering his own career, frittering away his meagre funds on wigs and cosmetics.

Never before had he had cause to question the Grand Maistre's orders. Now it weighed heavily upon his conscience: disobedience to the one he had sworn on his life to obey in all matters, both temporal and spiritual.

'Show me what I must do,' he said aloud. 'Send me a sign.'

A red haze of tiredness swam before his eyes; slowly his head slid forward until it was pillowed upon the open book and he slept.

Red haze. Heat haze.

He trudged on across the endless red sands. His throat was parched dry. Overhead the sun had burnished the cloudless sky to the patina of beaten copper.

Must keep going. Mustn't stop.

Sun-scorch in his eyes, sun-scorch searing his back.

A swirl of darkness on the distant horizon. Sandstorm.

Copper sky darkening fast, dust-daemons, whirling and twirling towards him. Sands singing, strange, high whine of the wind.

Must reach the citadel. Girim's message must get through.

He wrapped a scarf tightly about his face, head down to the oncoming storm.

Struck suddenly by the force of the dry wind – the storm spun him around – grit stung his skin, a fine rain of lacerating dust particles filled his eyes. Blinded, he dropped to his knees as the whirlwind of sand came eddying up about him.

Scarlet sand in his nose, his mouth, a dry, choking tide of it.

'Help me, Blessed Mhir, don't let your servant die –'

And then he heard a rushing – as if the convulsive beat of great wings was cleaving the swirling sand.

He was no longer alone. A presence hovered above him, dark as smoke.

Hands reached down to him, lifted him. He was rising slowly through the seething sandcloud, rising into the grey air.

Wingbeats throbbed in his ears, powerful wingbeats echoing the throbbing pulse of his own blood.

And then water, cool as spring rain, laved his sand-burned eyes, his cracked lips. Water flowed into his parched mouth.

Life-giving water. Now he had the strength to go on, to complete his mission.

'The message –'

'Look,' commanded a voice, a voice which trembled through him with the terrible majesty of thunder.

Far below, as the swirling dustclouds parted, Acir saw a figure sprawled in the sand, face-down. In the distance a white mirage shimmered: the gleaming walls of the citadel and the safe haven of the Commanderie.

Cloaked in storm-grey feathers tipped with flame they swooped down out of the sandclouds. And as they hovered closer, Acir's heart smote him. He recognised the prone figure.

Amaru Khassian. Alone and helpless in the red expanse of empty desert.

'Choose, Guerrior. Save him – or deliver your message.'

Agonised, Acir started down at Khassian. The shifting sands were already beginning to cover his body . . . No one could survive that storm for long. And yet if he stopped to save the musician, his message would not get through and the citadel would be destroyed.

'The choice is yours, Acir.'

Acir paused as he approached Mistress Permay's house in the Crescent.

Amaru Khassian stood at the window, staring out across the lawns to the misty hills beyond. His intended victim. The rebel he had been ordered to save – or kill.

Acir saw not the cynical, manipulative artist Girim had described but only a vulnerable young man, face pale and drawn with pain, brown eyes riven with a lost, hopeless expression.

His tousled hair was untied, unkempt, straying into his eyes; from time to time he irritably shook it back. His whole appearance was neglected, as if he no longer cared what image he presented to the world.

Mistress Permay showed Acir into the morning room where Khassian still stood staring out of the window.

'You have a visitor, Illustre,' she announced, bobbing a curtsey.

As Khassian glanced round, Acir saw the air of vulnerability vanish and his face set into a hostile scowl.

'What are you doing here?' he said sullenly.

'I come as the Grand Maistre's official emissary.'

'I told you – I have nothing to say to you.'

'At least listen to the Commanderie's proposition, Illustre,' Acir said earnestly.

'I'm surprised you propose anything to a madman. A lunatic.'

'I – I don't quite follow –'

'But all Allegonde knows, Captain. It was in the *Diurnal* – and as everyone knows, if the news is reported in the *Diurnal*, it must be true. The shock of the fire has made me lose my wits. I am at present confined in the Sulien Asylum for the Insane.'

'I knew nothing about this,' Acir said, puzzled.

'Neither did the Asylum Director.' The brown eyes mocked him. 'So. What is this proposition?'

'Come back to Bel'Esstar. Resume your rightful place at court.'

'That could be a little difficult.' Khassian raised his hands, shaking back the lace cuffs to display them fully. 'My touch is not so good as it was and I might play quite a few wrong notes. The Prince is known to be upset by clumsy playing.'

Acir swallowed; he had seen wounds as ugly as these many times before, he had helped cauterise amputated stumps in tent hospitals on the battlefield . . . and yet these burned, twisted claws seemed all the more obscene for the knowledge of what they were once capable of.

'Others will be your hands for you. You can still teach at the Conservatoire, rehearse your music with the –'

'You're not used to this kind of thing, are you?'

Acir shook his head, half-understanding.

'Bandying words. Don't you resent being asked to do this?'

'I am an officer of the Commanderie.' Acir found he had unconsciously thrust back his shoulders as if on parade. 'I do what I am commanded to do by my superiors.'

'And your superior gets your to do his dirty work for him. Doesn't it stick in your throat?' Malice still flickered in the brown eyes. Fox-fire. 'They didn't equip you for this in the desert, did they? The subtleties of political negotiation?'

'No,' Acir said. He would not allow himself to be provoked.

'Pray tell me, Captain Korentan,' Khassian shook the lace back to cover his hands; maybe he could not bear to look at them long himself, 'what are the Grand Maistre's conditions?'

'An affirmation of faith. To be made before the people of Bel'Esstar.'

'You mean a public confession of guilt? A public denunciation of my friends and fellow artists? Because that's what it would mean. You're asking me to stand up and announce that I've been living a lie, that all my works are meaningless. Worse than meaningless – degenerate.'

Acir stared steadily back at him.

'But your example would inspire others to return to the faith.'

'If I had wanted to convert infidels, I would have become one of the Commanderie long ago.' Khassian leaned forward, his eyes cold now, brown pebbles glittering beneath a clear ice-melt stream. 'Go back to your Grand Maistre nel Ghislain. Tell him I will never bow my knee to him.'

CHAPTER 5

The Museum of Sulien Antiquities, known locally as the Cabinet of Curiosities, was housed in a dilapidated building hidden away behind the imposing domed façade of the Guildhall.

As a child Orial was fascinated by the Cabinet of Curiosities. Her affection for the eccentric collection of antique objects – and its equally eccentric curator, Dame Jolaine Tradescar, the City Antiquarian – had not diminished over the years. With her ancient, moth-eaten periwig and her hobbling gait, she had seemed a hundred years old when Orial first met her. Yet they had discovered an immediate affinity, fuelled by a mutual interest in the city's past. Who else would have troubled to answer a child's questions about dragonflies or taken the time and trouble to research the origins of a shard of pottery she had unearthed in the Undercity? In recognition of their special understanding, Dame Jolaine had agreed, at Jerame Magelonne's request, to become Orial's soul-guardian, to foster her spiritual development, and – in the case of his death before her twenty-first year – to care for her and her affairs.

Orial knew now that if she was to find an answer to her question, she was going to have to confide in someone. And Jolaine Tradescar, her soul-guardian, seemed the only one she dared trust in all Sulien.

As she had hoped, the Museum was deserted at this early hour. She moved between the dusty glass cases, unable to restrain herself from stopping to gaze at one of her favourite displays. They glittered beneath the glass, their delicate wings an iridescent mosaic of tiny fragments of enamel and coloured glass.

Dragonflies.

The insect appeared on countless carvings and artefacts excavated from the remains of the Old City. Even then the dragonfly had evidently possessed some deep significance for the city-builders – though when it had become incorporated into the religious beliefs of the people of Sulien, no one seemed sure.

'Such exquisite craftsmanship,' said a voice behind her, a voice creaking rustily from lack of use.

'Jolaine!'

'You've always been fascinated by my dragonflies, haven't you?' She came limping down the aisle between the cases towards Orial, leaning heavily on her stick. 'When you were little, you had to stand on tiptoe to peer in. I can see you still, such a solemn, wan little mouse. Look at you now – quite the young demselle.'

Orial felt herself blushing.

'And look at you,' she said, countering the teasing. 'Your knee's troubling you again, isn't it? You must come into the Sanatorium and –'

'Ach!' Dame Tradescar waved one hand dismissively. 'Just a twinge from the morning's damp. I'll be fine by lunchtime. By tea you'll see me down at the Assembly Rooms cutting as fine a caper in the cotillion as any of the young demselles.'

Orial began to laugh in spite of herself.

'That's better, hm?' said her soul-guardian. 'You were looking quite dejected. Now, tell me, to what do I owe the pleasure of this visit?'

Orial slipped her hand through Jolaine's arm and together they went towards her study.

'There. Sit yourself down. Have I shown you this little beauty, hm? Found by a labourer digging a new drainage trench for the Nymphs' Bath, buried in the clay silt. It's been the devil to clean – but look at it now.'

As Jolaine bent over her, Orial could not help but notice that her fantastical wig seemed more motheaten than before and her hands trembled slightly as they unwrapped the treasure from its cloth covering.

A bronze brooch appeared, penannular; tiny lunar hares coursed around crescent moons in an intricately interwoven knot, picked out in scarlet enamel. Scarlet and bronze. The colours glowed as if they had been fired the day before . . . not hundreds upon hundreds of years.

'Oh!' Orial carefully turned it over, holding it to the light. 'It's – beautiful.'

'Quite a fascinating little horde. If I hadn't dug further down in the trench these artefacts would have been lost forever.' Jolaine pointed to a glass trough filled with a mud-clouded liquid.

'More treasures?' Orial wrapped the brooch up in its cloth.

'Maybe,' said Jolaine, an enigmatic glint in her eyes. 'Only when the silt of centuries has soaked away will I be able to tell. Of course they may be worthless . . .'

'But you don't believe that for one moment!' Why else would you be taking such trouble to clean and restore them?'

'Oh! That's just the peculiar obsession of an old woman. I'm a magpie, Orial. I collect anything that catches my eye. But how can I help you, my dear?' Jolaine eased herself into a chair opposite Orial's.

'You've read many old texts and manuscripts, Jolaine. I – I wanted to know if you'd ever come across an illness called – Accidie.'

'The . . . Accidie?'

'You have heard of it!' said Orial, sitting eagerly forward.

'I've unearthed many strange facts about this city and its inhabitants over the years. A place with as ancient and mysterious a past as Sulien engenders many fanciful theories amongst historians and scholars. Most are unproven. You must remember that if you are determined to pursue this enquiry any further.'

Jolaine rose rather unsteadily to her feet and tottered off towards a dark-shadowed book-stack; Orial heard her muttering to herself from the gloom.

Orial twisted her fingers together nervously, feeling them wet with perspiration. She began to wonder whether she had overturned a stone only to find a myriad scorpions nesting beneath.

'Aha!' Jolaine emerged triumphantly from behind the stack, carrying a cobwebbed ledger. As she placed it on the desk, Orial saw a spider hurriedly descending from her wig on a single silken thread, then scuttling away across the papers. Smothering the urge to giggle behind her hand, she brushed away the dusty webs from the cover and spelt out, *Sulien – Legends*.

'There's all kinds of fantastical foolishness in here. Moonshine. But maybe a thread of truth runs through it,' Jolaine said, untying the faded ribbon and pulling out a sheaf of manuscripts. 'Take a look at this old monograph: "A Discourse on the Auncient Citie of Sulien and its Healing Springs".'

Orial squinted at the indistinct handwriting, pushing her spectacles higher on her nose to try to decipher it more clearly:

Legend relates that the citie was founded by invaders from far across the seas. The strangers called themselves 'Lifhendil', which approximately translates into our modern tongue as *Songspinners*. The legend tells that their gift for music was so great, they could charm the birds from the trees with their singing.

I have heard it saide hereabouts that once in a generation or so, a child is born with Songspinner gifts. Apparently these unique individuals can be identified by their eyes which display multi-coloured irises of great beauty.

I attempted to seek one such out, curiouse to see for myself, and was tolde there was a poore girl, greatly afflicted, in the Asylum. I made haste to see her, onlye to arrive to the sad news that, in her confusion and despair, she had thrown herselfe from the uppermost room the day before and had dashed out her brains on the cobbles below.

'Oh,' Orial whispered. She wanted to stop reading, to put the manuscript from her, but she could not.

The gift is not a perfect gift. It carryes the curse of madness with it. Lyke the rare and graceful dragonflyes which haunt the water-meadows here, the Songspinners live a short intense life, gladdening all with their unique talents before their genius is brutally extinguished in a cruel and devastating loss of reason known as the Accidie.

'Madness.' Orial looked up, unseeing, from the manuscript. 'My mother went mad.'

The Temple of the Source stood in the very heart of the city. Here the people of Sulien gathered to pray at the source of the hot springs, to make votive offerings to Esstarel, Goddess of the Gap, and to celebrate the rites of passage. The original significance of many of the rituals had become lost in time . . . as had the true name of the Goddess. When, centuries ago, Allegondan invaders ransacked the city and massacred the Lifhendil, they had imposed their language, their customs, their religion. But they could not eradicate the potent influence of the Lifhendil tutelary goddess. Eventually the Allegondans identified her with Elesstar the Blessed, handmaiden of their god, Iel, and she endured in a strange fusion of the two beliefs. The Temple was rededicated to Iel but the older presence prevailed.

Orial went into the colonnades and entered the Temple. She paused a moment to dip her finger-tips in one of the founts of the living spring and mark her forehead with the warm mineral water, a gesture of respect she dimly remembered her mother making . . . and one she still practised if only to keep alive the memory of Iridial.

She moved swiftly through the dim, echoing spaces of the Temple, unable to rid herself of the impression she had first gained as a tiny child, clutching her mother's hand, that she was floating below water. Verdigris light filtered in, limpidly cool, from the high, green-glass windows, casting shifting shadows on the pillars, sunlight filtering into the depths of deep waters . . . Maybe this was what the Lifhendil had intended the worshipper to feel, Orial thought, the loose, bodiless sensation of drifting in water, freeing the mind to meditate on higher matters . . . Even the bronze prayer-bells, their carvings blurred by the touch of countless devout worshippers, had turned green with age and their muted vibrations dinned in the Temple depths like the bells of a drowned city, deep beneath the waves.

Below the Upper Temple lay the source of the sacred spring itself, the raw fissure in the natural rock from which the waters exploded, fizzing with heat. The Lifhendil had constructed a labyrinthine trail to lead the worshipper to the source of the sacred spring and as Orial passed beneath the ancient archway, she experienced a prickling shiver of apprehension. Steam clouded her spectacle-lenses and for a moment she was blind, lost in the gloom. She wiped the steam away and slowly groped her way forward, drawn by the roar of the bubbling waters until she found herself on the rim of the gaping fissure itself, a raw, iron-red gash in the living rock.

She gasped, gripping hold of the slender rail, balancing precariously above the churning energy of the swirling waters. The fine, warm spray dampened her face and she could taste the acrid tang of the life-giving minerals on her lips.

Silvered shafts of daylight dimly pierced the misty air from slits cut high above in the vaulted roof, slits that also served as vents to let out the drifting steam. As Orial's eyes became accustomed to the dim light, she saw curling green ferns growing from the walls.

And standing watching her, in the billowing steam, a dark-veiled figure.

Silent, mute as a revenant from the far shore.

For one terrified moment Orial stared back, transfixed. Then she remembered what had brought her here to the source of the spring.

The Priests and Priestesses of the Temple kept constant vigil here, day and night, each taking a turn to assume the cloudy veils of the Augurer.

'What do you seek, daughter?' The voice floated towards her, low and drowsy. Orial could not even be certain whether a man or a woman stood there, gauzed in night-spangled veils. It was said that the Augurer fasted before the vigil ... then inhaled the dark drugfumes of Arkendym dreamweed to lay their minds open to the will of the Goddess.

'I – I seek guidance. Answers, maybe . . .'

'I speak for Her whose place this is.' The Augurer began to move towards her through the clouds of steam. 'Ask your question.'

'It's ... difficult.' Orial twisted a straying lock of hair between finger and thumb. 'It's about my mother. I need to know – to know why she died?'

'Give me your hand.'

Orial stretched out her hand and felt the light finger-tips of the Augurer touch hers. The other hand reached out to brush her forehead. Beneath the starry veils, the drug-darkened eyes were mesmerised, smoky casements to another world.

Jewelled wings dart over black waters, leaving a comet-trail of light sparks in their wake: leaf-emerald, hyacinth-sapphire, white-opal –

'A flight of dragonflies . . .' The Augurer's voice was now so low, Orial could barely hear it.

'Dragonflies? On the Day of the Dead?' Orial asked. 'Or – on the stelae?'

'She comes through fire . . . through water . . . to set them free.'

A shudder ran through the Augurer's body and the fingers suddenly lifted from Orial's.

'She? The Goddess? Elesstar?'

The Augurer did not reply.

'Tell me,' Orial pleaded.

The Augurer turned and went drifting away until the cloud-gauzed figure was obscured by the gusting steam.

Orial sighed. She had come for answers – and had found only further questions.

Dragonflies. Even on the most ancient of Temple stone carvings, the stelae, the motif prevailed. Symbols of the souls of the dead, flying from the darkness of the Undercity to the light of day beyond.

The funerary stelae of the Lifhendil still lined the passageways of the Under Temple.

Orial's fingers hovered over the carving, tracing the worn images. She could never understand why the Lifhendil had abandoned all sense of proportion and scale in their engraving of these ancient stones. Here the dragonflies had been carved the same size as the officiating priests and priestesses. She peered more closely at the carved figures. The slim bodies of the dragonflies could almost be human; from this angle it was possible to see them as winged men and women, winged messengers from the otherworld, come to carry the souls of the dead . . .

Bordering the image were the intricately carved slashes and squirls that Jolaine Tradescar insisted were inscriptions in the lost tongue of the Lifhendil. But as she had failed so far to crack the code, her theories had been dismissed by eminent scholars and the true function of the stelae remained unknown.

'A flight of dragonflies?' Orial whispered.

In the Upper Temple stood the painted statue of Elesstar, one hand benignly extended, the other supporting a vase from which poured perpetually the spring waters which the worshippers dutifully drank, lukewarm and brackish. The Allegondan import stared smilingly down at the faithful, her features bland and regular; her carven hair was painted yellow, inlaid with gold leaf, her eyes painted blue and her lips red. Deified, she little resembled the Shultan's concubine who had given up her life of luxury at court to follow the prophet Mhir. Orial had always suspected that the historical Elesstar was Lifhendil – not this smiling Allegondan saint, eyes piously upraised to heaven.

Reason and enlightenment prevailed in the Upper Temple. But below . . . below she had just experienced the power of an older, darker, mysticism.

The legacy of the Lifhendil.

*

54

All night the notes rampaged around Khassian's head. Swirling, savage strettos; new melodies that swooped and darted like an arrow-flight of swallows; climaxes that climbed and climbed to teeter on the brink of a crumbling abyss.

Next morning at first light he blundered into Cramoisy's boudoir. He had devised a method of depressing the door handles with one elbow that permitted him to move – albeit clumsily – from room to room.

The Diva lay in a bed draped with primrose taffeta, a colour horribly at odds with his flamboyant hair.

'Cramoisy, you've got to help me.'

'Go away, Amar,' groaned Cramoisy, drawing the sheet up over his face.

'Please. I'm going crazy. It's the finale. Elesstar's transfiguration scene. It was weak, unsatisfying. Now I know how to improve it!'

'Elesstar?' The sheet slid down an inch or so, revealing two jet eyes, staring avariciously up at him. '*My* role?'

'*Your* role, Cramoisy. You have to write it down.'

'At this hour? You know I never rise before nine.'

'You'll never have a better role. It's written for you. I know your voice better than any other composer in the whole of Allegonde, you've said so yourself. Help me get the music on paper – before I lose it forever!'

'Oh . . . very well.' Cramoisy yawned. 'Give me five minutes.'

Khassian paced outside the door, his feet moving in time to the insistent pulse of music in his head.

Five minutes stretched to ten, fifteen, twenty. At length the Diva appeared, draped in a peignoir of celadon silk, his brilliant hair loose about his shoulders, a portrait of studied artlessness. Khassian could not bear to imagine the lengths the castrato had gone to to achieve the effect.

'You said five minutes.'

Cramoisy gave a little sigh, seated himself at the escritoire and began to fuss with the pens, nibs, ink bottle.

'Cramoisy –' Khassian growled.

'There now!' Cramoisy flashed him a glittering smile. 'I'm ready.'

It would have been a tedious business even if Khassian could have demonstrated at the keyboard what he intended. As it was he found himself obliged to enumerate each note, how long it lasted, where it lay in the octave compass. The process was so laborious that the notes kept wreathing out of his grasp, evanescent as woodsmoke.

'*Si bemol*. Dotted crotchet then *ut, re* –'

'When you say *si bemol*, Amar, is it the higher octave or –'

Khassian let out a roar of frustration.

Cramoisy flung down the pen, ink spattering the page.

'You singers are all alike!' Khassian cried. 'Not one ounce of musical theory in your empty brains!'

'And you are quite impossible, Amaru Khassian! I'm doing my best!'

'You call this your best? Two smudged lines of stave paper?'

'No one could keep up with your dictation! You need a transcription machine.'

'I could do better with a pencil between my teeth!'

'Then you can *try* with a pencil between your teeth! For I won't write another note for you, Illustre. Not one.'

'Very well,' Khassian said, trying to control his temper. 'Get me a pencil. Well-sharpened.'

'A sharpened pencil? Do you think I have nothing better to do than run your errands all day? I have visits to make, calls to pay in the city.'

'How insensitive of me. I quite forgot. Of course your social diary must take precedence over my music!'

'If you must know, I am going to try to arrange a series of recitals at the Assembly Rooms,' Cramoisy said in tones of chill disdain.

'And of course the Diva must satisfy the demands of his public, he must give freely of his talents, he must sing, sing, sing –'

'Who do you think is paying for our food and board? Someone has to earn a little money to ensure we are not cast out into the streets as penniless vagrants next week.'

'Just get me the pencil, Cramoisy,' Khassian said between gritted teeth.

Cramoisy started up from the escritoire and flounced from the room, slamming the door behind him.

Khassian had been too angry to hear clearly what the Diva was saying. He was vaguely aware he had offended him, wounded his feelings. And Cramoisy could be vicious when offended – as his rivals in the Opera House could testify.

Soon afterwards the vocal exercises began. The Diva adopted a bright, piercing quality, over-emphasising the vibrato. Cramoisy knew Khassian particularly hated him to employ that technique for the composer had spent long hours coaching him in the use of a more subtle, expressive method of sustaining the tone. But the castrato had never forgotten how to dazzle an audience – and with his supreme breath control, he could dazzle as no other singer could.

Now the Diva was doing it expressly to annoy him.

Each scale dinned into Khassian's aching head like a shower of silver nails until he could bear it no longer.

He stumbled into the morning room where Cramoisy stood as if on stage, hands formally clasped above his waist. The force of the sound, glossily shrill, made Khassian flinch.

'Cramoisy. Please.'

The Diva glared at him.

'I'm busy.' He began the next arpeggio; the notes seemed to rend the air with violent slashes of colour: shrieking yellow, skirling lightning-blue.

'Look – I'm – I'm sorry I shouted at you.' Khassian struggled to make himself heard above the rising arpeggios. 'It was – insensitive of me.'

'Yes. It was very insensitive.' Cramoisy paused for breath.

'If you could stop –'

'And why, pray, should I stop? I must sing, sing, sing, remember?'

'I have a headache.'

It was the plaint of a fractious child; the castrato hesitated but Khassian could see that this appeal to his sympathy had won.

'You great baby.' Cramoisy went to his reticule and took out a black bottle, pouring a measure into a glass. 'Here.' He held the little glass to Khassian's lips. 'Drink up, there's a good boy.'

The bitter dark liquid was smooth as syrup. One measure too many . . . and he would slip into that cold, endless sleep where his stillborn children, his unfinished works, would no longer torment him.

'Please, Cramoisy,' Khassian whispered, grimacing at the bitter taste of the medicine, 'get me some pencils?'

Whirling lines of music still tormented him, weaving in and out of his brain, unable to find resolution or release. He could not sleep for the clamour of the unfinished work that demanded to be completed.

The sharpened pencils Cramoisy had brought for him stood in a jar on the desk. He bent over the jar, dipping like an ungainly water-bird after its prey, trying to get one between his teeth.

At last he secured one and sat down over the stave paper. But the pencil was too long; it stabbed him in the palate, making him gag. A shorter one, then. Clamping the wood between his jaws, he tried to angle his head so that he could make the marks – any marks – on the stave lines.

Soon saliva began to dribble out between his teeth. It slid down the pencil and on to the paper, making slimy marks. The taste of the wood, graphite and saliva mingled, made his tongue burn. Disgusted, he spat the pencil out, wiping his mouth on his sleeve.

Then he looked down at what he had achieved.

A few clumsy strokes, smeared with the saliva from his mouth, were all he had managed. They were almost illegible.

And in his head, he could hear the brazen splendour of the music dinning on. No one else would ever hear it.

Cramoisy had left the sedative tincture on the top of the table. The bitter liquid, blacker than a starless night, numbingly cold as the rivers of hell, promised a slow drowning descent into the dark.

Close now, almost close enough. If he reached out, he could hook the bottle with his elbow into his lap – and wrench the cork out with his teeth.

He reached out for the phial –

The bottle fell to the floor and smashed in a dark-smeared puddle of viscous medicine. Khassian began to laugh: hard, painful laughter that hurt his heaving ribcage, that sent tears streaming down his cheeks.

He could not even kill himself.

Orial was carrying a tray of linaments along the Sanatorium corridor when she caught sight of Amaru Khassian. Pale and unsteady on his feet, the composer was being ushered into a treatment cubicle. The cubicle next to the one where she was to treat her first client of the day.

His eyes, in that one brief glimpse, seemed so bleak, so riven with despair, that she stopped still in mid-corridor, shocked.

The patient she was helping to treat was an elderly dowager whose knees were misshapen with rheumatism. She, unlike some of Dr Magelonne's more crotchety older patients, was indulgent with Orial's relative lack of experience and seemed delighted to have the opportunity to gossip about a minor society scandal at last week's Guildhall Ball.

'And the Mareschale must be at least as old as I am . . .'

Orial nodded and smiled as she worked, hardly noticing what was being said, remembering to look alternately surprised or shocked as each of the juicy details was related. At first she hardly noticed the music. It was distant, a faint trace of something she had heard long ago, perhaps, just a lingering fragment of melody, tantalising in its evanescence. Her fingers worked the hot mud which was to be applied into a manageable shape . . . and the music became more insistent.

'Disgraceful at her age . . . she could at least have tried to be discreet – ouch! Does the poultice have to be quite so hot, my dear?'

'I'm sorry.' Orial peeled it off again and tested the temperature of the mud with her elbow. What *was* that music? Where had she heard it before? It was quite unlike the usual Sulien repertoire, the charming little dance strains whose snatches she sometimes caught floating from the Upper Rooms, the cotillions, caprioles and badineries. This was something far darker, its leaps tormented by a bizarre intensity, the notes twisted into an utterance of a complexity she had never before experienced. It compelled and repelled at the same time.

'I said, it's gone quite cold!'

'Oh!' Startled, Orial looked up. How long had she been daydreaming? She hastily felt the poultice and discovered that it had indeed lost all its heat. The dowager glared up at her from rheumy eyes, glittering with indignation.

'I'll fetch some fresh mud.' Orial took up the bucket and hurried out of the cubicle.

Next door, Khassian pressed his lips together in grim concentration as Sister Crespine worked on his thumbs. The pain came in bursts: a dull, grinding ache suddenly shot through by jagged stabs of light.

He would not cry out.

Instead he carried on mentally orchestrating the final duet from the opera, the duet that had kept him from sleeping most of the night. Mental discipline. Concentrate on the music. Then the pain recedes to a tolerable level . . .

Final irony. That the way to improve the ending which had eluded him in Bel'Esstar should present itself to him now, when he was unable to transcribe it. Now it had become an apotheosis, imbued with a dark yet profound sense of bitter triumph, a hymn to the endurance of the human spirit in adversity. He knew it was good. He knew –

From outside in the corridor he heard a voice, low and sweet, singing. Singing the very notes he had been composing since before dawn!

'Bel'Mhir!' he whispered, sitting up.

'Did I hurt you, Illustre?' Sister Crespine said, surprised.

'No, no.' He was already off the couch, making for the door, following the sound of the voice.

'But where are you –'

'The singing. The singer.' His voice was hoarse with excitement. 'I have to know who it is.' Without thinking, he thrust his hand forward to tug back the curtain. The fingers missed their grip, clumsily jarring against the tiled archway. Pain shot like lightning from finger-tips to shoulder; he squeezed his eyes shut, fighting for self-control.

Sister Crespine briskly whisked the curtain open a moment, glanced up the corridor, then shut it again.

'You probably heard Demselle Magelonne. She's working in the adjoining cubicle.'

'Magelonne?' A wave of sickness queased through his body. 'The doctor's daughter?'

'Do lie down again, Illustre.' Sister Crespine's hand closed around his arm, coaxing him back towards the couch.

Orial Magelonne? How could she be singing his music? Did it mean that his triumphant apotheosis was nothing but a plagiarism of some existing work? The thought filled him with a deep and dragging sense of self-loathing. Had the fire so sapped his abilities that he could not even string together a series of notes without borrowing from some lesser composer?

Or – was there some other explanation?

'I must talk to her.' He reared up from the couch, only to be pressed gently back.

'I can't disturb her when she's with a patient,' Sister Crespine said firmly. 'Dr Magelonne would not approve.'

By dusk Amaru Khassian reached the River Gardens. He was not sure how long he had been aimlessly wandering the streets and terraces of the city. Now the clear light was fading from the hillsides and birds were twittering in the branches as they fluttered and settled to roost.

The pleasure gardens were all but deserted now; the winding paths that led amongst bosky groves were lit by little lanterns to show the few remaining promenaders the way to the gates.

The evening air was fresh and damp; heavy dew was already soaking the grass parterres. Khassian found himself in front of a little temple in the antique style, neglected amongst the cypresses. Entering beneath the crumbling pediment, he saw that the walls were painted with murals.

Dragonflies darted in a frieze of faded water-blue and rush-green above a black stream where pale lotos floated. He hardly noticed them. One thought alone obsessed him.

So it had come to this. His compositional powers were so enfeebled, so wasted by the accident, that all he was capable of was plagiarism.

He must have heard the melody in the Sanatorium whilst he lay in fever – and assimilated it as his own. It was probably some current Sulien ditty with a crude refrain, sung in all the taverns and qaffë shops.

How else could the girl have been singing the very notes he had been thinking? The realisation filled him with a rank feeling of disgust.

The River Avenne ran close by; in the evening's stillness he could hear the waters foaming over the wedge-shaped weir. Drawn to the tumultuous sound, he found himself walking up towards the rail that overlooked the river.

Swollen with spring rains and mountain snow-melt, the Avenne swirled in full torrent over the weir, sending up flecks of white spray.

Khassian stared down, unseeing, into the dark turbulence of the waters. The raw, untamed force of the river called to him.

They would not find his body until days later when it was washed up miles downstream.

Better to finish the work half-done by the Opera fire. He stood poised above the churning waters. Flecks of spray kissed his face, colder than snow. Frozen tears. His mind was as blank as the void below.

Now.

'Illustre!' Someone shouted his name. 'No!'

He glanced around and vaguely saw through the mist of spray the tall figure of Acir Korentan tearing up the path towards him. A defiant smile twisted his lips. At least he would die knowing he had eluded the Commanderie.

He turned back – and stepped out into nothingness.

CHAPTER 6

Acir saw Khassian poised on the edge of the swollen river. He saw him glance back – caught the look of defiant triumph – then throw himself into the waters.

Acir was pulling off his jacket as he ran forwards, kicking off his boots as he vaulted over the railings. He paused a moment to scan the bank for a branch, a loose railing, but there was nothing.

Khassian's head rose once above the churning waters at the centre of a swirling vortex – and then it sucked him down.

Acir took a breath – and plunged into the torrent.

The shock of the ice-cold water almost knocked the breath from his lungs. He went under – chaos of black water, white spray – then kicked upwards again, reaching out blindly for Khassian's current-tumbled body.

His hands caught hold, his arm crooked about Khassian's neck, dragging the head above the water.

Don't fight me. Don't fight me now.

The water tore at him, tugging Khassian's body as he fought to pull it to the shore. It was a limp weight now, dragging him down, he was struggling to keep a hold on it, he was losing feeling in his fingers, they were numbed with the icy cold –

The river had become a lethal adversary – he fought it for possession of Khassian. If he lost the fight, they would both drown. He took in a mouthful of water, coughed it out, spluttering . . .

One foot grazed against the muddy bank. He scrabbled to keep the foothold and heaved the water-sodden body half up out of the water. Rushing waters still dinned in his ears, a roar louder than the roar of his own pounding blood. Khassian's body seemed to be slipping back into the river. Acir slithered around in the mud until he could hook his arms beneath Khassian's and pull him right out of the water.

The last effort exhausted him; he slipped, falling over Khassian, water streaming from his sodden clothes.

'Khassian,' he whispered, coughing. 'Khassian!'

Khassian lay without moving, head lolling, muddy water running out from a corner of his slack mouth.

Sweet Mhir, let him not be dead.

Acir swept the soaked hair from his own face and bent over the composer, one hand on his chest. The ribs were still; he could feel no heartbeat beneath the wet jacket.

He looked desperately around for help – but the fast-darkening gardens were empty. Only a solitary bird sang, high in a bare-branched tree.

He tipped the composer on to his side, trying to empty the water from his open mouth. Still no stir of life.

'Help!' he shouted to the empty gardens. 'Help, here!' His voice echoed in the twilight – but no one appeared.

There was nothing for it. He knelt astride Khassian and covered the open mouth with his own, breathing in his own panting breath . . . then pressed his palms rhythmically on the still ribcage. Khassian's lips were cold and wet, slimed with the foul taste of riverwater.

'Breathe, Khassian.' Acir willed life into the limp body as he worked. 'Damn you, *breathe.*'

A faint shudder convulsed the composer's body. He turned his head a little to one side – and vomited up a gush of foul water into the grass.

'Why?' he said faintly, and then retched again, ribs heaving now as he gasped in lungfuls of air.

Khassian was alive. Acir began to shake with relief; relief – and cold. Only now did he realise that he too was soaked to the skin. And the evening chill was fast settling into the river valley.

'What's going on down there? I heard shouts!'

Acir looked up and saw a man approaching through the early-evening gloom.

'Can you fetch help?' Acir's teeth began to chatter. 'Th-there's been an accident.'

'You stay here. I'll get help.'

Stay here. The irony of the words would have made Acir smile if his mouth had not been so numbed with the cold.

He could just make out the crumpled shape of his jacket where he had flung it in the grass. He scrambled up the bank and retrieved it, tucking it about Khassian's body.

Khassian's eyelids flickered open.

'*Why*, damn you?' he whispered.

'Self-destruction is the ultimate sin,' Acir said, though the sternness of his words was lessened by the involuntary chattering of his teeth. He seemed unable to stop shivering. 'I c-could not let you put your immortal soul in danger of p-perdition.'

'You really – believe all that, don't you? Damnation, salvation. You poor deluded simpleton –'

And then torchlights illuminated the bank. The rescuers had brought blankets and a stretcher. They carried Khassian to the lodge-keeper's cottage at the gates to the gardens, Acir following, squelching as water dripped into his boots.

There the lodge-keeper and his wife helped them out of their wet clothes and wrapped them in blankets. Acir found himself thawing in front of the fire, hands clasped about a mug of mulled cider.

'A foolish accident,' he told them. 'My companion was leaning over the river when the wind carried his hat away. He tried to fish it out with a stick . . . and fell in . . .'

'Visitors, eh?' The lodge-keeper gave his wife a knowing look. 'The Avenne's treacherous this time of year. Sulien folk won't go near her till spring's past. Then she runs as smooth and placid as a minnow-stream.'

Khassian, sitting hunched in his cocoon of blankets and towels, slowly raised his head.

'You can't go back to your lodgings in those wet clothes,' the woman said. 'Shall we send for dry ones?'

'You've been most generous . . .' Now that the crisis was past, Acir found himself fighting off drowsiness; as the warmth of the fire and the spiced cider glowed in his veins, he felt an overwhelming urge to curl up in the flames' glow and sleep. Yet he must keep awake, keep vigilant. Given Khassian's morbid frame of mind, he might easily attempt to kill himself again.

'You lied, Captain Korentan.' Khassian's voice rasped, rough from retching up the riverwater he had swallowed. 'You lied to protect me. Doesn't that mean you've tarnished your immortal soul?'

Acir came awake with a start. Khassian was watching him, his eyes lit with a dull gleam. Hard as pebbles seen through riverwater . . .

'Does that bother you?' Acir asked.

'Why are you still here? Afraid I'll set fire to myself? Impale myself on the fire-poker?' He broke off, coughing. 'But then I'm no use to you dead, am I?'

Acir chose not to reply. He sensed that Khassian was spoiling for a fight. And he was too tired to fight. Too damned tired . . .

A little while later, the grating of carriage wheels on the gravel path outside woke Acir. He must have lapsed into a doze. He sat up, inwardly cursing himself for falling asleep on duty.

Cramoisy flung open the door and swept into the firelit parlour.

'I came as soon as I got your message! Whatever possessed you to fall into the river, Amar?'

Acir stood up, clutching the blanket to him.

'And you, Captain Korentan, you leapt in to rescue him. What a hero!'

The castrato seemed charged with the excitement of the situation, his gestures and voice too large for the little parlour.

'The clothes, Cramoisy,' Khassian said wearily. 'Have you brought the clothes?'

'Heavens, yes. And Mistress Permay's making a nourishing barley soup for you.'

Acir cleared his throat. It pained him to have to make the request, but he could not think of any alternative course of action.

'Diva, if I might borrow a pair of breeches and a shirt . . . I will have them laundered and returned to you on the morrow.'

'You have no other clothes with you, Captain?'

The Diva would not know, of course, of the vow of poverty he had made.

'We travel light in the Commanderie.'

'And it wouldn't do for you to wander the streets of Sulien naked beneath a blanket?' The castrato tweaked teasingly at the edge of Acir's blanket; horrified, he took a step backwards and sat down rather suddenly on the couch. Cramoisy laughed and turned away. 'How fortuitous that I gathered several items of clothing of Khassian's with me. I thought he might be cold.'

'Fortunate, Cramoisy,' Khassian said quietly. 'Fortunate.'

'Whatsoever,' Cramoisy said, ignoring him as he pulled out shirts, breeches, socks, and laid them on the fender to warm. 'There you are.'

Cramoisy stood looking at Acir expectantly. It was only then that he realised the castrato intended him to get dressed in front of him. Acir felt his face burning – and not from the heat of the fire.

'Why this modesty, Captain? I'm an old trouper, well used to cramped dressing rooms in provincial theatres. D'you think I haven't seen it all before?'

'Cramoisy,' Khassian said warningly. 'Go and give my thanks to the good people who have sheltered us. Some remuneration would be appropriate in the circumstances . . .'

Cramoisy paused a moment. Then, shooting a venomous glance at Khassian, he left the room, slamming the door.

Acir turned away from Khassian and, in the shadows, shed his blanket to pull on a pair of breeches. As he turned back into the light of the flames for a shirt, he saw Khassian regarding him with curiosity.

'What is *that*?'

Khassian was staring at his bare chest. Acir glanced down and felt a flush of heat sear his face again.

'A battle-scar?'

'What, this?' Acir touched the tattoo that covered his left breast, suddenly self-conscious. 'The mark of the Order of the Rosecoeur.' He tugged the shirt on, hastily covering it.

'No. Let me see.'

Acir found himself uncovering the sacred mark to show the composer. Perhaps if he could explain his devotion to Mhir he might win Khassian over . . .

Khassian raised one damaged hand as if he wanted to touch the dye-stained skin . . .

'A black-thorned rose . . . what are these three crimson spots, what do they signify?'

'It commemorates the miracle of the bleeding Rose. Mhir's martyrdom. The three drops of blood that fell from the Rose that grew from the dead Prophet's breast and restored Elesstar to life. The thorns represent the difficulties we encounter in our life's journey; the three drops of blood, the three virtues: love, fidelity and –'

'Yoo-hoo! Amaru!' Cramoisy's voice shrilled outside the room, shattering the moment's strange, still intimacy. 'Are you ready?'

Khassian let his hand drop back.

'Another minute, *miu caru*!'

Acir could not help but notice the immediate alteration in his tone as he called to Cramoisy; the voice he had heard a few seconds earlier betrayed a different Khassian entirely – gentle and sensitive.

'Pass me those clothes.'

Acir had handed him the warmed clothes and turned to look away as Khassian shrugged off the blanket. From the smothered grunts of effort he could tell that the composer was trying his best to dress himself. And only then did he realise that there was no way that Khassian would be able to do up the fastenings.

'You'll have to help me. If that's not too demeaning for a member of the secret Order of the Rosecoeur? Or perhaps you've taken a vow forbidding you to touch other people's clothing?'

'Would you rather I called the Diva?' Acir said, stung in spite of himself.

'Good gracious, no. I'll have to endure him fussing over me as he waits for me to develop a chill. Keep him away for a few moments longer.'

Acir turned around and saw that Khassian had managed to manoeuvre his arms through the shirt sleeves and wriggle into the breeches. The breeches however were flapping open.

This was no different, Acir told himself, from aiding a wounded confrère. He had stripped away blood-soiled, slashed uniforms, he had bathed and salved wounds, he had eased clean garments on over bandaged limbs.

And yet it *was* different. As he knelt beside the couch and leaned across to fasten the shirt ties, damp strands of his hair fell forward, brushing Khassian's bare chest. The leather thong that usually confined his hair must have been lost in the river. He raised one hand to push it out of his eyes and saw that Khassian was looking at him. Firelight burnished red glints in Khassian's water-tangled hair, glimmered in shadowed laughter in his eyes, at the corners of his mouth.

And it occurred to Acir that the composer was in some obscure way mocking him.

Only an hour or so ago he had covered that mocking mouth with his own, warmed it back to life with his own warmth, his own breath.

Angered, he snatched his hands away.

'What's the matter, Captain Korentan?' Khassian's voice was dark, fire-edged and dangerous. 'Burned your fingers?'

Riverdreams.

Orial sank down, down beneath the black waters. Dark shapes, long and sinuous, snaked past her.

Drowning.

Black waters, white shroud. Bound from head to foot, she could not kick free. Spiralling on down into the muddy depths.

Her jaw was bound, she could not move, she could not cry out. The lead weights dragged her down to the bottom. Weights, cerements –

They had given her to the waters, thinking she was dead.

But I'm alive!

She heard the snap and grind of razor-teeth close to her ear. The water swirled.

The water-snakes. They would devour her, alive or dead, they would strip the living flesh from her bones –

'Noooo!'

She was sitting up in her own bed, staring wildly into the darkness, her arms crossed against her breast, hands clutching her bare shoulders.

The Antiquarian, Dame Jolaine Tradescar, rubbed her eyes. Old age was an extreme irritation. Nothing worked properly anymore: hearing failed, sight dimmed – and just when she needed her senses to be at their most acute.

The desk was stacked with notebooks filled with page after tightly packed page of her small, neat script, her meticulous drawings of the hieroglyphs, a lifetime's scholarly obsession. A lifetime spent searching for hidden clues, following false trails.

Many times in the past, she had been certain she had been about to crack the code. She should know better by now! And yet she could not suppress a shiver of anticipation as she took out her eyeglasses to study the new find more closely.

A soaking in a bowl of clean water had removed the encrusted mud. She could see what it was now. A rolled sheet of fine pewter.

A curse.

With trembling fingers she took up tweezers and, with extreme delicacy, began to smooth the ancient pewter sheet flat.

The custom of inscribing a petition to the Goddess Elesstar and dropping it into the sacred spring was still popular amongst the people of Sulien. A generous donation towards the upkeep of the Temple was the customary fee. Most petitions were pleas for a cure for various ailments – but a few were vengeful curses, imploring the Goddess's aid. No one was certain when the custom had begun but the Priests and Priestesses did not discourage it, especially as the petitioners usually brought generous gifts of food and wine with them. And no one knew anymore why it was essential to scratch the petition backwards – it was merely the tradition.

But this petition was older and more fragile than any other Dame Jolaine had examined before. It might so easily have been lost for good if she had not spotted it in the silt the workmen had raked from a blocked drainage channel.

She peered at the faint scratches inscribed on the lead sheet. Backwards. Remember: transcribe the letters first, then reverse . . .

And then she peered more closely.

There were two inscriptions. The first was in what seemed to her eyes to be an archaic form of the Allegondan script. And the second below was in –

In the Lifhendil hieroglyphs!

Her heart pounded a wild jig against her ribs. She sat back, one hand on her breast, trying to control its leaping beats.

'Steady, Tradescar,' she murmured. 'It could be a fake. A forgery. No point having a seizure over a trifle.'

It could be a fake – but it could also be the petition of a long-dead worshipper from the Dark Age, child of an Allegondan-Lifhendil union. Certes, such children had been born. She let out a dragging sigh: little Orial was living proof of that.

And if it was what she hoped – maybe she had at last found the key to the lost language of the Lifhendil.

The faint script dimmed before her eyes. The room grew suddenly dark; shadows loomed across her vision. Pain burst in her chest, bright as an arrowstar. Her hands fumbled over the desk for her enamelled box of pills. Shakily, she opened the lid, picked one out and popped it under her tongue.

'Easy now. Easy.'

She leant back in her chair, waiting for the flaring pain to fizzle out.

This faulty heart was becoming a damn nuisance. Always letting her down just when she needed it. The doctors had told her to retire. Maybe they had a point . . .

Chronicle journalese flickered through her mind: 'Eminent scholar found dead in Museum. It is believed that Dr Tradescar was on the brink of a remarkable discovery. Her sudden death robbed us of the enlightenment . . .'

'No other scholar is going to get their hands on this! It's mine. I've waited a lifetime for this.'

And there was Orial to consider. Her soul-child. Orial was rapidly maturing – soon she would come into her full Lifhendil inheritance. The musical gifts to ravish and delight – and then the madness. Jolaine had to save her. She had to try. Maybe her theory was crackbrained, the ramblings of a crazy old academic. But suppose – just suppose she was right and the Lifhendil stelae held the key to the Accidie?

Khassian lay on the striped couch whilst Cramoisy paced to and fro. The Diva was twisting a lace handkerchief agitatedly between his fingers. The situation was, Khassian realised, curiously reminiscent of Flamilla's *scena* in the opera *The Fires of Fate*.

He knew Cramoisy was waiting for him to speak. To give him an explanation. But he would not explain himself – not to the Diva or anyone else.

'How could you do it?' The Diva's voice trembled with tears of accusation. 'Just – throw your life away! When we have all worked so hard to save you? It's so – so *selfish*!'

Khassian stared through him.

'Oh, don't go on pretending it was an accident. I know what you were about. I found the smashed bottle of opiate on the floor in your room. When that failed, you decided to drown yourself. If Korentan hadn't fished you out, you'd be dead – and what good would that do our cause?'

'So I'm to keep myself alive to further our cause? Even though I'm useless. I can't hold a sword, fire a pistol –'

Cramoisy flung himself on his knees beside him.

'You mustn't give up, Amar. If you lose hope, how will the rest of us carry on?'

'There's no point in carrying on. I'm no use to anyone. I can't compose.'

'But with an amanuensis –'

Why couldn't Cramoisy understand? Suddenly it all came spilling out, all the hopelessness, the despair.

'I thought I had found the will to compose again – Elesstar's duet. And today I heard one of the nurses singing the tune in the Sanatorium. Singing it aloud!'

'Which nurse?' Cramoisy asked.

'The girl who found us. Magelonne's child. Can't you see, Cramoisy? I'd been deluding myself. I hadn't composed anything new at all, I must have cribbed the tune from a common street ballad.'

'Orial Magelonne was singing one of your tunes?' said Cramoisy.

'I felt so cheap. So worthless. Elesstar's final duet – filched from some tawdry tavern song.'

'Amar. Listen to me.' Cramoisy cupped Khassian's face in his hands, suddenly earnest, the tragic mask of Flamilla abandoned. 'Think back. Had you been rehearsing the tune in your mind that morning?'

'But I don't see what relevance –'

'Think, Amar!' Cramoisy's finger-tips pressed into his cheeks.

'Well, I might have been . . . maybe I was . . .'

'Have you noticed her eyes?'

'What have her eyes got to do with this?'

'She's her mother's daughter. She has a gift, Amar. A gift that could save your life.'

'For God's sake explain, Cramoisy.'

'She's – *different*. And she doesn't know it yet. Rainbow eyes, Amar. I told you her mother was an exceptional musician, didn't I? They are descendants of a race of musicians. I sang her Firildys's arioso – and she sang it back to me, note for note. And she had never heard it before in her life.'

'So? My father taught me to do the same,' Khassian said dismissively. 'With discipline, children can develop remarkable memory skills.'

'And can they also hear the music in your mind?'

Khassian gave a sceptical snort.

'Oh, come now, Cramoisy.'

'Her mother Iridial could.'

'Musical telepathy? What kind of crazed fantasy did this Iridial spin you? To hear the music in other people's minds . . . it would send you mad.'

'Don't you understand? You didn't filch the tune. She learned it from you.'

'You're saying that Orial Magelonne could be my amanuensis? That she could transcribe what's up here –' Khassian nodded his head, ' – directly into written manuscript?'

'She'd need some training. From what I understand, she's self-taught. The good doctor has expressly forbidden her to take any kind of music lessons. But talent will out . . .'

'Ach, Cramoisy, this is like some bizarre faery tale. And I don't believe in faeries.'

'Just imagine, Amar,' Cramoisy leaned close to him, his breath warm on Khassian's face, 'the opera coming to life again, here in Sulien. You already have Valentan for the peace-bringer, Mhir. And you have your Elesstar here beside you. If other musicians can make it across the mountains, we can put a cast together –'

'But the girl. Orial. Suppose she doesn't want to do it? It will mean days, weeks, months of transcription. And if her father is so opposed to her coming into contact with music . . .' Khassian struggled to express the doubts that had already arisen in his mind. 'It seems – *wrong*, Cramoisy. To ask her to disobey her father.'

Father. The word still stirred unhappy memories: bitter words, slammed doors, letters returned unopened . . .

'After all I've done for you. All I've given up for you, Amar. My whole life

dedicated to the furthering of your career, your talents, to treat me so shabbily. My own son!'

'Let me talk to her. She's eighteen, old enough to make up her own mind about the matter.'

'Maybe.'

'And no more silly suicide attempts, *caru*?'

Silly. Khassian winced at the word. Was that how Cramoisy saw it? The petulant gesture of a child who can't get what he wants? There had been nothing petulant about the grey clouds of despair that had enveloped him, leeching all colour from the world.

'Promise me.' Cramoisy nuzzled his cheek, skin soft as rose-velvet against the unshaven stubble.

He nodded his head, wishing the Diva would leave him alone.

'Tried to drown himself?' Orial repeated, wide-eyed. She set down her bowl of tea and stared in alarm at the Diva.

The tea-shop echoed to the tinkle of cutlery and a low murmur of discreet conversation.

Cramoisy nodded – though not too vigorously. He was sporting an elaborately curled powdered wig of a construction as frothily light as the cream-filled pastries piled on the plate in front of him. Orial noticed that the wig had already occasioned several envious glances from the ladies of Sulien.

'Not a word of it to anyone, Orial. He was in such deep, deep despair.'

'Because of his hands?'

'Exactly so.' Cramoisy helped himself to a second meringue.

'How terrible.' Orial stared at the pastry which lay untouched on her own plate. She saw again the shambling figure of Amaru Khassian in the Sanatorium corridor, saw the pale face, the daemon-haunted eyes.

'And I fear he may try again – he can be so stubborn once he sets his heart on something – unless we can prevent him.'

'We?' Orial echoed. 'You mean I could help?'

'Mmm.' Cramoisy's rouged mouth was full of meringue; he lifted his napkin and delicately dabbed the traces of whipped cream from his lips. Orial saw the red rouge-stain on the white linen.

'But how could I help?' Orial picked up her fork and toyed with the cake, pushing it around the plate. 'I'm only in my first year of training. I haven't learned neurology or musculature yet –'

'I'm not referring to your medical skills, *carissa*. I'm referring to your other gifts.'

'I don't have any other gifts,' she said, confused.

'Let me share a confidence with you.' Cramoisy leaned closer across the tea-table. 'Amaru Khassian did not just lose the use of his hands in the fire. He lost the culmination of his life's work: his new opera. And now he just sits there, thinking through the lost music day and night. It haunts his dreams. At night I can hear him murmuring and weeping in his sleep. It's destroying him, Orial.'

'Because he can hear the music in his head but can't write it down?'

'To Amar music is much more than a profession. It's his own personal language, his means of expressing himself. "Music begins where words fail . . ." '

'But why me?'

'Think back to a morning last week. Amaru was being treated in the Sanatorium. You were singing in the next-door cubicle as you worked. What were you singing?'

Orial frowned. That melody. That dark, haunting melody with its sinous, twisted intervals . . . How did Cramoisy know she had been singing?

'I don't know its name. I don't know where I heard it. I just found myself humming it.'

Cramoisy reached out across the table and took her hand in his own, squeezing it reassuringly.

'Don't distress yourself, child. Listen to me. You were singing a fragment of Amaru's opera.'

'B-but you said it was burned. How could I have –'

Cramoisy raised his hand to stroke her cheek.

'You are your mother's daughter. You have inherited her talents, her gifts. You will need guidance in how to use them . . .'

'You mean – I heard the music in the Illustre's mind?' Orial could not begin to make sense of the revelation.

'It's a kind of musical telepathy. That's how your mother once described it to me. You will need to develop great mental discipline if you are to use it effectively.'

'And you want *me* to transcribe the Illustre's thoughts?'

'He needs you, Orial. You could be the one to save him from his own despair.'

'But I'm untrained. I've never had a lesson in my life.'

'Valentan and I will give you instruction in notation, theory, all you need to know.'

'Ohhh . . .' Orial let out a little sigh of excitement. It was more than she could bear. Her dearest wish come true. And then she remembered.

'*Papa* –'

Cramoisy's expression became pensive.

'I don't want to upset him.'

The sound of pastry forks on plates, spoons stirring tea-bowls, had suddenly become a clatter, intruding on Orial's thoughts.

'You're a loyal and loving daughter. I understand that. But whose interests is your father fostering? He has deprived you of the musical training that is your birthright. Forgive me if I speak plainly, Orial. If he cannot bear to hear music played, then so be it. But why should you suffer? It is wrong. Very wrong.'

Orial gasped.

'There. I've said it!' Cramoisy leaned back in his chair, triumphant.

'The decision is yours, Orial. Not your father's. You're no longer a child.'

Orial looked down at the table; her own hands, slender and unscathed, rested on the embroidered cloth.

Not my hands. But his . . .

She looked up.

'When can I meet the Illustre?'

CHAPTER 7

Dame Jolaine Tradescar rubbed sleepdust from her aching eyes and looked down at her work again, blinking.

What hour was it? She picked up the qaffë pot to pour herself another cup but only a cold, dark sediment dribbled out. The oil was burning low in the glass lamp . . . but daylight seemed already to be seeping in under the blinds. She had no need of oil-light now.

She tugged at the cord and the frayed linen blind slowly creaked up, letting more light into the study. Jolaine slowly stretched, groaning as stiff joints creaked.

She had been working all night. She should be tired. In fact, she had passed beyond tiredness to that state where she moved in a waking dream and a strange lucidity of mind illuminated her thoughts.

She sat down again, eager to look over the night's achievements. Yes, it was all there, she had not dreamed it! It had been slow, painstaking work to transcribe the indistinct scripts – and then to translate. But she had the beginnings of a match. She had traced enough concordances between early Allegondan script and the Lifhendil hieroglyphs to make a tentative translation:

To the *divine* [?] *Goddess* Elesstar. I give to you, Lady *Goddess*, the gold pendant that has been stolen from me this day. Let the thief, whether man or woman, Allegondan or *Lifhendil*, become as *liquid as the black waters* of the [[?]] *reservoir*. May his *soul* not fly to join the *winged ones* –

She had underlined certain words in the translation which seemed to link with hieroglyphs she recognised, hieroglyphs which appeared again and again on the temple stelae: divine, Goddess, Lifhendil, liquid, waters, reservoir, soul, winged ones . . .

She was so excited that, in spite of the stiffness, she stood up and went frollicking out of the Cabinet of Curiosities, seized with an insane desire to embrace the very first person she met.

It was a fine spring morning. The terraces and crescents of Sulien seemed to glow rose-gold. Wild jonquils carpeted the grassy banks in the River Gardens, like pale sunlight gilding the green. Blue tits twittered and chaffed in the branches; willow warblers piped liquid trills from the long strands of yellow willow hair that trailed in the Avenne.

And everywhere there was a stir of activity. Maids leaned out of upper windows to air quilts and blankets; housewives threw open shutters and doors to the sunlight to banish the frowsty humours of winter. Servants polished window panes, beat carpets, shook out dusters.

Acir Korentan walked slowly past the entrance to Mistress Permay's lodging house for the third time, oblivious to the domestic bustle that surrounded him. A convulsive sneeze shook his whole body; resignedly, he pulled a handkerchief from his pocket and wiped his streaming nose. The virulent cold had struck him down the very day after he had pulled Khassian from the river. He had been to the apothecary's who had given him infusions to be inhaled, infusions to be taken, and advised a visit to the steam bath to 'draw out the evil humours'. Now the brilliant sunshine made his streaming eyes worse and the pollen from the catkins seemed only to aggravate his ticklish throat.

The purpose of his visit was, he told himself, to return the parcel of neatly laundered and pressed clothes he had borrowed to Amaru Khassian's household. Why, then, did he find himself so reluctant to go up to the front door and ring the bell?

He sat down on a bench by the curved railings that separated the pavement from the wide green lawns that rolled down towards the river. Another sneeze racked him and, as he tugged out his handkerchief, the letter fell from his pocket. He sighed and read it for the second time that morning.

My dear Acir,

I am concerned to note that the dangerous revolutionary Valentan has arrived in Sulien. Watch him. He is a trouble-maker. Our intelligence tells us that others may try to join him and orchestrate their plots using Sulien as their base.

The Commanderie is currently discussing with the Prince the possibility of obtaining extradition orders so that you may arrest the revolutionaries in Sulien and bring them back to stand trial in Bel'Esstar. This requires subtle diplomatic negotiation with Tourmalise so *do not make mention of this to anyone*.

If there is still any means by which you can persuade *our friend* to return of his own accord, then in Mhir's blessed name, I beg you to do so. I thought I detected from the tone of your last letter that you may be experiencing doubts as to your suitability for carrying out this mission. Please assure me, dearest confrère, that I am wrong.

Yours, in the Blood of the Rose,
Girim nel Ghislain

Acir looked up at Mistress Permay's house, shading his eyes against the sheen of spring sunshine. A shadow passed across the tall first-floor window . . . the Diva maybe? Or Khassian himself, trapped in the prison of his mutilation?

Girim's letter left him with a sick, sour taste in his mouth. It smacked of conspiracy and underhand dealings, rather than a divinely inspired purpose.

As he rose to cross the wide curve of the Crescent, he noticed a woman, elegantly dressed, also staring curiously up at Mistress Permay's house. It was the brightness of her hair that caught his eye, a brightness that made his heart stop.

Gold of sun on marigold meadows in distant Allegonde . . .

'Fiammis,' he murmured. It must be coincidence. It must be a trick of the sunlight. And yet he had heard it rumoured that Fiammis assumed many disguises in her work for the Cause.

The woman was coming nearer unhurriedly, strolling across the cobbled street as if to gaze at the smooth lawns and the green hills beyond. Acir turned his head away.

'Good day to you, Captain Korentan.'

He gave a little gasp as if he had been shot.

'It *is* you.'

She nodded. She seemed as cool, as self-controlled, as he remembered her. And as perfect. To look on her heart-shaped face, translucent skin as pale as narcissus petals, tore open a deep wound he had thought healed long ago.

'Fiammis.' He heard the tremor in his voice, struggled to control it. 'What are you doing here?'

'Taking the waters, dear Acir. Why else does one come to Sulien?'

The Contesse Fiammis. Girim's secret agent.

'*He*'s sent you, hasn't he?'

'Did I take you by surprise, Captain? You look as if you've seen a ghost.'

A ghost from my past, the past that might have been.

He was seized with a sudden irrational urge to go in and warn Amaru Khassian.

But all he said was, 'This is my mission, Fiammis,' with as much dignity as his damaged pride could permit before another sneeeze threatened to explode. He fumbled for his handkerchief to smother it.

'Dear me. What a nasty cold. But then, you shouldn't go river-bathing at this time of year.'

She took out a folded newspaper from her reticule and showed it to him.

'Haven't you read the *Sulien Chronicle*? "Heroic rescue in swollen Avenne. Man swept away by flood waters rescued from drowning. The selfless rescuer, a visitor from Allegonde, modestly refused to reveal his name but was thought to be one Acir Korentan, a Captain of the Commanderie." '

Acir silently handed her back the *Chronicle*.

'Maybe Girim will see it as good publicity for the Cause, Captain. Or maybe . . . he will wonder why you did not let Amaru Khassian drown?'

Khassian lay watching golden motes slowly spiralling in a thin shaft of spring sunlight. The darkness of the curtained room by day suited the darkness of his mood; he shunned the sunlight, preferring to hide from its brilliance in his room.

A debilitating lassitude had overcome him; he had awoken from a night of troubled dreams to a feeling of dread and hopelessness. His breakfast tray lay untouched, his favourite cup of mocha cold, with a thick skin congealing on the top.

He did not share Cramoisy's confidence in Orial Magelonne's gift. The girl was so young, so inexperienced. Even if she possessed a telepathic ability to hear the music in his mind, he suspected she would not have the musical skills to notate it accurately.

'What! Still abed?' The Diva came in and dragged open the heavy swagged velvet curtains. Khassian turned his face away from the dazzling daylight. 'It's past noon! And are you to be still abed when Orial arrives? Look at you – unshaven, undressed. The valet tells me you'd have none of his help! Must I do everything for you?'

'I want you to cancel this meeting with Demselle Magelonne,' Khassian said, slowly swinging his legs over the side of the bed. 'There's no point. It's not going to work.'

'How can you be so sure?' Cramoisy continued to bustle about the room, pouring water into the wash-basin, gathering up brushes, razors, towels, in readiness. He patted the chair, inviting Khassian to sit down before the mirror.

'The mother. Iridial. Maybe if she were still alive, she could have helped me –'

Cramoisy smoothed shaving lather on to Khassian's cheeks.

'Iridial is dead, Iel rest her soul. Her early death was a tragedy and heaven knows what killed her off so young – some said it was a chill on the lungs . . . But the daughter lives and she wants to help you.'

'*Help* me!' The word was distasteful to Khassian; it smacked of genteel charitable work and condescension.

'This is the last time I do this for you.' With short, deft strokes the castrato drew the razor across Khassian's cheeks, complaining all the while. 'I pay good money for Mistress Permay's nephew to be your valet – and you send him away!' He wiped off the last of the lather with a flourish and slapped on some bay lotion; Khassian's eyes watered with its aromatic sting.

'At least give the girl a chance.' Cramoisy seized a brush and began to tug it through Khassian's tangled hair.

He caught sight of his reflection; caught the dull, weary glint of despair in his eyes.

'It won't work,' he said.

Orial sat on her bed, hastily turning over and over the worn pages of her mother's *Treatise*, trying to remind herself of all she had learned. How inadequate a training it seemed, now that she was to be put to the test by a real musician.

A pang of fear fluttered in her stomach. The flaws in her knowledge could so easily be exposed. She shut the *Treatise* and clutched it to her like a talisman.

'Isn't this what I've always wanted?' she whispered to herself as she knelt to put the book back in its hiding place. 'A chance to prove myself?'

The fluttering surged again, charged with exhilaration.

'Yes,' she said to her reflection as she tied on her bonnet, determinedly tugging the ribbons tight under her chin, 'this is my chance, the only chance that may ever come my way. I have to take it.'

She went down the stairs and was just crossing the hall when the door to her father's office opened. She froze.

'Where are you off to, my dear?' called Dr Magelonne.

'Out . . . to take the air.' She dared not turn around for fear he should see that she had blushed.

'Such a fine day! A walk in the gardens is an excellent idea. Shall we go together?'

Together! Orial bit her lip, at a loss to know what to say. If she demurred, he would become suspicious. But if she was late for her appointment with Amaru Khassian . . .

'I – I'd love to Papa. But –'

'Doctor, you're not busy, are you?' Sister Crespine appeared, looking flustered. 'I think you'd better take a look at General Talley's gout. I suspect he's been at the spirits again.'

Orial held her breath, hoping.

'I'm so sorry, my dear.' Dr Magelonne kissed her on the cheek. 'Enjoy your walk. Maybe we can go tomorrow?'

Spring sunshine gilded the plaster cornices of the elegant Crescent salon, glinted in the glass of the oval mirrors. Orial saw that Khassian was standing staring out of the tall windows; he did not even turn around as Cramoisy brought her forward.

'Orial, this is His Excellency the Illustre, Amaru Khassian.' Cramoisy took Orial by the arm and led her forward. 'Illustre – Demselle Orial Magelonne.'

Orial, well-trained in etiquette at the Academie, dipped a curtsey. When she raised her head she saw that Amaru Khassian was regarding her with a guarded air. She knew at once that he was bitterly sceptical, that he had already dismissed the whole plan as hopeless. And this realisation gave her a sudden surge of defiant energy. How dare he prejudge her? Was he too proud to accept her help – even if it was that of a mere novice?

'Demselle Magelonne.' He cleared his throat, evidently as ill at ease as she was. 'It is – generous of you to offer your help in this way. I hesitate to ask this of you – but if we are to proceed, would you be so kind as to seat yourself at this desk and transcribe a few notes for me?'

Cramoisy ushered Orial to the desk and patted her arm reassuringly. Stave paper, rulers, pens and ink were neatly laid out.

'What shall I write?' she asked.

Khassian went back to the window and leaned his arm against the pane in what seemed to Orial an attitude of weary melancholy.

'I'm rehearsing a simple four-bar melody. Shall I tell you the pitch it begins on?'

'No.' Orial shook her head, concentrating. 'It's *bémol* . . .'

The clarity of the Illustre's thoughts astonished her. She could 'hear' the melody almost as clearly as if he were playing it aloud for her. She reached for a pencil and began to scribble the notes down, stopping to chew the end as she puzzled over the number of beats in a bar. Was he trying to catch her out?

He walked over and stood behind her, looking over her shoulder. She held the paper up to him and watched with a certain self-satisfaction the way his dark brows rose – not in scepticism this time but in slow surprise. He turned on Cramoisy.

'This is a conspiracy. You planned it between you.'

'Me?' Cramoisy said sharply. 'How could I plan anything of the sort, Amar? How could I know what tune you were thinking?'

'Look. Look for yourself.' He gestured towards Orial and she noticed for the first time the ruined hand which the loose lace on his cuff had concealed, the stiffened claw coated in red scar-tissue.

'I don't need to look.' Cramoisy was regarding himself critically in the mirror, tucking back an errant curl. 'I know she can do it. You're the unbeliever.'

'The handwriting is somewhat crude.' Khassian seemed keen to find any reason to be critical. 'And she reverses the tails on the quavers.' He wheeled back to Orial. 'Did you know the stems should be on the left of the notes above the centre stave line?'

'For Mhir's sake, Amaru, don't be such a perfectionist! Could you have done as much?'

'So – in spite of the stems – I transcribed the tune correctly?' Orial asked.

The muscles in his face twitched with the passage of conflicting emotions. She saw that he could not begin to allow himself to hope again.

'A lucky coincidence. I need a professional amanuensis.'

'Give her another chance,' urged Cramoisy.

Orial was angry now. She had lied to her father to gain an hour's freedom to come here – and now he was treating her in this contemptuous fashion.

'I think I should go,' she said, rising.

'No, no.' Cramoisy rushed over to her, pressing her back into the seat. 'Amaru is being unpardonably rude. Amar – stop behaving like a boor. Show some courtesy to Demselle Magelonne.'

'I –' He stalked back to the window, his face a mask. 'Very well. A second chance.'

The music, when it came, took Orial by surprise. The first melody had been simple, a child's nursery-tune. But this echoed the dark-hued, twisting, tormented line of the music she had first 'heard' in the Sanatorium. It taxed her skills in notation to the limit. Her mind filled with darkness; the notes gashed the darkness with the brilliance of forked lightning. It was alien, unlike any music she had known before.

She looked up from the stave paper, blinking. What she had written was untidy, slashed out, altered as she struggled to notate unfamiliar intervals, rhythm patterns.

He stood above her, looking down at what she had written.

'You heard me think *that*?'

She sensed his hand, hidden beneath the soft lace, give an unconscious twitch – as though desperate to seize the pencil from her and score through the scrawl.

'I am unfamiliar with your style,' she said. Afterwards she would wonder how she had summoned the courage to do it.

'She's your only hope,' Cramoisy pleaded.

'I'll be difficult to work with. I'm impossible to please.' The eyes that met Orial's were suddenly the eyes of a mischievous boy, sulky yet seductive, used to getting his own way. The eyes of a spoiled child. 'Cramoisy said you wanted to learn. Your first devoir is to improve your hand. If we are to work together, I need to be able to read what you write.'

'I'm self-taught.' Indignant at the criticism, Orial felt her face go red. 'My mother had begun to teach me to read music when – when she died. I could just read the pitches. I worked the rest out for myself with a treatise.

You obviously need someone who has been properly trained –' She stood up and went towards the door, one hand blindly reaching for the handle.

'Wait.' There was a catch in his voice, the first genuine hint of emotion she had heard. She paused. 'I'm sorry if I have been a little – abrupt.'

'We can always employ a professional to make neat copies,' Cramoisy said. *Don't go*, his eyes implored Orial.

'So my transcription *was* accurate?'

'Yes. Untidy – but astonishingly accurate. An uncomfortable sensation . . . knowing that someone else is reading your mind.' The lambent brown eyes rested on her. 'Well, demselle. Are you prepared to try to work with this unreasonable, ill-tempered brute?'

'Yes,' said Orial. 'I am.'

Outside in the sunshine, the Crescent suddenly spun dizzyingly about her. Orial put out a hand to grip the spiked ornamental railings, steadying herself. The effort of concentrating on the mindmusic and the tension of the encounter must have taken a greater toll on her energies than she had realised. Now she felt achingly tired. The ten minutes' walk back to the Sanatorium seemed like ten miles.

Maybe I'm making a mistake. Maybe I'm not ready to take on such a responsibility . . .

She set out slowly, shading her eyes against the brilliant sunshine.

Crocuses, saffron-yellow, carpeted the grass, opening their gilded petals to the sun. She moved through a sea of sunlight, sniffing the saffron perfume of the ochre pollen dusting the heart of each waxen bloom.

Floating through golden waters . . .

She lifted her face to the sun and felt its light warming her, restoring her.

At the Sanatorium she hastily shrugged off her cape and, clutching her cap, went hurrying down to join Sister Crespine in the steam room.

The Sister looked up from her work and a slight frown passed across her face.

'I'm not late, am I, Sister?'

'No, no. Not late.'

A little later, the Sister whispered to her in passing, 'Who is he?'

Orial looked at her blankly.

'I promise I won't breathe a word to your father, but I can tell. There's a glow about you. It always shows.' She gave Orial a conspiratorial little nudge and a wink.

Astonished, Orial found herself nodding in reply.

A glow? As she passed the mirror she sneaked a glance at herself. Then she stopped and looked with more attention. Was it a trick of the light or had her eyes darkened again? And were those striations of topaz, striping the blue – the intense gold of the spring crocuses she had walked amongst on the Crescent lawns?

Passing the open kitchen door, she heard Sister murmuring to Cook, 'Have you seen our little Orial? She's growing up fast. Radiant. Quite radiant.'

And Cook, growling back a terse reply.

'That was how her mother was. *Before.*'

The Museum office was cluttered with rubbish. Empty mugs, stained with a dirty dried sediment of qaffë grounds, lined the windowsills and a faint odour of stale candlesmoke hung in the air.

'Jolaine?' Orial called.

Open notebooks lay strewn everywhere, showing meticulous sketches, line drawings of the Under Temple stelae and their hieroglyph inscriptions. The lifetime's work of a scholar.

And then Orial saw her.

Dame Jolaine Tradescar lay slumped over one of the open notebooks, her head on her arm, her wig tipped awry.

At first she lay so still, Orial thought she was dead.

Given Dame Jolaine's advanced years, this was, Orial allowed, a possibility – and yet her soul-guardian had always seemed indestructible, the one constant in her life on which she could rely.

Orial crept forwards . . . and as she came nearer, the Antiquarian sighed and let out a rattling snore.

She had fallen asleep at her desk.

Orial knelt beside Dame Jolaine and gently tried to replace the wig. Her scalp beneath was shinily pink, still tufted here and there with straggling white hairs.

'Jolaine,' Orial said again, close to her ear.

'Eh? What?' Jolaine Tradescar opened her eyes and stared blearily at her. 'Dear me, I must have nodded off for a few moments there.'

'More than a few moments! Have you been taking care of yourself? Have you been remembering to eat?'

Jolaine sat up, adjusting her wig.

'What hour is it?'

'Past ten.'

'Dear me. Dear me. More than a few moments, then.'

'Shall I go fetch you some breakfast from the pastry shop?'

'There's no need to fuss over me, child, I can look after myself,' Dame Jolaine said tetchily. Then she leaned across and patted Orial's hand. 'Been so busy here, I seem to have lost track of the hours . . . the days . . .'

Orial regarded Jolaine anxiously as the Antiquarian stood up and slowly stretched.

'It's my latest find,' she said apologetically. 'I think I may have stumbled on something of significance.' She winced as she tried to reach for a bound notebook that lay on the table beyond. 'A curse on this rheumatism.'

'A find?' Orial's curiosity was aroused.

'At first I feared someone was out to dupe me. I thought it must be a fake. But it seems genuine.'

'What seems genuine?'

'I've just got to . . . pop out the back a moment. Bladder plays tricks too at my age. Take a look at this whilst I'm gone.'

Jolaine handed her the notebook and hobbled out. Hieroglyphs had been copied on to the page . . . but below them Orial saw Jolaine had begun to enter tentative translations: 'Elesstar'; 'Goddess'; 'winged one/ soul/dragonfly?'

'Well? What do you think?' Jolaine appeared in the doorway.

'Is it – is it true? Have you really broken the code? Do you know what the stelae say?' Orial was so excited the questions came spilling, all jumbled up.

'I've cracked a little of the code. Thanks to the vindictive obsession of one of our distant ancestors. A curse, scratched backwards on pewter, thrown into the spring. Heaven knows if the Goddess read it! But because our curse-writer was unsure which language She best understood, he took the trouble to inscribe it in both tongues.'

'No wonder you lost track of the time.'

'Of course there are discrepancies. But the texts have symbols which recur – and thus I find myself able to begin to decipher them at last.'

'So what do they say?'

Jolaine Tradescar came to stand beside her.

'A strange people, the Lifhendil. With stranger beliefs. I can only surmise that much of this is religious – symbolic – but without full understanding of their myths and legends, I have to admit that most of it is utterly perplexing.'

'Stop tantalising me, Jolaine, and show me what you've translated!'

'Maybe you can make more sense of it than I can.'

Orial picked up the translation.

'*They [fall into the] long sleep – they lie many moons in the dark waters – sun warms [the waters] – they fly to the light –*'

'It's as you thought. The stelae must be memorial tablets. This describes funeral rites – an early version of what we do today.'

'Just as I thought too – *at first.*'

'What do you mean?'

'Sleep. Rest.' Jolaine Tradescar's eyes glimmered. 'We speak in metaphors. So much less distressing to talk of the "eternal rest" than death. "Rest in peace." But maybe here it actually means sleep. A dormant state.' She thumbed through the notebook and handed it back. 'Read this one.'

'Once I walked on the earth. Now – praise Ea-stil – I am transformed. I fly with the winged ones. I – – – through the time of the dark waters.'

Orial looked up to see that Jolaine was watching her intently, waiting expectantly for her reaction.

'Winged ones?' She found she was whispering as if they were sharing a secret of great import, and she feared they might be overheard.

'Look at the engravings. These are not dragonflies, they're winged people.'

'Angels, maybe?' Jolaine's excitement was infectious.

'We must go back into the Undercity and look carefully at your Lotos Princess. That's what you named her, didn't you? I seem to recall that there are two winged creatures hovering behind her. I have managed to unravel a little of her inscription. I know it will intrigue you.'

Orial looked at Jolaine questioningly as she took the book again and read:

'Spinner [of the] invisible songthreads/that knit us together/that [make us] One with Ea'stil.'

'Spinner?' she asked. 'Songspinner?'

'Songspinner. As in the monograph I showed you. It's not too fanciful, is it? The real title of the Lotos Princess was – Songspinner.'

CHAPTER 8

Khassian sat brooding over the first pages which Orial had transcribed for him.

What a strange creature she was, his little amanuensis – by turns eager to please, then wilful; shy, then acutely forthright. Not for the first time he found himself thinking that she was only a little younger than Fania would have been now, if she had lived – and not for the first time, found the thought so painful that he shut his mind to it. Fania, his beloved sister, dead of the smallpox at the tender age of twelve. Fania, his father's treasure. Fania, so gifted, so pretty . . . Was that why he was so awkward with Orial, so abrupt? Because she remained him of Fania and the disintegration of his family? She did not deserve this brusqueness.

But then there was her gift. It disturbed him. How could she hear the music in his head? And if she could hear what was in his head, how could she simultaneously block out all the music emanating from other people's minds, the repetitions, the scraps of tunes?

Yet here, on paper, painstakingly achieved, lay the first bars of the last act of the opera in short score, instruments sketched in . . . It had taken an hour to notate these thirty-one bars. She was slow, struggling still to sort out theoretical complexities which she had never had to contend with before. He found it hard to keep patient when he could not seize the pen from her fingers and show her how it should be done. Sometimes he could have bellowed aloud with frustration.

How long would it take before this blotted, untidy score could be handed to the copyists and work could begin on staging it?

He was so engrossed in thought that he did not hear the knock at the door. It was only as it opened and the visitor came in that he glanced up and saw Acir Korentan.

The sheets of music lay spread out on the table in front of him. He could not pick up a cloth to throw over them – or shuffle them hastily out of sight. He stood up and placed himself in front of them, hoping Acir would not notice.

'I'm disturbing you,' his visitor said.

'Yes. You are.'

'I came to return the clothes that Sieur Jordelayne lent me. My landlady has washed and pressed them.' Acir seemed all stiff courtesy once more.

'But it appears that he is out.' He placed the neat bundle of clothes on the couch.

'Out arranging a recital at the Guildhall, I believe,' Khassian said casually.

Acir nodded. He turned towards the door – and then turned back.

'Illustre,' he said, and there was a sudden urgency in his voice, quite unlike the earlier formal tone, 'I must talk to you. Have you any idea of the danger you are in?'

'Danger? Oh, you mean the danger to my immortal soul.'

'I mean personal danger.' He took a step nearer. 'Have you ever encountered the Contesse Fiammis?'

'The name is familiar.' Khassian was thrown off-course; the conversation had not taken a direction he had anticipated at all. 'I may have been introduced to her at court . . .'

'She is here. In Sulien.'

'I don't follow.'

'So you are unaware of her connections with the Commanderie?'

Khassian slowly nodded his head, uncertain what new tactic Acir was employing to sway him.

'She is dangerous, Illustre.'

'You're trying to threaten me!' he said, laughing.

'Threaten? Oh, no. Whatever differences there may be between us, I would not stoop to threaten – or to shadow my adversary like some Enhirran assassin. That is not the honourable way. That is not the way of the Guerrior.'

There was an earnestness in that steel-blue regard that profoundly unsettled Khassian. Acir Korentan was no fanatic, seared by dark fires raging within. No, the young man displayed a quite disarming frankness that – and Khassian had grudgingly to admit this to himself – had they not found themselves on opposing sides – he could well have found sympathetic.

'And the way of the Guerrior is to fight to defend the faith? It would have been so much easier for you if we could have settled this dispute, sword in hand, like men of honour.' Khassian could not prevent a smile from twitching at the corners of his mouth. And to his surprise he caught the ghost of a smile flickering across the Captain's stern face.

'You would have made a more than worthy opponent, Illustre,' he said, clicking his heels in a formal bow.

And, lacking real blades, Khassian thought, smiling too, *I can still duel with words, Captain Korentan.*

'So I am still "invited" to return to Bel'Esstar with you?'

'A reconciliation, that's all the Grand Maistre is seeking.'

Reconciliation. The word grated on Khassian's ear like an ill-tuned string.

'Humiliation would be more apt. Isn't that closer to the truth, Captain? Girim nel Ghislain would like nothing better than to see me prostrate myself at his feet in the holy name of the Poet-Prophet Mhir.'

'You misinterpret the doctrines of the Commanderie. Is it so hard to accept the teachings of Mhir? Are you so proud that you cannot accept a higher authority than your own?'

'I'm not talking of pride. I'm talking of spiritual honesty. Would it not be more contemptible if I dissembled? If I cynically professed a faith in which I did not believe – just to save my skin?'

Acir Korentan did not reply. But Khassian could see from the shadow that had darkened the piercing blue of those eyes that he was winning. Triumphant in that knowledge, he began to press his advantage.

'And miracles. Where does the Commanderie stand with regard to miracles?'

Acir Korentan was silent for a moment. When he spoke, his tone was pensive, as if he was still pondering Khassian's question.

'There has been no recorded miracle since the blood of the Rose restored the Beloved Elesstar to life. But a belief in miracles is an essential part of the doctrine.'

'And you would agree that only a miracle would restore my hands?'

Khassian saw to his bitter satisfaction Acir Korentan's expression betray first confusion – then anger; he had caught him off-guard.

'I tell you, Captain Korentan, that I would only consider public conversion to your faith if a miracle cure was guaranteed.'

The Captain shook his head slowly, sadly.

'Then there is no hope for you.'

'The Prince was miraculously cured of his wasting illness! Is that any different?'

'When the Prince knelt before the Grand Maistre in the shrine and asked forgiveness of his past sins, he was truly repentant. And from his belief came the remission of suffering, the gradual healing that restored his health.'

'So it wasn't a miracle!' Khassian said, bitterly triumphant.

'Why do you make mock of our faith?' Acir Korentan asked.

'Why did your Commanderie attack me and my opera?'

'You spoke earlier of cynicism. The Commanderie judged your opera an act of extreme cynicism, the work of a sick and amoral soul, deliberately designed to mislead and corrupt.'

'Oh, and you saw my opera, I suppose?' Khassian said, his voice crackling with sarcasm. 'You read the score? You heard the music?'

'You abused the one thing I hold most sacred. You twisted the holy texts to – *entertain*. I cannot condone that.'

'So that's what you believe?' Khassian moved closer. 'That my intentions were to corrupt?'

'Illustre? Is everything all right?' Mistress Permay rattled the door handle. Both men tensed, glancing towards the door. A second later, the mob-capped head of the mistress of the house appeared.

'I heard voices. Shouting. Old Lady Bartel in the apartments above has complained. I run a respectable establishment and I will not have my other guests upset.'

'Please give my abject apologies to Lady Bartel,' Khassian said with exaggerated courtesy. 'We were rehearsing a scene from my opera and must have allowed ourselves to be quite carried away by the – emotion of the situation.' He could not resist a malicious glance at the Captain as he delivered this coup de grâce.

'I was just about to leave.' Acir Korentan, all icy tact, gave a brusque nod of the head and retreated.

Khassian stood at the window and watched him stride hurriedly away along the curve of the Crescent. Korentan's tensed shoulders, his brisk pace, all betrayed his frustration.

'I win this bout,' Khassian said quietly. But he frowned as he said it.

Acir Korentan turned abruptly aside from the Crescent and plunged into the grove of great trees that bordered the Wilderness Garden beyond.

The arrogance of the man! The overweening arrogance!

He had gone to warn Khassian of the very real danger he was in – and Khassian had laughed in his face. He had baited him, he had mocked his beliefs! And yet . . .

Acir came to a standstill.

And yet he sensed there was an essential integrity of spirit beneath the cynical veneer. And in one respect, he had to admit, Khassian was right. He had never read the opera libretto. Girim nel Ghislain had described it to him, had recited aloud one or two of the passages of holy scripture which Khassian had, the Grand Maistre alleged, portrayed in his score in a blasphemous manner.

He stood amidst ancient cedars in a dark, mossy glade. A marble dryad glimmered on the far side, pale in the gloom; spirit of the grove, haunting the Wilderness. The air was damp, tinged with the green smell of moss and creeping lichens.

The chronicle of Mhir's death and transfiguration had been set down by an unknown disciple . . . though many, including Acir, believed that Elesstar the Beloved had written a substantial part of it. The ancient text was spare yet each incident was graven into Acir's memory as vividly as if he had been a witness to the events.

He sat on a marble bench, stained with damp, and pulled his breviary from his jacket.

When she heard the words of the Prophet Mhir, Elesstar felt her heart burn with longing. She looked on his face and saw the true radiance of Iel. She arose and put aside the fine raiment and costly jewels that the Shultan Arizhar had given her.

She found Mhir at work with his disciples around him, labouring to rebuild the fallen Temple of Mhir, the Temple which Arizhar the Cruel had razed to the ground in his impiety.

And there in that holy place Mhir and the slavewoman Elesstar were united before Iel . . .

Amaru Khassian had chosen to interpret these words as literally as any sensation-seeking crowd-pleaser would have done. Girim had told Acir that the opera required Mhir and Elesstar to be seen to come together – physically – on the stage. Acir found the thought of the castrato – and another man – play-acting physical consummation utterly repellent. It reduced Mhir's transcendent love – Acir's inspiration and his life's pattern – to a mere shudder of lust, contrived to titillate the jaded palates of the opera audience.

At the heart of the scripture was Elesstar: Elesstar the slave, the Shultan's concubine, whose love for Mhir redeemed her of her past sins. Elesstar's redemption was the essential metaphor illuminating the Thorny Path.

Khassian had spoken disparagingly, cynically, of miracles. But then he had reduced the miracle of Elesstar's resurrection to an acted charade, a mere theatrical device: a puff of smoke, a clap of a thunder board, a crash of the cymbals. He had robbed it of its mystery – and its meaning. Small wonder he could not begin to imagine the true power of the metaphor.

'If the sinner Elesstar could be saved – transfigured – by the Blood of the Rose,' Girim had cried to the assembled Commanderie, 'then have faith that you too can be saved!'

The damp seemed to be seeping into Acir's bones, oozing from dank cedar boughs. The darkness of the deserted glade only enhanced his morose mood; his task seemed impossible. Amaru Khassian was damaged in spirit as well as in body – yet too proud to ask for his help.

Maybe Fiammis was right. Maybe he should have let the composer drown. Maybe he should not have striven so hard to warm the limp body back to life with his own breath. Khassian had seemed so set on self-destruction. Maybe he should admit defeat, return to Bel'Esstar and let Fiammis finish the job for him –

'No!' Acir cried aloud. He sprang to his feet and began to pace the glade, feet squelching in the wet moss.

He did not like to acknowledge the fact but ever since he had breathed the life back into the half-drowned Khassian, he had felt in some intangible way . . . *connected* to the man.

Steam clouded the tiled walls of the Sanatorium pool, misting Orial's lenses. Annoyed, she took off her spectacles and, for the third time that morning, wiped them on her apron. Blinking, she gazed around at the ceramic tiles: the familiar blue and green motifs of whorled shells and water-lilies were still blurred. She examined the spectacle lenses again – but they were clean, clear of the smudging moisture.

Is my sight deteriorating? Do I need stronger lenses? Maybe I should consult Papa.

But then he might ask her what she had been doing to strain her eyes, he might wonder what kind of close work would cause such a deterioration. Close work such as the intricate notation of music –

No, best not to mention it to Papa.

All morning, Orial fretted over her tasks in the Sanatorium, impatient to be away to the Crescent and to Amaru Khassian. But when she had finished, her hands were shrivelled and wrinkled with constant immersion in the hot spring water and with slapping on noisome mineral-mud.

As Orial was drying her damp fingers, Sister Crespine came bustling past and slipped something into her apron pocket.

'What's this?' Orial brought out a little black jar.

'Calendula balm. Marigolds. Keeps the hands nice and soft,' Sister Crespine said and, to Orial's surprise, gave her a wink. 'Don't you worry, dear, your secret's safe with me.'

'Thank you.' Puzzled, Orial sniffed the white ointment; it gave off a scent of spring meadows, sweet as new-mown grass. What did Sister Crespine know? How much had her frequent absences been noticed – and remarked upon? Sister Crespine must believe she was keeping a tryst with a secret admirer.

Orial sighed and began to smooth a dab of the soft balm between her fingers. Amaru Khassian her admirer? The thought sent a strange shiver of warmth through her body. But theirs was no conventional friendship; she was the admirer, he the admired. On his side, the arrangement was one of obligation; she knew he would never have troubled to pay her the slightest attention if he had not needed her help.

But what links us?

She had read of an invisible thread of understanding discovered to link certain susceptible individuals. Was it possible that such a link existed between her and Amaru Khassian? Were they like two strings tuned to the same pitch; when one was plucked, the other vibrated too in sympathy?

Orial had devised a number of backstreet routes to reach the Crescent, each one designed to avoid recognition by any of her father's medical colleagues. She cut through alleyways and hurried along mews, past dairies, laundries and stables where horses whinnied and stamped in their stalls.

She was hurrying along Paragon Mews when she almost ran headlong into a young woman in scarlet riding habit coming out of one of the stables.

'Orial!' cried the young woman, reaching out to kiss her on both cheeks. 'It's been simply *ages*. You're looking a little peaky, my dear.'

'Alizaeth?' Orial said, stepping back. She and Alizaeth had been at the Academie for Young Ladies together. She had been dazzled by Alizaeth at school; with her glossy black curls and easy chatter, she had commanded the attention of a circle of admirers. But Orial had grown to realise they had little in common; Alizaeth's interests lay in balls and gowns.

'Aren't you going to congratulate me?' Her smile had become coy.

'Congratulate you?' Orial's brain had been filled with music; now the shock of encountering Alizaeth had made her mind go blank.

'I'm to be married!' Alizaeth said with a squeal of self-satisfaction. 'In four days' time. There's to be a banquet at the Rooms. I'd have asked you to be one of my maidens, but Alyn – that's his name, he's training to be an advocate – has so many sisters and female cousins . . .'

Orial nodded, smiling, starting to edge away. She must escape before Alizaeth started to tell her the wedding plans.

'I'd love to talk, but I'm late for an appointment. Some other time – '

'Don't you want to hear about my gown?'

'Oh yes, yes . . .' Orial backed down the mews, trying to sound enthusiastic.

'Orchid white silk, with an overlayer of gauze net – '

'You'll look ravishing,' Orial cried, turning on her heel and running.

'I'll tell Mama to send you an invitation,' Alizaeth called after her.

As Orial darted away, she experienced a sudden moment of self-revelation. A few weeks ago, she would have felt hurt to learn that Alizaeth had not bothered to invite her to be her wedding-maiden. But since Cramoisy and Khassian had arrived, she had not once thought of Alizaeth or her schooldays. She had been transported into a world more magical, more dangerous, than anything she could have imagined. There was more to life than an orchid silk gown and a wedding banquet at the Assembly Rooms.

'You're late,' Khassian said accusingly.

'I was – unavoidably detained.' Orial untied her cape and flung it over the couch.

'I've been looking over what you wrote down yesterday.' He seemed restless, irritable. 'There are errors of notation.'

She checked the retort that had sprung to her lips for she could sense he was in pain. An echo of the dull ache in his damaged hands resonated in her own fingers.

'I'll correct them,' she said quickly.

He nodded tersely.

'Is – anything else amiss?'

'Nothing.' He turned away from her.

She picked up her pen and had just opened the inkwell to check that it was full when she heard him speak again.

'How dare he accuse me of such a thing? How dare he presume to know me, know my most intimate thoughts and intentions!'

'I'm sorry?' She was uncertain whether he was muttering to himself or to her.

'Elesstar's aria. Where is it?'

She shuffled through the sheets and brought it out to show him.

'Read it again. Tell me if you think it is blasphemous.'

She gazed quizzically up at him, wondering what had provoked this outburst. He seemed distressed, his face contorted with suppressed anger. It would be best to humour him. She lifted the sheets and began to scan them rapidly; in her mind the raw passion of Elesstar's grief was reawakened, clothed in the sombre colours of Khassian's twisted harmonies. The music was strong, impassioned, sincere – and, to her untrained ears, difficult.

'Well?' he demanded impatiently. 'Has it corrupted you?'

'Corrupted, Illustre?' She did not understand what he meant.

'You observe that I have twisted the holy texts, I have distorted their meaning.'

'How can a piece of music such as this corrupt?'

'And yet, for writing this, they call me a blasphemer.'

'It *is* a little unconventional,' Orial ventured.

'And so it should be! Did they want pretty, simpering little tunes? Inoffensive harmonies to blunt the ear? The whole point was to make the story relevant in a cynical, jaded age. To make Mhir and Elesstar live again.'

Orial stared down at the sheets. She could hear the aria clearly in her head – but was her handwriting really so smudged? She held the paper nearer, closing one eye and then the other. Close to, it looked less indistinct. The music sang on in her head even though she could no longer focus upon the notes. She took off her spectacles and pinched her eyelids closed. Jagged pinpricks of light shot across the darkness in rhythmic patterns that mirrored the music.

What is wrong with my eyes?

'Are you all right, demselle?'

She opened her eyes again and forced a smile.

'I have a slight headache. May I take a glass of water before we begin?'

He gestured towards the crystal carafe which stood on a table beneath one of the gilt-swagged mirrors and went back to his habitual position by the window.

'No. It can't be . . .' Orial heard him murmur to himself. Suddenly he called excitedly, 'Cramoisy! Cramoisy!'

The Diva appeared in the doorway, yawning.

'Well, and what is it that you must wake me from my afternoon nap?'

'Look – down there in the Crescent –'

'*Miu Diu!*' cried Cramoisy, rushing into the hall. 'They've escaped.'

Khassian went to go after the Diva and then paused in the doorway.

'Those corrections, demselle.'

Perplexed, Orial sat down again at the escritoire and took up her pen. But the babble of voices in the hall was too noisy to allow for concentration.

'Were you seen? Did anyone pay attention to you?'

'Commanderie agents? In Sulien?'

'Even here. Come into the salon, come in. Cramoisy – what can we offer our guests? Tea? Wine?'

Orial laid down her pen as Khassian brought three strangers, shabbily dressed, into the salon.

'This is my amanuensis – Demselle Magelonne. Orial – meet three of the most gifted musicians it has been my privilege to work with. Azare – my repetiteur, a genius on the keyboard. Philamon – the deepest, most velvety bass voice in all Allegonde. And Astrel – the principal of the Opera orchestra.'

Orial dipped a curtsey. She could see the ravages of hunger etched into the visitors' hollow cheeks, weeks of neglect in their straggling beards and uncombed hair.

'But how did you evade the Commanderie?' cried Khassian.

'By spending weeks hidden in a damp cellar below the Conservatoire. They did not think to search in so obvious a place.'

'And papers? They could have arrested you at the border.'

'Clever forgeries. Astrel adapted that old music press in the cellar . . .'

Orial quietly began to tidy away the pens and pencils. Her presence, she sensed, was superfluous. Already the fugitives were pouring out the tale of their escape and Khassian's attention was focussed solely on them.

The pendule clock on the mantlepiece struck the hour. Heavens, it was five! She had lost track of the time and she was late for tea – Papa would be waiting for her to join him. She would have to run all the way.

Jerame Magelonne checked his fob watch again. Late for tea. Where was she? This sudden interest in helping the Antiquarian at the Cabinet of Curiosities seemed excessive. And her behaviour of late had been erratic. She often seemed preoccupied, lost in thought, even *distraite*.

Surely it could not be the beginnings of the Accidie . . .

No! He instantly banished the thought, refusing to acknowledge it could be a possibility. He had done his utmost to protect her from the baneful influence of music. And yet he had heard her singing tunes of her own making. It must not happen again. He had been unable to save Iridial from the curse of her inheritance, but he would give his last drop of blood to save his daughter.

He looked anxiously out into the courtyard. Eleven minutes past five. Didn't she know he would worry if she was late? Their afternoon tea ritual was something he cherished, looked forward to. When she was still at the Academie, she would come rushing in, cheeks flushed with excitement, to tell him the day's news. Charming things, schoolgirls' prattle, a distraction from the cares and worries of the Sanatorium.

'Tea's getting cold, Doctor,' called Cook through the open doorway.

'Er-hm. You haven't seen Orial, have you?' he asked.

'She not back yet? Ah,' said Cook knowingly.

'Cook,' said Jerame, hurrying after her, 'is everything all right with her?'

'So you've noticed at last!' she said with a cackle. Then she tapped the side of her nose. 'And about time too, I say. Head down in a book all the time – she'll be left on the shelf.'

'On the shelf?' Jerame realised what Cook was implying. Orial was courting? No. Impossible. And yet it might explain the distant look in her eyes, the sudden starts, the vague manner . . .

He caught sight of his own reflection in the mirror; watchful, mistrustful eyes, lips compressed in disapproval. Was that how she saw him? The repressive, over-protective father?

He went into the morning room and, sitting down, mechanically lifted the pot to pour tea, a task Orial usually performed. He lifted the bowl to his lips, unthinking; the heat of the pale liquid stung his tongue. Surprised, he set the bowl down. He had not been thinking about what he was doing. He had been thinking of Orial. He swallowed hard. The mouthful of tea scalded his throat.

He had not realised till now how much he had been dreading this moment. It was the natural cycle of things, after all. You cared for children, watched them grow . . . but when the time came to let them go, did it have to be so hard?

Harder for him to let go than for others. For in Orial, the echo of Iridial still lived and breathed. It was not so much in her physical appearance . . . although of late even that had begun to change . . . but in her gestures, the expressions which glided across her face, clouds across sunlight . . .

He reached blindly for the tea again, gulped down the hot liquid, ignoring the burn. She was still not back and it was a quarter past the hour. What did one say in these situations? You are confined to your room? You must never leave the Sanatorium unchaperoned again? He was not sure how adept he would be at playing the stern papa. He had no wish to turn her against him . . . and yet, damn it all, she was late and he was worried!

If only Iridial – He checked the thought. No point in wishing. At moments like this, a mother's subtle advice would be so much more appropriate. She would remember what it was like to be a girl of eighteen, to be young, admired . . .

And her secret admirer. Who was he? Some bespectacled student of Jolaine Tradescar's, perhaps, or some Academie boy . . .

What hurt him most was that she had not confided in him. Perhaps – he stood up and began to pace the room – she was ashamed of what she had done. Dear Goddess! She was sensible. Surely she would not have –

'Hallo, Papa, I'm so sorry I'm late!' She came into the room, casting her cape down over a chair. Her face seemed flushed, a becoming, rosy tinge warming her usual delicate pallor.

'It's nearly five-thirty,' he said stiffly.

'I'm starving. What has Cook prepared today?' She lifted the silver lid. 'Toasted teacakes! And they're still warm. Won't you have one, Papa?' She turned to him, holding out the teacake on a plate; a peace-offering.

He shook his head.

'I'm not hungry.'

'More tea, then?' she said a little plaintively. She must have sensed his anger.

'I was worried, Orial!'

'I was . . . delayed. That's all.'

Why wouldn't she tell him the truth? As she sipped her tea, cupping in her fingers the delicate bowl with its pattern of green and black cranes, her eyes were averted, fixed on some distant point beyond the steam rising from the bowl.

'Orial – is there anything you want to tell me?'

She started.

'I don't think you're being wholly truthful with me. I think you're hiding something, keeping something back. Now – I know all young girls are flattered by the advances of young men, I know it's spring, but –'

'Oh, Papa.' She went to him and put her arms around his neck, hugging him. She smelt clean and fresh, the pale fragrance of wild hyacinths. 'You mustn't worry about me. I won't abandon you. No matter what happens.'

All his intentions were fast ebbing away, already he could see what an unreasonable tyrant he must seem to her . . . And yet at the same time, as she gently disengaged her arms, he felt the needling sense of unease return. Since Iridial's death Orial had rarely lied to him . . . Though there had been the stray sable kitten, kept concealed in a basket in the laundry until it leapt playfully out at Sister Crespine, its tiny claws unsheathed . . . And the time she had been kept back after school for some schoolgirlish prank involving water, string and a loathed termagant of a needlework mistress . . . Trifles, really.

She had been such a biddable child, always eager to please. Which only made the present episode harder to understand.

He must keep a closer watch over her.

CHAPTER 9

Fiammis is floating just below the surface of the lake, her long yellow hair streaming about her pale body like ribbons of waterweed. Naked as a watersprite, her slender limbs shimmer with the fluorescent taint of floating algae.

Anguished, Acir goes wading into the green waters, catches hold of the limp body and drags it out on to the shore.

'Fia! Fia!' He can hear himself frantically calling Fiammis's name, her pet-name, the name he has not dared to use since childhood when they were constant companions.

Fiammis does not stir.

Acir leans over her, presses his mouth to Fiammis's and, encompassing the wet body with his own, begins to blow breath into the limp body.

The weed-stained lids open. Fiammis is staring directly into his eyes. Fiammis's arms, her waterweed hair, wind about him, binding their wet bodies together. Her mouth, no longer slack and cold, presses upon Acir's, her tongue . . .

They are rolling, rolling back into the water, floating down into the green depths, drowning slowly in this unending kiss . . .

Acir gasps for breath, each convulsive shudder wracking his body more profoundly than the last.

'Fia, oh Fia, Fia . . .'

Acir Korentan awoke, calling the name of his dream-lover. And then, with a groan of self-disgust, he felt a stickiness staining the sheet in which he had twisted himself.

How could I? *How could I?*

And he thought he had finally exorcised the ghost of her memory!

He lit a crimson candle before the rose reliquary and prostrated himself naked on the bare boards of his lodgings. He was shaking.

'Forgive me,' he said silently again and again. 'A lapse. A moment of foolish human frailty.'

The scourge still lay at the bottom of his travelling bag. He hardly felt the sting of its knotted cords as he struck himself in penance again and again. He was trying to score the image from his mind. The false dream-image. The dark succubus that had betrayed him into sins of incontinence and self-pollution.

The scourge dropped to the floor. He looked down at himself in the first light of dawn and winced. Angry weals had brought a brighter stain to the sign of the Rosecoeur. The rose wept real tears of blood.

Dawn cast pale shadows on to the grey and red slate tiles of the sloping roofs outside his window.

It was not as if he was still in love with Fiammis. He had purged himself of that hopeless love long ago in the deserts of Enhirrë, he had let the fierce sun burn her from his heart. His love for Mhir, selfless and all-encompassing, had filled the void she had left. It was just seeing her so unexpectedly –

How alone he felt in this foreign city. He sorely missed the spiritual counsel of his fellow Guerriors. Even if he had been in the barren deserts of Enhirrë, he could have sought advice from his confrères. Here he could not even find solace in prayer at the shrine of Mhir the Peacemaker.

And then he remembered the Temple. Elesstar the Beloved was venerated here in Sulien. It seemed the only place to go to shrive himself.

He winced as he pulled on his shirt, gritting his teeth, The pain scored his mind clean, it centred him.

A little while later, he went stiffly down the stairs and set off in the direction of the Temple.

It was not long past dawn and few people were about; a street sweeper pushed his cart across the Temple courtyard, sending the clustering Temple doves up into the air in a fluttering cloud of grey and white.

Drifts of steam blew across the Temple steps from the lustral baths.

Acir was used to the grey, echoing vaults of the Commanderie Abbaye, the austerity of unadorned pillars lit by the reflected fires shining through great rose windows. The Thorny Path began in stark stone gashed by a glory of blood-red light.

Elesstar. The name was Her name. But as he entered the Temple of the Source, he sensed he entered the presence of an older deity.

Acir gazed around, searching for a shrine, a plaque even, dedicated to Iel the All-Seeing. There was none. Till this moment he had not realised to what extent the influence of the Goddess of the Source still prevailed. In spite of the invaders' imposition of the worship of Iel, the Sulien people had managed to keep their allegiance to their Goddess alive through the cult of the handmaiden, Elesstar.

Elesstar's shrine was decorated with exquisite mosaics: water flowed in patterns of green and silver glass. And in the watery shadows stood Elesstar herself, a river-spirit arising from the darkness, one hand outstretched in blessing.

As Acir gazed he found himself drowning in the dream-memory again; watery reflections shimmered on the walls, like ripples on flowing river-water . . .

Elesstar was leaning forward from the water-shadows, offering her hand to him, her glimmering eyes fixed directly on his –

No!

He stepped back, moving too suddenly, and felt a raw, red pain grate through his wounds. It brought him back to himself.

He must be light-headed, weak from fasting.

The elderly Priest who oversaw the lustral baths showed Acir where to disrobe. The crumbling stones lining the bath were stained green with age and mineral deposits. Steam gusted in little clouds from the cloudy waters. Acir hesitated on the edge, steeling himself – and then eased himself in, a step at a time. Warm water swirled around him. He gasped as the open weals stung ... and then slowly let himself relax. Healing waters. He had come here to make penance – and the waters of the Goddess were soothing him, salving the self-inflicted injuries.

It was not at all what he had expected.

The Priest appeared on the rim of the lustral bath. He extended his hand until it gently touched Acir's head. Acir understood; complete immersion was required. He took a breath and dived beneath the surface of the water.

For a moment he floated there, a moment out of time. Water green as verdigris embalmed him, lulled him into a sense of immense and timeless calm.

And then the need to breathe forced him upwards. Shaking the water from his hair, he burst the surface, blinking in the daylight. The old Priest nodded at him and mumbled a few words of benediction.

It was over. Acir climbed out, shivering in the cold, and dried himself with a coarse towel. He felt light, cleansed, shriven. He pressed coins into the venerable Priest's hands and re-entered the Temple.

It was no longer empty. A trail of black-clad people was winding between the pillars, with movements solemn and slow. The women were veiled, the men bare-headed; all were carrying lotos candles in their cupped palms.

Curious to observe this unfamiliar religious rite, Acir drew nearer. The Priestess, also veiled, stood with a lighted taper beside the prayer-bells, making each candle blossom into flame.

A bier, borne by six men, was at the heart of the procession. The body lay on a curtained palanquin. The air filled with the milky smoke of perfumed wax.

Now he understood; a funeral procession. The Sulien way of death.

The mourners set the prayer-bells gently vibrating until the Temple filled with their bronze drone. He felt drawn to understand what the observance of the cult of Elesstar had come to mean to the people of Sulien.

The Priestess nodded to him as he approached.

'Where are they going?' he whispered.

'To the Under Temple.'

'Is it permitted for a stranger to observe?'

'Anyone may accompany the dead on their last journey. Here. Take one of these with you.'

She placed a waxen lotos candle in Acir's hand. The wax felt smooth and cold. It gave off a faint drowsy scent.

'What should I do with this?'

'You will see.'

The funeral cortège was winding its way below ground. Acir followed at a respectful distance. He had read of the underground reservoirs and cisterns beneath Sulien . . . but he had not until now realised the extent of the Undercity.

The tunnel opened out suddenly into a vast, dark hall. By the soft light of the lotos candles borne by the mourners, Acir saw that they stood on the rim of a great, dark reservoir, its waters as smooth and black as a polished mirror. The high-vaulted roof of the hall was supported by painted pillars, each carved with a pattern of lotos leaves and sinuous, twisting snake-creatures.

One by one, the mourners passed by the bier, respectfully touching it and murmuring words Acir could not catch. Then they knelt at the water's edge and gently placed their candles on the smooth black surface. Soon the cavernous hall gleamed with a myriad floating candle-stars, their white flames pale and insubstantial as will-o'-the-wisps.

Now they will seal the body in some subterranean tomb, Acir thought as the last mourner rose from the water's edge. One of the presiding Priests moved forward.

One voice began to sing . . . and the others joined it.

The bier-bearers lifted the bier on its poles and moved forward too. The two foremost bearers dropped to their knees on the edge of the reservoir and the bier tilted towards the waters. As the singing swelled, the shrouded body began to slowly slide into the water.

Acir stared, frozen in the shadowed archway. They buried their dead in the reservoirs? The singing echoed and re-echoed around the vaults as the body disappeared, sinking beneath the black waters. They must have weighted it with lead, he thought numbly.

The black water stirred; the lotos lights shivered and some went out, extinguished by the sudden violent turbulence. It was as if, Acir thought, horrified, some water creature – or creatures – lurked deep beneath . . . and the singing had brought them to the surface.

The singing had ceased. In the silence, all the mourners watched the writhing of the black waters, watched as one by one the lotus candles went out. And then the waters stilled as suddenly as they had erupted.

The Priestess with the torch stood on the rim of the reservoir, gazing calmly out over the waters.

Shaken, Acir waited until the last of the mourners had left the hall and only the Priestess remained. Only then did he venture to approach her, still holding his unlit lotos candle, the wax now warm and soft in his sweating fingers.

'What – what was *that*?' he asked her.

'They that are born of Elesstar return to Her. She takes back Her own.' She spoke dreamily, distantly, as if drugged.

'But – but I saw –'

'Elesstar's water-snakes. They strip the flesh from the bodies, the bones sink into the sediment.'

Acir swallowed back a sudden surge of nausea.

'This is not how we honour our dead in Allegonde. We treat them with respect.'

'You bury your dead in the earth to be eaten by worms. Is it so very different, Guerrior? Come back on the Day of the Dead. Then you will witness a miracle.'

Acir's hand automatically touched the sign of the Rose to ward off evil. He could still taste the lingering bitterness of bile at the back of his throat.

'On that day the sky-shaft is opened to let them fly free. The winged souls.'

She was talking in riddles. He tried to make sense of the skewed religious doctrine.

'The souls fly from the reservoir?'

'Dragonflies.' She pointed to the ancient carven stone and, peering by the light of her torch, he saw carved figures: stick men and women, over whose heads double-winged insectile creatures hovered. 'It is our belief that when the dragonflies hatch from the waters of the reservoir, they transport the souls of our dead as they fly to the light. It is a moment of supreme transcendence. You will not, cannot, understand until you have witnessed it.'

She was right. He did not, could not, understand. It seemed to contradict the teachings of Mhir on which he had based his life. His hands had become hot and sticky; looking down, he saw that he was still clutching the lotos candle and it had begun to melt.

The Priestess lit the wick and he watched it flower into light between his fingers.

'Stay a moment.' She raised her fingers to touch his forehead . . . and then his breast, lingering just over the place where the Rose was tattooed.

He gazed questioningly into her flame-warmed eyes and saw a frown pass, evanescent as a fast-moving cloud, across her calm gaze. Her lids fluttered, her eyes losing focus – and he was afraid she was going to faint.

'The Lotos is fading, dying . . .' Her voice was low, dream-drowsed. 'Blood blooms in the heart of the Rose. Listen! Elesstar calls to you, Rose-bearer. Can you not hear her voice?'

'Elesstar calls to me? What do you mean?' Acir's Guerrior training had made him suspicious of any such kind of religious trances or seeings. Yet the Priestess's words seemed unpremeditated – and spontaneous. 'What did you see?'

But the moment of Seeing had passed and the Priestess stared at him as if their conversation had never taken place.

'Go,' she said, turning away from him. 'Place your candle on the waters.'

Acir went to follow her – and then remembered where he was; a stranger in a foreign temple. He turned back, his questions unanswered.

Kneeling down on the rim of the reservoir, he let the candle float free; the lapping black water was chillingly cold to the touch.

Nothing stirred. The solitary candle floated out into the darkness, a single crocus-flame on the black waters of oblivion.

Khassian's fingers moved nimbly across the ebony and yellowed ivory keys as Cramoisy Jordelayne soared into the elaborate arpeggios of the cadenza . . .

Magelonne had worked his miracle and cured him. His hands were whole again. Healed!

And in that one moment of revelation, the illusion shattered.

He looked down at the keyboard.

The flesh had begun to peel from his fingers even as he played, the keys were stickily slippery with leaking blood, he could hear the hollow tap of the protruding bones on ivory –

His hands were disintegrating.

'No!' he whispered.

The discordant twang of snapped strings resonated about his head, the harmonic progression unresolved, Cramoisy's scream left hanging in the air.

He started up, staring at the bloody rags still clothing the skeletal fingers.

And in the candlelit salon, he became aware of a flurry of movement about him, a murmur of revulsion as the audience began to back away.

All so slow, so distant, fading into a blurred jangle of snapped strings –

In the pale brumelight of the Sulien dawn, Khassian slowly, shakily, examined his hands. The scar tissue knitting the fingers together felt lumpily coarse against his cheek, seamed with knots of rough skin. There was no sensation in the finger-tips – only the strange jabs of dull fire that sometimes irradiated the whole hand, making him cringe with pain. 'Damaged nerve-endings,' Dr Magelonne had said impassively at the last consultation. 'It may never improve. You will just have to learn to live with it, to ignore it.'

'I find I must speak plainly, Sieur Jordelayne.' Mistress Permay's voice rang out from the hallway, 'I don't like to have to talk of money – but you are well behind with your rent. I run a respectable establishment here, and some of these disreputable-looking individuals who have been calling upon you, well – it's giving my apartments a bad name in the city. People have been talking. Remarking upon it.'

Khassian held his breath. He could not be certain whether Cramoisy would react as Cramoisy Jordelayne, Prima Diva, or would use his charm to soothe the landlady. He prayed the Diva would choose charm.

'My dear Mistress Permay.' Cramoisy's voice oozed honey. 'How perfectly dreadful that our visitors should have occasioned ill comments – and comments that have been directed at you. May I share a confidence with you? A very important confidence? These individuals are musicians of the highest calibre –'

Khassian heard Mistress Permay give one of her disdainful sniffs.

'Highest calibre at begging on street corners, more like. I want my money, Sieur Jordelayne. And if I don't get it by midday tomorrow, I shall be obliged to evict you.'

Cramoisy entered Khassian's room, closing the door, standing with his back pressed against it as if to keep Mistress Permay out.

'You heard?'

'What's happened to our money, Cramoisy?'

The Diva gave a little shrug.

'We've spent it.'

'*All* of it? Even your jewel money?'

'Don't worry. The Mayor has invited me to give a series of recitals. And if that doesn't bring in enough, I'll start to give lessons. You could teach music theory.'

Khassian looked at him in horror.

'I am not teaching theory to Sulien brats!'

'*Miu caru*, you may have to.'

'We must find cheaper accommodation. We must live within our means.'

There was a shocked silence. Then Cramoisy said, each word clipped and precise, 'You may, if you wish. Composers are renowned for starving in garrets. But I have my reputation to consider. I shall remain here.'

Orial stood on the borders of an alien country. Clouds scudded overfast across a threatening sky, illuminating the unfamiliar terrain with brief snatches of stormlight. She was a stranger in this mindscape, wandering lost and confused, searching vainly for familiar landmarks.

She had begun to dread the daily mindjourney, the plunge into the darkness along unknown ways.

It was all happening too fast. Her brain could not assimilate Khassian's musical language.

Yet his influence was growing, shaping her own style. She sometimes experienced the unpleasant sensation that she was beginning to lose her identity, that his music was invading and altering her mind until her individuality was submerged in his.

Today they had been alone together, unchaperoned (Cramoisy was closeted elsewhere for fear his undisciplined thoughts might disturb

Orial's concentration). Khassian had walked close to her, his jacket brushing the corner of the escritoire. She had looked up and noticed the curve of his cheekbones, the shadow on his stubborn chin, the way his eyes softened when lost in the intricacies of his composition . . .

'Let me see that passage again.'

He leaned over her shoulder. So close that she wanted to reach out and push the errant strand of hair out of his eyes. So close she could breathe in the scent of his hair, a curiously clean scent, redolent of soap herbs, rosemary and mallow. But who had washed his hair for him, tugged a comb through the tangles –

'No, no, no, this is all wrong. You must do it again. It's free time here, *senza misura*. Recitative. Let's take it one bar at a time.'

Deflated, she took up the pen and scored lines through the passage.

'This leads into one of the key moments of the opera. I'm striving for something new here, something that goes far beyond convention . . .'

He wandered over to the window, still talking.

'You've never heard an opera, have you? The current convention is for the heroine to go mad – usually in Act Three. Her madness involves elaborate virtuoso vocal work – of the kind at which our Diva excels – and it usually brings the house down. Vocal acrobatics! I don't want such absurdities. My Elesstar is torn between her love for Mhir and her loyalty to the Shultan. When she hears that Mhir has been put to death, she loses her reason. It must be a moment of pathos – of poignancy – but also terror. The audience must become one with Elesstar. It must *terrify*.'

'Was that why the Grand Maistre wanted you to withdraw the opera?'

'*What?*'

The one word was as loud as the report of a mortar; he had obviously not expected her to interrupt him. But she wanted to know why so she braved another question.

'I still don't understand why he accused the opera of being blasphemous.' Khassian took in a breath.

'To understand fully you would need to have lived through the last year in Bel'Esstar. To have seen the personal freedoms you take for granted here in Sulien taken away, one by one. Opera is not a chaste entertainment, for a start. It takes passion, incest and intrigue as its subject matters. And the danseuses in the Interludes wear revealing costumes which inflame the lusts of the men in the audience and incite lewd thoughts.'

His moods seemed mercurial, unpredictable, the lowering gloom suddenly pierced by glints of wicked humour. Orial could feel a giggle threatening to burst out; she clapped one hand to her mouth to stifle it. But when she glanced up, she saw from the glint in his eyes that he had intended her to laugh.

*

Late-afternoon in Sulien, twilight slowly drawing a shadowveil over the sunlit hillside terraces ... Jerame Magelonne walked slowly, ruminatively, past the Cabinet of Curiosities on his way back to the Sanatorium – and then turned on his heel and went up the steps. A light burned in the depths of the Museum. Orial had mentioned she was spending some of her spare time assisting Jolaine with her work. He was suddenly seized with a pleasant inspiration; he would pay the ladies a surprise visit and take them to the Rooms for tea.

He pulled open the door and entered, gazing around him. The Museum seemed sadly neglected. Display cases were half-arranged, their treasures lacking labels or explanation. Signs had been removed, adding to the confusion. He ran his finger along the top of a display case; the tip left a trail in the grey dust. Had Dame Jolaine grown too old to manage the responsibilities of the position?

'What are you doing in here? We're closed!'

Her voice rang out, crisp as an arquebus shot; startled, he swung around to see Jolaine Tradescar framed in the lamplit doorway, glaring at him.

'Jerame.' She wagged her finger at him as if he were a naughty boy caught scrumping apples. 'I took you for . . . but no matter.'

'Who did you take me for?' he asked, a little disconcerted.

'One of the Mayor's minions, snooping around.'

Jerame followed her into the lamplit office; every surface was cluttered with open books and ledgers.

'To what do I owe the pleasure of this visit?' She swept up an armful of folders from a chair and patted it for him to sit down. 'I'd offer you some tea . . .'

He waved a hand in polite refusal; the tea leaves, he suspected, might be coated with the same dust that lay on the books and exhibits.

'I rather expected to find Orial here.'

'Orial? Whatever gave you that notion?'

'I see I was mistaken.' Jerame was a little perplexed. 'She gave me to understand she was helping you.'

'Oh, she's often in here,' Jolaine said vaguely. She let the folders drop in a heap.

'I came to invite you both to the Rooms. Would you care to take a dish of tea with me?'

Jolaine hesitated.

'Well, maybe for a half-hour – no longer! I have important work to complete.'

Jerame waited as she crammed notebooks into an old canvas bag and drew down the blinds, double-locking the back door. She seemed to be taking very elaborate precautions to protect the contents of the Museum.

'You wait for me outside. I must extinguish all the lights and it's easy to miss one's step in the dark. Go on, go on.' She shooed Jerame out.

Certes, she had become even more eccentric in her old age.

Jolaine Tradescar, his mother's bluestocking aunt, had always been a source of pride and exasperation to her family. And yet it was she who had proved the greatest comfort at the time of Iridial's death, her bluntness of manner a relief after all the polite, anguished whisperings. The disarray in the Museum perplexed him; her mental faculties seemed in no way diminished by age – so why had she neglected her duties as Antiquarian? And if Orial had been helping, why was everything so cluttered, so dusty?

The last light within was extinguished and Jolaine came out on to the steps. Jerame saw her glance all around as she double-locked the door, as if making sure there was no one suspicious lurking in the shadows. Even as he escorted her away from the Museum, she still glanced furtively around, clutching her canvas bag to her tightly.

They had already lit the candles in the crystal chandeliers at the Rooms and their brilliance spilled out on to the courtyard from the tall windows. Within, the tables were set out for cards and tea and a murmur of conversation blended with the more distant strain of country dances emanating from the ballroom. Jerame frowned. Maybe it was as well Orial had not accompanied them; he had forgotten there was a dance this afternoon.

The periwigged attendant ushered them to a table in the alcove. He offered to take Jolaine's wrap and bag but she refused, still clutching the bag possessively. Jerame hastily ordered tea and sat down, laying his gloves on the table.

'What a pity Orial could not join us,' Jolaine said, easing herself into a chair opposite his.

'I'd – hm – been meaning to come and see you about Orial.'

'Ah,' Jolaine said. 'So you've noticed too.'

'Noticed what precisely?'

'The eyes.' Jolaine eased herself into a chair opposite his. 'She has her mother's eyes.'

'But it usually skips a generation or two, often more.'

'Then how –'

Jerame looked up to see her gazing penetratingly at him. 'You don't think that I –'

'It is possible, Jerame.'

'But the Lifhendil inheritance only occurs in the female line.' He had begun to twist his gloves into a knot.

'Only shows itself in the female line. Who's to say that a strain has not lain dormant in your family for years?'

'You know very well I have no sisters.'

'My point precisely. You are the first of your line to sire a daughter for generations. The Lifhendil blood could have passed to her through you – as well as directly through her mother.'

'We have no proof.' To hear Jolaine confirm his suspicions only increased his disquiet. 'And I have kept her safe all these years, safe from the malign influence that music would exert over her. There is no certainty that she will develop the full-blown condition.' Who was he trying to convince with this show of bravado? Jolaine had noticed Orial's eyes too.

The attendant arrived, bearing the tea-tray, and Jerame tried to fix his attention on pouring tea into the bowls. But his hand shook and he spilled tea on to the cloth; a spreading yellow stain on the crisp white linen.

Jolaine leaned across and placed her hand on his arm.

'You must not blame yourself. No one could have foreseen such a thing.'

'But what am I going to do?' For a moment his composure deserted him and tremblingly he took out his kerchief to wipe his brow. The distant strains of the country dance no longer sounded merry but distorted, grotesque.

'It doesn't have to end the same way,' she said gently.

'But we know of no way to halt the progress of the Accidie once it manifests itself,' he said. 'I'm a doctor, Jolaine, *au fait* with the most recent discoveries in medical science. Why do I feel so helpless?'

Azare came into the salon carrying an elongated wooden case which he set down with extreme care. Cramoisy followed him, carelessly casting his new viridian jacket down on the couch, peeling off his kid gloves, finger by finger. But Khassian's sensitive ears had caught a slight vibration of sound as Azare put the case down, the tremor of tuned strings.

'What is *that*?' he demanded.

'What does it look like?' Cramoisy was critically examining his appearance in the mirror.

Azare knelt down and unlocked the case, opening the lid to reveal the ivory keyboard of a portable clavichord.

'They call it an epinette here – isn't that quaint?'

The hollow tap of the protruding bones on ivory –

Khassian stared at the epinette with loathing.

'You said we have no more money. Why this extravagance?'

'How am I to rehearse my recital if Azare has no instrument? What is he supposed to do? *Hum* the accompaniments? And if there is no recital, how shall I make money for us to pay the bills?'

Could Cramoisy not see how it exacerbated his feelings of uselessness, to have to hear Azare play the instrument at which Khassian had excelled . . .

Azare screwed the three legs into the case, stood it up and ran his fingers over the keys, setting up a sweet jangle. Khassian winced.

'Needs tuning,' Azare said, misinterpreting his reaction. Taking out a tuning key, he leaned over the case and started to tighten the tuning-pins securing the strings.

'For Mhir's sake!' Khassian flung himself out of the chair and went over to the door. Only as he reached it did he realise that it was firmly shut and he would have to attempt an undignified struggle with the handle – or wait for Cramoisy to let him out like an unruly lap-dog.

Orial slipped the gold-edged invitation from her apron pocket and gazed at it again. Her fingers smoothed the fine ivory card, traced the elegant black copperplate print:

A Vocal Recital of Divers Songs and Arias, including a selection from the new opera *Elesstar* by Amaru Khassian.

To be given by the incomparable Diva, Cramoisy Jordelayne, accompanied at the epinette by Oriste Azare.

The recital will take place at eight in the evening on the fifteenth day of Afril in the concert room of the Assembly Rooms in the presence of His Worship the Mayor of Sulien.

She pressed the card to her heart. A concert. A real concert – and she had been especially invited. The only problem was that Papa would never let her go.

Well, she would ask him nevertheless. And if he refused, she would go anyway. She was old enough to know her own mind.

Determined to have her own way, she went straight along to his office and rapped on the door. There was no reply.

'If you're looking for your father, he's been called out to a patient.' Sister Crespine was coming along the corridor in her cape and bonnet; she had finished her work for the day and was going home. 'He said he would probably be late. You're to sup without him. Cook's been told.'

It seemed too good an opportunity to miss.

Orial went to her closet and looked with dissatisfaction at her few gowns. Dowdy high-necked school gowns, girlish checks and sprigs. Nothing suitable for the Assembly Rooms.

She wandered around the upper floor until she found herself in her parents' room. Her fingers reached out to unlock the inlaid chest, to touch the delicate fabrics of Mama's gowns. A faint faded perfume drifted out, dried petals of orange blossom and lavender sprigs, as she lifted up the folds of muslin. She rubbed the smooth satin of some blue ribbons against her cheek, lost in a memory of distant childhood.

She carefully eased a gown out of the chest, shaking it loose from the protective folds of petal paper, and held it up against herself.

'Yes,' she whispered, looking with satisfaction at her shadowed reflection in the cheval mirror. 'Yes.'

'Orial?' Dr Magelonne opened the door of the parlour and looked in; the fire had burned down to embers. Perhaps she had gone to bed.

He was back much later than he had intended. He had known the old Mareschal many years; indeed he had helped him walk again after a hunting accident. It was difficult to get away without taking a glass or two of apple brandy and listening to the Mareschal's hunting anecdotes.

Cook had left him some bread and ripe blue-veined cheese; he felt too tired to eat much but chewed dutifully as he scanned tomorrow's schedule.

The last of the spent coals subsided with a soft hiss into ash. He started.

The house felt odd. Something was not quite right. Perhaps he should let Orial know he was back in case she heard the footsteps downstairs and feared robbers had broken in . . .

He tiptoed upstairs and tapped lightly on her door. No reply. Sleeping already. He opened the door a crack and gazed fondly in.

Her bed was empty.

CHAPTER 10

The Assembly Rooms were packed; all the glitterati of Sulien had come in
their jewels and feathered wigs to hear Cramoisy Jordelayne sing. Orial,
overwhelmed by the elegance of the crowd, shrank into Khassian's
shadow, hoping no one would recognise her.

Khassian, pale and austere, kept his hands concealed.

'Listen to them!' she heard him mutter. 'Gaudy starlings, all whistling,
jeering, chattering . . .'

The noisy chatter suddenly hushed. Cramoisy was there, on the
platform, in a suit of darkest kingfisher blue, embroidered with seed
pearls. In the shadows Orial saw a man silently, discreetly, seating
himself at the keyboard of a gilded harpsichord: Azare.

A glace passed between the performers.

'To start my recital I will be giving the first – the very first – performance
of Elesstar's aria, "O, Sacred Rose . . ."'

A murmur of interest greeted the announcement. Orial looked around
uneasily. Cramoisy was taking a considerable risk in starting the recital
with a new, unknown work – especially a work that was banned in
Allegonde.

Cramoisy began to sing.

This was the first aria Orial had transcribed for Khassian; every note
was graven on her memory. Till today this music had been an intimate
secret shared with Khassian alone. To perform it in public seemed a
violation of that intimacy.

And then she found her antipathy melting, seduced by Cramoisy's
exquisite singing. Slowly drowning in waves of sound, Orial resisted . . .
but resistance was no use and the music engulfed her.

Stillness hung in the room like a seafog over the waters.

Then came the applause. The audience shouted themselves hoarse,
they showered flowers on to the stage until the boards were covered in
green and white and gold: jonquils, lilies.

Orial sat silent, sad that the purity of the moment had been spoilt.

Cramoisy, smiling, dipped to pick up armfuls of the scented flowers,
kissing his hand to the enraptured audience. He turned to Khassian,
beckoning him with one hand.

Khassian, if anything paler than before, stood up and with a single bow of the head acknowledged the applause of the audience.

Orial heard excited whispers from the elegant women sitting behind her.

'How pale he is . . .'

'And yet uncommonly good-looking.'

'They say he only just escaped the tyrannical regime in Bel'Esstar with his life.'

'An escaped revolutionary, my dear, how thrilling!'

Orial ventured a sidelong glance at Khassian; he seemed utterly oblivious to the whispered compliments, lost in some memory of past triumphs, maybe . . . or else merely accustomed to audience acclaim.

And suddenly she knew the reason for his pallor. This was not just his first concert in Sulien – it was the first time he had appeared in public since the fire. Till now she had only seen him as the illustrious composer, unassailable in his craft. Now she saw how terribly vulnerable the fire had left him.

Please let no one ask him about his hands.

As was the custom in Sulien, the audience repaired to the salon for refreshments at the conclusion of the concert: tea punch was a favoured drink, lightly alcoholic yet refreshing.

Orial stood in the shadow of one of the fluted columns, cupping a bowl of punch in her fingers. Cramoisy and Azare had retired to the dressing room. Khassian was surrounded by a crowd of eager admirers. She felt herself invisible. Maybe she should slip away now, before anyone noticed her . . .

She set the glass bowl down on a side-table and began to move through the crowd.

Someone blocked her way.

'Where are you going?'

She looked up, startled, to see Khassian had moved away from his admirers.

'We must talk.'

He ushered her towards an alcove, curved like a shell, painted pink and gold. As they sat down together, she became aware of eyes resting on her: curious eyes, envious eyes. Had anyone recognised her? Would anyone tell her father? She looked questioningly at Khassian.

'Do not think, I beg you, demselle, that I am not sensible of your role in tonight's triumph. Indeed, it would not have been possible were it not for the part you have played in transcribing my music so swiftly and so accurately.'

She nodded, hardly hearing the compliment, seeing only his eyes, brown as tortoiseshell, gazing earnestly into hers.

'I want to stage the opera here. In Sulien.' His voice was husky with excitement.

'Here?'

'But it will mean a great deal of work – especially for you. Do you feel equal to the task?'

'Oh, yes, *yes*!' Orial heard herself agreeing before she had even thought about it.

'How much longer can you go on keeping it from your father? You're going to have to tell him.'

Her father. The delicious trance was broken.

'He would be so angry.'

'But you're a born musician. You should be studying at the Conservatoire. When the opera is complete, I shall write you letters of introduction to the Director.'

So often she had dreamed of this. Here, at last, was confirmation of her deepest hopes and aspirations. *A born musician.* The words sang in her mind.

'And you mustn't leave it too late. You've so much to catch up on – and you're already eighteen.'

Orial had begun to twist one of the blue satin ribbons around her fingers.

'How could I leave Papa? He has no one but me.'

'If he truly loves you, he will let you go. For if he tries to hold on, he will just as surely lose you.'

Jerame Magelonne had created his own personal shrine where he could be alone with his memories, alone with the few relics of his life with Iridial. He felt closer to her here, in the room they had shared, than in the eternal silence of the Undercity. And in the dead of night, when he was certain he could not be overheard, he spoke aloud to her.

It was well past midnight. The blue-painted room seemed to mirror the starry spring night outside, the dusky folds of the silk hangings dusted with white-embroidered daisies and star-lilies. She had chosen the material herself, holding its softness up to her cheek, delighted with the delicacy of the embroidery.

Now he drew aside the curtain that veiled her portrait and placed a lamp beneath it. The golden light warmed glints in her hair, almost lending the illusion of life to the dazzling eyes that gazed out far beyond the canvas.

Rainbow eyes.

'What am I to do?' he asked her. He sat down in front of her, trying to evoke the fading memories of lost intimacy. 'Oh, Iridial, what am I to do?'

The painted image stared on into the far distance. Into eternity.

'Should I have told her? Warned her? I didn't want to cloud her life – when it was clouded already. And besides, there was no guarantee she would inherit the . . . the gift.'

Even as he spoke the word aloud, he knew he had been deceiving himself with false hopes, false securities, all these years. Orial had the gift as surely as she was her mother's daughter.

'Have I done wrong in denying her? Would it have developed anyway, no matter what I did?' And then, wrung out of him, 'Does she have to die too?'

A floorboard creaked outside. He sprang up and, grabbing hold of the oil-lamp, flung open the bedroom door.

The landing was in darkness – but by the light of the lamp, he saw the pale figure of a girl, a slender girl in a gown of white and blue muslin . . .

'Iridial,' he gasped, and clutched his chest.

The girl turned, looking over her shoulder.

Eyes. Dazzling rainbow eyes, Irises a multi-coloured striation of prismed light strands, violet, sapphire –

It was not Iridial but Orial – creeping in like a sneakthief, her eyes wide with guilt

'How – *could* – you?' He was choked with fury now. How could she violate her mother's memory, stealing one of her dresses to attend her secret assignation? Double betrayal. 'Take it off! And before you go to your room, you will tell me where you have been. And with whom.'

'I have – been at the Assembly Rooms. With Sieur Jordelayne. He brought me back in his carriage.' The rainbows suddenly dulled with brimming tears.

'You have been with – *that creature*? Listening to *music*?'

'You never said I couldn't listen to music outside the house! Never expressly. And it was so wonderful, Papa.' Tears began to trickle down her cheeks. He had made her cry and he could not remember her crying in many years. 'So wonderful I wanted to be a part of it. Punish me if you must – but please don't keep me from the music. *Please*!'

Her words made him chill with sudden fear. She meant what she was saying. He had never seen her so in earnest before. And abject fear made him stern, impervious to her tears.

'You will go to your room and stay there until I give you permission to come out.'

The Sulien Asylum had been built outside the city on the edge of the River Avenne, a rambling, ramshackle bastion, its neglected gardens rank with strangling creepers.

Jerame Magelonne stood before the massive doors, hand upraised to tug the rusted bell-pull. A thin wind blew off the river marsh, a mean wind, piercing and damp. He had avoided coming this way for the past thirteen years. He would not have come at all had it not been for last night's scene with Orial.

He gave the bell-pull a sharp tug. Deep within he heard the bell clang, a harsh, cracked sonority. Bolts were tugged back, clinking chains disconnected, the heavy door dragged open, grating over the uneven flagstones.

A prison, Jerame thought as he crossed the inner courtyard.

'Jerame!' Ophil Tartarus, the Asylum Director, came out to greet him. 'I've been expecting you.'

'Expecting me?' Jerame glanced at him warily, wondering if in the intervening years since they studied at Medical School together, Tartarus had become as mad as his patients. How could he have known Jerame was coming today?

'Let's talk in my office.'

Brownish light filtered into the dark-walled room; Jerame placed his gloves and hat on the desk.

'Drink?' Tartarus held up a glass decanter containing a brackish liquid, looking suspiciously, Jerame thought, like old embalming fluid. He shook his head. Tartarus poured himself a glass and drank it down.

'Ahh. Keeps out the damp.' He grimaced, showing teeth stained as yellow as the liquid he had just swallowed.

Jerame began to wonder if he had been wise in coming. But Tartarus was the only expert on disorders of the brain in Sulien – and at Medical School his quirkily enquiring mind had distinguished him as the genius of the year, the star pupil.

'Long years ago I asked you a question. A question you could not then answer.'

'Why? That was the question you asked, I seem to recall. A hundred questions in that one word. Why the Accidie? Why is it irreversible? Why Iridial –'

'Yes, yes. And you said to me you would investigate the Accidie from the viewpoint of modern medical thought. Away with the superstitions, the legends. Observed facts and scientific conclusions – that was the only way forward.'

'But you wouldn't let me draw my own conclusions,' Tartarus said; a gleam of resentment lit his eyes, dull as old varnish in the brown light.

'I wouldn't let you dissect her!' Jerame cried.

Tartarus shrugged and reached for the decanter.

'So much for modern scientific investigation. But Iridial is long dead. Why are you here today?'

'It's my daughter Orial. She –' Jerame faltered, hands toying with the fingers of his gloves. 'She is showing all the same signs.'

'Your daughter too. So I was right?' The gleam had become acquisitive. 'Intriguing. It so often skips a generation. It would be most instructive to examine her –'

'Impossible. You see – I haven't told her. I – I didn't want to alarm her.'

Tartarus folded his arms across his chest.

'So why are you here?'

'To consult you. You're the expert.'

Tartarus paused. He seemed to be considering the matter.

'You must give me your word – on our sacred Doctor's Oath – that you won't poach my research.'

'Damn your research! I want to save my daughter.'

'Very well.'

Jerame followed the glimmer of Tartarus's shabby white coat down interminable gloomy corridors until he stopped and ushered Jerame into an ill-lit chamber lined with shelves.

The sour stink of the room was overpowering; some vile stale chymical miasma that seemed to have pickled the dusty interior and stained the window pane.

'There! A fine specimen. A unique specimen.'

Tartarus brought out a glass jar.

Jerame saw that it was a brain. A human brain, floating in a hideous discoloured liquid.

'The only one of its kind. Look at the right hemisphere – over-developed, hm? If I lift the top section so that you can see better –'

'Whose –?' Jerame, experienced practitioner that he was, felt a sudden rising surge of nausea.

'You can clearly see these extraordinary neural pathways –'

The pungent stench of the cloudy chymical vinegar was making Jerame's stomach heave.

'Ophil!'

'The subject's name was Serafine. I didn't perform the dissection, you understand. That honour fell to my predecessor.'

'How can you be sure she had the Accidie?' The suffocating stink was sickening Jerame, filling his nostrils with its pungent odour of decay.

'Read this entry in the Register here. "Serafine in an extreme manic state. She cannot abide a note of music to be sung or whistled within earshot. It sends her crazy. She also claims she can hear the music in others' minds. All the time."'

'A kind of musical telepathy?'

'A cacophony. A din. A chaos . . .'

Jerame nodded slowly.

She sits naked on the floor, her hands clutched over her ears, rocking to and fro, to and fro. Her pale face is twisted with a silent agony, her hair, unwashed, unbound, streams wildly about her shoulders, tarnished golden snakelocks. 'Make it stop, Jerame,' she whispers, 'make it stop!'

'. . . caused no doubt by this rapid degeneration of the neural pathways.'

'What are you suggesting?' Jerame struggled to make sense of the information. 'That the musical gift is nothing but the result of some –

physical defect in the brain? This – malformation?' He tapped at the clouded jar with his finger.

'Defect, malformation . . . what can we do but speculate? If it is a Lifhendil inheritance – what were they like, these Lifhendil? Did they practise some form of telepathy? Oh, I've many theories, Jerame. All hypothetical. This is the only evidence. Apart –' and his eyes seemed to gleam again in the dusty room '– from your daughter Orial.'

'You are not laying a finger on her! I will not have her used as part of your experiments, to prove some crackpot hypothesis –'

'Then you'll let her go the same way as Iridial? Your decision, Doctor.' Tartarus lifted the jar and placed it back on the shelf alongside the other diseased specimens.

'Let her go? You speak as if there were some cure!'

'By the time you brought Iridial to me, she was past help. Her mind was irreparably damaged and I could see no pattern to it.'

'You're certain there *is* a pattern?'

'Oh, come now, Jerame. Don't tell me, after all these years as a medical practitioner, you still subscribe to the "madness is possession by evil spirits" school of thought? Neural pathways.' He tapped the jar again, disturbing the cloudy ichor. 'That's the clue. Dissect a normal brain . . . and compare the two. The Lifhendil brain is distinctly different.'

From somewhere deep inside the Asylum came the echo of distant laughter.

Jerame took out his handkerchief and mopped at his brow. He had broken out in a sick, cold sweat.

'Wait till you see what I've installed upstairs. Come.'

Tartarus locked the specimen closet and, taking Jerame's arm, led him back along the corridor. Even in the sepia light filtering in through the high grilled windows, Jerame could see damp stains on the walls, cracked plaster, signs of neglect.

Up the winding tower stair they went until Tartarus flung open a door at the top.

'What is this place?'

Coils of wire dangled from the ceiling; tall glass vats of transparent liquids stood beneath. A wooden chair was placed in between the vats; leathern restraints hung at the arms and seat. A curious smell made Jerame sniff, trying to identify the chemical. Acid; yes, it was definitely acid.

'My electric chamber.'

'Hm! Torture chamber, more like.'

'You are looking at the most revolutionary method of treating the insane in all Tourmalise. You are looking at the future.' Tartarus danced around the bizarre equipment, fingers conducting an imaginary experiment. 'It's in its earliest stages – but the results are quite astounding.'

'Electric? You're harnessing the power of lightning?' A helmet stood beneath the chair; Jerame picked it up and turned it round in his hands.

'Not harnessing. Creating, controlling!'

The helmet consisted of a circular band of metal with crossed bars, like a crude crown, and the whole was encased in leather straps.

'You direct electrical currents into the brain through this? But – that's an appalling thought! You could fry your patients alive –'

Tartarus snatched the helmet from Jerame's hands.

'D'you think I'd use it on my patients if I hadn't tested it on myself first?' He popped it on to his wild hair and grinned at Jerame.

'You?'

'After the initial shock I felt completely restored. Renewed! There was some blurring of the memory. But as we only administer the minutest of doses, that was soon restored. The treatment seems to re-order the thought patterns in the brain most satisfactorily.'

Jerame sat down heavily in the chair.

'You must meet Adelys.' Tartarus prowled around the chamber, a jagged black shadow. 'The poor woman was in the most desperate state. Since I treated her, she has quietened down and is docile and calm once more –'

Jerame slid his hands slowly along the wooden arm-rests. He tried to imagine what it would feel like to be strapped in, to feel the metal band tightening around the forehead. And then the juddering shock of the electrical spark, the ensuing convulsions –

'No. I won't let you experiment on Orial.'

'There was a time when you put your trust in science. What's happened to that trust?' Tartarus took off the helmet and hooked it over the chair back.

Jerame regarded it with loathing and suspicion. Instrument of torture, devil's instrument. He went over to the slit window and gazed out. And yet . . . what other treatment was there? Suppose he was rejecting the only possible hope of a cure?

Far below the Avenne glistened like a slick of oil in the river marshes. Water. The ever-present lure . . . and the ever-present threat to her life.

A sudden violent commotion broke out below.

'Doctor Tartarus!' a desperate voice called as the sounds of a struggle grew louder. 'A sedative! Quick!'

'We're never off-duty here,' Tartarus said with a wry curl of the lips. He seemed in no hurry to go to the aid of the nurse. 'Fool! I warned him she was in a violent humour today. He never listens.'

'I'm keeping you from your patients,' Jerame said hastily. 'I'd better be on my way.'

The great door clanged shut behind him. He stood on the weed-cracked path, listening to the screams and cries of the unfortunate inmate and her attendant until they dwindled to nothing and all he could hear was the faint, sad whine of the wind off the river marshes.

The woman lies weeping on the ground, her shoulders heaving. Orial approaches slowly, cautiously. She wants to comfort her – and yet she is afraid. The terrible weeping makes her sad. So sad.

She kneels down beside her and puts her arm around her.

'Orial make it better, Mammie . . .'

'NO!' *The woman rears up. Her face is distorted, her rainbow eyes wild, waterfall torrents streaming down her pale cheeks.* 'Go away. Go away!'

Orial shrinks away. Now she is crying too, crying that her mammie has shouted at her, crying that everything is so wrong –

'Aiieeeee. . . .'

And what has happened to Mammie's face? Raw claw marks stripe the white skin with red, she has torn the earrings from her lobes, has raked her own nails down her cheeks.

Orial stares, too terrified to move.

'Take the child away! Don't let her – let her –'

Someone scoops Orial up, carries her away, but still she can hear Mammie crying, so lost, so pitiful.

'Don't – let her – remember me like this –'

'Mammie!' Orial sat up in bed, still rigid with terror.

Iridial's gown lay on the floor in a heap where she had cast it last night, the blue ribbons crumpled.

She gathered the gown up and, smoothing out its folds, laid it on the bed. In the daylight it seemed to have lost its glamour, like the bruised petals of a flower that had faded in the night.

She dressed and came slowly, uncertainly, down the stairs, dreading to hear his voice suddenly shouting at her in anger.

I am old enough to make my own decisions. And I will not be kept a prisoner in my own room.

But his office was locked.

She peeped into the dining room and saw that the breakfast Cook had set out had hardly been touched; the qaffë had gone cold in the pot. Even as she stood gazing down at the congealing mess of scrambled eggs, wondering if the empty feeling in the pit of her stomach was hunger, Cook came in.

'Heaven's sakes, why do I bother preparing food if neither of you is going to eat it?' She began to pile dishes on to her tray, muttering to herself. Orial helped her.

'Where is my father?' she asked.

'Out. Went out. Gone to visit some rich old so-and-so with more money than sense, like as not.'

If Jerame could go out, then so could she. Orial took her cape from the hook and set out for the Crescent.

The aria came to a sudden halt in mid-phrase. Orial looked up and saw that Khassian was staring at his hands. He seemed to have forgotten she was there.

'Illustre?'

He started.

'I'm sorry. We'll . . . take a few minutes' rest . . .'

'I – I wondered if you could give me some advice.'

'Musical advice?'

Maybe it was not the best moment to mention the matter.

'I compose too. A little –' she added hastily. 'I've never had any guidance. I know our style in Sulien must seem somewhat . . . provincial. But –'

'Show me,' he said tersely.

She took the folded manuscript paper from her pocket and smoothed it out on the table in front of him: '*Moon Eyes and Silver Hare.*' She was ashamed to see how untidy it looked, how the notes which had excited her so much as she spun them together looked so dull on paper.

He sat down to study them. His maimed hand twitched impatiently under the concealing drifts of lace.

'Well?' she said quietly.

'It's – it's –' He seemed to be casting around for words. 'It's a pretty tune. It has a – a certain naive charm.'

His hesitation told her that he did not really regard it as worthy of his attention.

'If I had my cithara I would play it to you. It's based on an old Sulien tale. This part – the leaping figure – is the hare.'

'You seem undecided here as to the correct way to notate the rhythm of the accompaniment figure. Was it de-*da*-de-de? Or *de*-da-de-de? You have to be precise. And look at this part-writing. Doubled notes . . .'

'Grammatical errors. I'll correct them.'

'Mm.' He appeared bored with it already. 'You've much to learn.'

His curtness shocked her into silence; a sigh escaped her lips, so soft it was hardly audible. It was all she could permit herself; she was, after all, only an untutored girl – and he was the Illustre Khassian. She should be grateful for his advice . . .

Why, then, was it that she felt as if his criticism had blighted her creation, as if a lethal breath of frost had shrivelled the life from the simple song?

Khassian crossed the broad sweep of lawns that curved down from the Crescent, making for the shade of the great cedars. A worn path led to a verdant walk beyond, past moss-encrusted statues and crumbling urns, tumbled with cascades of ivy.

As he walked, scuffing up cedar needles from the soft carpet underfoot, notes came floating into his head, light as soap bubbles. He ignored them.

They would not be ignored.

Damn it, why were they so persistent? It was a child's tune, a simple melody, absurdly simple, plaguing his memory.

Where had he heard it before?

He sang a few notes aloud, hoping to exorcise it –

And remembered.

It was Orial's tune.

Now the tune seemed skewed, its simplicity tainted by his feelings of guilt. He had treated her badly, and for reasons which were nothing to do with her but with emotions he had thought long-buried.

He had forgotten her youth, her inexperience. He had criticised her work as brutally as if she were a Conservatoire student.

Why, when he looked at her, had he seen – for a moment – *Fania?*

It was not her fault she remined him of long-dead Fania. She did not know, she could not know, he had had a sister, a sister who had not lived to fulfil the promise of her early years.

He sat down on a wrought-iron bench painted a dark and flaking green and watched a flutter of sparrows squabbling over crumbs of bread.

Maybe there had been guilt mingled with a child's uncomprehending grief. The golden, gifted boy, who had envied Fania's promise, her brilliance that threatened to overshadow his . . . Could the dark thoughts that had clouded his mind have made her vulnerable to the smallpox?

The boy Amaru shrinks into the shadow of a doorway as another doctor is ushered into the house and hurried upstairs. Hushed voices whisper, the bitter smoke of fever herbs wafts down the stairs, barely disguising the foetid smell of the darkened sickroom. He has become invisible; his parents stare through him as they confer in urgent undertones with the doctors, the servants rush past unseeing, bearing bowls of water, towels . . .

And once or twice, once or twice he hears a thin, high voice crying out, crying out his name. 'A . . . mar . . .'

When he tries to go to her, they won't let him in. They hold him back. Their strained faces, their dark, sunken eyes, terrify him.

'You can't go in. You mustn't go in.'

'She's calling for me!'

'She's feverish, she no longer knows what she's saying –'

He stares at the gilded icon of the Prophet Mhir, the painted wreath of jagged rose-thorns framing the Prophet's face, gold leaf and dark jewelled colours. Only the thorns, long and jagged, look real. The boy can feel them tearing at his heart –

'Don't let her die. Please don't let her die.'

Unanswered prayers . . .

The ethereal angel's voice that had made Prince Ilsevir and the court weep no longer called his name. It was silenced for all eternity.

'Fania,' he whispered to the sparrows.

Maybe since that day he had been courting death, seeking expiation for the quirk of fate that had allowed him to live – and Fania to die. Maybe that was what had sent him back into the burning Opera House . . .

Orial took a taper, held it to the lantern flame and then lit, one by one, the lotos candles she had brought to perfume her mother's shrine.

White for purification. Hyacinth-blue for mourning. And willow-green for hope, life beyond death . . .

The blue scent of hyacinths drifted through the painted room, imbuing it with the wistful memory of past springs.

Orial breathed in the scent as she tuned her cithara. She had come to work on her new composition, a prelude dedicated to the memory of Iridial.

But after playing a few bars, she stopped. Khassian's music still resonated in her mind, its tortured complexities making mock of her own simple, brightly coloured harmonies.

Her music darted with the jewelled brightness of a dragonfly skimming the surface of the waters. His music rose from the depths, it spoke of despair and madness, it aspired vainly towards stars too far to reach.

He had told her she had much to learn. Now she sat in silence, listening to the dark echoes in her head.

'What should I do?' she whispered to the silence. 'Iridial. Mother. I wish you could tell me what to do. I wish you were –'

I wish you were still alive.

She began the prelude again. Soon her fingers strayed, plucking other notes, unfamiliar notes.

Not her music, but his.

He was slowly infecting her mind.

Her fingers crept from the cithara strings to press against her temples, as if they could force the alien shadow-sounds from her mind.

What's happening to me?

Shadow-sounds ravelled themselves around her prelude, distorting, mocking. She shut her eyes – but still her melody continued to disintegrate in her head.

She stands alone in a ruined hall of broken mirrors. In the distance a rainbow shimmers. Slowly, yearningly, she moves towards it, hands outstretched. Her feet crunch over shards of broken mirror-glass until they bleed, each step releasing a harsher burst of cacophony until the stones of the ruined hall start to tremble. Yet with each painful step, the iridescent bow seems further and further away . . .

Orial opened her eyes.

She wanted to weep for her spoiled prelude, for its bright and innocent spontaneity – but her sore eyes felt too dry for tears. Or maybe she wanted to weep for the loss of her mother; the two had become inextricably entwined.

Loss: an aching emptiness, mingled with a child's uncomprehending anger . . .

How had she thought she could ever adequately express her feelings in such naive musical language?

Orial wrapped up the cithara and replaced it behind the memorial stone.

She took the lantern and began to wander aimlessly through the Undercity. But now the raw, rekindled anger began to conjure shadows from the silence of the Lifhendil necropolis. She started at the sound of her own footfall, began to glimpse spirit-shapes, pale and formless, out of the corner of her eye. Were the souls of the dead still lingering here, waiting for the Day of the Dead to release them?

Was that slight sound the whispering of dead voices . . . or her own hesistant breathing?

She found that she had come to the door of the Lotos Chamber; within, the Lotos Princess still held court, playing the cithara to an enraptured Lifhendil audience.

Holding the lantern high, Orial tried to scry the winged figures Jolaine Tradescar had described to her.

She had never paid them much attention before . . . but now she saw that they hovered, like tutelary spirits, behind the Princess's head. The insubstantial gauzes that streamed from their shoulders could be . . . wings?

The air behind her seemed – for one brief moment – to *twitch*. A breath fanned her hair.

Startled, she wheeled around, almost dropping the lantern.

'Who's there?' she whispered into the darkness.

It was almost as if something – or someone – had flitted past her. And yet there was no sound of footsteps or voices.

She was alone. And yet not alone.

For the first time in the Undercity, Orial Magelonne found herself overwhelmed by a sudden sense of mindless terror.

She gathered up her skirts – and ran.

CHAPTER 11

Orial was sorting through the first pages of Act Three with Khassian when the Diva wandered yawning into the salon, patch box and mirror in hand. He had obviously only just risen from sleep even though it was well past midday.

'Orial, sweet.' Cramoisy kissed the tips of his fingers to her.

'We're busy,' Khassian said, reading the sheets over Orial's shoulder.

'I met such a charming woman at the Mayor's reception last night.' Cramoisy was applying a beauty spot to his cheek, a black-sequinned star just above the upper lip. 'A Contesse, no less. An exile, *miu caru*, just like us.'

'An exile?' Khassian looked up, frowning. 'From Allegonde?'

'Another fugitive from the tyranny of the Grand Maistre. She had seen me in *Firildys* – three times! It is so very agreeable to meet one's admirers when far from home . . .'

'You didn't tell her anything of our plans, I trust?'

'She could be of great help to us, Amar. She has connections . . . and she is such a fan of your music. You would have blushed to hear the compliments she paid you.'

'Cramoisy,' Khassian said warningly, 'have you been indiscreet?'

'How could you!' His mouth twisted from its perfect painted bow to an expression of mortification. 'Oh, Khassian, how *could* you accuse me of such a thing? You know I am the soul of discretion. I would never betray you.'

'I know that you love to hear the sound of your own voice,' Khassian said brutally.

'Oh! Oh! Oh!' Cramoisy's voice began to rise; Orial winced at the shrillness of the pitch.

'What was her name, Cramoisy, this charming Allegondan Contesse?'

'Fiammis.'

'Cramoisy, you will be the undoing of us! Why do you never think before you open your mouth?'

'Pardon me, Illustre, but what precisely have I done wrong? Tell me!'

'I was warned . . . to beware of a Contesse called Fiammis.'

'And did you warn me?'

'I had no idea you would encounter her.'

'Fa! A fine excuse!'

'So I should have told you. But you should have known when to keep your mouth shut.'

'What harm's been done? And why is she such a threat?'

'I have it on good authority that she is an agent of the Grand Maistre.'

'Whose authority?' demanded Cramoisy.

'Captain Korentan's.'

'Oh!' Cramoisy threw up his hands. 'And you believe *him*?'

'What exactly did you confide in the Contesse?'

Cramoisy suddenly seemed engrossed in putting the sequinned patches back into the enamelled box.

'Cramoisy?' said Khassian warningly.

'I might have mentioned the opera . . .'

Khassian closed his eyes.

'Well?' Cramoisy said defensively. 'It's no secret!'

'Why didn't you also tell her we were plotting to assassinate Girim nel Ghislain whilst you were about it?'

'Great heavens –'

His sarcasm seemed lost on Cramoisy who stared back at Khassian uncomprehendingly.

'We must all be more careful. We cannot afford to take risks. We cannot rehearse in a public hall. We need a room where we will not be overheard.'

'But where in Sulien would one find such a place?'

Orial realised they were both looking at her.

'The Undercity?' she said.

'Rehearsing in a necropolis. That has a certain ghoulish appeal.'

Cramoisy gave a fastidious little shudder.

'I don't think it is seemly. We should show respect for the dead.'

'I have always practised my music in the Undercity. I don't think it is disrespectful,' said Orial.

'I will make contact with the other musicians. Let us agree to meet in the Parade Gardens tomorrow – say around three in the afternoon? That way, anyone who observes us will think we have come to listen to the band.'

Amaru Khassian left Mistress Permay's house in a rainstorm. Acir Korentan watched him check the Crescent to see if anyone was watching and then, head down, plunge out into the pouring rain.

Acir followed – at a distance.

The composer seemed to know where he was going. He dodged through the umbrellas in broad Millisom's Street and crossed the rain-glossed cobbles at a run. Acir just caught sight of him slipping into a qaffë shop. With a sigh, he positioned himself under the striped awning of a milliner's and prepared to wait.

By midday the louring rainclouds had lifted from the city, revealing a sun-sheened sky of delicate blue. By the afternoon, it seemed to Acir that all Sulien had come out to take the warm spring air, to see and be seen . . .

Numbed with boredom, he almost missed Khassian as the composer came out of the qaffë shop in the company of three men.

Three strangers, all unfamiliar to Acir.

He slipped out into the jostling crowd and followed them.

North Parade was thronged with people, all taking their afternoon promenade. Posy-sellers thrust little bunches of violets and anemones under his nose; confectioners offered him dishes of junket sprinkled with nutmeg or brown-bread ices. In the Parade Gardens below the band had begun to play country dances: quaint old-fashioned quadrilles and rigadoons.

Silken ribbons streamed from spring bonnets and straw hats, fluttering like pastel pennants in a skirmish of fashion. Even the men had entered into the spring spirit and sported brightly embroidered waistcoats; lace, white as cow parsley, frothed at necks and wrists.

Acir passed like a sombre shadow between the cheerful promenaders, keeping his quarry in sight. In the Undercity he had experienced the visceral power of an ancient religion. Could these muslin-gowned women, these periwigged men, be the same people he had witnessed at the subterranean funeral?

Khassian and his companions had reached the bridge across the Avenne; they turned abruptly aside and took the steps down to the gardens. Acir stopped in the shadow of the bridge's arch. No longer raging and swollen with snowmelt, the Avenne lapped placidly at the bridge's foot.

Acir watched Khassian talking with his companions in the shade of a snow-blossomed cherry tree. Who were these three shabbily dressed strangers with whom he seemed so intimate?

A woman came strolling towards Acir, idly twirling a lacy parasol on her shoulder.

The sun dazzled in her tumbled marigold curls; yellow and gold, echoed in the faint dusting of freckles on her nose that even the most clever maquillage failed to disguise. Golden pollen.

'Contesse,' he said formally – though his heart had begun to beat faster at the sight of her.

'Captain,' Fiammis said. Her tone was equally cool.

He placed himself so that the sun was behind him; he saw her dazzled eyes narrow to try to read what was in his face.

'What are you doing here?'

'The same as you – taking the air. And if we are not to draw attention to ourselves, we had better do as the other visitors,' she said, sliding one delicate hand under his arm, 'and . . . promenade.'

He flinched at her touch – but, seeing Khassian glance around, reluctantly submitted. He hoped he had not been seen.

'I wonder if you have read the latest issue of the *Sulien Chronicle*?' She handed the paper to him. The front headline proclaimed:

THE DIVINE JORDELAYNE TAKES SULIEN BY STORM

No singer has received such a rapturous reception in Sulien since the days of the late, lamented Nightingale, Iridial Magelonne. The pure tone of the world-renowned castrato Cramoisy Jordelayne, the majestic command of the expressive art, all combined to make the recital at the Assembly Rooms an unforgettable evening.

But the item which provoked the most controversy was the first performance of an aria from the Illustre Amaru Khassian's new opera *Elesstar*. Such passion! Such fervour! When, the Sulien audience are asking, may we expect to hear more from this remarkable young composer?

'Well?' said Acir, handing it back to her. 'I understood you were here to take the waters. How can this possibly be of interest to you?'

'It should be of interest to *you*.'

Irritated at her interference, he turned to pull away but Fiammis's fingers suddenly tightened on his arm.

'Look,' she said softly.

A young woman was threading her way through the crowd towards Khassian, clutching a portfolio of papers.

'The Magelonne girl,' he murmured.

Behind her came Cramoisy Jordelayne in an outrageous perruque, long powdered kiss-curls adorned with little crimson bows. The Diva blew kisses to left and right as people in the gardens recognised him.

'They're coming this way.' Fiammis pulled Acir aside from the gravel river-walk.

The musicians went along the gravel walk and passed beneath the arches of the bridge. Fiammis waited a few moments and then darted after them. Acir followed.

'Where –?' She gazed around her. The riverbank was deserted, there was no one in sight. 'They can't just have vanished!'

Beyond the bridge, the formal gardens with their neatly planted flowerbeds ended in another shady river-walk meandering away beneath the willows.

'This looks like some kind of grotto.' Acir pointed to the entrance to a mossy cave which had been skilfully carved out of the rocks to look like a ruined chapel.

'What are you waiting for!' Fiammis gathered her skirts in one hand and, gracefully ducking her head so as not to dislodge her hat, went inside.

The grotto was empty; its rough walls glistened with whorled patterns of shiny pebbles inlaid with shells from the far-distant sea. The muddy floor was damp, showing the prints of many feet.

'There must be a secret way through here.' Fiammis began to twist the shells, to press on the stones, but the sequence – if there was one – eluded her. Frustrated, she stamped her foot on the floor in vexation. 'We've lost them.'

'We?' Acir said. 'Why are you here, Fiammis? Why are you shadowing Amaru Khassian? Or are you shadowing me?'

'Maybe I was bored . . . these spa cures are not very diverting. Then when I spotted an old acquaintance, maybe I was curious to see what he was doing.'

Her explanation did not convince him.

'There's a bench beneath that willow tree.'

She drew him out on to the bank and seated herself beneath the slender willow branches which formed a rustling canopy of tender green streamers.

'And while we wait and watch,' she said, re-arranging the folds of her gown – taffeta, pale as buttermilk, the underskirts striped, grey on cream – 'we can pass the time agreeably enough in conversation.'

'Conversation!' Acir turned away from her, his eyes fixed on the grotto. 'What is there to say?'

'So . . . I am not forgiven?'

He said nothing. He knew what she was up to, recognised her wiles of old. He would not be tricked into revealing his feelings for her. Not this time.

'I can tell from your silence that I am not.'

Was this the true purpose for her visit to Sulien? He felt doubly confused now. Was he hunter – or hunted?

'Why didn't you wait for me, Acir?'

'I? Wait for *you*?' He wished he had bitten his tongue. Too late now, the words were out. Besides, all the while he was angry with her, he could not listen to the deeper voice that whispered of more tender feelings, long repressed. 'You were the one who couldn't wait. You married the Conte. Because I, a nobody, a nothing, could not give you what you wanted. Money – lands – titles.'

'The Conte was old.'

'You shared his bed.'

'It was a contractual obligation, that was all. If you'd waited –'

'There's no point in discussing this. It's all in the past, all behind us now.'

Perhaps she did not hear what he was saying, for she carried on, 'Instead of which you renounced the world on my wedding day and joined the Commanderie.'

'I had found my vocation.'

'That was not what I heard.' The little smile on her lips was provocative, openly challenging him.

'Don't flatter yourself, Fiammis.'

'But what a perfect opportunity this is to renew our acquaintance.' She had moved closer, close enough for him to become aware of the scent of her skin, a milky jasmine

'We're far from the Commanderie here, Acir. Who would know if we –'

He stood up and went to lean one arm against the coarse-grained trunk of the willow, staring at the river.

She followed him. He closed his eyes, willing himself not to be swayed by her soft voice.

'I took a vow. For seven years I have kept that vow. I don't intend to break it now.'

'No,' she said. 'Of course you don't.' Her words were silvered with laughter, light and inconsequential as the willow-shadowed sun flickering on the riverwater.

'You're certain we've lost him?' Khassian glanced back into the darkness.

Orial was busy with the lanterns they had brought, nursing a tiny spark to flame between cupped hands.

'The grotto door to the Undercity is only known to a few people. Jolaine Tradescar let me into the secret. I can assure you that Captain Korentan will be utterly confounded!' She smiled to herself as she replaced the glass cylinder around the flame. 'Besides – even if he were to follow us, I could easily lead him astray. He'd be days finding his way out again.'

'What is this place?' Valentan shifted uneasily from foot to foot.

'The necropolis,' Azare said, laughing in the darkness. 'The city of the dead. The realm of shades and shadows.'

'Must you, Azare?' Cramoisy hissed, tapping him sharply with his quizzing stick.

Orial handed him a lantern.

'Shall I lead the way?'

They followed her in silence along the descending passage until she found the pillared portal to the chamber she had chosen.

'In here.'

Black-rimmed eyes stared at them, unblinking from the shadows.

'Aiii! We're being watched!' Cramoisy let out a shriek which echoed around the dark hall.

'Paintings,' Orial said, raising her lantern to illuminate the frescos. 'Wall-paintings.'

Khassian moved closer to examine the paintings. The light from Orial's lantern revealed the painted ripples of water, beds of reeds, ochre-spotted fish finning through them . . . and long-limbed, graceful people on the banks, many playing instruments: five-stringed citharas, aulos and timbrels.

'Who are they?' he asked.

'They called themselves Lifhendil,' Orial said, gazing up at the painted figures. 'The city-builders. The musicians.'

'I thought I glimpsed other paintings on our way here.'

'The whole Undercity is painted. No one is certain why. Necropolis, temple . . . or gate to the other world.'

'They give me the shivers.' Cramoisy pulled his jacket closer about his shoulders. 'Those *eyes*.'

'Musicians, you said?' Khassian turned questioningly to Orial. She nodded.

'Renowned for their music. Dame Tradescar is trying to decipher their script.'

Khassian knelt down to examine the mural more closely.

'Is this it?' He pointed to the formal border of painted reeds that fringed the frieze.

'Why – yes!' Kneeling down beside him, Orial saw a pattern of hieroglyphs cunningly concealed to look like tiny insects amongst the reeds: spotted ladybirds, cranetails and three-tailed damsel-nymphs. 'What keen eyesight you have, Illustre. I don't believe anyone has ever noticed these before. I must tell Jolaine.'

'It's too chilly down here. Damp. Bad for the vocal chords,' Cramoisy complained.

'A lost race of musicians,' Khassian murmured. 'What better place to rehearse?'

'But what am I to do?' demanded Cramoisy. 'You know how powerful my voice is, Amaru. Suppose I were to set off a rockfall? We could all be buried alive!'

Khassian had been walking around the hall, looking at the paintings. Now he stopped, smiling. Orial was astonished at the difference the smile made to his face; the hard eyes warmed, the stubborn set of the mouth creased into an endearingly boyish expression, sunshine on a barren landscape.

'I like this place. I feel an affinity with these people. They were musicians too. They would understand.'

'Shouldn't we obtain permission from someone?' Cramoisy was still determined to make objections.

'From whom? The Lifhendil are long dead.'

'How should I know! The Mayor?' Cramoisy blustered.

'Ah. Well, as you keep telling us that you are on such good terms with

His Worship the Mayor, maybe you should speak with him? Does this chamber have a name, Orial?'

He had called her by her first name, not the usual formality of 'demselle'. If it had not been so dark, he would have seen a sudden flush of colour warm her pale cheeks.

'I call it the Hall of Whispering Reeds,' she said softly.

'The Hall of Whispering Reeds,' he repeated her words. 'I like that.'

Orial felt her face burning with pleasure.

What's the matter with me? Blushing when he speaks to me. Wanting to be near him yet whenever he moves closer, wanting to move away . . .

She found herself wondering what links bound Khassian and Cramoisy together. She had assumed that they were lovers; there was a bantering quality to their exchanges that spoke of an easy intimacy established long ago. Yet they seemed oddly matched: Cramoisy, whose every gesture was exaggerated, whose every utterance was a little performance, and Khassian, whose whole bearing spoke of sensitivity and self-restraint.

Now she kept darting little glances at them whenever they spoke together, looking for clues – yet hoping against hope not to find them.

Acir Korentan was a haunted man.

As he walked the twilit streets of Sulien, he kept thinking he caught sight of Fiammis's reflection in the bow windows of the boutiques. He glimpsed her in the swirl of taffeta petticoats, the provocative tilt of a ribboned straw hat, the frills on a pretty parasol.

Each time he felt his heart miss a beat – and then, as he realised it was not – could not be – her, a ridiculous sensation of disappointment dulled his spirit. Even the sweet scents of the warm evening air stirred his senses as he remembered the lingering fragrance of her milky skin.

It was dusk and most of the shopkeepers were boarding up their shop windows for the night. One alone at the end of the row was still open, lanterns burning within and without. Acir was about to pass by when his heart stuttered again.

She was inside.

He swiftly drew back into the doorway of the neighbouring boutique.

This time it was no trick of the imagination. It was Fiammis. But what was she about? The little shop was dark and fusty, not the fashionable kind of boutique she preferred to patronise.

Acir looked up at the sign overhead: a pestle and mortar proclaimed the shop to be an apothecary's. Was she ill? Maybe she was not deceiving him after all; maybe she had come to Sulien for her health.

He heard voices and shrank back into the doorway as the shop bell tinkled and Fiammis appeared. He saw her glance up and down the street, then push a little package into her reticule. A moment later, she was away, nonchalantly walking alone into the dusk.

Should he pursue her? Should he offer to escort her through the darkening streets?

No, no. Acir stopped himself. Whatever was he thinking of? She could defend herself easily against whatever dangers she might encounter in Sulien at night.

The apothecary came out into the street to close his shop, a stooped little man who seemed hardly strong enough to pull the heavy shutters across.

Acir stepped out of the shadows.

'Good heavens, sieur, you made me jump!' The apothecary blinked at him in the lamplight. 'Can I help you? I was just shutting up for the night –'

'The customer you served . . . The one who just left your shop.'

'The lady?' The apothecary regarded him with his straggle-bearded head cocked to one side like a wary bird.

'What did she purchase?'

'Oh, I couldn't reveal the details of another customer's purchases –'

Acir drew two golden courons from his pocket.

'On the other hand, if you care to come into the shop, I could refer to the receipt book to refresh my memory.'

The shop was dingily lit by a single lamp. The shelves were lined with wooden boxes and ceramic jars, the painted names of the drugs within flaking away: Arnica; Calomel; Nux Vomica; Quassia. Bottles of luridly coloured water glowed in the lamplight. The counter-top was covered in a fine layer of powder . . . though whether it was from pounded herbs or dust, it was difficult to tell. Certainly the air had the dry taste of dust.

But what drew Acir's attention was a glass tank, filled with cloudy water, in which he could vaguely discern creatures, snaking through the water with restless, thready movement, to and fro, to and fro. They reminded him of –

But no. Surely that was impossible. Who would want to keep the carnivorous reservoir water-snakes in an aquarium? What possible purpose could they serve?

'That's what the lady bought.' The apothecary pointed to the tank. 'Sulien water-snake venom. My most expensive remedy.'

'She bought venom?'

'She had a prescription. It was all perfectly legal, I assure you.'

'And what is this venom prescribed for?'

The apothecary seemed reluctant to explain.

'Certain physicians here regard the treatment as their secret. If word were to get out . . .'

Acir brought out another two gold courons and laid them on the dusty counter.

130

'Administered in minuscule doses, it is the most efficient pain-killer. When laudanum and the poppy drugs cease to be effective, water-snake venom can bring relief.'

'But what ails the lady?'

'Megrims. Very severe megrims. The physicians only prescribe the venom in the worst cases – because of the risk.'

'What risk?' Acir heard the edge to his voice.

'A bite from one of these creatures can fell a full-grown man in a matter of minutes. The venom is injected through the front fangs. It numbs the prey almost instantly. So it's tricky trying to milk the slippery little devils. See?' He put the scoop into the tank and instantly the water became a wild froth as the water-snakes seemed to go into a frenzy, attacking with their teeth and their tails.

Acir drew back but his clothes were already spattered with water.

'And is there no antidote?'

'None. If they were to bite me, my head would soon start to spin, my sight would blur, my breathing would slow – I'd be dead within hours. So I keep 'em well-fed.'

Fiammis a sufferer from blinding headaches? He could never once recall her complaining of the megrim. What did she want with such a lethal poison?

A chilling suspicion began to form in his mind. The dusty little shop seemed suddenly airless; he had to get out.

'I could furnish you with more details if you so wish...' the apothecary called after him.

Orial went running up the steps to the Cabinet of Curiosities, eager to tell Jolaine Tradescar of Khassian's discovery. But when she reached the door she saw that a sign had been placed in the window, proclaiming:

'Museum closed until further notice for renovations'.

'Jolaine! Jolaine!' Orial tried the door handle: it was locked.

'What's amiss? Is the building on fire?'

Orial heard Jolaine's voice, sharp with irritation, from deep inside the Museum as her shuffling footsteps came nearer.

'I'm very busy. I haven't the time –'

Heavy chains rattled against the door panel as the Antiquarian shot the last bolt and opened the door, peering suspiciously with light-starved eyes into the sunshine. For one moment, Orial was irresistibly reminded of a mouldiwarp poking its snout out of its burrow.

'Oh – it's you. You can come in. I thought it was some interfering Guildhall clerk come poking his nose into my affairs.' Jolaine closed the door firmly behind her and locked it again. 'They want me to open the Museum to visitors by next month! I've told them it's impossible.'

Dustsheets lay over the cabinets; obviously nothing had been made ready for the summer season. The Antiquarian had been neglecting her duties.

'And they had the effrontery to suggest I should make some display of the new artefacts!' Muttering in an aggrieved tone, Jolaine set off towards her office. 'As if I had the time –'

Orial tapped her on the shoulder.

'We've found some new inscriptions. In the Hall of Whispering Reeds.'

'New inscriptions, eh?' She had caught Jolaine's attention now. 'I'd better take a look. Come into the office – I need to get my notebook and pencils.'

Orial followed her into the dusty office and waited whilst she gathered her notebooks into an artist's bag with pockets for pencils, humming jauntily to herself.

'What's this, Jolaine?' Orial picked up a volume she had left open and looked at the title on the worn leather spine. '*Faerie Tales and Legends*? Has the strain of translation become too great, Dame Antiquarian, that you've turned to reading children's stories?'

'There's a lot more sense in children's stories than most adults would care to admit.'

Orial had already begun to read:

THE FAERIE BRIDE

No one knew where she came from but all in the village acknowledged her to be a rare beauty. The young shepherd had been slaking his thirst at the waterfall, when he had heard a girl singing. Creeping closer, he had seen her sitting beside the water, combing her golden hair and singing so bewitchingly that it made his heart yearn with longing. From that hour he vowed not to eat or sleep until he had made her his bride.

At length she took pity on him and gave him her hand – but on one condition: once every year at midsummer she must leave him for a few days to return to her own folk far beyond the mountains. He must let her go – and he must give her his solemn promise not to follow, for if he tried to come after her, she would be lost to him forever. And so he gave her his promise and they lived in perfect happiness for a while . . . until she began to pine, growing pale and silent.

'What ails you, dear heart?' her husband asked her.

'The time has come when I must leave you,' she replied. 'But never fear, I will return – so long as you keep your promise.'

'Then give me something as a keepsake, a token that you will keep faith with me.'

So she cut off a lock of her golden hair and gave it to him as a keepsake.

Days passed and the bride did not return. The young shepherd began to grow suspicious. On Midsummer Eve he went back to the waterfall where he had first met her and he heard the strains of a strange, sad music drifting from a distant glade. Curious, he followed the sounds of the music and came upon a company of the Faer Folk beside the waters, dancing and making such music as he had never heard before. And foremost amongst them he recognised his bride.

Forgetting his promise, he called her name aloud – and in that instant, she gave a terrible cry and threw herself into the waterfall. A mist swirled about them – and when it cleared, he was alone on the bare hillside.

Nothing would console him. For years he roamed the hills searching in vain for his faerie bride, clutching the lock of golden hair she had left as a keepsake. And some say she came to him on his deathbed, as young and as beautiful as when he had first seen her . . . for in their halls of Faerie, the passing of mortal time is but the blinking of an eye . . .

'That story always used to make me cry when I was little,' Orial said, setting the book slowly down, 'though I was never sure why. Was it because the shepherd died for love? Or because I wanted to find the Faer Folk for myself and everyone kept telling me it was just a silly story and, besides, faeries don't exist?'

'I'm sure I never told you that.'

'Oh, not you, Jolaine, never you.'

'It was always my theory, as you remember, that these faerie tales contained a grain of truth. A folk memory, maybe, of events long since forgotten, unrecorded in the written annals of Sulien.'

'But a memory of what?'

'The Lifhendil.'

'Now you're going to tell me I've faerie blood in my veins. Should I expect to sprout little wings and fly?' Orial said teasingly, making her hands flutter upwards like a butterfly.

'Lifhendil blood.' Jolaine was not to be distracted from the line of thought she was pursuing. 'Suliens called it "faerie" to explain away a phenomenon they would not, could not, understand. By reducing it to a children's fantasy, they defused the myth of its potency. There's nothing too threatening about rainbow-winged sprites, is there?'

'Threatening? The Lifhendil were a peaceful race. The Allegondans slaughtered them.'

'The Allegondans did not understand the Lifhendil. Their religious rites must have seemed utterly incomprehensible. Confronted by such alien beliefs, they reacted in the time-honoured way.'

'The religious rites?'

'At first I thought the rites must be some form of ancestor-worship. And then, more and more of the inscriptions led me to believe they were . . . something else. What have the Lifhendil bequeathed us? Our funeral customs – and the Accidie. A terrible legacy. And yet they were a serene, gifted people – all the wall-paintings and writings confirm that. Something went wrong, Orial.'

'No, I'm wrong,' she said slowly, with growing understanding. 'I'm a freak. Can't you imagine how it happened? Allegondans captured and raped the few surviving Lifhendil women. The Allegondans and Lifhendil were never meant to intermarry. I am the result of some ancient atrocity.'

'But no freak, my dear.' Jolaine took her hands; the Antiquarian's fingers felt as gnarled and knotted as willow twigs but Orial was grateful for the comfort of her firm grip. 'The wrong that was done to your Lifhendil ancestors was that their culture was obliterated. Until now.'

'What have you discovered?' Orial whispered, not taking her eyes from Jolaine's.

'To the Lifhendil, this life was but one stage in their development. The first stage.'

'The first stage?'

'The reservoirs were designed as – as –' Jolaine Tradescar searched for words. 'Places of transition. Birthing pools. Are you with me? Not burial places – but somewhere where the mortal shell could be shrugged off, where a new, transfigured being would emerge. Like the dragonflies.'

'But that would mean my mother –' Orial had begun to tremble. 'She went mad. She – she was buried in the dark waters, the reservoir. Oh, Jolaine –'

'If it's upsetting you –'

'Go on.'

'The madness was regarded as a sign from the Goddess. A sign that the one divinely afflicted was ready to be translated to a higher state. To join the winged ones.'

'The faeries?'

'Faeries, angels, that's our modern, inadequate translation . . . the Lifhendil had no words like these.' Hoisting the canvas artist's bag on to her shoulder, Jolaine locked the door to her office and ushered Orial down the Museum between the shrouded cabinets.

'But surely it's just a metaphor, Jolaine. The body dies and the spirit takes wing towards the light.'

'Not for the Lifhendil,' Jolaine said firmly.

Orial saw that there was no gleam of eccentric fervour in Jolaine's eyes. She was in earnest.

'You really believe it.'

'There's too much evidence to the contrary.' Jolaine shot back the bolts and opened the door; cloudy daylight spilled into the Museum.

'B-but – where are they now? The winged ones?'

'Now?' Jolaine's eyes lifted beyond hers, towards the distant hills. 'On the lonely mountainside, behind the waterfall? Over the hills and faraway . . .'

'Dame Tradescar!'

Two men were coming swiftly towards them, climbing the steps two-at-a-time.

'Hell and damnation!' Jolaine swore under her breath and attempted to retreat into the Museum. But her canvas bag-strap caught on the door handle and before she could slam the door shut, the brawnier of the two men wedged his foot and shoulder in between.

'You can't come in,' Jolaine said defensively. 'See the notice?'

'I see it.' The second of the men, impeccably dressed, took a letter from his breast pocket and handed it to Jolaine.

'What does this mean?' Orial said, bewildered.

'I represent the Sulien Council, demselle,' he said with a nod of the head. 'I have attempted to serve this order upon Dame Tradescar on several occasions and each time I have been turned away. You are my witness that she has taken the order and is now obliged to read it.'

'Jolaine –' Orial turned to the Antiquarian who had already torn the order open and was scanning the page, muttering venomously all the while about petty officials and bureaucrats.

'So now you will let us in?'

The brawny man made as if to push the door wide open; Jolaine neatly jabbed him in the foot with her walking-stick. There was a smothered curse and the foot was hastily withdrawn, enabling her to slam the door shut in his face.

'I am in the middle of important new researches,' she shouted from behind the door. 'I will *not* be disturbed.'

'As you are disinclined to co-operate, Dame Tradescar, His Worship the Mayor wishes me to inform you that he has recently received an application from a gifted young scholar, a certain Dr Theophil Philemot from the University of Can Tabrien.' The official took a step forward, as if confident Jolaine would admit him. 'He also wishes me to remind you that you are deemed by the City Council to be well past the usual retirement age.'

Orial saw Jolaine's shoulders sag; it seemed as if all the fight had suddenly leaked out of her.

'Jolaine – there must be something I can do!'

The Antiquarian shook her head. *Keep your counsel,* her eyes implored Orial through the glass.

'I'm so sorry, my dear. Our little outing will have to wait for another day.'

CHAPTER 12

Acir Korentan was no longer certain whether he was shadowing Amaru Khassian to spy on him – or to protect him.

Until that sun-gilded afternoon in the Parade Gardens, he had been steeling himself to bring his mission to a conclusion. He had planned one more meeting with the composer, a meeting at which he would convince him that the only course of action left to him was to return to Bel'Esstar. He would appeal to Khassian's better nature, would talk of reconciliation and a new dawn.

And then Fiammis had thrown all his plans awry.

Was she acting on her own initiative? Or was there some more sinister reason for her appearance? Even in Enhirrë he had heard rumours . . . sudden, inexplicable deaths in Bel'Esstar of prominent people opposed to Ilsevir's new regime. There was, of course, no proof that the deaths had been deliberately contrived . . . And there was no proof that Fiammis had not come to Sulien for her health.

Each day Acir had observed Khassian leave the Crescent house in company with the Magelonne girl. And each day he had followed them, only to lose them in the back streets of the city – or, more accurately, they lost him.

But today Acir kept the musicians in sight; today he saw them turn aside from the busy market thoroughfare and – disappear.

Acir followed, hastening his pace. Steep steps, with only an iron handrail to cling to, plunged down the hillside between ramshackle terraces. There were many of these precipitate stairways in Sulien, winding down beneath ancient arches into squalid courtyards or weed-grown lanes, behind the ornate façades of the crescents and squares.

This stair led nowhere. A blind alleyway, the sheer walls on either side windowless, blackened with soot, damp and clinging moss.

Acir turned around. There was no other way out. The Magelonne girl had tricked him again.

Then he saw it. At the far end of the alley, an archway, overhung with dark, dusty ivy, concealed an iron grille. A carved stone face stared out from between its leafy crown of glossy green, its sunken eye sockets empty, seeing nothing: a sightless mask of death. The grille beneath led down into darkness. Into the Undercity.

Acir came closer. He had no lantern to light his way below ground. But he was certain he was still on Khassian's trail. This was not the moment to turn back for want of a torch. He slipped beneath the trailing curtain of ivy and tested the handle of the grille. The rusted iron hinges groaned – then, as he exerted greater pressure, slowly opened. Far ahead in the darkness he caught the dwindling flicker of lanterns.

Darkness, secrecy, concealment – the whole escapade stank of conspiracy.

He sighed. He had no choice now; he must follow them into the dark. And the lights were so far ahead, he would soon lose them altogether.

He pulled the grille to behind him and set out warily in the darkness. He had not forgotten the vast reservoirs that lay below ground . . . or the vicious water-snakes that lived in their murky depths.

The flickering lights went on some way ahead of him. This was too easy. Had the composer become careless? Or did he just not care any longer?

The lights suddenly vanished.

Acir stood alone, lost in the utter blackness, listening in vain for a footfall, a dislodged stone, even the distant drip of water.

Should he feel his way back to the entrance, hand over hand? And which way was the entrance? Was the only alternative now to go on into the dark?

Slowly, uncertainly, he went blindly forward, still listening attentively.

He had expected to hear the murmur of voices, hushed, conspiratorial. But all he could hear was – singing.

They were musicians, after all. And musicians needed to practise their craft.

He crept closer, drawn towards the faint strains of music until he reached a tall doorway cut into the rock.

Voice intertwined with voice, clashing then resolving into a melting sweetness.

Only gradually did he begin to distinguish words . . . and with a shock, realised that he knew those words as if they had been branded upon his heart. He and his brothers had chanted them at dawn and at dusk in the echoing rock-temple in the Enhirran desert. The *Vineyard Verses*. The verses in which Mhir described the appearance of the angel in the hillside vineyard: the moment of divine revelation.

And now, through Khassian's music, it was as if he was hearing them for the first time.

Notes swirled like dark smoke, and in the smoky darkness a third voice soared, a column of flame, searing the darkness.

'Mhir, Mhir, open your eyes, look on me!'

The pulsing of the swirling keyboard figurations became the throb of great wings, fanning a hot, dry wind, a wind of fire that would burn away all disbelief, all sin.

'*Then he put His mouth to my mouth and His tongue was as a scorching flame. The fire of His words flowed into my body. Though I was burned to the core of my soul, yet was I made whole again . . .*'

Tears pricked Acir's eyes; the lighted chamber beyond blurred in the darkness.

Angrily, he pulled the back of his hand across his eyes, wiping away the wetness. This was wrong. The composer's music should merely act as a vessel for the words, it should remain remote, unemotional, allowing the words to speak for themselves. The repetition of the words in free chant was an act of devotion in itself, devoid of anything extraneous to sully their purity. The worshipper should contemplate the meaning of the words – not the beauty or expressive power of the music.

This music was sacrilegious.

And yet its power to move was indisputable.

Was this why Girim wanted Khassian? To use his gifts to glorify the Commanderie's achievements? Was this what lay behind these long, frustrating weeks in Sulien?

The music suddenly broke off – and the golden vision vanished as swiftly as a pricked bubble. The Diva began a petulant complaint. Acir moved closer until he stood in the chamber doorway, unnoticed.

They had hung lanterns around the walls of the painted chamber, filling it with pools of watery light. One musician sat at a keyboard instrument; Khassian and the Magelonne girl leaned over his shoulders, peering at the music. The Diva paced up and down, remonstrating with them. In another corner, Acir noted that the other singers were observing him and hiding smiles behind their hands.

It was the Magelonne girl who spotted Acir. It was almost as if she sensed he was there for she slowly raised her golden head and stared directly at him. The Diva followed her gaze – and let out a piercing scream that echoed to the roof of the chamber.

'A ghost! *A ghost*!'

Cramoisy sank to the floor in a faint.

The other singers sprang to their feet, closing ranks. Acir was outnumbered. He would not retreat now; that would be undignified. Open confrontation was inevitable.

He entered the chamber.

'Korentan.' Khassian straightened up.

Orial was fanning Cramoisy's face; she glared at Acir as he walked past her. The other singers closed in around him but he kept on walking until he had reached the keyboard.

'For one moment then, Captain, I truly believed you had come to kill us,' said Khassian.

Acir picked up the sheets of music from the keyboard.

' *"Elesstar* – Act Three, " ' he read aloud. ' "Enter Elesstar, distracted." '
He threw the sheets down again. The keyboard player grabbed them,
clutching them to his breast as if he feared Acir would tear them up.

'So now you have discovered our secret,' Khassian said quietly, 'what
are you going to do about it?'

'There is no law against the practising of music in Sulien,' Valentan put
in.

'Why do you persist with this opera?' Acir asked, ignoring Valentan,
addressing Khassian alone.

'Because I have to.'

'No. Because it's seditious. Because it warps the words of the poet-
prophet, bends them to suit your aims. Because you alter Mhir from a
visionary to a revolutionary.'

The other singers drew closer still.

'Some might say that the two were the same. Mhir spoke out against
the oppressive rule of the Shultan. What was that if not revolutionary?'
Khassian had turned to the others. 'Let's give the Captain a further taste
of sedition. The "Freedom" chorus.'

Valentan struck a chord on the keyboard and Khassian began to sing.
The other singers glanced uncertainly at each other, and then first one,
then the others, joined in until the chamber throbbed to their mingled
voices.

'You can't stop it!' cried Khassian. 'You can kill the singer – but the song
will still be sung.'

A sudden thrilling swerve of key brought all the voices in unison, all
singing the refrain together:

'Freedom, freedom!'

Sunset had warmed the roseate stone of the city of Sulien to flame and
gold; window panes were afire with the last glory of the dying light.

Acir stood at the railing and gazed down over the darkening city.

Khassian's music smouldered on in Acir's mind, dark as holy fire. It
had touched his heart, his soul. He had been unprepared for this assault,
unprotected.

How could the mind that had conceived and fashioned such ravishing
sounds be labelled corrupt?

Amaru Khassian was a true visionary.

'Good evening, Acir.'

She sat in his chair, one hand resting on the table, the other caressing
the handle of the parasol which lay across her lap.

'F-Fiammis.' He stumbled over her name, shocked to see her here in
his lodgings. 'How did you –'

'Oh, don't worry. I'm not here to assail your virtue.' She rose to her feet; in the cramped little room, there was barely any distance between them. 'I know it is unassailable.' Her voice was dry, mocking him. 'Your reputation is safe – the landlady didn't catch sight of me.'

'Why have you come?'

She turned away from him, trailing her finger-tips over the table, the wooden bedhead . . .

'Just the barest necessities. A hard bed, a table, a chair.' She lifted the knotted scourge from the case which he had left beneath his bed and turned it over in her hands. 'What are you punishing yourself for, Acir?' Her fingers stroked the handle of the scourge suggestively.

He blushed and reached out to take it from her.

'I must ask you to leave, Fiammis.'

She had obviously been through all his possessions. But what had she been searching for?

'Don't you want to hear the message I've brought you from Commanderie headquarters?'

'The message?' Acir said. He had no desire to prolong the encounter. To be so near to her again was torment enough.

'Girim nel Ghislain wants to see you. In Bel'Esstar. Do I need to elaborate?'

'Elaborate,' he said shortly.

'You haven't fulfilled the task he set you, Acir. So you are recalled to Commanderie headquarters.'

'And you?' he said, frowning. 'He hasn't sent you here merely to relay a message.'

She looked up at him; her cornflower eyes hard, bright as jewelled enamel.

'I am to replace you.'

'You!' The implied criticism wounded him deeply. Girim nel Ghislain no longer trusted him. How had he come to fall from favour so fast?

'Until you have received new instructions from the Grand Maistre. Whatever they may be,' she said, smiling again. The smile which he had once found so bewitching now seemed charged with menace.

'Your authority?' he said coldly formal, hand extended, palm upwards.

She slid her fingers into the soft cleft between her breasts and drew out a token and placed it on his outstretched palm. He tried to stifle a shiver as he realised the token was still warm from the heat of her body. He looked down and saw the crimson rose of the Order of the Rose-coeur enamelled on the metal token, weeping its jewelled tears of black blood.

The badge of the inner circle of the Commanderie.

Without a word he returned it to her.

*

Orial could hear Dame Jolaine puffing as the Antiquarian followed her down the steep path into the Hall of Whispering Reeds.

'I'm afraid I must be a little out of condition. Give me a moment or two to get my breath.'

Orial held her lantern high to illuminate the border of painted reeds. Jolaine hobbled up to the wall and, head on one side, began to copy down the hieroglyphs with swift, rapid pencil strokes.

'And we thought it was merely a hunting scene, decorative . . . but not very significant. How perceptive of your friend to notice these concealed inscriptions.'

Orial was glad that Jolaine had not asked her precisely what she was doing with Amaru Khassian down here in the Undercity. After a while, Jolaine began to read aloud:

' *"She hears the voices of the winged ones calling her. She falls to the ground, possessed by the divine madness. It is time to go down into the dark waters."* '

On the frieze the naked diver cleaving the green waters seemed sexless, the slender body clothed only in long strands of hair and a loincloth.

'My predecessor called this "The Boy Diving for Fish",' Jolaine muttered. 'But look at the skin colour. Ivory for a woman, light terracotta for a man. This is a young woman. And now the next picture in the cycle begins to make sense . . .'

'Water-snakes? Or dragonfly nymphs?'

Dark, wormlike shapes writhed through black waters. Sun, moon, dawn and duskstars shone in the sky together. On the shores of the water, a riot of confused seasons was in progress. Stylised trees bore blossom, fruit, bare branches simultaneously.

' *"Years go?"* Ah! Years pass!' Jolaine cried excitedly. 'Of course! It shows the passing of time. The artist was not merely being fanciful. It's a calendar – of sorts.'

'And this picture?' Orial moved on to illuminate the last image. ' "The Day of the Dead"?'

Dragonflies, gauze wings limned with jewel-shards of emerald and sapphire, hovered in a ring above the waters.

'The unbroken circle. Symbol of eternity. We can but guess . . . for look, Orial, the last hieroglyphs that would have given us the clue have flaked away.'

'Trodden into the dust in this chamber.' Orial felt she might weep from disappointment. 'And now we'll never know.' She set the lantern down on the floor and knelt to search the dust with her finger-tips, vainly hoping she might find a fragment of broken plaster.

'Ah . . . but all is not lost. Your friend has made a discovery of some significance. These chambers are of immense importance – not just to you and me, but to the history of Sulien. They must be properly preserved or these priceless records of our past will end as dust blowing through empty chambers.'

A wisp of melody floated into Orial's mind. She began to hum softly as she searched.

'We always thought the Lifhendil sense of perspective less sophisticated than our own.' Jolaine halted her swift pencil strokes to contemplate the spinning circle of dragonflies. 'Giant dragonflies – little people, little trees. How charmingly primitive, we said.'

'They're not dragonflies?'

'Winged Ones. Eä-Endil.'

'Eä-Endil.' Orial resumed her humming. What *was* the tune? She couldn't remember where she had heard it before – and now it circled her brain as she continued her search, round and round . . .

'What's that you're singing?' Jolaine looked up from her notebook.

Orial broke off, surprised. She was unaware she was singing aloud.

'I don't know. Some dance-tune from the gardens, most like. I don't remember where I first heard it. Do you recognise it?'

'No. I can't say I do.'

Orial's fingernail clicked against something hard. She moved the lantern closer.

'Look. Look at this, Jolaine. I've found something.'

A glimmer of white had appeared in the caked dirt.

Jolaine swore under her breath and, kneeling down beside Orial, took two brushes from her pocket, giving one to Orial. With careful strokes, they set about brushing the earth away.

'What is it?' Orial whispered.

'Look. Oh, look,' crooned Jolaine. 'Isn't it beautiful? Have you ever seen anything so perfect?'

Slowly, their careful brushwork revealed a fragment of an enamelled lotos flower: ivory-white set on green and gold. Producing a palette knife, Jolaine slipped it beneath the fragment and gently began to lever.

'It's coming, it's coming –'

'Be careful,' begged Orial.

'Seems to be set in some kind of stone plinth.' Jolaine wiped her sweating brow.

'Perhaps we shouldn't remove it.'

'I'm only going to examine it, clean it, record it. I'll put it back.'

There was an acquisitive glint in Jolaine's eyes; she was not to be diverted from her purpose. 'In a few days or so . . .'

Orial sat back on her heels and watched the Antiquarian work.

'That's it . . . out you come, my beauty, out you come . . .'

Jolaine lifted the enamel out from the encrusted dirt that had held it in place over the centuries and cupped it in her palms.

'But where's the other half?' Orial asked.

Jolaine began to dig again – but only uncovered an indentation in the stone where the other half-lotos had been.

'Damme if it isn't gone!' she said, exasperated. 'Someone's been here before us. Still, one half is better than none and this is the finest piece of Lifhendil enamel work I have ever seen. How did you know it was here?'

'I didn't,' Orial said. 'I just . . . had an intuition.'

'There may be other treasures concealed beneath this dirt floor.' Jolaine spread her hands, encompassing the whole chamber. 'I have a theory that this chamber is of far greater significance than anyone has ever imagined. The inscriptions on the walls, the ritual paintings –' She rubbed her hands together in anticipation. 'There's no way the Mayor can force me to retire now. Not when I'm on the brink of my greatest discovery!'

CHAPTER 13

Orial stood beneath the bleak walls of the Sulien Asylum, shivering in the rain-damp wind.

Better to turn back now. Better not to know.

An attendant ushered her across a windswept, weedy courtyard. Barred blank windows stared down at her. And from deep within the building, she heard someone laughing, a cracked, crazy laughter that echoed on and on.

The Asylum Director looked as dishevelled as his Asylum, his stained white coat unbuttoned, his hair ruffled, ill-combed. Orial began to wonder if she had made a grave error of judgement in coming. The gloomy office into which he ushered her did nothing to improve her first impressions: a yellowing skull leered at her from the desk. The walls were covered in a gloomy dark brown wallpaper with faded medical charts showing sections of the brain, highlighted in lurid greens and pinks.

'How can I help you, demselle?' He was staring at her in a way that made her feel distinctly uncomfortable, as if she were a laboratory specimen pinned out on a board. 'I'm sorry, I didn't catch your name?'

'Magelonne.'

He let out a sudden, wild bark of laughter that made her jump.

'Orial Magelonne! Let me introduce myself: Tartarus. Ophil Tartarus. Your father may have mentioned my name . . .'

Orial looked at him blankly.

'Or maybe not.'

'Dr Tartarus – what can you tell me of an illness called the Accidie?'

'It's rare. Exceptionally rare, demselle.' He was still staring at her. 'Before we proceed – does your father know you have come to consult me?'

Orial hesitated. If she said no, would he send her away?

'I can tell from your silence that he does not.'

'And does that prevent you answering my questions?' Orial asked. She had summoned the courage to make the journey here; she would not come away unsatisfied.

'Please. Sit down.' He held out a chair for her; the worn leather upholstery creaked as she sat down.

'If you know my father – then you know what happened to my mother?'

He sat opposite her

'Iridial Magelonne? Yes, I treated her.'

His prompt reply took her by surprise.

'So she *did* go mad?'

'Mad? Such an imprecise term. Your mother was suffering from a kind of mania. She claimed she could hear the music in other people's minds. Constantly.'

'The Accidie?'

'Before we proceed you'd better read this – a monograph written by my predecessor.'

He pulled out a bound ledger and smoothed it open: the page he presented to Orial was filled with a tightly written script in fading brown ink:

As the Accidie only seems to affect females at or after puberty, how can we be sure that the patient is suffering from the Accidie and not hysteria? The eyes (cf. my pamphlet on this subject) show a tendency to myopia and astigmatism. If the irises have developed marked striations of several colours, then this is a certain indicator.

The patient will manifest musical ability of a prodigious nature.

The madness begins with a state of confusion. The patient claims to hear music emanating from the minds of other individuals. Anyone who has ever been plagued by a melody 'on the brain' will understand what a terrible affliction this must be. This stage may last – with remissions – for anything between a few months to several years. The confusion culminates in a sudden devastating deterioration from which there is no recovery.

'No recovery?' Orial whispered.

'When I was called to your mother, she had already tried to drown herself. In the end, of course, she succeeded.'

'She – *drowned*?' Orial stared at Ophil Tartarus. She had gone rigid with shock.

'I'm sorry. You didn't know?'

She numbly shook her head.

'Here.' He poured liquid from a flask into a glass and placed it in her shaking hand, guiding it to her lips. 'Drink this.'

A few drops slid down Orial's throat; she choked on their bitter fire, waving the glass away as tears clouded her eyes.

'I assumed your father had told you.'

'My – father –' Orial said between coughs, 'has told me – nothing.'

'Then maybe –'

'No. I appreciate your frankness. Where did she drown?'

'In the River Avenne. It was most unfortunate. After a week or so here, our regime seemed to have calmed her. So when your father came to visit her, we let him take her to walk in the gardens. Suddenly she broke free, ran to the riverbank – and threw herself in. By the time he had pulled her out, she was dead. Drowned.'

'Dead,' Orial repeated. 'You are *sure* she was dead?'

'Great heavens, demselle, both your father and I are doctors! What are you implying?'

Orial sat silent a moment. The sour taste of the spirit still stung the inside of her mouth; she centred her mind on that one sensation. After a while she said, more to herself than Tartarus, 'So that's why.'

'Why what, demselle?'

'Why my father has kept all music out of the house. To protect me.'

'An intriguing theory. Most intriguing.' Tartarus began to scribble in a notebook, murmuring to himself, 'By eliminating the stimulus . . . maybe hoped to delay or even avert the onset of the symptoms of the degeneration . . .'

'But has it worked?' Orial asked.

'Demselle?' Tartarus said, regarding her warily.

'Please be frank, Doctor. What are my chances?'

'It's impossible to make an accurate prediction without examining you properly.' He leaned closer across the desk, staring into her eyes. Orial, suddenly uneasy, sprang to her feet.

'Well, thank you, Dr Tartarus. If I need to consult you again . . .'

He was still staring at her in that disconcerting way.

'Maybe if I could just visit the gardens and see where my mother . . .'

'Please.' He did not rise from the desk but she felt his piercing stare follow her out of the office.

Outside in the courtyard, she took in several breaths of fresh air. The spirit had made her light-headed and her heart was pounding.

A sudden devastating deterioration from which there is no recovery.

Orial wandered through the neglected Asylum gardens. Weeds choked the borders; the path led past a sundial, half-smothered in bindweed. She parted the clinging stems, revealing the slate dial beneath.

The faint shadow of the broken finger flickered across the dial . . . backwards?

Overhead, clouds scudded on fitful gusts of wind, obliterating the faint sun.

This was where Iridial had spent her last moments. This was where, distracted beyond endurance, she had turned towards the river, seeking oblivion.

The rusting iron gates that led out into the river marsh should have been locked . . . but the links of the chain securing them had snapped. Orial pushed open one of the gates and went out to stand on the bleak banks of the Avenne beneath the fast-scudding clouds. Here the lonely marsh seemed to stretch on forever into the distant hills. No birds, no stir of life, only the wind: just sky . . . and rippled water.

Banks of dry reeds whispered, moving to the wind's incessant whine. She closed her eyes a moment, listening.

'Or – i – al . . .'

'Who's there?' she cried aloud.

The green riverwater shivered. Where the stooping willows trailed their yellow tresses in the river, Orial caught a tremor of movement.

She squeezed her eyes shut – and half-opened them again.

Fingers part the rippling riverwater. Hair, green as riverweed, drifting on the current. A woman is floating in the cold waters of the Avenne, her naked body tinged with the chill grey of the river's sediment.

Drowned . . .

Orial's fingers cage her eyes, she dare not look, she dare not – for if she looks, who will she see?

Dead Iridial . . . or her own body floating past?

Jerame Magelonne hung up his white coat, washed and dried his hands and set out along the Sanatorium corridor for the parlour.

It was time for tea. Even if the pendule clock had not struck the hour, he would have known for Cook had been making girdle cakes: he had smelt them sizzling on the range. He rubbed his hands together in anticipation; his mother had made girdle cakes for him when he came in from school and that warm, comforting smell of eggs, flour and buttermilk always made him remember his own childhood with happiness.

Orial stood in the parlour, staring out the window.

'Girdle cakes, eh?' he said, lifting the cover off the dish and looking with pleasure at the round, crisp pancakes, helping himself to several.

'Tuck in, Orial!'

She did not move.

'Mmm. They're very good.'

She turned around. Her face was taut, her fists clenched at her sides. And when she spoke, the words were wrenched out of her in a tortured whisper.

'Why? Why did you never tell me?'

He shook his head, not understanding precisely what he had not told her, yet dreading to hear.

'That she *drowned*.'

She raised her face to him and for a moment he saw Iridial's drenched face, water pouring from her water-logged hair. He swallowed the half-chewed mouthful of girdle cake as if it were bitter medicine; it had lost all its savour.

'Who's been talking to you?' he said. The question rasped out more roughly than he had intended; fear for her sanity filled him with anger. 'What mischief has someone been stirring up? Has Dr Tartarus been here behind my back?'

'No one's stirred up anything but me,' she said defiantly. She had begun to twist a loose strand of hair repetitively round and round her finger. The obsessiveness of the gesture disturbed him.

'Then how did you find out –'

'I went to the Asylum.'

'Dear Goddess.' His legs felt weak all of a sudden; he sat down, fumbling for his kerchief to wipe his brow. 'Orial – why didn't you come to me?'

'Why do you think?' *Blue-ice stare, streaked with frost.*

He had forgotten how the rainbow eyes could change with different emotions, could reinforce those emotions with startling impact.

'I –' He lifted his hands as if to protest – and then slowly let them fall back. 'I wanted to protect you. To shield you.'

'But you could see I was changing.' The accusing eyes still bored whitefrost into him; he almost shivered under their chill. 'I needed to know.'

'What exactly did Tartarus tell you?'

She pressed her lips together; he could see from the trembling of the lower lip that she was fighting to keep from crying.

'That there is no cure.'

'Such insensitivity!' Jerame got up again, almost knocking over the chair; she flinched as she had always flinched from loud noises as a child. 'He had no right.' He turned on her. 'He had no right to tell you such things.'

'On the contrary,' she said in a flat, hard little voice. 'He was honest with me.'

The implied criticism hurt more than he could ever have anticipated.

'What else haven't you told me? What else am I going to have to learn from strangers about my life? About my own mother?'

'How dare you!' He was shouting now. She had touched the rawness of his secret pain. 'You will not speak to me like that! You will go to your room!'

'Yes, I'll go.' She retreated, one step at a time. 'But not to my room. I'm not a child anymore, Papa. I'm going out.'

'Come back, Orial!' He went after her but she grabbed her cloak and evaded him, slamming the front door behind her.

'Tsk, tsk.' Cook had appeared with her tray. 'Another unfinished meal. Why do I go to all the trouble to prepare it, I ask myself . . .'

Jerame found he was still clutching his napkin. He threw it down on the table.

'I'm not very hungry, Cook.'

The Hall of Whispering Reeds echoed to the voices of Cramoisy Jordelayne and Celestion Valentan. Khassian stood behind Azare's shoulder, following the score.

Orial sat close by, hugging her knees to her, listening.

The sight of her face, transfigured by an intense delight, caught Khassian's attention. She seemed utterly absorbed in his music.

And was it a trick of the lantern-light – or had the colours in her eyes deepened, intensified? She had been such an awkward, sallow chit of a girl when he had first encountered her, bespectacled and gauche. Now her gaucheness seemed nothing more than a charming shyness.

Cramoisy and Valentan reached the end of their duet – and the keyboard notes suddenly came to a stop.

'What's the problem?' Khassian asked.

'We have no one to sing the Angel,' Cramoisy pointed out. 'Why you had to write it for a boy treble when we have no boys –'

'Orial can sing it,' Khassian said.

'Me?' she said, startled. 'But I can't sing. I –'

'You transcribed the notes. You can sing.'

Valentan handed her the manuscript; Khassian saw her hands tremble as she took the sheets.

'Two bars from the cadence,' Azare said.

Orial missed the cue.

'Sorry,' she whispered.

'Two bars,' Azare said, starting again.

This time she caught the cue – just – and in a thin, true voice began to sing. Khassian closed his eyes. He could hear her fear – she could barely sustain the longer notes, dying away into a whisper. But there was an ethereal quality to her singing that sent chills through his body. For a moment he believed he was listening to a voice from another world –

The soft light of the lanterns reflected the rainbow shadows in her eyes. Ripples of iridescent notes spread through the hall, a shifting spectrum of sound, as the song reached its climax . . . and final cadence.

'Forgive me.' She cast down her eyes, blushing. 'That was awful. So many silly mistakes.'

'No,' he said, dazed. 'It was – different. Maybe I'd better rethink my original concept. Maybe a girl's voice . . . Maybe yours . . .'

The eyes softened, glimmered silver-rose.

'Me? Sing the Angel?' She clasped her hands together, thrilled as a little child who has been given an unexpected present. Her pleasure touched him; he was so used to seeing singers fight each other over roles they felt to be rightfully theirs.

'Go practise with Azare,' he said. She seized the sheets and ran back to the keyboard.

The Diva drew near; his lips tightly pursed, his eyes narrowed, purposeful.

'You're making a mistake, Amar.'

'She will in no way rival you, Diva,' Khassian said, still watching Orial as she repeated the first phrase with Azare.

'That's not what I'm saying.'

'Isn't it?'

'I've taken a liking to the girl.' Cramoisy snapped open a pocket mirror case and re-adjusted his beauty spot, a tiny crescent of black velvet. 'I feel responsible for her.'

'This is most unlike you, Diva.'

'A debt to her mother. That's why I say you should be careful.' Then she added in a stage whisper, 'Besides – I think she is growing fond of you.'

Acir Korentan saw Fiammis pause at the entrance to the Botanical Gardens and then go in. He followed at a discreet distance.

He had taken care to make sure she knew he had left Sulien on the overnight diligence. A little distance outside Sulien, he had asked the coachman to set him down and had walked back to the city before dawn.

By the time he called at Mistress Permay's, Khassian had already left. Mistress Permay told him that a letter had come for the composer; she thought it might have been an assignation with a lady, for he had asked her how to find the Botanical Gardens, and if young gentlemen visited the Botanical Gardens, with their shady arbours and hidden pavilions, it was rarely to examine the plants.

A lady.

When Acir caught sight of Fiammis in the dappled shadows, slowly twirling her parasol over one shoulder as she walked, he knew his suspicion had been correct.

Winding paths led around an ornamental lake covered with pallid water-lilies whose crimson stamens seemed to exude a peculiarly foetid scent. Beneath the jade leaves finned silver-spotted carp, nosing up to the surface, then diving in a trail of bubbles.

Did Fiammis know she was being followed? There seemed little purpose to her meandering walk; she stopped to look at the carp, she stopped to sniff a geranium leaf . . .

It was damply warm beneath the heavy foliage; the dappling sun drew out earthy odours of rotting bark and leafmould.

A little further ahead, the path divided: a curving bridge of lichened stone led upwards into a dark-arched tunnel of knotted rhododendrons; beneath the bridge the lake path wound on towards a summer pavilion heavy with wistaria.

Fiammis took the path that led up on to the narrow bridge. Acir hung back, unable to follow without being discovered.

The Botanical Gardens drowsed in the humid afternoon.

Fiammis's languid walk became swift, purposeful. Acir cast a quick glance around, wondering what had provoked this change.

And then he saw Khassian coming along the lake path below.

Fiammis leaned out over the bridge parapet, her frilled parasol balanced on her forearm, almost as if she were lining up the sights of an arquebus.

Suddenly Acir realised what she was about. Suddenly he understood.

He threw himself forward, gripped the parasol in both hands and wrenched it from her.

She tried to grab it back.

Beneath them, oblivious to the danger, Khassian strolled on towards the pavilion.

Acir twisted the parasol out of her grip and, with shaking hands, tried to disable the concealed mechanism.

'Be careful!' Her shriek came almost too late. His fingers tripped a hidden catch – and something shot from the point of the parasol, rebounding off the parapet on the other side of the bridge with a metallic twang.

Astonished, he looked up and saw that she had flung herself to the ground.

'Give it here!' she cried, snatching the parasol back.

Acir hurried over to search for the projectile amidst the weeds and grit. He could see the graze where it had scarred the stone. He prodded about with a twig, sifting through the gravel and dandelion leaves until he caught the faint glint of metal. Parting the leaves, he extricated the tiny dart and gingerly examined it.

'A clever device,' he said.

'A *moustiq*.' Fiammis was brushing the dirt from her clothes as she came towards him, hand outstretched to take it. 'Ingenious little device, isn't it? It goes in as smoothly as a gnat's sting.'

It was exquisitely crafted – if something so lethal could be described as exquisite. The impact against the stone had hardly dented its streamlined precision.

'Oh, and don't touch the tip. I took the precaution of dipping it in water-snake venom.'

Acir handed it back to her without a word. His palms were sweating. Fiammis – frail, beautiful Fiammis – was a cold and calculating assassin.

'Girim sent you to kill him.'

She carefully took the dart and, slipping a cachou box from her reticule, opened the enamel lid and placed it inside. Each movement was calculated and precise.

'Girim sent me to bring affairs to a conclusion. One way or the other.'

'But murder –'

'Who would have been able to tell it was not an insect sting? Such things are not unknown. Poisoning of the blood following the sting of an insect – oedema of the body tissues, difficulty with breathing. There would have been no *proof*.' She seemed consumed with cold fury, snapping at him in short, stabbing phrases. 'And look what you've done to my parasol! It cost me a fortune to have it adapted. Now it's ruined.'

'Fiammis, what's happened to you?'

'I learned to survive. That's what happened to me.'

A waft of the foetid water-lily scent rose on the breeze, cloyingly sweet.

'Survival meant killing for a living?'

'Oh – and the men you've killed in the name of the Commanderie, that's different?'

He had no answer to that. She, the stealthy killer, the shadow assassin, had no right to employ that argument against him – and yet he knew his silence acknowledged that the accusation was just.

'You should be in Bel'Esstar. You have no business to be here. You deliberately disobeyed Commanderie orders – you, the model Guerrior. What hold has this Khassian over you?'

'Destroy him and you destroy all hope of reconciliation in Bel'Esstar.'

'On the contrary. One bite from the *moustiq* and the rebels lose their hero. The rebellion collapses like a burst balloon. I won't miss next time.'

Her callousness shocked him. What had become of the young girl, golden-haired Fia, whom he had loved so passionately? Who had corrupted her, who had trained her to kill? Before he knew what he was doing, he had gripped her by the shoulders, forcing her to look into his face.

'Spare Khassian. Let him live. There has to be another way.'

Her eyes opened wide, curious, questioning.

'I have my orders. Why should I disobey them?'

Still that infuriating air of nonchalance, taunting him, teasing him.

'For my sake, Fia.'

'I propose a compromise.' She slipped out of his grasp as lightly as a dancer. 'I will find . . . another way, as you put it. He will live. But in return, you will grant me a favour when next we meet.'

'What manner of favour?'

'Whatever I ask.'

He was caught in her snare.

'If it is in my power to grant that favour –'

'Oh, it is, Acir.' She lifted her hand and let her finger-tip brush across his lips. 'It is.'

Amused watchers in the Gardens below had seen the fine gentlewoman and the man on the bridge tussling over the pretty parasol.

Their raised voices had been too faint to distinguish the words. Seasoned observers of the Sulien social scene could easily guess the theme. They pleased themselves with constructing little scenarios: she had bought another outrageously expensive outfit; he had caught her flirting with a rival and had decided to assert himself; the parasol was a present from her lover and proof positive that he had been cuckolded . . . It was generally decided that the latter interpretation was the most likely: she was an uncommonly handsome woman – whereas he, soberly dressed, stern-faced, was obviously too boorish a companion for such a rare creature.

In the wistaria-wreathed pavilion, Amaru Khassian sat alone, wondering if he had misread the time – or the day – on Azare's note. Or perhaps there was another pavilion in the Botanical Gardens.

Either way, he had wasted an afternoon when he could have been composing.

Fiammis threw the broken parasol down upon her bed.

He had touched her. He had caught hold of her – she could feel his touch still, as if his fingers had burned her skin.

She closed her eyes a moment, reliving the sensation.

Against her closed lids she saw a marigold meadow under a blue sky, she heard the echo of distant teasing laughter. A dark-browed boy caught her in his arms – and she pushed him away, mocking.

Then he had vowed himself forever hers and she had rejected him. Now she burned to possess him, to melt that stern resolve.

But now he knows me for what I truly am. An assassin.

She opened her eyes. On the bed lay the twisted frame of the parasol, irrefutable evidence of her trade.

She picked it up and examined the mechanism. The delicate concealed spring-action mechanism was wrecked beyond hope of repair.

She was becoming careless.

Never let your feelings interfere with your work.

It was as well that she had taken the precaution of having a second parasol adapted in Bel'Esstar. A skilled agent anticipates every eventuality.

She checked her reflection in the mirror.

A tiny blemish marked her red-rouged mouth where she had bitten her lip in vexation. A fleck of a darker red – blood – marred the delicate shade

154

the perfumier had made up to her instructions.

She seized her rouge pot and brush and began to repair the damage, dabbing with tiny, precise strokes until the imperfection was concealed.

He loved her still, she was sure of that. She had seen it in his eyes, a darkness shadowing their clear blue. But he would not betray his calling. He would rather abjure her, rather endure a lifetime of self-denial, than break his vows. His honour meant more to him than she did.

But now she had snared him. Snared him with a promise on his honour. He must grant her that one favour she most desired.

And as for Khassian . . . she would now put her second scheme into operation.

A skilled agent anticipates every eventuality.

CHAPTER 14

Bel'Esstar. City of a Million Lights. The glittering star illuminating all Allegonde.

Acir Korentan crossed the wide, windswept boulevards, passing elegant town houses, mansions in grey stone. Each boulevard radiated outwards, rays of a star, from the Winter Palace, seat of the Princes of Allegonde.

A city of light: pale stone and glass. And yet a city steeped in blood. Here the Poet-Prophet Mhir, Mhir the well-beloved, had died a martyr's death defending the faith against a despotic and cruel Shultan.

Acir shivered. At this time of year a dry, cold wind blew from the mountains, delaying the arrival of the summer's heat. It stung the eyes, left a taste of dust on the lips and tongue.

The grand buildings did not impress him, nor did the glimpses of crystal chandeliers and gilded splendour. The grey stone façades seemed austere, forbidding, after the warm, rose-tinged sandstone terraces of Sulien.

Bel'Esstar had lost its soul. It was a city of mirrors and reflections – but all it reflected was a chill heart.

Acir shaded his eyes against the midday sun, gazing up at the scaffolding towers and pulleys, the fast-growing walls of the Fortress of Faith.

Already the little shrine where the Poet-Prophet Mhir was buried was dwarfed by the foundation trenches being dug around it, the marker posts, the scaffolding. Acir looked at it sadly, remembering how only a few weeks ago he had stood in its candlelit silence and had felt a sense of peace such as he had not experienced since the day he was called; a warmth, golden as amber, intense as candleflame. Now that stillness was broken by the sound of shovels and pickaxes, the tapping of chisels on blocks of stone, the rough shouts of the overseers.

He hoped that its tranquillity had not been destroyed forever.

'The realisation of a dream, Acir.'

He turned around and saw Girim nel Ghislain, Grand Maistre of the Commanderie and Leader of the Order of the Rosecoeur, watching him intently.

Acir crossed the churned turf and, sinking to his knees, pressed the

Grand Maistre's hands to his lips, kissing the rose-stone ring.

'Have you seen the plans?'

The Grand Maistre unrolled some architect's drawings. An imposing edifice was revealed, its massive walls more a fortified citadel than a place of worship.

'Mhir's tomb enshrined, preserved forever, a jewel in a precious casket. The finest sculptors and masons working with painters, mosaicists, glaziers, to create a building without parallel in all Allegonde.'

'It's – it's vast. I had no idea –'

'You are looking at the future of the Commanderie. This will be our headquarters. The heart of the Rose. Close your eyes and imagine the day of dedication. The rose-strewn aisles thronged with the faithful, countless more crowding outside . . .'

For a moment Acir's head was filled with Girim's vision of echoing chapels reverberant with the murmured prayers of pilgrims, swimming with a misty light, cloud and distant sunlight, vaulted arches high as heaven . . .

'A great lantern tower will be constructed over the tomb.' Girim stopped at the entrance, his gesture encompassing a structure of immense proportions. 'An architect's psalm of praise realised in stone and glass. Carven vines tendrilling up the columns . . . thorns of stone . . .'

'But the funds.' The vision vanished. 'How can the Commanderie possibly afford to pay for this?'

'Prince Ilsevir has decreed that the assets confiscated from convicted dissenters be added to our building funds. And those convicted are providing us with our workforce.'

Acir looked at him, puzzled. 'Convicts?'

'Our brothers have already established a second Sanctuary in the mountains to quarry stone. See those men over there –'

A band of workers were struggling to unload massive blocks of rose-red stone from a wagon, watched over by several of the Commanderie.

'Sulien stone?' The stone that had weathered to a warm rose in the rain-washed light of Sulien, looked harsh and red under the unforgiving glare of the Bel'Esstar sun.

'The mountains are not owned solely by Tourmalise. If we wish to quarry stone, it is our right to do so.'

Acir had been watching the Sanctuarees labouring as Girim spoke. 'Why are they shackled like slaves?' he asked.

'Don't forget they are convicted criminals,' Girim said sharply. 'What would you have us do, Acir? Leave them chained up, forgotten in some foul-smelling oubliette?'

'But to build the holy Stronghold with forced labour –'

'Not so long ago these dissenters would have been hung, burned, crucified for spreading their heresies.' The light in Girim's pale eyes pierced Acir like a spear. 'But we are giving them the chance to work to redeem themselves.'

In the Enhirran desert Girim had never lost faith; when they were all parched for want of water, half-starved, weak with dysentery, he had urged them on. Girim's vision had sustained them even when their own courage had faltered.

So why did Acir doubt him now?

'But this is not the reason I called you back.'

Girim laid his hand on Acir's arm and led him towards the shrine.

The workers had covered the little building with heavy oiled cloths to protect it. Girim pushed aside the cloths and held open the door to the tomb. Acir followed him.

A bitter breath of frankincense fumes stung his eyes; a thousand petals of flame burned in the niches, rose candles of crimson wax.

This was where the Blessed Mhir lay buried. Mhir who had dared to defy the dissolute Shultan of Bel'Esstar, and in defending the rights of the faithful, had died a martyr's death. A stone slab, worn away by the kisses and caresses of the faithful, covered the holy place where the first miracle had taken place. Here the Rose had sprung from the buried Prophet's breast, the perfect crimson Rose that wept drops of blood, heart's blood. Here the miraculous roseblood had restored Beloved Elesstar to life – and she had led the people of Bel'Esstar to overthrow the Shultan. The story had never failed to move Acir; the selfless sacrifice of the Poet-Prophet whose love for Elesstar and his people had endured beyond death.

Girim prostrated himself, his forehead brushing the worn stone; Acir knelt beside him and remained several minutes lost in silent prayer.

'Where is Amaru Khassian?'

Girim's voice startled Acir out of his reverie.

'He should be here, at Mhir's tomb, making a public affirmation of faith. And where is he? Still in Sulien.'

'You know me, Girim. I'm a soldier. I have no skill with words.'

'My dear friend, you still don't see how dangerous Amaru Khassian is.'

'Dangerous?' Acir shook his head. 'Intelligent, yes. Proud. But he is no threat to the Commanderie –'

'The Contesse Fiammis is right! He's blinded you with his charm.'

'Fiammis . . .' Acir echoed.

'The Contesse is a devour supporter of the cause. If she had succeeded, the situation would now be resolved. The blasphemer would be dead.'

'And a new martyr created.'

'Why did you ignore my instructions? You had my written authority to do whatever the situation merited.'

Girim's eyes glittered in the darkness; Acir stared at him, not certain what he was witnessing. A dull, cold horror had begun to seep into his soul. He had been a long while in Enhirrë and maybe the change in Girim nel Ghislain had not been apparent when he was first summoned home to undertake this mission.

'Have you been blind to what's happening in Sulien? Dissenters are drawn to Amaru Khassian, like wasps to a honeycomb. He's been plotting his retaliation right under your nose. It could mean the end of all our plans, all our dreams, Acir. He must be stopped.'

'I – I need time to think.'

'The time for thinking is past. This cell of revolutionaries must be broken up. Crushed. Eradicated.'

'They're only musicians –'

Girim moved closer still.

'Am I your superior officer?' he whispered.

'Yes,' Acir said wretchedly.

'Then do not question my orders again. Your vow, Acir.' Girim thrust out his hand. 'Obedience. In all things.'

Torn, Acir hesitated – and then slowly sank to his knees to kiss the ring.

'Come to my apartments in the Palace tonight. I have new instructions for you.'

As Acir emerged from Mhir's shrine into the daylight, he caught a distant snatch of song that made him stop and gaze upwards.

A single voice at first, from high up in the scaffolding, faint, ragged, as the singer gasped in breath as he worked . . . and then another joined in, and another, until the melody swelled and soared. The singing was rough, rhythmical – and fervent. And the song – he recognised it, he knew he had heard it before.

'Silence those men!' ordered Girim. He could hardly be heard above the singing.

Guerriors went swarming up the ladders to the high platform.

The singing faltered – and died, to be replaced by muffled cries and grunts of pain.

Acir turned to Girim, shocked at the brutality of the punishment.

'What's the harm in singing?' he asked. 'Didn't we sing in Enhirrë when we were restoring the birthplace shrine?'

'But we sang the Psalms of Mhir. This is no work-song but an act of blatant defiance. Don't you recognise it?' Girim was regarding him with keen attention.

'It was too faint to catch the sense of the words.'

' "Freedom freedom . . ." by Amaru Khassian. Now do you see what damage your failure to complete your mission has done?'

Girim nel Ghislain had been given apartments in the Winter Palace at the request of His August Highness the Prince Ilsevir.

As Acir made his way to the Grand Maistre's headquarters, the panelled walls painted in grey and creamy white, the delicate plasterwork adorning the ceiling and cornices with gilded bows and knots of flowers, all presented a significant contrast with the austerity of the Commanderie headquarters where he had first taken his vows.

'Your orders, Captain.' A secretary handed a sealed paper to Acir.

'I thought I was to see the Grand Maistre in person.'

The secretary regarded him coldly over his spectacles.

'I have no record of an appointment. The Grand Maistre is dining with the Prince tonight.'

Acir broke the seal and scanned the page.

'Why is this assigning me to the Sanctuary?' he said, shaking his head in confusion. 'I understood I was to return to Sulien –'

'Those are your orders.' The secretary turned back to his work.

Orial hummed to herself as she combed her hair. She kept snatching little critical glances at herself in the mirror. First she pulled her hair back with a ribbon. Then she let it fall loose about her shoulders. Still unsatisfied, she took the two side locks and looped and pinned them . . . Which was the most becoming? Perhaps, after years at court, he preferred the natural, less artifical style. Perhaps –

What am I doing! She threw down her brush in dismay. Preening like a silly schoolgirl!

'Say aloud three times, "The arrangement between us is strictly professional"', she ordered her reflection.

One moment, life was so enchanting she wanted to laugh aloud; the next, she was seized with a sense of its poignancy that brought her close to tears. And *he* had made her see this way, *he* had opened her eyes . . .

Amaru Khassian.

She could not even whisper his name without feeling a shiver of illicit delight.

This obsession was ridiculous. What would he, a man ten years older than she, ever find to intrigue him in a Sulien schoolgirl? She was wasting time on Amaru Khassian that she should have spent on her own compositions. His music dominated her waking life. His presence dominated her waking dreams: wounded, brooding, enigmatic.

Cramoisy was preparing to go shopping as Orial arrived at Mistress Permay's house.

'I was just saying to Amaru that I have not seen our dour-faced Captain for several days,' the Diva announced. 'Have you seen him, Orial?'

Orial shook her head. 'Not since he came upon us rehearsing in the Undercity.'

'Do you know what I think, Amar?'

'No . . . but I know you're going to tell me.'

'I believe he has given up. He's gone back to Allegonde. At last we are to be left in peace.'

'Left in peace?' Khassian gave a wry laugh. 'He's just biding his time. Waiting for the right moment to make his next move.'

The silence of the salon was broken only by the soft scritch-scratch of Orial's pen. Khassian stood at the window, his back to her, silently dictating.

Across the sublimely agonised line of Elesstar's aria, another tune suddenly intruded, a cracked tune, a lewd tune that broke her concentration.

Orial looked up.

'Is there someone in the street?'

'I can't see anyone,' Khassian said, scanning the Crescent below.

'I – I thought I – There! Can't you hear it now?' Orial, frowning, put one hand to her head as if she could erase the intrusive tune with her fingers.

'No. But it doesn't matter.' He came to her side and looked at what she had written. 'Maybe you should take a rest. We're making good progress. Soon we will have completed Elesstar's mad scene. Then comes the final transfiguration and apotheosis.'

He might not be able to touch her with his ruined hands but it seemed that his voice caressed her.

'This is good. Very good.' He leant over her, closer still. The warmth was tangible now, the warmth of his breath on the back of her neck. 'You have understood my intentions . . . perfectly . . .'

'I have?' she whispered, turning her face to his.

'I'm back!' Cramoisy threw open the doors. Khassian drew away from Orial; she, blushing, began to assemble her pencils, pens and rulers.

Cramoisy deposited a number of little packages on the couch, talking loudly all the while, as if he had noticed nothing.

'The perfumier's only had the citrus pomade, the astringent, so I bought a bottle of the bay lotion though it is somewhat inferior to the Bel'Esstar kind. I thought you must have finished for this afternoon. It is nearly time to meet Azare.'

'I'll get my cloak,' Orial said, eyes lowered so as not to meet Cramoisy's gaze.

'Let me help you, child.' He followed her out into the hall and, lifting down Orial's cloak, placed it around her shoulders. As he did so, the castrato whispered, 'Listen to me, Orial. Don't be taken in by Khassian's charm. He loves only himself. He cares only for his own music.'

Orial started and took a step away from the Diva.

'Why are you saying this to me? Do you think I plan to take him away from you?'

'From *me*?' Cramoisy placed one lace-gloved hand on his heart and began to laugh. 'Oh, my dear, he's never truly been mine.'

'But I thought –' Orial stopped, confused. She was floundering, out of her depth.

'That I was his lover? That's a little charade we've kept up for years. Well, there was a time . . .' The mischievous glitter in Cramoisy's eyes faded. 'But we were not suited to each other, not in that way . . .'

'I never meant to pry –'

'Composers are curious creatures. Self-absorbed. Selfish. Single-minded. The music always comes first.'

The Commissaire of the Sulien Constabulary heard a gentle tap at his door. He glanced at the pile of warrants awaiting his signature. Paperwork, always more paperwork. He took up his pen.

'I'm busy.'

The door opened.

'I said, I'm busy.' He set down his pen, ready to blast the intruder with a volley of words.

'Not too busy to see me, I trust, Commissaire?'

He looked up and saw a young woman, ravishingly attired in jonquil colours: white, lemon-yellow, saffron-gold.

'Madame, I –' He rose clumsily to his feet. 'Never too busy to see a lady as – as –' Beautiful? Desirable? Words deserted him. 'As yourself.'

'I am here on a confidential matter.'

'How can I assist you, madame? Stolen valuables, maybe? Some undesirable characters haunt Sulien in the season. But let me assure you, you can place complete confidence in me and my men –'

'Are you aware, Commissaire, that there are Allegondan revolutionaries here in Sulien?'

He had been expecting the usual tale of a stolen necklace, a pilfered jewel box – not revolutionaries.

She laid one hand on her creamy breast and closed her eyes, obviously greatly distressed. 'I . . . I fear for my life.'

She seemed about to faint. Alarmed, he went to her side and, one arm around her slender shoulders, helped her into a chair.

'I'm . . . so sorry,' she said in a whisper.

'Let me get you some water?'

'No . . . no . . .' She weakly raised one delicate hand in negation. 'I'll be all right in a moment.'

'My dear madame, tell me your story.'

'My late husband . . . the Conte . . . died loyal to the Prince. I came to Sulien to . . . get over his death. But they followed me here. Now I fear I have become a target in his place.' She raised her eyes to him, brimming with unshed tears. 'They are desperate men, Commissaire. And I am so afraid.'

Desperate men. She had come to consult him in a professional capacity. He went back to his chair, placing the desk between them.

'You have papers, madame, to prove your identity? I am obliged to ask, you understand.'

'But of course.' She handed him a folded document.

He opened it.

An Allegondan passport, stamped by the Sulien office, a visa for a stay of six months from Fevriar to Iul in Tourmalise. It gave her name as Fiammis, Contesse of Tal'Mont and Reial, her age as twenty-seven, hair – fair, eyes – blue, height – eight and a half spans. Other distinguishing feature – a small rose-mole on the right upper lip. The description in no way did justice to her beauty, or to her desperate vulnerability. But she was a noblewoman – and as a good citizen of the republic, he felt uncomfortable dealing with the privileged scion of an antiquated system Tourmalise had long ago rejected.

'This seems to be in order,' he said gruffly, handing her back the passport. 'But as to your concerns . . . I am powerless to act.'

'Even though they are dangerous revolutionaries?'

'They may have been revolutionaries in Allegonde but here in Tourmalise they are merely visitors. We are a citizens' republic, madame.' He would not call her Contesse.

The brimming eyes implored him. 'So I am defenceless.'

'I can only arrest these individuals if you have proof. Or if a formal complaint has been made against them by a citizen of Sulien.'

'They could attack me here and you would not lift a finger to protect me?'

'Sulien is a spa, madame. Many foreign visitors pass through our city. The role of the Sulien Constabulary is to keep the peace. So far there has been no untoward occurrence.' He rose, hoping she would take his cue. Her presence was disturbing him. 'Let me assure you, madame, that you are in no danger. Write down the address of your lodgings . . . and I will request the constable who patrols that quarter to be especially vigilant.'

CHAPTER 15

Khassian watched the morning mists slowly drift from the roofs of Sulien to reveal a glorious day.

Yet the windows in the first-floor apartment in Mistress Permay's house were shut to seal out the noise of the street, the clatter of barouche wheels on the Crescent cobbles, the rowdy whistling of the coachmen.

Orial sat at the escritoire, her pale face rapt, utterly absorbed in the task of transcription. Occasionally one hand would move upwards to tuck back a straying lock of hair. Yet all the while not one word was spoken, not one sound disturbed the stillness of the salon.

Khassian moved across to look over her shoulder.

'What is this?'

This was not his opera. He did not recognise what she had been notating at all. It was utterly unfamiliar.

She shook her golden head.

He looked up from the score and met her eyes, dazzling in their iridescent glitter.

'I – don't understand.'

Her vagueness irritated him. He had been struggling to articulate the moment of Elesstar's death – and she was not paying attention.

'What in the name of hell is this?'

It was as if some other music had intruded upon her consciousness and she, unaware, had continued to notate it, nurturing the parasite within his own work.

'I don't know.' She stared at the five bars, frowning. 'I thought it was you.'

'This is nothing like my style!' He was angry now, insulted that she could have confused this aberration with his own distinctive musical voice.

'I wrote down what I heard.' She stood her ground. Bravely, for he could see the tears in her eyes.

'Strike it out. We'll have to start again.'

She nodded dumbly and lifted her pen to score through the alien fragment. Then he saw her – almost as if guided by a will other than her own – take the page and surreptitiously slip it beneath the others.

*

The River Avenne flowed serenely through the Parade Gardens. The mellow light of late-afternoon gilded the west-facing terraces on the surrounding hills but the riverwater was dark with secrets, untouched by the sun.

Orial stood at the railings, staring down into the water.

What am I doing here?

She could not remember walking this way, could not even remember leaving the Crescent house.

Notes formed themselves into a melody, a repetitive, insistent, obsessive melody. It flowed through her consciousness like a current of dark water. Where had she heard it before? The Parade band? She glanced over her shoulder to where the musicians were packing away their instruments beneath the striped awning.

She softly sang a few notes aloud.

No. It was not one of the simple country jigs or gavottes favoured by the band; its intervals were too wayward, its mode too melancholy. Neither was it a part of Khassian's opera; it bore none of the characteristics of his style. Whenever she closed her eyes, waters lapped into her mind, cloud-dark waters, stirring with a breath of current . . .

The melody and the waters seemed inextricably linked, one with the other.

She wandered on alongside the Avenne, holding the iron rail, the feel of the cold metal against her finger-tips centring her, keeping the weaving spell of the melody at bay.

She lifted her hands from the railing and closed her eyes, waiting.

The music flooded back into her brain, a rushing current, eddying, swirling into a vortex. A whirlpool.

Orial gasped. The notes spun faster, faster, dragging her towards the black chasm at the centre of the spinning vortex. Whirled giddily around, she felt her knees buckling, she was falling, falling –

She opened her eyes. She was leaning out over the railing, dangerously far over the placid riverwaters below.

'What is happening to me?' she whispered.

A cheerful whistling cut across the insistent river-music, a drinking catch, robust and simple. The drinking catch argued with the river-music in Orial's mind. She tried to concentrate on the catch, on its bright major intervals, thirds, clean, clear fifths, sixths . . .

'Are you all right, demselle?' The park-keeper was coming along the path towards her; the last sunlight burnished the brass buttons on his uniform.

'A – little – dizzy –' Orial whispered. *Keep whistling. Please keep whistling.*

'You could have fallen in the river!' He caught hold of her, prising her fingers from the railings.

Normally she would have shrunk from such intimate contact with a stranger. But now she sank thankfully against his broad shoulder, utterly spent. He smelt strongly of pipe tobacco, his breath warm, tainted with the stale smoke. A real smell. A comforting smell.

'Shall I call you a barouche, demselle? Have you far to go?'

'Dr Magelonne's Sanatorium,' she said faintly.

'Let's sit you on this bench to recover.'

Shadows were lengthening, birds were fluttering in the ornamental cherry branches overhead, settling to roost. Underfoot the dewy grass was white with cherry and crab apple blossom. She stared at the fallen blossom. Spring was passing. It would soon be the Day of the Dead.

'Dr Magelonne?'

Jerame looked up from his notes.

A woman stood on the threshold.

He got up, frowning slightly. It was not yet time for his first patient of the morning.

'You have me at a disadvantage.'

'Fiammis, Contesse of Tal'mont.' She held out one gloved hand. 'I have no appointment.' It was a statement, not an apology. A trace of a foreign accent subtly coloured her speech.

'How can I help you?'

She sat opposite him, placing the frilled parasol she was carrying across her lap.

'We will not be disturbed?'

Mesmerised, he shook his head.

'You have a daughter, Dr Magelonne?'

'Orial.' Jerame felt a slight unease; he had been expecting the Contesse to make discreet enquiries about the treatments he had to offer. Wealthy women frequently came to the Sanatorium hoping for a cure for infertility or the removal of some unsightly skin blemish. Over the centuries, the Sulien waters had gained a miraculous reputation.

'I don't like to interfere in your personal affairs, Doctor, but are you aware that she has been regularly visiting Amaru Khassian?'

'Amaru Khassian?' At first he was too astonished by the information to wonder why she had taken it upon herself to impart it to him.

'I see that you were unaware of this.'

Orial had deliberately disobeyed him! She must have been taking music lessons with the composer – and in doing so, had unknowingly exposed herself to the very danger from which he had sought to shield her. Dear Goddess, what damage might she have unwittingly inflicted upon herself?

He made an effort to collect his thoughts.

'Why have you come here to tell me this?'

'Because I believe Khassian is plotting some kind of insurrection, using

Sulien as his base. He is a wanted man, Doctor Magelonne.'

Magelonne blinked, pushing his spectacles higher up the bridge of his nose as if to see the Contesse more clearly. This elegant stranger could have no idea of the reason for his distress; who – save Tartarus and Jolaine – knew of the dangers of the Accidie?

'Now, wait. How can I be sure you are telling me the truth, Contesse? What precisely have *you* to gain from telling me? For all you know, my sympathies might already lie with Khassian's cause. What's to stop me going to warn him?'

'Your daughter's wellbeing.'

He gazed at her in disbelief. She was still smiling; a self-composed, calm smile that belied the threat in her words.

'You're threatening my daughter?'

'I am merely informing you of the facts, Doctor.' She stood up, shaking out the frills of her parasol. 'Act upon them as you see fit.'

He sat down at his desk again, dumbfounded. His neat writing in the open ledger no longer made any sense as he stared at it, through it.

Orial – visiting Amaru Khassian? Was Khassian the secret suitor who had brought such a becoming flush to her cheeks, who had caused her to lie and dissemble?

No. He slammed the ledger shut. It must be a mistake. She was helping Jolaine Tradescar – she had told him so.

He grabbed his hat and cane and made for the door; outside he almost bumped into Sister Crespine who, starched and immaculate as ever, was bustling down the corridor.

'Where are you going, Doctor? You've a patient at nine-thirty –'

The nine-thirty patient would have to wait.

Pigeons fluttered out of the way as Jerame crossed the Guildhall Square at a brisk pace and climbed the steps leading to the Museum two at a time.

A sign on the door proclaimed the Museum closed for renovations. He ignored it and tried the handle, rattling it loudly. Locked, of course. What had Orial told him? Jolaine Tradescar had made some kind of discovery in the Undercity and was jealously guarding it from other scholars.

He walked around the side of the building, along a narrow alleyway where the walls of the Museum were stained with green streaks of damp. He peered in through the windows which were filmed with a thin layer of grime – but the blinds were pulled down.

He went round to the back where he remembered Jolaine had a rickety privy housed in a shed. The alleyway was darkest here, noisome, with a slime of dead leaves underfoot. Jerame gave a grount of disgust; the old scholar, obsessed with her studies, had neglected the upkeep of the building. He did not like to think that Orial had been working in this dirty, insanitary environment.

The side door was also locked; he rapped on the glass pane which was clouded in cobwebs.

'Jolaine! Jolaine!'

'Who's there?' a voice demanded querulously.

'It's me – Jerame Magelonne.'

'I'm in perfect health, Doctor. And I'm busy.'

'I need to talk to you.'

'This really is most inconvenient.'

'Five minutes of your time, that's all.'

There was a pause. Then Jerame heard a key turn in the lock and Jolaine Tradescar's face appeared, wispy wig awry, staring at him suspiciously.

'Well?'

'Is Orial with you?'

'Not strictly speaking "with me" at this precise moment in time.'

'Let me in, Jolaine.'

The Museum office was still in a state of disorder. Stale fragments of half-finished rolls littered the tables alongside chipped mugs with puddles of cold qaffë inside.

'How can you live like this!'

'At my age, one lives as one pleases,' she said.

'And have you been following the regime I prescribed for you?'

Jolaine gave a little shrug.

'Orial told me she had been coming here to help you. Is that true?'

'She has been helping me, yes.' Jolaine shook the crumbs off an open ledger, affording Jerame a glimpse of line upon line of meticulous drawings.

'Was she here yesterday afternoon? And the day before?'

'The day before yesterday?' Jolaine took off her pince-nez, polished the lenses on her skirt and put them on again. 'I seem to lose track of the time . . .'

Jerame was not convinced by her performance. 'If you've been conniving with her to deceive me –'

'To deceive you?'

'Don't deny it. She's been lying to me and you've been shielding her. Turning her against her own father.'

'Sit down, Jerame.' Jolaine's manner was no longer that of the eccentric scholar; her voice was stern, even commanding. Surprised, he sat down.

'If I didn't know you as well as I do, I would take exception to your tone of voice. Bursting in here, making all manner of wild accusations! But as it's concern for your daughter that's made you forget your manners, I'll forgive you. If you hear me out.'

'Now wait a –'

'Did you think you could keep her from the music forever? It is as necessary to her as food and drink.'

'But the Accidie,' Jerame said in a whisper. 'You know it will kill her, as surely as it killed Iridial. First the radiance – then the confusion. Madness. Death.'

'You must listen to me, Jerame. The madness is not what it seems. The death – may not be death as we understand it. She is Lifhendil. Ach, if you would only read what I have been transcribing –'

'I haven't time. I have to find her. And I have a good idea where she is.' Jerame seized his hat and gloves and made to stand up.

'I have not finished,' Dame Tradescar said in a voice of iron. Jerame hesitated . . . then put the gloves down again.

'Well?' he said brusquely.

'To the city-builders, children gifted as Orial now is were special. When the "madness" came, it was regarded as a divine sign. Unchecked, it precipitated the sufferer into a trance-like state where all outward life-signs ceased.'

'No.' Jerame slowly shook his head in denial. 'Not . . . possible.'

'Read what I have written. It is all based on accounts left by the Lifhendil themselves.' Jolaine pushed the open book around so that Jerame could read for himself.

A NEW PERSPECTIVE ON THE ACCIDIE

The one possessed could choose either to leave her family and become immortal as one of the Winged Ones, *Eä-Endil* – or to forego her chance of immortality and bear children who might themselves become *Endil*. The madness could only be lifted by the ministrations of the Winged Ones who –

At this point Jolaine's writing trailed away.

Jerame stared at the translation in disbelief. If this were true, then Iridial . . .

'Winged Ones? Immortals?' All the solitary years of study had finally turned the old woman's brain. 'This is mythology! Moonshine!' He brought down his clenched fist upon the open book. 'I know only medical certainties. When the heart stops pumping, then the blood supply to the brain ceases and death ensues. Her heart had stopped. She was dead when we dragged her from the Avenne.'

'Had you never stopped to ask yourself if there might not be a grain of truth in the old legends? That if you stripped away the veneer of centuries, there might be an underlying constant beneath the distortions and elaborations? That there might be an ancient wisdom we could use to preserve Orial?'

'Then why is modern medical science ignorant of it? I consulted the greatest authorities in Tourmalise over Ir— Ir—.' He could not bring himself to say her name out loud.

'That was because the answer was here in Sulien. And maybe Iridial was trying to tell us so – but we did not understand her.'

'There is no proof!' cried Jerame. 'And all the while we waste time arguing over maybe and what-might-have, Orial is with Amaru Khassian. And every moment she spends with him is shortening her life, hastening the onset of the Accidie.'

Sun-glints on green water . . .

Orial had set out to walk to the Crescent. But now she found herself walking once more beside the Avenne.

What am I doing here? I should be with the Illustre. He'll be displeased if I'm late again.

She had hardly slept all night for the music in her head. She had covered sheets of paper, trying to notate the different melodies, trying to disentangle the knotted threads. Now she was so tired that the bright flowerbeds of the River Gardens had all merged into a blur.

She stopped beside a willow and sat on the grassy riverbank to take off her spectacles and rest her sore eyes. The soft plashing of the water, the breath of the breeze through the willow leaves, wove a thread of green melody, pulsing spring sap, into her mind.

Riversong, lulling her to sleep . . .

If she closed her eyes a moment . . .

Sleep . . .

A bright burst of sound awoke her. The band had begun to tune up in the River Gardens and the cacophony as they endeavoured to reach the same pitch pierced like a white-hot blade through her spinning thoughts.

If the band was tuning up, it must already be three in the afternoon. And she should have been with Khassian by three.

Must go to the Crescent . . . must . . .

Slowly, exhaustedly, she forced herself up the grassy bank. So tired . . . she was so very tired . . .

Khassian, standing at his usual vantage point at the window, saw Orial meandering along the sunny Crescent. What was the matter with the girl? Why was she so late? He was impatient to get started, his mind bursting with fresh ideas.

Two men in uniform appeared, walking briskly along the Crescent; they passed Orial and came up the path to knock at Mistress Permay's door. Their dark blue jackets and crimson-trimmed tricorne hats proclaimed them members of the Sulien Constabulory. Khassian leaned closer to the glass, trying to hear what they were saying.

'I keep a respectable house, Officer, as well you know,' Mistress Permay was protesting.

170

Khassian moved hastily away from the window.

'Cramoisy!' he shouted, crossing the salon. 'Cramoisy!'

He heard the tread of the constables' boots on the stairs – and then Mistress Permay's sharp rap on the door. Cramoisy emerged from his room in déshabillé, his hair undressed. Before he opened the door, he shot Khassian a quick, questioning look.

'These two gentlemen want to have words with you.' Mistress Permay's voice was querulous; her eyes darted suspiciously from Cramoisy to Khassian and back again. The unspoken message was blatant: 'Any trouble with the law and you're both out in the street.'

'Sulien Constabulary,' the first of the constables said, tipping his tricorne hat to the Diva. 'If we might step in a moment?'

Orial appeared on the landing behind the constables, her white face floating like a ghost in the gloom. Khassian irritably beckoned her inside and pointed towards the music room.

'Practise on the epinette,' he ordered. 'I won't be long.'

Cramoisy smartly shut the outer door in Mistress Permay's face.

'I'm sorry to disturb you,' the constable said, 'but we've been asked to check the papers of all foreign visitors in Sulien. A formality, you understand.'

Papers. By Mhir's blood, they still had no official papers! Khassian felt his heart begin to drum a desperate tattoo.

'Do sit down,' Cramoisy said, ushering them into the salon.

'This will only take a minute,' the officer replied. Neither sat down and the silent one took out a notebook, licked a stub of pencil and began to take notes.

'If you know my name then you will also know that I am intimately acquainted with His Worship the Mayor,' Cramoisy said with one of his most gracious smiles. 'He will vouch for me – and for my compatriot, the Illustre Khassian.'

The two constables looked at each other; they seemed somewhat discomfited.

'We are nevertheless required to check your papers, so if you would be so good –'

Cramoisy shot Khassian another glance. He sensed that the castrato was as nervous now as he.

'We were in a fire,' Khassian said. 'Our papers and passports were destroyed, along with all our possessions. I came here to recover from my injuries. No one insisted on seeing our papers then. We can, of course, send to the Allegondan Embassy for new passports . . . but this might take some time.'

'So you have no papers,' the officer said. The other constable was busily scribbling away.

'Is this a problem?' Khassian said edgily.

'My orders are to arrest any illegal immigrants. And without papers –'

'Take me to the Guildhall!' Cramoisy cried imperiously. 'I demand to see the Mayor at once. Let him speak for me and my compatriot. I take it you will not argue with *him*?'

'Exactly how long have you been in Sulien?' said the constable.

'Eight or nine weeks, maybe more. It's difficult to be precise . . .'

'If you had come on a temporary permit, it would have expired after eight weeks. It would have had to be renewed,' he said sternly.

'Are you threatening me, officer?' said Cramoisy, giving him one of his most withering glances.

In reply, he drew an order out of his breast pocket and handed it to Cramoisy.

'Well, and what is this?'

'Notice. If you and the gentleman here have not produced the necessary papers within three days, I will be obliged to arrest you and take you to the border where you will be handed into the custody of officials of your own country.'

He gave a little bow and placed his hat back on his head. The other constable snapped his notebook shut, pocketed it and stuck his pencil stub behind his ear.

'We'll see ourselves out.'

The instant they had closed the door behind them, Cramoisy threw the order of repatriation on the floor and stamped on it.

'Who has done this to us? Who has reported us? I'll wager it's that cursed Captain Korentan!'

'Three days,' Khassian said numbly. 'Three days.'

'All's not lost yet, Amar. The Mayor will grant us a reprieve. And if he won't – then we'll have to go underground.'

'Always hiding, always on the run.' Khassian's head was aching; the tension of the interview with the constables had tightened a band around his temples. 'How long can we keep this up?'

'As long as we have to,' the Diva said brightly. 'Ask yourself – what is the alternative? To go back to Bel'Esstar? To kneel before Girim nel Ghislain and beg forgiveness? To repudiate your works, denounce your friends publicly? To reject everything you have ever valued?'

'I'm tired, Cram,' he said.

The Diva drew Khassian's head towards his shoulder and let it rest there a moment or so. Then he patted his cheek.

'Orial's waiting. Get back to work.'

The music flowed from Orial's fingers in a flood that she could no longer control, it possessed her whole being utterly.

Rivermusic.

She was a channel through which the music poured in a torrent, unchecked. But where all had been golden glints on green water, now a chill darkness slowly shadowed the notes until the onward rush had become an underworld river moving through a still, sad landscape . . .

Distant voices whisper over the black water, calling her name . . .

'No . . .' she whispers back.

'Orial . . .'

She can see them now, waiting on the far shore, a host of pale spirit-shades, calling to her.

The voices of the dead . . .

The notes of the epinette floated into the salon, the melody eldritch, haunting, the underlying harmonies subtle and sad.

It was a warm day. Yet Khassian sat shivering as the music wove its wanton spell. The notes of his score seemed to shrivel into insignificance on the page before his eyes. Even this, his most inspired, his most complex, work lacked that unique quality of spontaneity.

'Orial!' he shouted. '*Orial!*'

She appeared in the doorway, pale-faced, gold-brown hair escaping its ribbons.

'Let's get started.'

'But, Illustre, I –' The glittering rainbows were unfocussed, as though half-veiled in distant mists.

'Now. I want to complete the aria today.'

One slender hand rose tremblingly to touch her forehead as though it ached.

'My own music. I can't –'

'*Your* composition?' Khassian's temper flared. 'You dare to put your inconsequential ramblings before *my* work?'

'You don't understand.' A stifled sob escaped from behind the hand that had risen to cover her mouth. The other fumbled for the pen, dipping it into the ink.

'Listen to the first phrase.'

He saw her hand begin to move over the sheet. The first flight of string fanfares, as he had thought them to her, note for note. Then the pen faltered. Another blot.

'Again,' she whispered.

He re-rehearsed the opening bars and watched, frowning. Her hand seemed to be arguing with itself. Notes appeared – were scratched out – reappeared again. The clean sheet was criss-crossed and cross-hatched with a fretwork of fine lines. She was transcribing nonsense.

'Orial!'

'One more time . . .' There was a soft pleading tone to her voice which might have mollified him, had he not been so aware of the pressure he was under to complete the work.

She suddenly flung down the pen. Ink seeped all over the manuscript. When he looked at her, her hands were clutched to her head, fingers slowly clawing her pale cheeks.

'I – I – can't. Your music – my music – all *jumbled* –'

A thunderous knocking at the front door drowned her words.

'Where is my daughter? I demand to see my daughter!'

Mistress Permay's cry of protest went unheeded as someone came running up the stairs.

'Orial! Orial!' Dr Magelonne flung open the doors. 'What have you done to her? What have you done to my child?'

Bewildered, Khassian turned back to Orial.

'Orial. Oh, no, no . . .'

Where her nails had dragged down her cheeks, crimson scoremarks had appeared.

It looked as if she was weeping blood.

CHAPTER 16

Bel'Esstar was swarming with patrols, Guerriors of the Commanderie policing the streets. Everywhere Acir went, he passed marching columns of grey-uniformed soldiers, heard the tread of their booted feet echoing along the wide boulevards of Bel'Esstar.

But where were the ordinary people?

Those Acir glimpsed were subdued, creeping along in the shadows, moving warily as though fearful of being stopped and questioned. When they saw him coming in his Commanderie uniform, they shrank into doorways or turned swiftly aside.

Was this the vision of Mhir's heavenly city made manifest on earth that had first inspired him to follow Girim?

Acir stopped on a street corner, transfixed by a sudden vivid memory.

He had been on night-watch, warming his hands at a smoking brazier – the nights were bitter-cold in the desert – when Girim nel Ghislain had appeared.

'Prince Ilsevir has fallen grievously ill.' Girim withdrew a letter from the breast of his robe and Acir saw the royal seal attached to it. 'He is asking to see me. I am recalled to Bel'Esstar, Acir!' Girim took him by the shoulders, gripping him hard. 'This is the moment we have long dreamed of. We have taken back the Poet-Prophet's birthplace and now we shall restore His shrine. We will make His city a fit place for His second coming.'

Acir, left in command of the desert garrison, had often imagined by the watchfires in the dead of the empty desert night, the scenes of rejoicing in Bel'Esstar that greeted the Prince's restoration to health. Acir had built a gilded picture in his mind from Girim's letters of a city reborn to faith, a city triumphant. Girim had described how warmly the citizens had welcomed the Guerriors; the streets had been strewn with flowers. Soldiers had begged to leave the Palace Guard to enlist as members of the Commanderie.

'We shall defend our own,' Girim wrote, 'from the infidel and from the unbeliever. Bel'Esstar is a fortress of faith and there we shall build our Stronghold.'

Acir looked around him. Dust blew across the empty street. In the distance he could hear the faint, frenetic chip of metal on stone from the site of the Fortress of Faith.

The gilded city of his desert dreams did not exist, maybe had never existed, he had conjured it from Girim's letters.

There was no sense of joy – only an all-pervading fear.

The Sanctuary for the Correction and Improvement of Unbelievers had been established in the old Debtors' Prison on scrubby waste ground to the north of the city.

As Acir approached, he noted the high fences, the watchtowers, the locked gates. He wished he did not have the feeling that Girim had assigned him here as punishment; that he too would have to be forcibly 'corrected' from his deviant behaviour. And this dull feeling of dread only increased as he approached the sentries at the gate and saw the look of suspicion in their eyes as his papers were demanded.

'Please wait in the gatehouse, Captain. I will inform the Governor you have arrived.'

Captain nel Macy, Governor of the Sanctuary, came striding briskly across the courtyard to greet him. He walked with the stiff strut of a seasoned soldier who has survived many campaigns.

'Captain Korentan! Welcome! Glad to have you with us. Let me show you what we've been doing here.'

Beyond nel Macy's broad shoulders, Acir could see a group of Sanctuarees being herded across the yard; to Acir they looked like convicts, men and women dressed alike in coarse grey tunics and loose trousers.

'Where are they going?' he asked.

'To work on the Fortress. Have you seen it? Isn't it magnificent?'

'But I understood the purpose of the Sanctuary was essentially spiritual. Not a labour camp.'

'Healthy labour, confrère! Nothing better to improve the spirit. Keep the body active in the service of God.'

'But look at them – exhausted, dispirited.'

One of the Sanctuarees began to cough, a racking, shuddering cough that shook his stooping frame.

'And ill.'

'We have a dispensary here,' nel Macy said defensively.

'Are you feeding them? They look thin. Wasted.'

'They get two substantial meals a day.' Nel Macy stopped. 'Look, Captain Korentan, is this some kind of Rosecoeur inspection? Be frank with me. I am well aware of your long association with the Grand Maistre.'

'I am assigned here to join your staff,' said Acir. 'That is all.' So nel Macy suspected him to be an agent of the Rosecoeur; all to the better.

A cry rang out across the yard, a shrill cry of pain and outrage. Acir swung around, hand automatically reaching for the hilt of his sword.

'Nothing to bother about. They're just tagging a new inmate.'

'Tagging him? Like an animal? Why is this necessary?'

'Identification, confrère. They suffer no more pain than a woman suffers when she has her ears pierced to display her gold and pearl earrings.' Before Acir could pursue the subject, nel Macy had steered him towards an open doorway, saying, 'Let me show you the dormitories.'

The dank walls of the old prison had been coated with whitewash but a musty prison smell still lingered. The Governor unlocked a door and showed Acir a bare chamber fitted with bunk beds, six along each side.

'See? All clean, all functional. Every man has his own sheet and blanket. The Sanctuarees run the laundry. We are self-sufficient here.'

On the far wall, Acir caught sight of a wooden rose, crudely painted crimson and green. The only evidence of the Faith he had seen so far in the Sanctuary.

'We observe our devotions every morning and every night. Each officer is assigned a different dormitory,' said the Governor, as though reading Acir's thoughts. 'Now – it may happen that one of our charges experiences the desire to convert. He must then undergo a series of spiritual trials. If at the end of this period he is still strong in his convictions, then we open our arms to him and welcome him into the faith.'

'Does this happen often?'

'The spiritual trials are, of necessity, rigorous. We have to be certain, Captain. Very certain.'

Acir stood at the barred window of his cell and gazed down into the yard.

How could the dream have turned out like this, in dour prison walls and cowed prisoners, tagged like animals? In the shadow of fear, fear which had settled over the whole city like a chill cloud, which blew through the deserted streets like the cold, dry Fevre wind?

Acir's faith still burned in his breast, a vision of warmth, of joy, of reconciliation. How had his fellow Guerriors lost their vision, how had they come to perpetrate this atrocity upon their fellow men in the sacred name of Mhir?

'Do not desert us in our hour of need,' he whispered, one hand pressed to his breast. Beneath his fingers he felt the Rose graven into his flesh. The physical pain he had endured as the tattooist's needle pricked out the intricate pattern of petals and thorns was as nothing to the agony of knowing that the cause he followed had wrought so much damage and despair.

The sky is darkening above the Fortress of Faith, a cloud rides fast on the Fevre wind, sweeping in to blot out the sun.

Duststorm – here in Bel'Esstar?

Acir gazes frantically around for somewhere to shelter – but the walls of the Fortress are open to the sky.

Dry particles of dust, grey dust, begin to swirl about the city. Dust stings his face, his upraised hands – cold, ice-cold as stinging hail. The icy dust settles over the city, choking the streets. Soon the whole city will be filled with it, smothered in it, stifled to silence.

Acir staggers into the Fortress, fighting against the gusting Fevre wind to reach the entrance to the Poet-Prophet's shrine. Drifts of grey snowdust lie across the doorway: he tears at them with his hands, feeling each icy particle sharp as shattered glass. When he looks down at his hands, they are bleeding from a myriad tiny dust-grazes.

At last he tugs open the door and slithers down into the darkness. Dust blows in after him: he puts his shoulder to the door, straining with all his strength to close it. A gust of wind blows it open again, sending showers of dust cascading down into the tomb below.

He throws himself across the tomb, trying to protect it from the encroaching dust with his body. His lacerated hands leave smears of blood across the worn stone.

The tomb shudders.

Acir draws back, terrified.

Something has penetrated the worn stone, and is spearing its way upwards.

A thin branch of green, prickled with black thorns. At its tip a bud unfurls, crimson petals unfold.

A rose. A perfect crimson rose.

The miracle renewed. The sign of divine forgiveness.

The shrine door slams open again and the whirlwind comes tearing in.

'No!' he cries aloud, vainly trying to encompass the miraculous Rose in his arms.

The Rose droops in the death-cold blast. Its velvet petals, red as heart's blood, begin to wither, frostburned.

One by one, the seared petals drop. Even as he watches the fresh green of the branch turns brown – and the dry stick crumbles away.

CHAPTER 17

Clutching her worn canvas bag with her precious notebooks stuffed inside, Dame Jolaine Tradescar crossed the forecourt of the Temple of the Source, all the while glancing back over her shoulder to see if anyone had followed her.

Inside the Temple, she dipped her handkerchief in the shell of sacred spring water and dabbed the perspiration from her brow.

A curse on the Mayor and his meddling clerks! And, more particularly, a curse on erudite young Dr Philemot. A wicked thought flitted across Jolaine's mind, a scholar's revenge. Perhaps she should inscribe her rival's name backwards on a thin sheet of pewter and cast a curse into the spring as her ancestors had done! Boils. Boils were particularly irksome and unsightly. Yes, boils would do nicely for a start . . . and maybe a touch of scrofula?

Why couldn't they have waited a week or two more? Her life's work was so very nearly complete. And there was no way that her successor was going to snatch it from her now.

She took up her bag and made towards the stair to the Under Temple. A Priest rose up from the shadows to bar her way.

'You cannot enter the Under Temple today.'

'Whyever not?' cried Jolaine, exasperated.

'It has begun. They must not be disturbed.'

'What the deuce has begun?' Why must the Priests always speak in riddles?

'They are almost ready to be born again into the Light.'

'The dragonflies!' Jolaine struck her palm to her temple. The Day of the Dead was approaching – and sooner than she had anticipated. This was a double blow. But there was no way accurately to predict the hatching patterns of dragonflies.

'And besides, Dame Tradescar,' the Priest said, 'there has been some concern expressed in the Temple Court about your excavations.'

'This is a fine time to start expressing concern!'

'There have been portents. Warnings.'

'This is the first I've heard of it –'

'Disturbing the ancient sacred sites. The unravelling of mysteries that are better left unravelled. It must cease.'

'Portents? Hocus-pocus! A fig to you and your silly superstitions!' blustered Jolaine. 'I'm City Antiquarian – I have unlimited access to all the historic sites. I'll be taking this up with the highest authorities. I'll go straight to the Mayor!'

The Priest did not budge, his face bland, expressionless.

Fizzling with frustration, Jolaine hefted her bulging canvas bag under her arm and left the Temple.

In the Temple forecourt she sat down on a bench to think. She knew all the hidden ways into the Undercity . . . but the stelae she wished to re-examine were all located on the rim of the Main Reservoir.

A little boy ran past, scattering breadcrumbs. Soon he was surrounded by an attentive, pecking flock of Temple doves. Jolaine heard the child's sudden shout of delight as he spotted the bustle about the stalls in the forecourt. Chandlers were setting out trays of scented lotos candles; there were rainbow streamers, dragonfly paper kites, and the traditional striped lotos bonbons, their curved sugar petals flavoured with strawberry, lemon and spearmint.

All in readiness for the Day of the Dead.

'Dame Tradescar?'

Jolaine looked up, shading her eyes against the morning sun, to try to make out who was addressing her. A young man stood before her, soberly attired, with a plain, pug-like face, rather endearingly ugly.

'Do I know you, sieur?'

'I don't believe we have ever been introduced.' The young man held out his hand. 'Theophil Philemot. Of the University of Can Tabrien.'

Jolaine's manners deserted her. She stared with hostility at the outstretched hand.

'How did you know to find me here, hm? Did you follow me?'

Dr Philemot slowly let his hand drop; his face had flushed bright red.

'It must be quite a wrench to relinquish the collection to another curator after so many years, Dame Tradescar. I must say I'd never have guessed you were eighty-one! Taking the waters must keep one youthful –'

'Relinquish the collection?' Jolaine interrupted. 'Maybe I'm a little hard of hearing at my very great age – but did I hear you say I had relinquished the collection?'

'Why else would I be here?' Dr Philemot seemed flustered. 'I was appointed – I understood – as you had retired –'

'*Retired*?'

'See for yourself. My letter of appointment.' Dr Philemot rummaged in his pockets and brought out a letter which he put into Jolaine's hands.

'My dear young man, there has been a mistake. A clerical error. I have most definitely not retired, as you can see. I –' Jolaine was seized with a sudden apprehension. She grabbed the canvas bag and started off across the Temple forecourt. Dr Philemot followed, moderating his lanky stride to Jolaine's hobbling pace.

She was puffing for breath by the time she reached the Guildhall steps; halfway up, she could see that she was too late. The blinds were up and her sign had been removed. She fished out her key to unlock the door – and saw the shiny new lock and the pile of sawdust beneath, left by the Guildhall locksmith.

'Ingrates!' she cried, hurrying around to the back door. It too sported a new lock. Jolaine sank down on to the doorstep, defeated.

'I deeply regret –' began Dr Philemot, and then subsided as she flashed him a look that would have withered a braver man. 'I will personally ensure that all your possessions are safely packaged up and taken to your lodgings.'

'My life's work,' muttered Jolaine, not listening. 'Fifty-five years of service to the city – and they throw me out into the gutter like a beggar!'

Jolaine Tradescar gave the Sanatorium bell-pull another vigorous tug.

The peephole in the door shot open and the porter's eye appeared.

'We're closed.'

'Closed! My dear fellow, it's two in the afternoon, not two in the morning. Let me in. Tell the good doctor I'm here to see him. It's urgent.'

'Like I said – we're closed.'

'I'm a family friend. Don't you know me? Tradescar. Dame Jolaine Tradescar. I've two silver courons here for you if you'll admit me.'

There was a silence, a considering silence. Then Jolaine heard the key turn and a calloused hand appeared, palm turned expectantly upwards. She placed the coins in the upturned palm which instantly shot back out of sight. The door opened.

'Don't tell *him* I let you in,' the porter said, hastily ushering her into the courtyard.

'What's the matter? Why is the place shut up like a tomb, the blinds down? Is there plague? Is someone dead?'

'It's his daughter. Taken ill.'

'Orial?' Jolaine stopped. 'Damn it all to hell!' she muttered. 'Am I too late, even now?'

'You all right, Dame Tradescar?' The porter was staring at her warily. 'You've turned a funny colour.'

'Just take me to Dr Magelonne,' Jolaine ordered, her own troubles forgotten.

Cook appeared in the corridor carrying a tray.

'Tragic,' she said to Jolaine, shaking her grizzled head. Her eyes were red-rimmed. 'Just like her poor dear mother. Tragic.'

'How's the doctor taking it?'

'Bad. Very bad. Won't even touch his food.'

'Shall I go up?'

Cook gave a shrug, setting the cutlery rattling on the tray.

The stairs seemed steeper than before; Jolaine had to stop and pause for breath several times, clutching on to the polished handrail. At last she reached the top and tottered towards Orial's room. The door was ajar.

Orial lay on her bed, one arm across her breast, her hair trailing across the white pillows like strands of waterweed.

Jerame Magelonne rose from her bedside and came across to Jolaine. Even in the shadowed room, Jolaine could see the unshaven stubble darkening his face; he had neglected his own needs to stay at her side.

'The Accidie?' Jolaine said.

'I can't be sure. I've sedated her.' Magelonne spoke in a whisper as though frightened a louder tone might disturb Orial.

'Why didn't you let me know, Jerame? I would have stayed with her. You need rest. I don't need so much sleep at my age.'

Magelonne beckoned her out on to the landing.

'What use will you be to her if you fall sick too?' she said sternly. 'You must eat, you must sleep. Go to bed – I'll watch over her.'

'But –' Magelonne began to protest but his voice was slurred with tiredness.

'Go.'

'I'll be in my room. You'll wake me if there's any change?' he added anxiously.

'Yes, yes.' Jolaine waved him away. 'Just get some sleep.'

She settled herself in the chair at Orial's bedside. The girl's pale skin seemed almost translucent in the darkness – except for the long red weals marring her cheeks.

How Jolaine hated to have the blinds drawn by day; it reminded her of far-distant childhood sickrooms, of fever and bowls of gruel, beef tea and barley water . . .

'Mmm . . .' Orial murmured in her sleep.

Jolaine leaned over her, listening, watching for any sign of a change. Her pale lips moved, mumbling a word.

'Ama . . .'

'Ama?' Jolaine repeated out loud, perplexed. What did it mean? Was it a name? Or was it 'Mama', was she calling for Iridial?

But Orial did not speak again, drifting back into drugged slumber.

Jolaine raised one of the blinds, took a book from her canvas bag and began to read, moistening her finger-tips as she turned the pages.

'Tea, Dame Tradescar?' Cook stood in the doorway.

'That's remarkably good of you,' Jolaine said.

Cook came in and placed the tea-tray on the table beside the bed. All the time, her eyes were on Orial; she softly clicked her tongue in disapproval as she gazed down at her.

'Poor lamb. She doesn't even know we're here.'

'Cook.' Jolaine laid down her book. 'Won't you join me for tea?'

'But the doctor –'

'Is asleep.'

'I'll pour then. Can't stay long. Left the soup simmering on the hob.' Cook wiped her bony fingers on her apron and poured tea for the two of them. 'As I recall you like your tea with sliced lemon and two sugars, Dame Tradescar?'

'What an excellent memory you have!' Jolaine took the bowl and pressed her spoon against the slice of lemon, releasing its sharp fragrance. 'I'll wager you can remember when they pulled down the old town hall and started work on the Guildhall dome?'

'Lady bless us, I do indeed.' Cook eased herself down into a chair with her tea. 'Such a fine building. Not that all the changes you and I have seen have been for the better.'

'Too many of the old ways forgotten or pushed aside to make way for the new.'

'These young people – excepting our Orial here – they want to make change for change's sake.'

Dr Philemot's eager face briefly floated before Jolaine's eyes.

'True, true . . . Look how the old traditions are swept away. I'll also wager you know tales and songs that the young today have never even heard?'

'When I was a girl, there used to be this custom – surely you remember it? The morning after the souls flew free on the Day of the Dead, you had to get up before dawn and go into the hills. The Faer Folk held their revels that night. If you could catch one, they were bound to grant you a wish.'

'Well, I saw one of them. With these very eyes. And no one ever believed me – they all laughed when I told them. I was nine years old at the time. We were up in the hills over Illyn way, collecting bilberries. At the rocks, near the waterfall. You know how the sun on the spray makes rainbows? That's what they said I'd seen. But I know different.'

'One of the Faer Folk?' Jolaine said softly.

'I heard something. It was like – a bird flying over my head. Wingbeats. But when I looked up, I *saw*. Behind the waterfall. A figure. It knew it had seen me, for it was gone in a flash. But I've never forgotten the way it looked on me. Never forgotten the eyes. Rainbow eyes, Dame. But not human. Wild. Wild like a wildcat's eyes. *Faïe*.'

'Faïe. Now that's a word I haven't heard in many a year.'

'An old word and none the worse for being old!' said Cook, noisily draining the last of her tea. 'I dearly wanted them to grant me a wish.' She gave a wry little sigh. 'I'd go chasing them again if a wish would bring Orial back to us.'

'Perhaps it might,' Jolaine said pensively.

'A wish? Now you're supposed to be a learned woman.'

'And if the old tales hold a grain of truth?'

Cook gathered the tea things on to the tray. 'Well, I'd best away to my soup, I don't want it boiling the pot dry.'

'Amar . . .' murmured Orial again.

'Did you hear?' Cook turned to Jolaine.

'I heard. A name.'

'Sister Crespine and I, we thought she had a sweetheart. A beau.'

'Amaru,' Jolaine said. 'Of course. Amaru Khassian, the musician.'

'Ohhh . . .' Cramoisy raised his handkerchief to his mouth to stifle his sobs. 'It's all my fault. I should never have brought you together.'

Khassian paused in his pacing.

'How was it I didn't know? Why didn't you tell me?'

'I didn't know. I never knew till now. I heard Iridial was dead – but they said it was from fever. Not this . . . Accidie.'

'Then why didn't *she* tell me? Why did she have to play the martyr? Why?'

But Khassian already knew the answer. And it only made him more disgusted with himself. She had given him her gifts because she wanted – more than anything – to become part of the musical world he inhabited. And he had used her, he had played on her sympathy, on the generosity of her character.

And now it was too late.

The score lay on the table, the last pages smudged with her tears.

Even to look on it made his stomach crawl. It recorded the disintegration of a mind. Her mind. It was evidence of the insidious progress of a mental disorder so devastating it could kill her.

He should have recognised her distress earlier. But instead he had forced her to continue.

And now the score lay there, a constant reminder of his wanton selfishness.

A sharp rat-tat at the front door made them both start.

'Suppose it's the police?' whispered Cramoisy. 'The permits.'

'You said you would go to the Mayor.'

Cramoisy waved his damp handkerchief. 'All this business with Orial has quite put it out of my mind.'

They stared at each other as footsteps could be heard coming up the stair.

'Out of your mind!' began Khassian.

Mistress Permay appeared.

'There's a Dame Jolaine Tradescar downstairs wanting to speak to you.'

'I'm not at home to visitors.'

'She's most insistent. Says it's urgent.'

'Tradescar?' The name was familiar to Khassian but he could not remember where he had heard it before.

'You won't know me,' announced a voice from the hallway, 'but I come on behalf of a mutual acquaintance. My soul-child, Orial Magelonne.'

Orial. Khassian closed his eyes. When he opened them again, he saw a crook-backed old woman in the doorway, eccentrically attired and periwigged in the fashion of some thirty years ago.

'May I come in?'

Khassian shrugged; Dame Tradescar was in already. He dreaded what she might have come to say to him – and yet there was something in the sprightly bearing of the old woman that belied the bearing of bad news.

'Please . . . sit down.'

Jolaine Tradescar spread the panniers of her ancient gown and sat.

'I'll come straight to the point, Illustre. Orial's affliction is very grave – but I believe there may be a way to restore her sanity.'

'I understood the condition was incurable.'

'Did you know that she has been calling your name?'

'My name?' Khassian felt his face flood with fire. Sweet Mhir, this woman obviously believed he had made some kind of advance to her soul-child. Who would begin to understand the true nature of their relationship? Should he blurt out that he had never so much as laid a finger on her?

'I hoped you would want to help,' Jolaine Tradescar said bluntly. There was something of the directness of Acir Korentan's stare in the old woman's blue eyes, light as a summer's sky.

'I wouldn't be of much use,' Khassian said, revealing his hands.

Jolaine Tradescar seemed barely to notice them. 'Maybe you can reach her in ways the rest of us cannot. Through music.'

'My music has wrought the damage! I don't want to make matters worse.'

'Tell me, Illustre,' Jolaine Tradescar said, leaning forward, 'exactly what happened before her collapse?'

Khassian swallowed hard; even to recall that afternoon gave him a feeling of nausea, the griping headache that precedes a storm.

'I should have noticed she was not . . . herself. She was playing a tune, over and over again on the keyboard. Obsessively.' He could not suppress a shudder as the notes of the bizarre melody wound their way back into his brain.

'Over and over again?' repeated Jolaine Tradescar. She seemed excited. 'I don't suppose you recall the melody?'

'I find it hard to forget.'

'Could you sing it?'

'Of course. But I fail to see –'

'The melody may be of some significance to her. It may act as a stimulus to restore her to herself. Or it may lead us to *others* who can help save her.'

There was something in the way she pronounced the word *'others'* that made the hair at the back of Khassian's neck rise.

'D'you know, I owe you a debt of gratitude, Illustre?'

'Me? How?' he said, surprised.

'It was you, wasn't it, who discovered the hidden hieroglyphs in the Hall of Whispering Reeds? And those hieroglyphs may hold the key to solving Orial's predicament.'

'You're the Antiquarian!' At last Khassian realised who his visitor was.

'*Was* the Antiquarian,' said Jolaine Tradescar. 'I have just been replaced without so much as a by-your-leave – but that's a story for another day. I'd like to propose that you come with me into the Undercity. Your keen eyes may yet discover some hidden hieroglyphs that we scholars have missed.'

'Oh, I don't think I could possibly be of any use to you –'. began Khassian. A polite but firm refusal, his customary response in such circumstances. And then he was seized by a curious impulse and heard himself saying, 'But, seeing as I have no other pressing engagements, I think I might accompany you, Dame Tradescar.'

Jerame replaced the sedative tincture in the drugs cabinet and turned the key in the lock; each movement slow, automatic, as his thoughts chased each other in a frenetic fugue whose subject was Orial, Orial, Orial.

Wild eyes staring at him through a cage of slender fingers, eyes whose iridescent colours were muddied with tears.

'*Iridial?*' *Time somersaulted, spinning him back to a chaotic vortex where all was madness and despair.*

The revenant raised one trembling hand to him: the finger-tips were stained with blood.

'*Papa . . . make it stop. Please make it stop.*'

Not Iridial, but Orial, their daughter, flesh of his flesh, blood of his blood, her face torn by her own nails, her body hunched, drawn in on itself, shaking . . .

The Accidie.

Why had he not kept better watch over her? Why had he not recognised the signs of imminent collapse? Should he consult the experts from the Medical School? They had been of no use at all when Iridial had shown the first symptoms of the Accidie. Which left one alternative: should he call in Ophil Tartarus?

No. Not Tartarus. He would not have that man poking and prodding with his yellowed finger-tips, peering into her wandering eyes with his glass, pawing her – and all in the name of his research.

'Dr Magelonne.' Sister Crespine tapped discreetly at the half-open door. 'There is a woman here to see you.'

'Send her away. I cannot see anyone. My daughter is ill. Desperately ill.'

'I think you may wish to see *me*, Doctor.'

That grave, cool voice subtly inflected with its Allegondan accent – he turned to see the Contesse Fiammis in the doorway.

'I cannot see anyone –' he began again, but she came in and closed the door, placing herself in front of it.

'Are the rumours correct? Your daughter was taken ill in the apartments of Amaru Khassian?'

'Him and his damned music!' Jerame choked on the words.

She drew close.

'Are you prepared to lodge a formal complaint against him? With the Constabulary?'

'On what charge?' Grief-drunk, he almost laughed aloud at the thought. 'Abusing my daughter – with *music*?'

'Corrupting your daughter's mind.'

'I don't know, I don't know.' Jerame let his head sink into his hands.

'You want him out of your daughter's life?'

'I – don't know if my daughter has any hope of a life now –'

'Then make a formal complaint.'

Jerame slowly raised his head to gaze at the Contesse.

'Were you aware he was making your daughter work long hours transcribing his music?'

'No, I was not aware,' he heard himself saying in a voice bleared with fatigue. Even though Khassian could not have known of Orial's condition, the composer must have sensed he was pushing her to the limits, he must have seen her pallor, her exhaustion. Doubtless he thought he was bestowing some privilege upon her in using her as his assistant. And Orial had such a kind, giving nature, she would have striven to please, not heeding the cost to her own health.

'And can we be certain that is all he was making her do?' said the Contesse in a silk-soft voice.

Her words conjured lewd images of seduction, as loathsome as they were lascivious. All those long hours they had spent together, alone, unchaperoned . . .

'I have no proof, of course, but . . .'

'Orial,' whispered Jerame. His beloved daughter wasting all the promise of her young life on a selfish, over-indulged composer.

A father's anger, pure animal instinct, raw and primitive, flared up within him. His child, his only child . . .

'I am on my way to see the Commissaire now,' said the Contesse. 'Can I count on your support, Doctor?' She opened the door and went out into the hall, her taffeta gown whispering with the soft rustle of willow leaves as she walked.

'Wait!' Jerame took up his hat and gloves and strode swiftly after her. Amaru Khassian must answer for the consequences of his actions.

CHAPTER 18

Faint strains of music drifted from the centre of the city, transient as windscattered petals.

Khassian paused on the doorstep of Mistress Permay's house, listening intently.

'D'ye hear that?' Jolaine Tradescar cried. 'Damme if we're not already too late.'

'Too late?'

'Have you never before seen Sulien on the Day of the Dead?'

'I am a visitor. I know nothing of your ways, your customs.' Khassian was fast becoming irritated with Tradescar's oblique comments.

'They'll have sealed off all the doors into the Undercity – all but the doors in the Temple. The only way in is through the Temple with all the crowds.'

'Then let's join them.'

'My dear young man, have you any idea what you're suggesting? It's such a crush.'

'A crush in which we can slip into the Undercity unnoticed.'

'Hm.' Jolaine Tradescar was fingering her collar as if it were too tight. 'It's worth a try.'

The Day of the Dead. To Khassian, the name evoked a sombre, macabre festival. Already he could imagine leaping figures wearing grotesque death masks, dangling skeletons, candles set inside human skulls. Perhaps the staid, provincial people of Sulien practised some bizarre ritual of death, such as he had read of in the far islands of Ta Ni Gohoa, carrying the wrapped mummified corpses of their venerated ancestors around the city to the sounds of music and firecrackers . . .

The reality could not have been more different. The shops and boutiques approaching the Temple forecourt were hung with rainbow banners and paper star-lilies. The most grisly souvenirs Khassian saw were the wriggling water-snakes made of blackcurrant jelly which a confectioner was selling to a crowd of clamouring children.

'It's too commercial nowadays,' complained Jolaine Tradescar. 'Too many stallholders making a profit out of it. Prefer to remember the dead my own way, not in some public jamboree.'

*

'So – where is the patient?' Ophil Tartarus handed his cloak and hat to Sister Crespine.

'I've sedated her.' Jerame led the way upstairs. 'But she's very weak – she's taken no nourishment for two days now.'

'Two days!' Tartarus's wild eyebrows lifted. 'Why didn't you call me sooner?'

Jerame gruanted an inaudible reply. He could not tell Tartarus the real reason; he had only called him now because nothing he had tried had worked. He was desperate.

In the darkened sickroom, Orial seemed no more than a pale shadow on the bed.

Tartarus checked her pulse at wrist and throat, raised her eyelids, one at a time. Orial murmured, twitching at his touch. Jerame clenched his fists, willing himself not to interfere. He must respect Tartarus's professional judgement, he must remember that the man's medical methods might be unorthodox – but they were Orial's only hope.

'How much longer can you keep her sedated? She's fighting it,' Tartarus said. 'And how great a dose can her body tolerate? There's little enough of her as it is.' His fingers passed over the scars striping Orial's pale cheeks. 'Self-inflicted?'

Jerame nodded.

'But no other indications?'

'Well, no . . .'

'Then how can you be certain it is the Accidie? You must stop the sedation at once.'

A band went along the street below, squeaking out a carnival tune: strident pipes and fiddles scraping to the hectic beat of a tambourin.

'You hear that?' Tartarus said.

Jerame nodded grimly. 'The Day of the Dead.'

Orial twitched again, jerking her head to one side. Her hand fluttered up, moving involuntarily towards her temples.

'See? She can hear it too. Maybe she can even sense the music from other bands further away. Or maybe all we're observing is an adverse reaction to the sedative drugs.'

'That's ridiculous.'

'Your medical judgement seems more than a little clouded by your feelings as a father. Let me take her back to the Asylum, away from the festivities.'

'No,' Jerame said instantly.

'Of course you want to keep her here, in familiar surroundings. But at the Asylum she will have calm, quiet, experienced nursing. If the fit comes upon her again, we can restrain her safely.'

'I will not have her tied down to the bed like a madwoman.'

'How else can we be sure this is fully developed Accidie – and not just hysteria, induced by excitement and overwork? I need to observe her to confirm your diagnosis – and I can tell nothing whilst she's so heavily sedated. At the Asylum we can employ the new electrical methods if the fit comes upon her again.'

'You will not subject her to your accursed electrical contraption! She is not a laboratory rat to be used in your experiments.'

'Then, my dear Jerame, if you refuse all the treatments I have to offer, why did you call me in?'

Jerame did not reply.

'What is worse? To poison her slowly with laudanum, or to risk loss of memory?' Tartarus came closer, closer, until he stood just behind Jerame, his voice low and persuasive. 'Ask yourself, what are the alternatives?'

When Tartarus had gone, Jerame stood looking down at his daughter for a while, a long while.

Tartarus's accusations still stung. How could Ophil suggest his medical judgement had become impaired?

Orial stirred; her lashes fluttered open a slit . . . then closed again. She was slowly surfacing from the drugged sleep – and it was time to administer another measure of the sedative.

He went to the cabinet, took out the bottle and uncorked it. The smell, sickly and bitter, made him grimace.

How dare Tartarus imply his treatment was wrong? Safely sedated, she could do no harm to herself. And yet . . . he knew as well as Tartarus the risks of continuous sedation.

His hand hovered over the cork.

It was as much of a risk to stop the treatment.

But suppose Tartarus was right and the sedative was slowly poisoning her? He had done all he could to end the insidious influence of Amaru Khassian. Once the musician had been removed from Sulien, the most immediate danger to Orial's sanity was over.

He stoppered the bottle tightly and replaced the sedative in the cabinet.

The Commissaire of the Sulien Constabulary rapped loudly on Mistress Permay's door with his staff.

'Where is Amaru Khassian? I have a warrant for his arrest.'

Constables burst into the Diva's apartment, flinging open doors, peering under couches.

'What are you all *doing*?' The question, released at full opera-house volume, made the crystals of the chandeliers tremble. The constables paused mid-search, disconcerted.

Cramoisy Jordelayne had appeared in the doorway of his room.

The Commissaire took off his gold-tasselled tricorne and approached him, warrant in hand.

'If you could tell us where he is –'

'I have no idea where he is,' Cramoisy said in a low voice, all the more menacing for the contrast with his earlier ear-splitting shriek.

'If you are not prepared to co-operate with us, then –'

'I told you. Are you deaf? I don't know where he is.'

One of the constables came up to the Commissaire, respectfully touching his forehead.

'He's right, Commissaire. There's no one else here.'

'I told you so!' Cramoisy said.

The Commissaire let out a little sigh.

'And precisely what crime does this warrant accuse Khassian of?' demanded Cramoisy.

'I'm not at liberty to divulge the details.'

'What will you do with him? Lock him up?'

'Until he can be taken under escort to the border. I understand that there are serious charges to be answered in his own country.'

'You're deporting him?' Cramoisy cried. 'But you can't!'

'Good day to you.' The Commissaire beckoned his men and hastily retreated towards the door.

Khassian found himself caught up in the jostling crowd, drawn downwards through the echoing Temple, towards the Undercity. He could just see Dame Tradescar ahead of him, the old scholar still clutching her canvas bag closely to her chest.

The vast vaulted hall of the Main Reservoir glimmered with a thousand lotos candles, lily-white, rose and gold. The people of Sulien thronged the rim of the glimmering waters: even little children waited, wide-eyed with excitement, clutching rainbow streamers.

A holiday atmosphere pervaded the hall, a sense of contained anticipation.

'This way!' Jolaine Tradescar signalled to him over the heads of the crowd. She was slowly forging a passageway through to the back of the hall. Khassian followed, slipping after her into one of the narrow passageways that wound away from the reservoir.

The Undercity was no longer pitch black; lotos candles burned in every niche and alcove in the wall. When they came to a pillared doorway, Khassian suddenly recognised where they were.

'The Hall of Whispering Reeds,' he said.

'Tread carefully,' Jolaine Tradescar said. Her voice trembled with excitement.

In the centre of the dusty floor a circular shape had been revealed, decorated with fragments of tile stained with bright glazes: blue, turquoise and grass-green.

'A mosaic pavement.' Khassian knelt down to look more closely.

'Isn't it exquisite?'

'A flight of dragonflies...' Khassian's hands hovered above the mosaic, slowly tracing the pattern Jolaine Tradescar had uncovered.

'And you led me to them.'

'I? It was as much Orial as myself.'

'Orial has always had a particular affection for this chamber.' Jolaine Tradescar gestured to the painted walls. Khassian could vaguely make out the figure of a woman, hands crossed on her breast. She stood knee-high in a meadow of white star-lilies on the borders of a stream. Dragonflies encircled her head, in a winged cloud.

'Star-lilies. A symbol of death for the Lifhendil. These meadows represent the Other World, the afterlife.'

Khassian was only half-listening. He could see Orial, wandering through that lily meadow, her hair unbound about her thin shoulders.

A symbol of death . . .

At that moment he could not have identified the bright pain that lit his heart, the reason for the sudden quickening of his breath. The image melted away, as swiftly as it had come, spring snow in sunlight.

'The circle. The spinning circle. The image recurs throughout the depictions of their mysteries.'

'"The ceaseless round . . ."' Khassian murmured, recalling the words of the ancient psalm he had sung as a boy.

'"The harmony of the spinning spheres" . . . yes, yes, I recall it too. But I don't think the Lifhendil understood it merely in a metaphysical, cosmological sense. To them it was a reality. The Winged Ones, the Eä-Endil. Orial's illness is the sign that she is ready to be translated, to become part of the circle.'

'To die,' Khassian said bluntly.

'No.' Jolaine Tradescar's response was so vehement it took him by surprise. 'We're such sceptics. In Tourmalise, reason and enlightenment prevail. We cannot begin to imagine a world which moves to a different rhythm, a world where the numinous is made manifest. It contradicts everything we have been taught –'

'*Trespassers!*'

Khassian spun around to see a Priestess standing in the entrance to the hall. In the flickering lotos-light she looked, in her starry veils, as if she had stepped down from one of the wall-paintings. But when she came closer, shaking her finger at Jolaine Tradescar, the momentary illusion passed.

'Dame Tradescar, you were expressly forbidden to enter the Undercity today. I am sent to escort you both back to the Main Hall.'

Jolaine Tradescar sighed and reluctantly gathered up her belongings.

'Why do you violate the sanctity of our ceremony?' The Priestess asked. Khassian sensed that they had held this conversation before. 'It only comes once a year. You know how important it is.'

As they drew near to the Main Reservoir, the perfumed scent of the lotos-candles filled the vaults with the drowsy sweetness of a summer's meadow.

The dark air throbbed with sound: a chanted song surged from one corner of the hall to the other, like a translucent wave. Khassian, pressed so tightly up against Jolaine Tradescar he could hardly move, wanted to reach out and catch it as it passed – and instead found himself engulfed in it.

At the same moment there began a grinding sound as if some great stone wheel had been set in motion.

Khassian strained to see what was happening; Priests and Priestesses in an obscure corner seemed to be straining to work an elaborate system of cogs and pulleys.

'Up! Look up!' Jolaine Tradescar cried.

A ray of sunlight pierced the vault.

Khassian raised his head – to see a thin crescent of pale sky appear in the roof far overhead. The mechanism had opened a concealed window in the vaulted roof of the reservoir.

A breath of clean air wafted into the drowse-fumed hall.

'This is it,' murmured Jolaine Tradescar. 'Will they fly?'

The crowd fell silent, as if waiting, collectively holding in a breath that could not be released until –

Until –

'Well, I'll be damned,' Jolaine Tradescar muttered.

A murmur of apprehension passed through the onlookers. The Priests and Priestesses stood staring, dumbfounded. Amidst the murmuring, Khassian began to distinguish words, hushed words.

'A sign. A portent. An omen.'

'Ill luck . . .'

'Mammie,' came a little child's voice, clear as a glass bell, 'why won't they fly?'

There was an uneasy ripple of laughter.

'What does it mean?' Khassian whispered to Jolaine Tradescar.

The Antiquarian scratched her ear. 'I've never known such a thing. Not in eighty years.'

'Is the weather not warm enough?'

'Perhaps their breeding grounds have been disturbed.'

The elder Priestess came to the rim of the reservoir and passed her hands over the dark waters in a series of ritual gestures. As her hands moved, she began the chant again – and gradually, hesitantly, the onlookers joined their voices to hers.

The Priestess had closed her eyes and was drawing in deep, shuddering breaths.

The chant faded – as she fell backwards into the arms of her acolytes. A voice, hollow and inhuman, issued from her gaping mouth.

'*The souls of the Dead shall not be One with the Light . . .*'

The hairs at the back of Khassian's neck rose. He had been sceptical about the ceremony. Now he felt a deep and visceral terror.

'*Until the Rose and the Lotos are One . . .*'

The Priestess's hand lifted and – as though moved by a power more potent than her own – slowly pointed. Directly at himself and Jolaine Tradescar.

'*Violator of the sacred places . . .*'

The people beside him began to edge away.

Her eyes, whites showing, stared sightlessly towards them.

'*Put back what you have taken.*'

'I? What have I taken?' Jolaine Tradescar began to splutter. 'I've been digging down here for over half a century. No one has ever made such an accusation before!'

'The dragonflies have never refused to fly before!' cried one of the Priests.

'Pshaw! You miscalculated! Look to your calendars and check before you start blaming me. What taboos have I broken? Surely the Goddess would have struck me down if I had violated her shrine, hm?'

'I came to see my mother's soul fly free,' a woman said, and burst into tears. Others turned around, staring.

'Dame Tradescar,' Khassian said, 'I think we should leave.'

He hooked his arm through Jolaine's and began to draw her backwards towards the stairs as the murmurs of the crowd grew louder and more fingers began to point in their direction.

'Violators!'

Orial walks through a darkling meadow. Flowers, waist-high, brush her skirts, star-lilies whose petals seem to gleam with the burnished glow of sunset.

As she passes, her footfall sets the petals trembling. She leans closer. Vibrations emanate from the fire-flushed flowers, audible vibrations, tickling her ears.

'*Orial!*' *Someone is calling her name. She glances up and sees a shadowed figure on the edge of the fiery meadow, arms outstretched towards her.*

Suddenly the petals go swooping up into the air. A trail of notes falls from the wings on to her upturned face like pollen.

They swirl around her, dazzling her with their rainbow pollen. Dizzied, delighted, she feels herself slowly lifting, rising with them in their circling flight into the air.

'*Orial!*' *The calling voice seems very faint and faraway now.*

She gazes down – and sees a body sprawled on the grass in the darkened meadow. The flowers have withered, the stalks are brown and dry. Whose is the body lying there so still, so lifeless, crumpled like a discarded dress?

*

A carriage was stationed outside Mistress Permay's house. As Khassian approached, one of the blinkered horses snorted and struck the cobbles with an iron-shod hoof. It must be waiting to take the dowager Lady Bartel to the Assembly Rooms; the old lady always kept her carriages waiting whilst she fretted over her toilette . . .

He heard the carriage door open and footsteps hastening towards him. A hand clamped on to his shoulder, firmly turning him around.

'Let go of . . .' he began to protest – and found himself confronted by two constables of the Sulien Constabulary.

'Amaru Khassian?'

He nodded. His mouth had suddenly gone dry.

A third man stood in the half-light, holding open the carriage door.

'I am the Commissaire. Please be so good, Illustre, as to get into the carriage with me.'

'Are you arresting me?' Khassian began to shout. 'And if so, on what charge? I demand to know why I am arrested!'

The grip on his shoulder tightened; the two constables tried to manoeuvre him towards the carriage.

'At least tell me what I am charged with!' Khassian cried.

'Now, sieur, let's not make a scene. We don't want to distress the neighbours, do we?'

Glancing back over his shoulder, Khassian saw shadows appear at the lighted window on the first floor.

Cramoisy. Let it be Cramoisy.

They bundled him into the carriage and, clambering in after him, pulled the door to. The Commissaire rapped on the roof with his staff and the carriage lurched away over the cobbles.

Orial started up, wildly staring around her.

She had been in a sunset garden. There had been flowers, colours, sounds . . . oh, such ravishing sounds . . .

But then she had heard the voice calling to her from beyond the garden. And there was such anguish in the voice that she had felt compelled to go to the gate to see who was calling. Looking all around, she ventured outside –

The garden gate slammed shut behind her. Outside, all was darkness, beneath a confusion of windblown clouds – and when she strove to find her way back into the garden –

'She's awake.'

Orial blinked Cook's face into focus, haloed in soft lamplight.

'Cook? Have I overslept? It must be late . . .'

'Praise the Goddess, she's awake!'

She struggled to sit up but sank back, her head swimming.

'Why . . . do I feel . . . so muzzy?'

'You've been ill, my lamb. Now you just lie there quietly and let Cook bring you a nice drink of barley water.'

'Ill? How long . . . have I been . . . ill? And where's . . . Papa?'

Cook hesitated.

'He's been called out to – on business. Oh, but he'll be so happy when he hears the news.'

The oil-light cast a striped pattern through the barred grille of Khassian's cell door. He sat hunched on the wooden bed, staring fixedly at the barred shadow. It could be an empty segment of stave, waiting for notes to be inscribed upon it.

Or a bar of silence.

The Sulien Constabulary had treated him with firm but detached courtesy. They had locked him in a single cell, away from the drunks and petty thieves. He had demanded to see a lawyer, he had demanded that they send for Cramoisy, he had demanded to know the charges on which they were holding him. But no further explanation had been given.

Now he sat here on the bare-boarded bed in the darkness, starting at the slightest sound, tense and anxious.

Why? Why had he been arrested? Who had accused him of a crime? What crime had he unwittingly committed? The Mayor had assured Cramoisy that they could stay in Sulien as long as they wished . . .

'On your feet!'

The two constables unlocked the door and beckoned him out.

The first thing Khassian noticed was the Sulien coat of arms on the wall, dominating the courtroom, blue and flaking gilt.

The Commissaire sat at a table beneath the coat of arms, his hat and staff of office before him. He yawned behind his hand, evidently weary of the affair, looking to bring it to a swift conclusion. A clerk sat at his right, pen in hand, ready to record the session.

'Your name is Amaru Khassian, native of Allegonde?'

'It is,' Khassian said, 'but –'

The Commissaire raised his hand to silence him.

'Amaru Khassian, you are charged with a serious crime: the moral seduction of the young woman, Orial Magelonne.'

'Moral seduction! What manner of crime is that?' Khassian stared at the Commissaire incredulously. 'And who brings this charge against me?'

'Let the plaintiff come forward,' said the Commissaire in disinterested tones.

Jerame Magelonne stepped out of the shadows. He moved like a sleepwalker, his eyes staring staright ahead at the Sulien coat of arms.

'Magelonne?' Khassian whispered. Magelonne still stared fixedly at the coat of arms.

197

'Jerame Magelonne, do you bring this charge on your daughter Orial's behalf against Amaru Khassian?'

'I do,' Magelonne said in a low voice. 'I took this man in when he came to Sulien, a fugitive from Allegondan justice, I healed his wounds. And how has he repaid me? By ruining my daughter's life.' Magelonne's eyes, glazed with tiredness, focussed on Khassian. 'By driving her to the point of distraction.'

'No!' cried Khassian. 'It's not true! I never wished her harm, I –'

'The accused will remain silent until spoken to,' said the Commissaire coldly. 'Dr Magelonne, you say this man is a fugitive from Allegondan justice. Is there any other here with evidence to support those claims?'

'Yes,' said a voice. A woman's voice.

Khassian gazed wildly around, seeking out the speaker. She had been standing behind Jerame Magelonne and now she came forward. She was dressed for travel in dark riding garments.

'Your name?'

'Fiammis, Contesse of Tal'Mont and Reial. I speak as the official representative of the government of His August Highness Prince Ilsevir of Allegonde.'

Fiammis. Now Khassian understood. Acir Korentan had returned to Bel'Esstar – but in his place this clever agent had contrived Khassian's arrest. He should have heeded Korentan's warning. And now, now it was too late.

'This man, Khassian, is wanted by the courts in Bel'Esstar. I have a warrant for his extradition.' She drew a paper from the breast of her jacket and laid it on the table before the Commissaire.

'I do not recognise the courts of Bel'Esstar!' said Khassian, starting forward. The constables caught hold of him by the arms and pulled him back. 'I am a musician, persecuted for my beliefs. I have committed no crime – neither here, nor in Bel'Esstar. I request asylum in Tourmalise.'

The Commissaire had been reading Fiammis's warrant; now he handed it to the clerk who began to copy it into his ledger.

'It's too late to request asylum,' he said. 'The extradition papers are in order. The matter is out of my hands.'

'Wait!' Khassian cried as the constables placed their hands on his shoulders. 'Dr Magelonne! Don't let them do this to me! I can help Orial. I want to help her! Please – make them listen.'

For a moment he thought he had moved Magelonne as he saw a doubting frown pass across the doctor's face. Then as the constables hustled Khassian out, Magelonne pointedly turned his face away.

'This man may try to do himself some mischief,' Fiammis said to the constables. 'He should be restrained.'

'As you wish, Contesse.'

They drew Khassian's wrists together in front of him; the fine lace fell away, revealing the raw-scarred remains of his hands. He sensed them hesitate – then clamp on the manacles. Cold metal chafed his damaged flesh as they forced him back into the closed carriage. Fiammis delicately lifted her dark skirts and climbed up after them, closing the door. She sat, placing her parasol across her lap, smoothing out her skirts, each movement elegant yet precise.

'At least let me leave word for Cramoisy,' Khassian said.

'He will be informed. In good time.'

The carriage rolled out into the silent streets of Sulien, the ring of the iron-bound wheels echoing in the night. Khassian eyed the door, wondering if it would be possible to throw himself against it – and out on to the street. But he was wedged too tightly between the burly constables to make any sudden move. And the carriage was going faster now, leaving the city, making for the border road. Soon it would start the slow, winding climb towards the gorge and the foothills of the mountains.

He was to be handed over to the faceless inquisitors of the Commanderie.

They would order him to recant, to make public confession of his sins. He would refuse – less out of bravery than sheer stubbornness. Then they would work on him mentally, physically, until he broke. And when they broke him, he would lose the last tatters of dignity, of self-respect.

He would rather die than endure the humiliation.

Numb and cold with dread, Khassian began to shiver.

The exchange took place not long after midnight at a lonely watchpost high in the mountains above Sulien.

As the Sulien Constabulary carriage slowed, stopped, Khassian became aware of a mosaic of tiny sounds embellishing the silence of the mountain night: the fretful rattle of nightjars, the distant hooting of a snow-owl, the sighing of wind in the tall cinder pines.

Another carriage stood waiting beyond the borderline. The constables helped Khassian down. One tripped on the rough, stony road, lost his grip – and Khassian ducked free.

Vain fantasies of escape danced through his brain as he ran. And then he caught a rush of movement from the shadow of the pines.

Guerriors.

'Stay where you are!' cried Fiammis. Her voice pierced the cold air, keen as a crossbow bolt.

As his eyes adjusted to the night, he saw them more clearly. Half a dozen armed men, grey as night shadows, swiftly closing in on him.

And she stood blocking his way, still clutching that absurd parasol – as though she could fend him off with its laces and ribbons.

In that one instant's hesitation, the constables grabbed hold of him.

'You may return to Sulien,' she said to them, coldly dismissive. 'My thanks to the Commissaire for his co-operation. But from here *I* take full charge of the prisoner.'

CHAPTER 19

'So. You are Amaru Khassian?'

Khassian shaded his eyes, squinting into the rising sun. Girim nel Ghislain, Grand Maistre of the Commanderie, was a shadow silhouetted against the blinding glare.

'I had not realised you were quite so young. So young and so talented. A god-given talent. Only once or twice a century one as gifted as you is born, Illustre. Come into the light. I want to look at you.'

When Khassian did not move, two Guerriors seized hold of him by the arms and dragged him forward.

'Let go of me!' Khassian shook himself free. The two Guerriors stood at his side, staring into the dazzling sun, faces unmoving.

The Grand Maistre gestured to one of the officers.

'A chair for the Illustre Khassian.'

A gilt chair was placed behind him. He shook his head.

'Oh, please sit down, Illustre Khassian. This interview may take a little time.'

Hands were placed on Khassian's shoulders. He was pressed down, gently but firmly.

'Interview? Wouldn't interrogation be a more accurate term?' he said.

'Your words, not mine.'

'Then why the secretary?' Khassian nodded towards the grey-suited officer discreetly writing in a ledger.

'For your protection as much as my own.'

'So that you can twist my words to condemn me.'

'If you have nothing to hide from us, Illustre, then you need not fear a record being kept of our conversation.' Girim sat back in his chair. 'You showed such promise, even as a young child. All that burgeoning talent so sadly misused. Abused. Frittered away in sick, sad projects like this . . . what did you call it? . . . *Elesstar – or Litanies of Transubstantiation*?'

'Only a working title.'

'But blasphemous. Even the title reeks of heresy. You arrogant young intellectuals – why must you mock and deride what you do not understand? I am called back to Bel'Esstar, Jewel of Cities, my spiritual home – and what do I find? The Blessed Mhir's shrine neglected – even

His name, His holy writings, desecrated in – in vulgar *entertainments*.'

'*Elesstar* is not an entertainment!' cried Khassian. 'It is my interpretation of Mhir's writings. The *Vineyard Verses*.'

'Your misinterpretation,' said Girim coldly. 'Your blatant distortion of holy texts. It seems a remarkably contentious work to me, Illustre. A work calculated to disturb. To provoke. Inflame.'

'I don't understand.'

'Oh, I think you understand very well, Illustre. For a young man, you demonstrate a great degree of understanding. In the Opera House you know how to rouse the passions of your audience. You manipulate them through your art.'

'Manipulate!' Khassian echoed.

'Music is the most powerful manipulator of the emotions. In the hands of the corrupt, the spiritually warped, it can be a terrifying weapon. My role is to protect the vulnerable, the innocent, the untainted, Illustre. I have to guard my flock from the wolves.'

'And you've marked me down as a wolf?' Khassian smiled, an ironic smile.

'If I read this libretto aright, you planned to depict the seduction of the Blessed Mhir by the Angel Messenger sent by Iel the All-Seeing. The carnal seduction.'

'Mhir's words are explicit: "*Then he put His mouth to my mouth and His tongue was a scorching flame. The fire of His words flowed into –*" '

'You have no need to quote the holy texts to *me*, Illustre. I have spent a lifetime in study and contemplation of Mhir's words. And I find your interpretation a lewd distortion of what is essentially a poetic metaphor.'

'So you deny the power of the metaphor? Mhir's metaphor?'

'I question your motives in portraying literally what was meant to be interpreted metaphysically. I question your motives in portraying Mhir on stage in a work of entertainment. In my opinion this opera of yours is a blasphemous abomination. The anger it arouses amongst true believers is justified.'

'Oh, so they were justified in trying to burn us alive?'

'I do not condone the arson attack upon you and your company. But your opera has stirred up strong feelings, Illustre. Dangerous feelings.'

Khassian had focussed his attention on the Grand Maistre's hands; the nails perfectly manicured, the skin smooth and pale and supple. The hands of an aesthete, one who does not sully his fingers with everyday matters, Khassian thought. Before the fire his own hands had always been stained with ink, the nails chewed: craftsman's hands; honest hands.

'Together, Illustre, we could re-fashion your opera into a celebration of Mhir's life. The aggressive musical language of your recent works would be wholly inappropriate, of course. But a composer as versatile as you would have no problem adapting his style to create a less contentious work.'

Girim was looking at him over steepled fingers. His eyes were colourless; neither the grey of winter skies nor the pale brown of endless sands. For a moment Khassian was balancing on the top of a dizzy precipice; far below the clouds eddied and swirled.

He gasped in a deep breath.

'Impossible.'

The steepled fingers slowly lowered. There was silence in the panelled chamber; even the scratching pen stopped.

'I beg you to reconsider,' Girim said quietly. 'We can find you an amanuensis.'

'You understand nothing about music! Even with an amanuensis, it would be impossible. You ask me to compromise my name as a composer, to compromise my own style, my own voice – I will not do it.'

'So be it.' Girim turned to the secretary. 'Let it be set down that I offered the Illustre Khassian the opportunity to recant. And he refused.'

Khassian closed his eyes. He had condemned himself.

'I will give you one more chance to change your mind. So I am sending you to the Sanctuary, Illustre. There, in a solitary cell, you will have time to reflect upon the answer you have just given me.'

Voices outside the bedroom door drifted into Orial's consciousness.

'A remarkable recovery, wouldn't you say, Tartarus?'

She smiled drowsily to herself: Papa's voice, reassuringly confident.

'Remarkable, indeed. But for how long will it last?'

'For as long as I can keep her away from the music.'

'Ha! And you really believe you can do it?'

'If music overstimulates certain areas of her brain, provoking these manic episodes, then yes, I must do it. She'll come to see the sense of it in time.'

What was Papa saying?

No music meant never to see Amaru Khassian again. Never to share again the unique melding of musical consciousness that had bonded their minds.

How could Papa say he loved her – and deprive her of the one thing she cherished most?

'If you change your mind, Jerame, you know where to find me.'

The voices faded as the men moved away down the corridor.

Orial lay motionless.

There was still a choice.

To live a sterile life, safe from the dangerous influence of music, a sheltered life, trapped within the silent walls of the Sanatorium . . .

203

. . . or to break free, to follow the glamour of the music wherever it led her, to dance to its tune until the madness finally claimed her.

'Good morning, Papa.'

Jerame looked up from his breakfast to see Orial propping herself against the doorframe.

'Why are my legs still so weak?' she complained.

'My dear, you have been very ill.' Jerame tenderly helped her into a chair. 'You must try to regain your strength slowly, not rush at everything.'

'But there is so much to be done! The Illustre will be wondering what has become of me –' She stopped, one hand flying up to cover her mouth.

'I know,' Jerame said, steeling himself to tell her what had happened. 'I know what you were doing.' Better he told her the truth than that she heard some garbled version from Cramoisy Jordelayne. 'Listen, Orial. Khassian has gone back to Bel'Esstar.'

'Gone back!' she echoed in an incredulous whisper. 'And he left no word for me?'

'He had very little time, I believe, to leave word for anyone. There was an extradition order.' He moved to the window, pretending to look out at the weather. 'He had to go.'

'But, Papa – do you know what this means? They'll *kill* him.'

The volatility of youth. Everything was a life-or-death issue. He sighed.

'There were charges he was obliged to answer in Allegonde. He was fulfilling his duty as a citizen –'

'Who have you been talking to?' She was looking at him shrewdly. 'Because don't you believe for one moment, Papa, that his rights as a citizen will be respected in Bel'Esstar. I must see the Diva. We must organise a petition on his behalf. We – we must –' She tried to raise herself from the chair but sank back, drained.

'All in good time,' soothed Jerame, tucking a shawl about her legs. 'Right now you must conserve your strength.'

'This is most vexing,' she said in a small voice. 'Can you not at least invite the Diva here, Papa? Talking should not exhaust me.'

'I have much work to catch up with, my dear. Maybe in a week or so . . . when you are stronger. Rest now. And don't forget to drink your restorative tincture; it is made from mountain herbs and flowers.'

He did not tell Orial that the Diva had been calling every day, begging to see him – and every day Jerame had somehow managed to avoid him, to send him away.

But how long would it be before Orial discovered the part he had played in Khassian's deportation?

Another sad band of Sanctuarees had arrived. Acir Korentan stood and watched the prisoners trail after nel Macy as he marched them to their quarters, barking out orders.

They had taken one away from the others and were hurrying him towards a separate wing of the Sanctuary. Acir frowned into the sunlight. There was something oddly familiar about that defiant stance, that shock of tousled dark hair.

Khassian?

Acir hurried down the steps after the prisoner and his escort. But before he could reach them, nel Macy hailed him.

'A new batch, Captain Korentan!'

'So I see.'

'Will you take charge of their induction? I've been called to the Fortress.'

Take charge. A chance at last to assess what processes were at work within the Sanctuary. A chance to find out how it was that Amaru Khassian had come – in spite of all Acir's efforts – to be imprisoned here.

'And the last prisoner?' he asked casually. 'What are the instructions regarding him?'

'Who? 654? He's marked down for Meditation. Special instructions. A hard one to break, apparently.'

Meditation. Another of Girim nel Ghislain's euphemisms. Meditation meant solitary confinement. Acir's hopes of making contact with Khassian were immediately dashed.

'You were sent here as a spiritual advisor, Korentan.' Nel Macy clapped him on the shoulder. 'You can take charge of the weekly confessionals.'

'And what,' Acir said levelly, 'is the precise purpose of these confessionals?'

'When these rebels arrive at the Sanctuary, they're in poor shape spiritually. Morally weak. We talk to them. We give counsel. We keep a check on their spiritual progress. And if any feel ready to make a public renunciation of their old beliefs, then we welcome them back into the faith. There have been torchlight ceremonies in Bel'Esstar – crowds of onlookers. A stirring sight!'

Acir listened in silence, arms folded across his chest.

'And if they are not ready?'

'We have our methods. Even the most stubborn breaks . . . eventually.'

Everywhere the posters advertising the second appearance at the Guildhall of Cramoisy Jordelayne *By Public Demand* were slashed across with red writing proclaiming the blunt message: CANCELLED.

The sky was filling with clouds as Orial hurried towards the Crescent; the first drops of rain began to patter on to the pavements as she went up to Mistress Permay's door and rapped loudly with the knocker.

'Ho! It's you, demselle,' said Mistress Permay suspiciously.

Raindrops spattered Orial's head; the sky had darkened and the pavements were already glistening with the downpour.

'I've come to see the Diva.'

'He's not receiving any visitors.'

'He'll receive me.' Orial could feel the rain trickling into her hair. She took a step forward. Mistress Permay blocked her way.

'No more musicians. They're nothing but trouble.'

Orial thought swiftly.

'But I've come from the Sanatorium.'

'Oh? Well, that's different, then, I suppose you'd better come in.' Mistress Permay grudgingly moved aside to allow her into the hall. 'Mind you wipe your feet. The floor's just been polished. Can't have mud and filth trodden in everywhere.'

Orial wiped her feet on the mat and hastened across the shiny floor under Mistress Permay's watchful eyes.

She tapped on the door of Cramoisy's apartments. There was no reply. She quietly pressed the handle and opened the door.

The salon was exactly as it was the day she had been taken ill – except for the absence of Amaru Khassian. She had half-expected to see him in his customary position by the window, turning to greet her.

Now she felt a bleak chill wrap round her heart as she gazed around the empty room.

It was only then that she saw Cramoisy Jordelayne.

The Diva was sitting staring into empty air. His hair was unkempt, lying lank and straggling about his shoulders. He was still in déshabillé, not having bothered to dress; from time to time he pulled at the lace on a crumpled handkerchief clutched in one hand.

'Cramoisy?' Orial called his name softly. The Diva started and glanced around; his face was streaked with black-stained tear runnels.

'Orial?' Cramoisy said bemusedly. 'But – but I thought you – they said –'

Orial crossed the salon.

'I'm here.'

'I had feared the worst.' The Diva hesitated a moment – and then he enveloped her in his arms, crushing her in a pomade-scented embrace. His fingers tremblingly touched her face. 'And here you are – healed.'

Orial, overwhelmed by this unexpected show of emotion, gently extricated herself from the Diva's fond embrace.

'Listen to me, babbling on.' Cramoisy made an effort to control himself. 'But it is so good to see you – when everything else –' his voice cracked again '– everything else is in ruins.' The tears began to well again and he raised the handkerchief to his mouth as though to smother them.

Orial reached out and shyly touched his hand.

'Tell me.'

'So – upset – my voice –' He could not finish; one hand pointed at his throat.

'You've lost your voice?'

Cramoisy nodded.

'Your singing voice?'

'It can happen, you know. Shock. And once it's gone, it's gone for good. It never comes back. My performing career is over,' he said starkly.

'But tell me what brought this about?' Orial persisted.

'Amaru – was arrested.' This was no performance; Cramoisy's distress was genuine. 'Deported – no word now – for days –' He turned to Orial, mouth contorted with anguish. 'How could he do it? Didn't he know he was sending him to his death?'

'How could who do it?'

'I'm sorry to speak ill of your father, *carissa*. Doubtless he thought he was doing it for the right reasons. He was acting as a responsible citizen. He –'

'My father?' Orial said sharply. 'My father had Amaru arrested?'

Cramoisy nodded, dabbing at his eyes.

'But why?' Even as she asked the question, Orial realised that she knew the answer. 'Oh, no. Not because of me?'

Cramoisy's eyes brimmed above the handkerchief.

'My collapse? He blamed Khassian?'

'Apparently so.'

Orial started up from the couch. Her heart was beating too fast.

'Then I must put this to rights.'

'It's too late. He's already in Bel'Esstar.'

'Then I will go after him.'

The Diva's eyes widened.

'Go to Allegonde?'

'I will plead his case with the Grand Maistre – with Prince Ilsevir himself, if he'll see me.'

'No. Oh, no.' Cramoisy made a tutting noise. 'Have you any idea what it is like in Bel'Esstar? You've heard the horrific stories Azare and Valentan have to tell. It's no place for a young girl –'

'At least we could find Captain Korentan. He would help.'

'And how can you be so sure? How can we trust him? He was in league with that so-called Contesse, that brassy strumpet parading herself in her fine gowns and millinery . . .'

Orial went to the window and looked out through the rivulets of rain darkening the panes.

'When does the Bel'Esstar diligence leave?'

'Your father will never allow you to go.'

'I shan't ask his permission,' Orial said, gazing out over the rainswept city. She swung around and looked the Diva directly in the eyes. 'Will you come with me?'

'Me?' The Diva tried to get to his feet but instantly sank back as though exhausted by the effort. 'Oh, it's hopeless, hopeless . . . every time I think of Amaru in Bel'Esstar, I come over so faint . . .'

'What's worse? To go or stay here, worrying and waiting?' Orial demanded.

'And there's the problem of papers. Of course, there might be another solution . . .'

Orial saw a faint glint of malice light the Diva's dull eyes.

'You've devised a plan?'

'I have a mind to play the Commanderie at their own game. Yes, that's it!' Cramoisy clasped his hands together, as though clutching the idea tight to his breast. 'I'll play the penitent. I'll tell the Grand Maistre in a heart-rending scene that I have seen the error of my ways. The Diva decides to be converted – what a *coup* for the Commanderie!'

'But that would mean –' Orial stopped. 'I couldn't ask you to compromise your principles, that would be too great a sacrifice.'

Cramoisy flapped one hand dismissively.

'Fa to principles! Listen, *carissa*, a Diva can't afford to have principles. He sings for whoever pays the highest price.'

Orial gave the castrato a long, pensive look. It seemed as if he was in earnest, in spite of the extravagant words and gestures . . . though it was always hard to tell.

'But we'll need funds.' He rose from the couch and went to unlock a walnut casket on a side-table, talking all the while. 'I could sell this jacinth brooch, I suppose it might fetch fifty courons or so. And the matching buckles – I always thought they were a trifle tawdry.' He took out one piece of jewellery at a time, laying them side by side on the table. 'That pays for our passage. Now for the lodgings . . .' Cramoisy began to count on his fingers, silently calculating the sums.

'So you'll come?'

'Well, there's precious little to do here in Sulien. Besides, I have a pressing desire to see what is being worn at court this summer.'

Orial stood on tiptoe to kiss the Diva's cheek.

'I'll go and pack!'

On the curved staircase, Orial faltered, grasping at the rail to steady herself.

What am I doing?

She could still hear her own voice, clear and determined, ringing out across the echoing salon:

'*I must put this to rights.*'

She reached the front door; outside, shafts of light penetrated the looming clouds and puddles glistened between the paving stones. The rain had stopped.

Where had the courage come from to speak out? Now that she had time to think about what she had said, she was astonished at her own boldness.

How long have I got before the Accidie finally claims me? Is it long enough to repair the damage my father has done?

Is it long enough to save his life?

Orial drew out her leather valise from beneath her bed. The rain drummed relentlessly on the window panes. What did one take on such an unpredictable journey? And was the weather hot at this time of year across the mountains in Bel'Esstar – or grey and stormy, as in Sulien? She knelt back on her heels, perplexed. Where to start?

Why am I fussing about packing? Does it matter what I take?

She knew she was living on borrowed time. But if there was only a little time left to her, she wanted to use it to the full. She felt a strange sense of calm now that she had made her decision to go. Besides, who could foretell what the future might bring? Anything might happen.

A door banged downstairs. Her heart pattered as fast as the falling rain.

A man's voice called up the stairs.

'I'm off to the apothecary's, Orial. I'll see you at tea.'

Papa.

How was it possible to love someone – and yet be so desperately ashamed of what they had done?

If it were not for you, Papa, I would not have to make this journey.

She went to the window and saw him striding purposefully away down the street, case in hand. But from this height she could see the little patch on the top of his head where his immaculately trimmed hair was thinning. In spite of his brisk step and his neat appearance, he was ageing. And who would care for him when she was gone?

Her heart gave a little twist of anguish.

She unfolded the brief note she had written him and re-read it:

I have to go away for a little while. Don't worry about me, Papa, please, I shall be quite safe – and you know I am more than capable of looking after myself.

Your loving daughter,
Orial

It seemed so inadequate a way to say goodbye.

She went to the drawer and took out her only jewellery: a necklace of black and ivory pearls with ear-drops of matching pearls that had belonged to her mother. Maybe they would act as a talisman, a token of good luck. She could not bear to leave them behind – but to wear them might attract unwelcome attention.

It would be sensible to sew them into the hem of her dress; she had heard tales of unscrupulous thieves and pickpockets in Bel'Esstar.

She swiftly unpicked a few stitches and threaded the pearls inside the hem, sewing them tightly in. She stood up, smoothing out the folds; no one would guess the pearls were there.

Now she was ready.

She took up the valise and placed the note on her coverlet next to her old rag doll and much-loved book of faery tales.

'Farewell,' she whispered, softly closing the door.

The diligence to Bel'Esstar stopped in the courtyard of the Moon and Sickle inn in the centre of Sulien. Carriages and mail coaches for all other destinations in Tourmalise used the Three Hares tavern on the far side of the city.

Orial approached the busy yard warily, glancing all around, hoping no one would recognise her. She had collected her travel permit from the Guildhall, her valise was packed – now all that was needed was the Diva and the tickets.

Ostlers bustled about within the cobbled yard, leading fresh horses from their stalls. There was a rich, all-pervading odour of trampled hay and horse-manure.

The passengers from the capital were descending and collecting their luggage. But where was Cramoisy?

A sudden shrill whistling pierced her mind, a bolt of blue lightning, icily cold. She stumbled, clutching at the wall to support herself.

One of the stable lads passed in front of her, laden with fresh nose-bags for the horses. He was whistling 'Come Kiss Me Now', a popular dance air. An innocuous little tune in itself, it threatened to bring all her plans to a premature conclusion.

She squeezed her eyes tight shut but 'Come Kiss Me Now' etched itself across the darkness in zig-zags of dazzling light.

The Accidie.

'You all right, demselle?'

She opened her eyes and saw the stable lad staring at her.

'Yes . . .' she said, embarrassed.

He gave her a peculiar look, hefted up the nose-bags and disappeared into the nearest stall. At least he had stopped whistling.

'*Orial!*'

She looked around to see Alizaeth coming towards her, arms out-stretched, ribbons and laces streaming from an absurd little feathered hat perched like a sparrow on one side of her head.

There was no escape. Alizaeth's arms enfolded her and she dutifully kissed her friend on the cheek, almost overpowered by the sweet fragrance of lilac water.

'We've just returned this very minute from the capital. Such modish fashions, Orial! Look at my new bonnet – isn't it becoming? Alyn bought it for me – he's such a darling. Have you met him yet? There he is – collecting our baggage. Alyn – yoo-hoo! Come and meet my old school friend Orial.'

Of all Orial's acquaintance in Sulien, gossiping Alizaeth was the last she would have chosen to encounter.

'What are you doing here?' Alizaeth asked brightly. 'Going on a journey?'

Orial forced a smile, hoping that Alyn would take Alizaeth away.

'Bel'Esstar coach leaves in five minutes!' cried the coachman from the inn steps.

Where, oh where, was Cramoisy?

'Bel'Esstar? You're going to Bel'Esstar?' shrieked Alizaeth.

There was one ruse that might silence her old friend. Orial placed one finger to her lips.

'Can you keep a secret, Alizaeth? I'm eloping.'

'Eloping? How thrilling! But – with whom?'

'Hush. You're not to breathe a word. I would not have confided in you – if it were not for our long friendship.'

Alizaeth took Orial's hands in her own.

'I promise you. Not a word. But is *he* trustworthy, my sweet?'

'Bel'Esstar coach ready to depart!' The coachman had climbed up on to the driver's seat and was settling himself, spreading his cloak around him. He clicked his tongue to the horses, drawing the reins together in one hand. Stableboys ran to drag open the doors.

And there was still no sign of the Diva.

Orial bit her lip in vexation.

'Wait! Wait!'

The Diva came sweeping into the yard, one bejewelled hand imperiously upraised, scattering ostlers and stableboys. Behind him, two servants struggled with a heavy trunk.

Cramoisy climbed up into the diligence. He paused on the step and turned around and, with an arch smile, grandly beckoned to Orial.

'Hurry along now, *carissa*! You're holding up the driver.'

Alizaeth's mouth had dropped open in astonishment. Orial could just imagine what she would tell her friends: *'Orial Magelonne has eloped with a castrato, but then you know what they say about those castrati, my dear!'*

She gave Alizaeth's hand a farewell squeeze and, picking up her valise, ran across the yard to board the diligence.

*

211

'Ohh – ohh,' moaned Cramoisy. 'They've stopped the coach. They're going to arrest us.'

'Hush,' Orial said curtly. It was warm in the coach and the sickly scent of Alizaeth's lilac water still clung to her clothes. She was beginning to tire of the Diva's attacks of the vapours – partly because they were occurring with increasing frequency and partly because they were beginning to make her feel apprehensive too. She feared that Jerame might have set out after her – although she had done her best to ensure he would not discover her absence until they had crossed the border into Allegonde. And there was a far deeper fear. How long before the Accidie took hold again? How long before –

The coach door was opened.

'Your papers, please.' A Guerrior of the Commanderie stood at the open door; another stood further off, observing.

Orial presented their passes. Beyond the Guerrior she glimpsed vertiginous crags, brown cinder pines, a tumble of scree. From high above came the keening cry of a mountain hawk.

Cramoisy lay back against the cracked leather seat, fanning himself.

'Demselle Orial Magelonne? Eighteen years? Native of Tourmalise? A three-month permit to attend the Conservatoire in Bel'Esstar?' The Guerrior gave her a searching look and then glanced past her at Cramoisy.

'Cramoisy Jordelayne. The Diva.' He pronounced the name slowly, consideringly. 'You have been away a long while from Bel'Esstar, Diva.'

'I've been giving recitals,' Cramoisy snapped. 'That's what I do. I'm a singer. Is that a crime?'

'And the purpose of your journey, Diva?'

'I've had time to reflect . . . and I have decided to seek an audience with the Grand Maistre –'

A deep, distant rumble interrupted the Diva. The ground trembled and the horses twitched their heads uneasily, setting their bridles jingling.

'What's that noise? Thunder?' Cramoisy craned his neck to stare up at the sky. 'I can't see any clouds. Is there a storm coming?'

Orial saw the Guerrior glance at his companion; the papers were hastily stamped and handed back.

'Continue with your journey.'

The coach pulled away from the border post.

'Didn't you think that strange?' Orial said. 'Thunder – without a cloud in the sky? What exactly *are* the Commanderie doing up here, so close to Sulien?'

'Just be thankful they didn't ask any more questions.'

'It sounded like firedust. Are they testing out new weapons? Arquebuses? Cannons?'

'You should never have come.' Cramoisy was not paying attention to what she was saying. 'Your father will never forgive me for allowing it.'

'But there was no problem! They stamped our papers, they let us through!'

'And now news of my return will reach the capital long before us. Grand Maistre Girim will have his reception party prepared.'

'Shall we turn back then?' Orial cried. 'Shall we leave Khassian to his fate?'

'You should turn back, yes. It's not your battle, *carissa*.'

'All we need to do is to find Captain Korentan and explain the mistake. He seemed a fair-minded man. I believe he might be prevailed upon to help us.'

'Tcha! So naive!' Cramoisy began fanning himself again.

'How so?' Orial asked, flushing. 'How naive?'

'Since when has the Commanderie been fair in its dealings?'

The coach juddered and creaked as it began its erratic descent towards the river plain far below.

'But the case my father brought against Khassian can be quashed.' Orial caught hold of the leather strap as the coach swerved to the right. 'Here I am! Living proof!'

'My dear child, the Commanderie would have seized on any excuse to get Khassian back into their clutches. He is their trump card. If he capitulates then all resistance to the Commanderie will collapse. Don't misunderstand me, I admire what you are doing. And I know you are doing it for the best of reasons. But Girim nel Ghislain will not give up until Khassian has prostrated himself at his feet in Mhir's shrine and made full public confession that his opera was decadent and dissolute. I fear we are wasting our time.'

'Ouf!' Cramoisy reached into his reticule and brought out a metal flask. 'More cordial?'

Orial listlessly shook her head. Cramoisy had added a little spirit to the dilute elderflower cordial but even the dash of alcohol did not improve the metallic taste of the lukewarm liquid.

It was bakingly hot inside the coach and the tannery smell of hot leather was beginning to make her feel queasy. She opened the window – but a cloud of dust from the road forced her to close it again to just a crack.

'Is it always this hot in summer?'

'On the Dniera plain? Always. Sometimes there are thunderstorms – terrifying thunderstorms that sweep across the plain till it boils with water like a vast lake.'

Orial gazed out of the window, checking for clouds. There were none against the burning sheen of the sky – but there was a distant shadow on the horizon.

'Is that Bel'Esstar?'

Cramoisy leaned across to take a look.

'And not before time. If I have to spend much longer in this oven of a coach, I shall expire!'

'City of a Million Lights,' Orial said softly. The name conjured visions of candle-lit concerts, the royal chapel echoing to the sweet voices of the boys' choir, the glittering stage of the great Opera House itself . . .

The visions faded into smoke, dispersing like charred fragments of a burning manuscript.

There was no Opera House. The Prince's preferred music nowadays, Cramoisy had said with a sniff, was the Psalms of Mhir or the battle-hymns of the Commanderie.

A small, persistent voice kept whispering that she was on a fool's errand. Who would pay attention to an insignificant doctor's daughter? She was wasting her time.

Too late to turn back now. She must finish what she had begun.

She kept her gaze fixed on the shadow of the city as it slowly grew – until it filled the horizon.

'Mind your head, Captain Korentan,' called the Guerrior.

Acir ducked just in time to avoid grazing his forehead on the low arch. His feet slopped through muddy water that seemed perpetually to drip off the glistening walls. The old prison stank of mould; it would take more than a coat of whitewash to make it habitable. Demolition was the most appropriate solution, he thought wryly. Ironic that so many men and women should be imprisoned here in squalor – and forced to labour all their waking hours to build a house for a god.

'This wing has still to be fully restored.' said the Guerrior over his shoulder. He stopped and, selecting a key from the ring he wore at his belt, unlocked the door at the far end of the low-arched passageway.

The Sanctuaree was gaunt and hollow-cheeked. Shabby work overalls, powdered with stone dust, hung loosely on his emaciated frame. Acir noticed that he flinched whenever the Guerriors touched him. Only in his sunken eyes a dark spark of defiance still glimmered.

'Sanctuaree number 137, Captain,' announced the one of the Guerriors.

'That will be all, confrères,' he said. 'You may go.'

The Guerriors glanced at each other.

'Is anything wrong?' Acir looked up at them.

'Our orders are to stay, in case the prisoner –'

'Then your orders are changed. You will stay outside until I call you.'

Acir waited until the door was closed and he was alone with number 137.

'You have a name?'

'What's it to you?' the Sanctuaree said.

Acir opened the folder containing the record of the man's imprisonment.

The stark facts in front of him told him that Gualtier Tomasin had been a claveciniste and repetiteur at the Opera. He was also the composer of several 'degenerate works of music, written in an uncompromising style wholly unsuited to the needs of the new regime in Bel'Esstar'.

'I see that you have been brought here regularly for spiritual counselling since your arrival.'

A tremor animated the man's lips, the twisted parody of a smile.

'So what is it to be this week? Another letter from my wife? Our son is sick, she has no more money for medicine, no money for food. If only I would overcome my pride and do as the Commanderie wish . . .'

'There are no letters,' Acir said, searching the folder.

'Oh, so that's the tactic now? Leave me wondering why, what's become of them? You won't break me that way, confrère. I've listened to your Commanderie fabrications for too long.'

Acir did not respond. Shame had tied his tongue. Nothing he said would change Gualtier Tomasin's view of the Commanderie – but what Gualtier Tomasin had said revealed a great deal about the Guerriors in the Sanctuary.

He closed the folder.

'You call yourselves men of god. What kind of a god has priests who starve and torture their charges? Who imprison a man for stringing together a few notes of music in the wrong style? Your god couldn't give a fig about my music.' Tomasin's thin face was twisted with anger. 'Surely gods have better things to do than concern themselves with such petty issues? Surely –'

The door was flung open and the Guerriors ran in, seizing hold of the musician, pinning his arms behind his back.

'No, no!' shouted Tomasin. He went on shouting as they wrestled him to the floor.

Acir rose to his feet, furious.

'Who summoned you?'

'Sanctuaree's out of control. Governor's orders – to intervene.'

One flung open the small door beyond Acir's table.

'Not the inner chamber! Not the inner chamber!' screamed Tomasin hoarsely.

They bundled him into the lightless room and slammed the door shut. Tomasin beat on the door with his fists, still screaming.

'Governor's orders!' repeated Acir coldly above his screams. 'What about *my* orders?'

'This one's a trouble-maker. He stirs the others up.'

'Because he has been maltreated. Locked and left in the dark. Beaten. Now take him out of there before he has a fit.'

The Guerriors looked at each other.

'The Governor won't like it.'

'The Governor can bring his complaint to me. Get him out of there.'

They unlocked the door and Tomasin fell out on to his knees. He looked up at Acir and his bloodshot eyes narrowed.

'You won't break me this way. They've tried that trick too. *You'll never break me.*'

The Fortress of Faith towered above Acir Korentan.

A group of Sanctuarees were hauling a block of stone up to the second tier, using a pulley; Acir could hear the creak and groan of wood and rope, strained to the utmost by the weight of the massive block, the grunts of the men as they heaved on the rope.

Gazing upwards, he saw the stone rise slowly, jerkily above his head – too jerkily.

Instinct saved him – he flung himself to the ground and rolled away as the stone came crashing back down, thudding into the earth at the exact spot where he had been standing.

Guerriors rushed towards him.

'Captain, are you all right?'

Stumbling to his feet, Acir brushed the earth from his uniform.

'Unharmed,' he said shakily.

The whole site had stilled; even the incessant din of chisels and mallets fell silent. Everyone stared up at the Sanctuarees high above on the platform.

'The rope,' cried one of the Guerriors, picking up the still-dangling end. 'It's been cut.'

'Show me.' Acir took the rope from the Guerrior. The rope had not frayed with wear – the strands were evenly severed. A deliberate act of sabotage. They had meant to kill him. To crush him with the block which now lay before him, half-buried by the impact in the earth.

'Bring those men down!' The Guerriors made for the ladders and began to climb towards the huddle of Sanctuarees on the platform.

'Wait!' Acir detected a flicker of movement, the brief glint of light on an upraised blade.

High above, one of the Sanctuarees teetered on the edge of the platform – and suddenly came toppling down to land sprawled on the trampled grass at Acir's feet. The sharpened chisel he had clutched speared into the earth a foot away.

Acir knelt and tried to raise the dying man in his arms. Blood glistened on the Sanctuaree's face.

'Careful, Captain!' shouted the Guerrior.

'Gualtier Tomasin,' whispered Acir, recognising him. 'Why? Why this way?'

The Sanctuaree's eyes opened. His mouth strove to form words.

'My blood be on . . . your conscience, Guerrior . . .' The musician choked and a gush of crimson flooded from his mouth. The broken body convulsed as the eyes slid skywards.

Acir laid him down and closed the sightless eyes.

'Go in peace,' he said softly.

Looking up, he saw the Guerriors had brought down number 137's companions from the platform; he saw the fear and hostility in their eyes.

'Don't you worry, Captain. We'll get confessions from all three. Attempted murder.'

'No.' Acir stood up. 'There is no need. 137 confessed.'

'But these were his accomplices –'

'The incident is over. I'll be writing a report. There'll be no further charges.' Mechanically he began to straighten his jacket – and his hands came away sticky with 137's blood.

' "And I believe it was his intention to kill me – or die in the attempt. The attack on my person was unpremeditated, clumsy and spontaneous. Further investigation is therefore unnecessary." '

Acir finished reading his report aloud to the Grand Maistre and stood waiting for his response.

After several moments' silence, Girim looked up.

'I'm afraid I must disagree with you. I smell dissent. I want those men interrogated.'

Acir was still shaken after the morning's events. He had spent all afternoon trying to find details of the whereabouts of the dead Sanctuaree's family. No one seemed to know – or maybe to want to tell him. If his sources were correct, Gualtier Tomasin's wife had fled the capital to her parents' farm on the plain of Dniera. A messenger had been sent bearing the terse report of 137's death. Acir had wanted to go himself but had been denied permission.

The whole business disgusted him.

'I can't see that interrogation – torture – will be of any use. Under extreme duress men will say anything.'

Girim rose from his desk and came over to him.

'I know you are saying this for the very best of reasons, Acir. But these unbelievers are subtle. Can't you see what they are doing to you? Take a firm line with them. Force is the only thing they understand.'

'But why can we not co-exist with those who wish to follow their own beliefs? Why must we use force?'

'These liberal ideas are the flowers lining the way to the pit of despair. Exotically beautiful, alluring – but to breathe their scent is to breathe a deadly poison. Why else did Mhir call the path of righteousness the "Path of Thorns"? It was never an easy path.'

217

For years Acir had followed Mhir's banner, followed the Thorny Path, strong in the belief that it led to the realisation of a dream: Girim's dream, the dream he had shared.

'Look, Acir.' Girim drew back the heavy curtains. 'Look at the city.'

In the blue twilight, lights glimmered in windows, street lights illuminated squares and boulevards. An inky lake filled with a myriad reflected star-shards.

City of a Million Lights.

'We have carried Mhir's banner back to his city. We have set up his standard so that all may know this is his Holy city. Now we must ensure all is in readiness for His coming.'

Acir stared out unseeing at the starry lights of Bel'Esstar.

They had brought the banner back – but now it was tattered, battle-torn, soaked in the blood of innocents.

The Commanderie had lost its way. Led by Girim nel Ghislain, the Guerriors had taken the wrong road, they had followed the path of vanity and self-delusion. They were marching to damnation, dragging down the people they had sought to save, dragging them into the mire.

Couldn't Girim see what he had done?

The city lights suddenly dimmed and blurred. Acir blinked – and felt wetness on his cheeks.

'I see tears in your eyes, Acir. You know what I say to be true.'

Yes, he thought. *I was dazzled by your rhetoric. But my tears have washed away the dazzle and I see you as you truly are. A man drunk with his own powers, inflated with his own self-importance.*

I worshipped you. Girim. You were my ideal. The man I most looked up to, the man with a dream. I would have followed you into the dark.

He saw his path only too clearly now. He was the standard bearer, he had to take up the tattered remnants of Mhir's banner and lave away the stains that besmirched it. He must carry it through the last of the light – no matter what the cost.

CHAPTER 20

Khassian's face itched with several days' dark growth of beard. His stomach rumbled.

God, he was starving. Why was his empty stomach the only thing he could think of?

At first he had disdained to eat the Sanctuary food. Then by the end of the second day he was so ravenous he had got down on hands and knees on the flagstones and gulped the millet porridge from the bowl like a dog.

Now he had become quite skilful at raising the bowl to his mouth, using his stiffened hands as a crude scoop. The process was inelegant – but who was to see if porridge dribbled out of one side of his mouth, if he slopped soup down his shirt?

Two meagre meals a day. Were they trying to starve him into submission?

He kicked at the door of his cell until his stubbed toes protested.

'Get me a lawyer. You have no right to hold me here against my will. I want to see a lawyer.'

No response, as usual. He waited a while and then shouted out again.

'The Prince is my patron! I demand to send a message to the Prince!'

He had nearly shouted himself hoarse when the door was suddenly unlocked and a bearded Guerrior appeared, his broad bulk filling the doorway.

'This is a place of silence and meditation. You are disturbing the concentration of the other Sanctuarees.'

'I don't care!' Khassian snarled. 'I demand my rights as a citizen of Bel'Esstar. I demand –'

The Guerrior struck him across the head. Khassian fell to the floor, dizzy, ears ringing from the blow.

'H-how dare you!'

'You will keep silence,' said the Guerrior, slamming the door.

Khassian put one hand up to his stinging ear and brought it away, moist with blood.

The Diva had been gone five hours.

Orial went to the window of the villa and gazed out again over the street. No sign or sound of a carriage. The River Faubourg drowsed under a heavy sky.

They had been installed for several days in the Diva's riverside residence, the Villa of Yellow Vines, days which had been filled with writing letters and petitions on Khassian's behalf. This morning the Commanderie carriage had arrived without warning to escort the Diva to the Winter Palace. The invitation – to attend upon the Prince at his levee – was most pressing. The Guerriors would not even wait for the Diva to change into a costume more fitting for the occasion.

Since then, there had been no word and Orial had fretted away the hours alone. The housekeeper had brought her some lunch; she had tried to eat but felt so sick with apprehension that she only managed to swallow a spoonful or two of the delicious iced tea-cream dessert.

The Diva must have been arrested. That was the only explanation for so long an absence. All her plans had been aborted before there was time to put them into action.

There came a distant rattle of hoofs over gravel. Orial sped to the open window, leaning far out over the vine-covered sill. A carriage drew up at the gates; a man climbed out.

'Diva!' cried Orial.

She ran down the stairs and flung open the door to greet him, hugging him tight.

'Such effusion!' said Cramoisy. 'Anyone would think you had not seen me in years.'

'What happened? Why were you gone so long? Did you see the Prince?'

Cramoisy sank into a fauteuil and kicked off his shoes.

'My ankles are quite swollen with standing so long. Court levees are a terrible trial on the legs, *carissa*.' His voice was hoarse with strain.

'But did you see Prince Ilsevir?'

'His Royal Highness was gracious enough to grant me an audience. We agreed that I will make my confession before the court in the royal chapel. He wanted me to sing an aria or two from Talfieri's new oratorio *The Path of Thorns*.' Cramoisy made a little moue of disgust. 'I was almost glad to tell him that my voice is ruined for I cannot abide the man's music. And do you know, Orial, what Ilsevir then said to me?'

'No . . .'

' "We shall pray together for your voice to be restored. Perhaps the Blessed Mhir will restore your voice as He restored me to health." ' Cramoisy pulled a grimace. 'I preferred Ilsevir as he was before – this sanctimoniousness makes me queasy.'

'But what of Khassian?'

'Ilsevir would not talk of him. I know he heard what I said. We may yet achieve something . . .' There was a slight tic at the corner of Cramoisy's left eye; the strain of the encounter had not left him unscathed. 'And you'll never guess who I saw as the carriage was driving through the Winter Gardens?'

Orial shook her head.

'Captain Korentan! Striding along with a face as dark as thunder.'

'Captain Korentan?' Orial said consideringly. 'Maybe he would help us. Maybe I should go in search of him . . .'

'Heavens, no, *carissa*! A young girl out alone in Bel'Esstar? You must remember you are not in Sulien now. Men can go where women cannot. You must leave the negotiating to me.'

Time seemed to have lost its meaning. The sun set and the solitary cell grew dark. The sun rose again.

Khassian hunched in a corner.

He would not recant.

If only they would let him send a message to Prince Ilsevir. If the Prince knew they were holding him here like an animal in a cage, he would surely order Girim to release him? Even if Ilsevir no longer cherished him as his favourite, he still respected him as a musician.

Khassian let his eyes drift slowly shut, remembering . . .

There had always been a special understanding between the Prince and his young protégé. It had begun when Amaru and Fania had been brought to perform before the court and Ilsevir had smiled at the 'charming moppets' and given them each a bag of sugared almonds and a gold medal. A year or so later, the young chorister from the royal chapel had been singled out to sing and play for the Prince . . . and not long after Fania's death, Khassian had found himself the royal favourite, showered with money and favours, his training paid for by the Prince himself.

At first, Khassian had felt desperately out of his depth. He was aware of his own beauty, yet not certain how to react to the Prince's admiration. And then, as he grew more self-assured, he had begun to enjoy the attention, to manipulate it ruthlessly to his own advantage.

He had taken all that Ilsevir had to offer in gifts, honours – and commissions.

And in return, he'd granted the Prince . . . the occasional favour.

Khassian let his head drop back until it rested against the white-washed wall of the cell. White of lime-washed walls . . . Ilsevir had always favoured the pale, bleached colours of winter. Through half-closed lids Khassian glimpsed again Ilsevir's bedchamber with its stucco walls: a winter landscape of white, grey and gold, Ilsevir, lingering in the ivory-draped bed, calling for him to come back to his side . . . whilst Khassian, all physical passion forgotten, sat at the desk scribbling away feverishly, his head filled with a glory of sound . . .

Ilsevir had always been seeking after the unattainable, Khassian saw it now so clearly. For years the Prince had pursued him, hoping perhaps that he might absorb a little of his beautiful boy's genius by some mysterious, carnal alchemy . . .

Maybe if he could have shown more kindness to his benefactor, maybe if he had not been so absorbed in his own musical projects, Ilsevir would not have turned his back on earthly pleasures – or have been so easily swayed by the visionary sermons of Girim nel Ghislain.

But Ilsevir had wanted more than kindness from his protégé. He had wanted his heart, his soul. Unable to create his own compositions, Ilsevir had sought to gain control of Khassian's music. *This phrase was too angular, that modulation too unexpected, too harsh . . .*

Khassian shuddered, remembering disagreements, clashes, ugly scenes. Words that should never have been spoken; cruel, bitter words. Words that could not be unsaid. His head drooped slowly forward until his forehead rested on his updrawn knees.

Ilsevir would not help him now . . . not unless he capitulated to all Girim's demands.

And he would not recant. He would never recant.

Khassian's cell door was flung open and two Guerriors came in. One grabbed his wrists and twisted them behind his back, forcing him to his knees. Khassian struggled. Another seized his head between his hands, twisting it sideways.

Pincers bit into Khassian's ear-lobe. He yelped aloud, outraged at the indignity. A metal tag was forced into his tender flesh and firmly clamped down with tongs. The metal tag, heavy and cold, grazed against his neck, pulling the torn lobe down. Blood spattered his grey tunic.

His pierced ear on fire, he stared at his oppressors, speechless.

'Now, move.'

'Wh-where are you taking me?'

'You can't leave the Sanctuary without a tag.'

In the yard outside, the daylight hurt his eyes. The Guerriors pushed him up a ramp into a wagon where they chained his wrists to the seat.

The wagon left the Sanctuary and trundled away across the heath.

Narrowing his eyes against the sunglare, he saw an extraordinary structure on the horizon, a monstrous unfinished building whose jagged walls were swarming with workers.

At first he had not recognised them. And then, as face after face had slowly turned towards him, he had seen the flicker of recognition in their eyes – and he had known them.

The unlucky ones. The ones who had not got away in time. His musicians. His singers, his orchestra. The cast of the ill-fated opera.

Clad only in filthy overalls, they laboured to move the huge blocks of stone. They were covered in stone-dust, their hair and faces powdered.

The air was thick with the choking dust; it dried Khassian's throat, it settled on his lashes. He could see how their efforts to shift the stones had lacerated their hands; fingers which had once moved over strings and keys to produce sounds of delicacy and subtlety, were now bleeding, torn by the coarse stones.

They did not dare to acknowledge him. He saw how their eyes slid away, avoiding contact, how their shoulders drooped as they turned from him back to their work.

He wanted to cry out to them, 'Don't give up! Don't let them break you!' but the wagon moved on, taking the road into the city.

The twilit avenue was filled with a sea of bobbing torches; a procession of citizens was winding down towards the Winter Palace. They were singing, chanting the Psalms of Mhir.

'What is this? Why are they singing?'

His guards still did not answer; the wagon followed the procession to the Winter Palace.

On the torchlit balcony of the Grand Maistre's appartments, Khassian saw the figure of a man, clad in a simple white robe. Girim nel Ghislain stood beside him, attended upon by several of the Commanderie.

As the chanted psalm died away, Girim nel Ghislain lifted his arms to the crowd.

'The unbeliever repents. Rejoice with me as yet another convert is born again into the Faith.' He turned to the white-clad man beside him who dropped to his knees and kissed the hem of his robe. Girim nel Ghislain placed his hands upon his bowed head – and then raised the man to his feet again, embracing him.

A cheer rose from the crowd and the chanting began again.

'The moment is drawing nearer,' Girim cried. 'The time is almost upon us. But not until all have bowed to the name of Mhir will He know that His city is ready to receive Him again.'

Khassian watched in growing fury.

'Why insult my intelligence by forcing me to watch this charade? Who ordered me to be brought here?'

'The Grand Maistre himself. He felt it would prove edifying.'

That night as Khassian lay sleepless in his cell, he saw nothing but the musicians' eyes – empty of accusation, empty of hope, empty of everything except exhaustion.

So many fine musicians, sensitive, skilled performers, whose only crime had been to make music – *his* music – condemned to an endless misery of hard labour.

'Next.' Acir pretended to be examining the nib of his pen and did not even glance up as the two Guerriors brought Amaru Khassian into the chamber.

'Sit down,' he said. He would not look Khassian in the eyes, not in the presence of the Guerriors. He was too afraid he would betray their familiarity – and now everything hinged on his remaining aloof, preserving the appearance of the dedicated Commanderie officer.

'I prefer to stand.'

Acir flinched, hearing blatant defiance in Khassian's voice. He looked up and saw what the ravages of Sanctuary life had done to the musician. Hair matted, unkempt, face grimy beneath a ragged growth of beard, Sanctuary overalls stained with slopped food. Only the eyes were recognisable – though now they stared wildly back at Acir, burning with an ungovernable fury.

'Leave us,' he said to the Guerriors.

'The Sanctuaree could be violent, Captain.'

Had they been given orders not to leave them alone together? Exactly what had Fiammis told Girim – and what had the Grand Maistre deduced from her report?

Acir slowly turned around. He allowed his mouth to curve in an ironic smile.

'I think I am well able to look after myself, confrère.'

The two Guerriors released Khassian's arms and stepped back, saluting. The door clicked shut behind them.

Acir hastily came round the desk to Khassian, reaching out to him.

Khassian raised his unkempt head and spat, hitting him in the face.

Acir stopped.

He felt the spittle trickling down his cheek.

A riot of conflicting feelings burst in his heart – but he willed himself to betray no emotion. He reached into his pocket and drew out a handkerchief, slowly wiping Khassian's spittle from his cheek.

'Come on, Captain Korentan. Aren't you going to hit me?'

Acir put away his handkerchief, each movement deliberately slow and considered, taking time to regain his self-control. This was going to need as much skill as he could summon – and even then the risk of failure was great. At least there was no grille in the door through which they could spy on the interview.

'I respected you. I came to believe you were different from the rest of your cursed Commanderie. Why don't you just hand me over to those thugs outside and let them beat me senseless?'

'Have you quite finished?' Acir said briskly.

'No. The food's inedible. I'm crawling with lice, I can't even scratch –'

'Amar! For Mhir's sake, listen to me!' Acir wanted to grip him by the shoulders, to shake him until the bitter, incoherent stream of complaints ceased. 'I want to help you. But you've got to trust me.'

'Trust you!' Khassian threw back his head and began to laugh. And then the laughter choked into sobs; his shoulders began to heave.

Anguished, Acir could only stand lamely by and watch. After a while he began to speak; quietly, insistently, hoping the sound of his voice would eventually penetrate Khassian's grief.

'You are going to have to call on all your theatrical skills. You are going to have to act the unwilling convert. Just as I will have to act the interrogator. We are going to play at priest and penitent. There is no other way I can get time alone with you – to relay messages to you, to plan your escape. Are you hearing what I'm saying? This is the only way no one will suspect.'

Khassian wiped his streaming eyes and nose on the filthy sleeve of his tunic.

'It's just another game. Cat and mouse. You played this game with me in Sulien. I'm not playing this time.'

'Maybe you saw it as a game in Sulien. Now there are others, many others, relying on you. But if you want to give up . . .' Acir shrugged. 'It's your choice.'

'Wait,' Khassian said, voice still thick with tears. 'Others? This is just another trap. I play along with you – implicate others – and then the Commanderie arrests us all. No promise of conversion this time. Conspiracy trial, and execution.'

Behind the desk Acir dug his nails into his palms. Damn the man! Was he always going to be this stubborn?

'I heard them singing your song at the Fortress of Faith: "Freedom". Until they were beaten into silence. But they won't be silenced forever. You've given them hope. They'll be singing "Freedom" again.'

'Why are you doing this? Is this some kind of Commanderie power struggle? Perhaps you want to be Grand Maistre in Girim's stead?'

'Me – Grand Maistre!' The preposterous suggestion incensed Acir.

'It doesn't make sense.' Khassian gazed doubtingly into Acir's face. 'I thought you really believed it? When you spoke of your faith, you spoke from the heart.'

The door opened and the two Guerriors appeared.

'How dare you interrupt this interview?' Acir cried.

'Governor's orders. Each Sanctuaree is entitled to a half-hour. No less, no more.'

'And so you interrupt without even the courtesy of a knock at the door?'

'We have our orders, Captain.'

Had they overheard the last of the conversation? Were they well-trained at spying – or merely doing as they were ordered?

'Very well. But when you are interrupting *my* interviews, you will knock at the door and you will wait for me to tell you to enter.' He fixed each Guerrior in turn with his eyes, unblinking. 'Do you understand?'

'Understood, Captain!' barked the elder of the two.

'And bring me no more Sanctuarees until I have completed my reports for the Grand Maistre.' Acir sat down again and drew out a clean piece of paper from the sheaf on his desk. When they made no move, he looked up again, feigning irritation. 'Well, what are you waiting for? Take this one away.'

The Guerriors took hold of Khassian by the arms and hurried him out of the chamber. Acir listened as their footsteps died away into the distance, listened until all he could hear was the pounding of his own heart and the perpetual slow drip-drip of water.

He exhaled slowly, raggedly. He picked up the pen, dipped it in the inkwell, and then saw that his hand was trembling so much that spots of black ink spattered down upon the clean page even before the nib had touched the paper.

Khassian let the Guerriors manhandle him back to his cell. He was glad to rely on their rough strength as his head was light with hunger. There was a clean, scrubbed smell to them: even their sweat smelt of strong soap. He concentrated on the physical sensation, trying to forget what had just happened.

But he could not forget. The shock of seeing those steel-blue eyes in the interrogation cell had quite unmanned him. Time had flickered about them and he had found himself back staring into those same eyes, as freezing riverwater cascaded from Acir's hair on to his face.

'You should have let me drown . . .'

And the irony of the situation had suddenly seemed foolishly, crazily funny. When the laughter began, he just could not stop it. Painful, racking laughter that seemed to tear from his throat, convulsing his body until the tears started from his eyes.

Of course he had not been crying. They were tears of laughter, scornful, defiant laughter.

If it had been anyone but Acir Korentan –

Now that he was alone, he began to recall fragments of the extraordinary interview.

'You've got to trust me.'

And had he imagined it – or had Acir Korentan really called him by his first name? How dare he be so familiar! And yet just remembering sent a shiver through him . . . a shiver of hope.

No.

It must be a deliberate ploy.

He had heard of such tricks of interrogation. The interrogator would befriend the prisoner, win his trust . . . and then draw the information he needed from him by stealth.

And yet Acir Korentan had never played him false. He had been open in all his dealings with him. Acir Korentan had even warned him of

Fiammis – and he, like a fool, had laughed the warning aside.

'*Trust me . . .*'

How much he ached to trust him. To know there was one person in Bel'Esstar upon whom he could rely.

Khassian drew his legs up to his chest, resting his chin on his knees, holding in the gnawing pain in his empty belly.

At that moment he would have betrayed his own father for a loaf of fresh-baked bread.

'Dr Magelonne – there's something wrong with the water supply to the treatment pools.'

Sister Crespine's voice penetrated Jerame's consciousness – but as if from a great distance away. All he could think about was Orial's note.

She was gone.

'What are we to do? I shall have to send the patients away. Without spa water for the treatments –'

'Mm? What's that?' He looked at her, blinking. He realised he had not heard a word she said.

'The patients, Doctor!' Her voice was crisp with exasperation. 'Do I send them away? I've called for the ingenieur to come and check the pipes.'

'The water supply?' Jerame began to take notice of what she was saying. 'Have we a leaky pipe? A fault in the hydraulic system?'

The first thing he noticed as they approached the treatment pools was the absence of humidity. His spectacle lenses did not steam over. The little hot bath and the exercise pool were almost empty, the tiles covered with a thin film of greenish water.

'A crack beneath the tiles?' He squatted on the edge of the pool to get a closer look.

'Message for Doctor Magelonne!' An errand boy appeared in the doorway, waving a paper.

'What's this?' Jerame unfolded the paper. ' "Unavoidable delay in answering your request for assistance." This is unacceptable! I have patients waiting for treatment!' He hadn't the time to go chasing after ingenieurs, sorting out plumbing faults. He had to start looking for Orial.

'It's the same all over,' stammered the boy.

'What d'you mean, all over?'

'All over the city, Doctor. All the baths, all the pools.'

Jerame looked at Sister Crespine. She gave a perplexed little shrug.

'Shoddy maintenance! Scrimping on essential works! I've been warning them about this for years. I trust the Mayor has been informed.'

'They're saying it's bad luck 'cause the dragonflies didn't fly.'

'Silly superstitions!' snorted Jerame. He spun the boy a coin. 'Go on, boy. Here's for your pains. Tell your master I'll be pleased to see him just as soon as he can get here.'

'I've heard the self-same rumours,' Sister Crespine said when the boy had pocketed his tip and gone. 'It's not just the Sanatorium. The Temple is closed. They say the sacred springs have dried to a trickle . . .'

'Impossible,' Jerame said. 'We've had plentiful rain in the past years. Springs don't just dry up overnight.'

'Not without divine intervention . . .'

'Oh, Crespine, I'd believed better of you! Don't tell me you give credence to all this talk of the vengeance of the Goddess?'

Sister Crespine opened her mouth – and then snapped it shut again.

'We can offer manipulation today.' Jerame turned and made for the stairs. 'Any patient who can be treated without immersion or hot mud can still be seen.'

'And if they want to see you?' Sister Crespine called from the foot of the stairs.

'I have to go to the Constabulary. Book them an appointment later . . .'

A noisy crowd filled the street outside the Guildhall. Crudely painted banners proclaimed 'Restore Our Hot Water'. Jerame hastily skirted around the edge of crowd, hoping no one would recognise him and ask him to join their protest. He had no time to spare in his search for Orial.

But as he reached the Constabulary, he met the Commissaire coming down the steps in company with several of his constables.

Jerame hailed him.

'Any news of my daughter?'

'I'm sorry, Doctor Magelonne, all my men have been busy investigating this business at the springs. Now there's unrest outside the Guildhall. And as you have no proof of forced entry into your property – or abduction – there's little I can do.'

And the Commissaire walked on past him.

'Damn!' Jerame sat down on the Constabulary steps. Every trail he followed petered out. He had had posters put up about the city, offering a reward for information as to Orial's whereabouts. But the disappearance of one girl seemed to matter little to a spa city whose water supply had suddenly, inexplicably, dried up.

Acir reined his horse to a halt in the shade of a clump of silver-leaved poplars and dismounted.

A thin stream trickled over gravel beneath the poplars; he led the bay to the water and let it drink. Swarms of black flies buzzed under the leaves; the horse swished its tail vigorously as it drank. Acir drew out his water-bottle and drank too. It was hot and humid, even in the shade of the fluttering leaves, but it was not the dry, intense heat of the desert which seared the skin and made the air taste of fire and dust. On balance, he

228

thought, wiping the sweat from his face, he preferred that intense desert heat to this uncomfortable stickiness.

Propping himself against a poplar trunk, he took out his orders from his jacket and re-read them.

'Report to me on progress at the Sanctuary Quarry. Marcien is the Commanderie officer in charge. Assess the situation. We need more stone for the Fortress. Do they need more Sanctuarees?'

A junior officer could have carried out this mission equally competently. So there must be a reason why Girim wanted Captain Korentan out of Bel'Esstar today.

In the distance the mountains that divided Allegonde from verdant Tourmalise shimmered in a blue haze of heat.

Inscribed below the written orders was a map; when he looked at the site of the Quarry, it seemed more close to Tourmalise than Allegonde. Girim could have elected to build his Fortress from Allegondan granite. This insistence on costly red stone could be seen as further proof of a disordered mind – or as an act of ultimate devotion to the Faith.

It was past midday when Acir reached the shade of the mountains. Glad of the fresher air, he stopped again to check his map.

Suddenly the ground rocked as a dull thud reverberated through the air. Choughs rose up in a black cloud, circling and cawing in panic.

His startled horse whinnied and shied. He pulled hard on the reins, stroking the brown head and murmuring reassuringly.

An explosion – deep within the mountain.

As he rode on up the road, he saw indisputable evidence of quarrying: traces of fine red dust powdered the bushes and brambles.

A little further on he had to pull his horse in to the side of the road to make way for a cart drawn by a team of oxen, laden with blocks of fresh-quarried stone, heading down to the Dniera and the stone barges.

Around the next bend, the road suddenly opened up and Acir found himself gazing at a vast excavation in the mountainside, a raw, red gash.

Here everything was clogged with red dust; the road, the few stunted trees, the rocks. In this barren hollow, men were working, tiny as ants against the sides of the cavernous bowl that had been hacked out of the hill.

'Good day to you, confrère.'

A Guerrior approached Acir, striking his hand to his heart in salute.

Acir returned the salute.

'Where is Captain Marcien? I've come from the Grand Maistre with new instructions.'

'I'll take you to him. Follow me.'

Clouds of choking dust blew into their faces as they entered the quarry.

'We've been blasting a new tunnel,' said the Guerrior, taking out a kerchief to cover his nose and mouth.

'Blasting?' Acir wiped the dust from his watering eyes. 'Do you use explosive charges often?'

'The best stone is in the heart of the mountain. We have to go in deep.'

Acir frowned. 'Into Tourmalise?'

A look of suspicion flashed across the Guerrior's face.

'Have there been complaints?'

They had reached a wooden shack tucked under an overhang. The Guerrior gestured to Acir to dismount and took his horse's reins.

An officer came storming out. He was caked in stone dust; even his beard and eyebrows were thick with red powder.

'Who the deuce are –' He stopped, seeing Acir's badge of office. 'Ah, Captain. Welcome.' His eyes, startlingly green amidst the dust, belied the words of welcome, staring at Acir with overt hostility.

Acir began to relay the Grand Maistre's message. Before he had finished, Marcien erupted.

'More stone! Tell him we need more workers. More Sanctuarees. There's been sickness with the heat. Bad water.'

'Heat sickness?' Acir said, suddenly alert. 'Let me see them. I served in the desert. I have some expertise in these matters –'

'That won't be possible,' Marcien said hurriedly.

Now Acir was certain: Marcien was hiding something.

'Take me to them.'

'You've come at a most inopportune time.'

'I'll be making a full report, Marcien. If you have been concealing anything from the Commanderie –'

'Confound you and your report.' Marcien glared at him. 'You pen-pushers – what do you know about the risks of quarrying stone?'

He led Acir towards the entrance to a cave.

In the dank, cool air, he saw forms lying on the cave floor, human forms covered in bloodstained sacking.

Bodies.

Marcien flicked back the sacking from the nearest, watching Acir's face. He forced himself to show no emotion; he sensed that Marcien wanted to shock him – and yet it was hard not to feel pity at the sight of the twisted, crushed corpse.

'How?' he asked.

'Rockfall. We were blasting deeper into the mountain and the tunnel caved in.'

'Any survivors?'

'One. He's so badly injured he won't last the night.'

'I'll need a list of the names of the dead to take back to Bel'Esstar. For the records.'

'You and your damned Commanderie records. *I* need fresh men. Fresh supplies. Tell Girim that. Then he'll get more stone.' Marcien went out of the cave towards the shack.

Acir knelt down and gently replaced the sacking over the dead Sanctuaree, murmuring the Obsequy from the Requiem Canticles. There was already a buzz of flies at the cave entrance; he feared this perfunctory farewell would be the only form of funeral rites granted to the dead Sanctuarees.

'Here's your list.' Marcien thrust a paper in front of Acir's face. Acir glanced down the list of numbers and names beside them.

'All Sanctuarees.'

'The Sanctuarees are here to work the stone – and we're here to see that they get on with it.'

Acir swung around to face him.

'I take exception to your attitude, confrère. Men cannot work in these inhuman conditions!'

'Oh, but they can – and they do.' Marcien smiled at him, an openly provocative smile, baring his teeth.

'You'll have no workforce left if you make them labour through the heat of midday – and keep them in the tunnels when you're blasting.'

'You make my heart bleed,' Marcien was jeering at him. 'Have you forgotten who these men are? Convicted criminals. Rebels. They'd slit our throats and make off across the border if we didn't watch them night and day.'

'But these names!' Acir struck the sheet with his hand. 'These men were not murderers. They were intellectuals. Musicians. Poets.'

'Intellectuals?' Marcien spat into the dust. 'Word-twisters. Rabble-rousers. And they make cursed useless stoneworkers, I can tell you.'

'Have you no sense of compassion?'

'Compassion? This is a place of correction, not a convent.'

Furious, Acir turned away and began to retrace his steps; he could not trust himself not to strike Marcien down.

'For a Guerrior you seem uncommonly sympathetic to these revolutionaries.' Marcien called after him. 'Where do *your* allegiances lie, Korentan?'

'Bring in the next witness!'

Khassian stared about him in dismay. Guerriors lined the walls of the courtroom. High up in the public gallery he caught sight – behind the ranks of Guerriors – of anxious faces peering down: wives, mothers, children.

Three men stood chained together before a bench at which a panel of three judges sat in their indigo robes and wide-brimmed hats of office.

'Is your name Amaru Khassian?' said one of the judges.

'It is. But –'

'Bring him forward.'

'Is this a trial? Who is being tried?' Khassian cried as his guards caught hold of him by the arms and hustled him to the front of the court.

'Amaru Khassian. Do you recognise these men?'

They were gaunt. Their sunken eyes seemed to burn with fever, and their faces showed the livid marks of brutal treatment: swollen mouths, half-healed cuts and weeping sores. But changed as they were, he knew them. They were his musicians.

Wordlessly he begged them to let him know if he should identify them – or plead ignorance. But they would not meet his eyes.

'Do you know these men?' repeated the judge. 'Did you employ them?'

'Yes,' Khassian said miserably.

'Their names, please. And former occupations.'

'Saturnin – bass. Teriel – hautboy. Ignace – viola d'amore,' he whispered.

'Thank you.'

'Shall we take him back to the Sanctuary?' asked one of the guards.

'No. The Grand Maistre has specifically requested that he should be present throughout the proceedings.'

The judge turned back to the three musicians.

'Now that you have been formally identified, we shall proceed. You have been charged with conspiring to assassinate an officer of the Commanderie. How do you plead?'

There was silence.

'This is your chance to defend yourselves.'

Still the accused remained silent.

'We have many witnesses who saw you deliberately cut through the rope holding the masonry when an officer of the Commanderie was passing beneath. What have you to say in your defence?'

Saturnin, the bass, cleared his throat.

'We do not recognise this as a court of justice.' His words were slurred; Khassian saw that he moved his bruised jaw with difficulty. 'This is a travesty of a fair trial. We demand a civil hearing – with a lawyer to defend us against these accusations.'

'Your protestations do not alter the facts of the case. You plotted to kill one of our officers. And for that, the Grand Maistre demands the ultimate penalty – death.'

'*No!*' cried Khassian, straining forward. His guards caught hold of him and pulled him back.

'It is the sentence of this court that you be taken from here to a place of execution and hung by the neck until you are dead. Let your deaths be a warning to all those who seek to conspire against the Commanderie.'

There was a cry from the public gallery, a woman's voice, harsh and sobbing. Khassian thought he caught sight of her, arms outstretched over the balcony – and then the Guerriors closed in and in the ensuing pandemonium, he found himself being dragged away by his guards.

'Saturnin!' he shouted. 'I didn't know, I didn't –'

'Fight on, Amaru!' cried the bass. 'Don't let them defeat you! Don't –'

Khassian did not hear his last words as his guards pushed him back into the passageway that led beneath the court.

Acir Korentan stopped in a vineyard to rest and water his horse. He felt weary and dispirited by what he had seen; the raw, red gash in the mountainside was an atrocity, an Allegondan rape of Tourmalise's resources. But worse still was this wanton squandering of the miners' lives.

Acir took the remains of the rations he had brought with him from his saddle bag: unleavened bread, olives, cheese . . . but after a mouthful or two he found he was not hungry.

He lay back beside the young vines, gazing up at the brilliant stars, his eyelids slowly closing . . .

He walks alone through the verdant vineyard in the last light of the setting sun. The fiery sky is streaked with flame and gold: thunderclouds are massing overhead.

The new grapes on the vine tremble in the rising stormwind which comes gusting through the vineyard. It is growing dark.

Acir is gripped with a sudden and inexplicable sense of terror.

'Acir.'

A man stands between the young vines. A hood covers his face, shadowing the features. How does he know Acir by name? The voice, though low, is sweet as the taste of new wine on the tongue, sweet and strong.

'I have a gift for you, Acir.'

'A gift?'

The hooded stranger draws from the breast of his robe a green spray and offers it to Acir.

He slowly stretches out his hands to take the spray – and as his fingers close around the branch, he sees the drops of living blood on the fresh leaves from the torn and lacerated hands of the stranger, red as new wine.

The spray is a rose branch, prickled with vicious thorns that pierce deep into his own flesh. His blood begins to trickle, mingling with the blood of the stranger.

'Ahh . . . it burns!' Seared by the fiery pain. Acir looks up into the shadowed face.

'What do you want of me?' His whispered question is almost drowned in a distant grumble of thunder.

For answer, the stranger beckons him towards the vines. In the stormlight, Acir sees the new grapes have shrivelled, the green leaves have turned dry and brown.

'They are dying.' The stranger begins to walk away into the darkness of the oncoming storm. 'Save them. Save my harvest, Acir.'

'What must I do to save them? Tell me what I must do!'

The stranger turns and looks back and in the sudden pale brilliance of lightning, Acir sees his face.

'Now do you know me?'

Acir awoke with a start, heart pounding with exhilaration. The young vine leaves rustled softly, stirred not by the stormwind but a faint, warm breeze. Overhead the stars glittered in a cloudless sky.

He knew it had only been a dream – and yet such a vivid dream that he gazed down at his hands in the starlight, half-expecting to see the bleeding thorn-scratches where the burning blood of the Poet-Prophet had mingled with his own.

It was dawn by the time Acir reached Bel'Esstar.

Even as he approached the city, he sensed that something was wrong.

Three bodies swung slowly from the gallows on Pasperdu Hill. A guard of four Guerriors was stationed beneath the gallows.

Acir dismounted and strode over to the guard.

'What's happened? Who were these men? Why were they hanged?'

'Conspirators, Captain. Revolutionaries. They tried to murder an officer of the Commanderie.'

Acir gazed up at the bodies. Sacks had been tied over their heads. But he knew only too well who they were. Girim had deliberately disregarded his recommendations. He had made an example of the musicians.

'Cut them down.'

'But our orders were to –'

'Your orders have changed. Cut them down. And let their families have the bodies for burial.'

When the Guerrior still stood there, hesitating, Acir climbed up on on the platform and began to set about the grim task. Reluctantly, the four Guerriors clambered up to help him.

When all three bodies were laid out beneath the gallows, Acir called the Guerriors together.

'If anyone questions what you have done today, tell them that you were ordered to do it by Captain Korentan.'

As he turned to go back to his horse, he thought he glimpsed shadowy figures, women watching, waiting in a passageway, supporting each other, clinging to each other for comfort.

CHAPTER 21

'Wake up.'

The darkened Meditation cell was suddenly blindingly bright with lantern-light. Dazzled, Khassian thrust up one arm to shield his eyes.

'Wh-what do you want?' He tried to conceal the tremor in his voice as grey-clad Guerriors threw a hood over his face and bundled him towards the open cell door. 'Where are you taking me?'

'No questions. Just do as you are told.'

The voice of the commanding officer was unfamiliar. Khassian began to panic. They were going to execute him.

'But why now? I demand to know wh—'

'No questions,' repeated the officer curtly.

A closed carriage was waiting in the courtyard below; Khassian was pushed inside and the carriage started off. Blind, half-stifled by the thick muffling hood, he began to conjure terrifying fantasies.

Surely if they were going to execute him, they would have hung him yesterday with Saturnin, Ignace and Teriel, as an example to the other Sanctuarees?

Or was this an act of assassination to be carried out in secret, his body thrown ignominiously in a pit, never to be found? Was his fate to become just another of the many dissidents who had simply *disappeared*?

The carriage slowed to a halt and the Guerriors pulled him out into the fresh air. Into another building, forced to stumble up a winding flight of stairs, along another endless corridor.

A door clicked quietly shut. The hood was untied and removed from his head.

Khassian opened his eyes to see a servitor clad in the grey and white livery of the Prince's household bowing before him.

'Your bath is ready, Illustre. Let me help you off with your clothes.'

Khassian took an unsteady step backwards.

'Is this some kind of a joke?'

'Not in the least, Illustre. I am instructed by His Altesse the Prince, to assist you with your toilette.'

Khassian gazed around him. The restrained elegance of the chamber, the walls painted cloud-grey, embellished with delicate plaster mouldings in cream and gilt, the pale polished wood of the floor . . . all was in the refined style favoured by Ilsevir.

'Then I'm dreaming.'

Behind a blue and white painted screen, a porcelain hip bath stood, a gentle steam arising from its herb-strewn waters. A hot bath!

The servitor's hands were already deftly removing the stained Sanctuary tunic from Khassian's shoulders. He stood and let the servitor strip away the rest of the filthy garments and help him into the bath. A long sigh of contentment escaped him as the water rose around him and he lay back, closing his eyes.

He would not think of anything but the bliss of the hot water and the astringent sting of the wash-herbs. The servitor soaped his matted hair, fingers expertly scrubbing the engrained dirt from his skin.

Later, wrapped in soft towels, Khassian sat before a mirror whilst the servitor shaved away the ragged beard and trimmed the tangles from his hair.

A soft tap at the door announced the arrival of a second servitor bearing a tray of breakfast: Khassian's starved stomach contracted painfully at the warm aroma of fresh-baked butter-rolls and quince marmalade, and hot, fragrant mocha. His favourite breakfast – Ilsevir must have remembered.

'Shall I pour the mocha for you, Illustre?'

Khassian nodded avidly. He watched the fragrant liquid as it filled the bowl. His mouth was watering painfully at the mere smell of it. Yet as he tried to chew into a roll, his throat seemed to contract. After so many days' near-starvation, he could hardly swallow down the delicious food.

'Would the Illustre care to dress now for the morning levee?'

The servitor brought out a suit of clothes; subtly tailored, elegantly understated. The Prince had also remembered his preference for dark yew-green, though the sombre shade was alleviated by delicate embroidery in bronzed thread at revers and cuffs. Even the silky cream chemise was embroidered.

Khassian stood looking at himself critically in the cheval mirror. The shaving had revealed a dark bruise marring the left side of his face; the elegant court costume concealed the other marks of Commanderie brutality. A stranger gazed back at him. The dark, curling hair of the slim young courtier was like his own – but the eyes, the haunted, mistrustful eyes in that bruised face . . .

A distant bell sounded, sweet-toned yet penetrating. The servitor cleared his throat.

'His Altesse will see you now, Illustre.'

Khassian's earliest memory of the Royal Apartments in the Winter Palace was of the sheen of gold-veined marble columns, of gilded mirrors that reflected vista upon candlelit vista, receding into infinity . . .

All the mirrors had been removed.

A man knelt, head bowed upon a prayer book, before a candle-lit shrine on which glowed the blood-red image of the thorn-pierced Rose.

The stab of pain that Khassian felt on seeing Ilsevir was as vivid as if one of the holy thorns had pierced his breast.

The Prince rose to his feet and turned around, hands outstretched in welcome.

'Amaru.'

Khassian dropped to his knees.

He could not look on the Prince's face. Not yet. For fear the crowding emotions would betray him and he would cry out, 'Why? Why did you abandon me?'

He felt the Prince's fingers absent-mindedly stroke his hair . . . a gesture that once had meant so much and now seemed no more than an old habit, not yet abandoned.

'Amaru,' said Ilsevir again. 'Look at me.'

He could not disobey. Trembling, Khassian raised his head. The sickly-sweet smell that had tainted Ilsevir's breath had gone; his skin had lost the translucent grey pallor of the last days of his illness.

'You are looking in the . . . the very best of health, Altesse.'

'My physicians tell me my recovery is nothing short of a miracle. I feel young again, Amar. My sight is clear. I've been riding. I've even sailed the barque on the lake.'

'We were all praying for your recovery.'

'And your prayers were answered.' Ilsevir placed his hands on Khassian's shoulders and raised him to his feet. 'I feel renewed, Amar. Reborn. To come so close to death . . . It made me reflect on what I had done with my life. But he opened my eyes. He made me see the meaninglessness, the emptiness, of my existence . . . That's all behind me now.'

He. Girim nel Ghislain. The golden dream of the past, in which Khassian had been floating since he had entered the Royal Apartments, popped like a frail soap bubble.

'Come, sit with me. Let's talk.' Ilsevir gestured to a couch of brocade, golden and black.

'Talk?' Khassian glanced around, wondering where the unseen listeners were concealed.

'As we used to.' The Prince leaned comfortably back, one arm over the corner of the couch; Khassian sat, as he was bidden – but on the edge.

What was there to say? Khassian remained silent.

'My poor Amaru. You've suffered needlessly.'

Ilsevir's fingers touched his bruised face; he winced.

'Put it all behind you. The suffering. The pain. Come back to me. Resume your rightful place at court. Be my court composer again.'

Ilsevir still knew how to speak seductively, still knew how to charm.

'And the charges against me?'

'All dropped.'

'On what conditions?'

Ilsevir flicked one hand dismissively. The glint of a rose-red jewel caught the candlelight.

'The details can be discussed later.' The jewel was cut in the shape of a rose. Carnelian, with a blood-ruby at its heart. The thorn-pierced heart. Symbol of the inner circle of the Commanderie.

'And my hands?' Khassian slowly raised them to show the Prince. 'How can a court composer perform his role with hands like these?'

For an instant he saw a expression of repugnance pass across Ilsevir's calm countenance – a breeze glancing across limpid water. Then the Prince's eyes fixed on his, ignoring the burned hands.

'You are still that rare creature, an intuitive. You can direct, conduct, instruct others. Who else in Bel'Esstar has your sensitivity, your musicianship? Not even old Talfieri. Of course there's Lissier . . . but his style is brash, unrefined.'

'What if I refuse?'

Ilsevir looked at him a moment in astonishment – and then began to laugh.

'My dear Amaru, *refuse*? I do not make such offers twice.'

Ilsevir rose to his feet and beckoned. Khassian followed him to the window. The Prince pulled a golden cord and as the heavy swagged brocades whispered aside, a vista of Bel'Esstar appeared, a shimmer of grey stone and glass, cupolas, balconies and weathervanes.

A civilised façade.

'A fine sight, still, would you not agree? Yet my city is stricken with a mortal canker, slowly eating it away from within. And what is the reason? Pride, Amar. The pride that comes between man and his Maker. The pride that makes a man turn away from his god and set his own needs first.'

Ilsevir placed his hands on his shoulders. Khassian tensed, remembering the gesture of old. Once this had meant the prelude to a drawing closer, the touch of mouth on mouth . . . And maybe Ilsevir knew it too, maybe he had done it on purpose, evoking an intimacy long-since dead to serve his present intent.

'*You* have it within your power to heal this canker.'

Khassian tried to move away but Ilsevir's hands still held him, his eyes still held him.

'Yes, you, Amar. You are still loved, respected amongst the artistic community. You have immense influence.'

'I have nothing –' began Khassian.

'You underestimate yourself. If you were to make this one gesture of reconciliation, others would follow. There would be no need for a

Sanctuary. No more hunger . . . no more suffering.'

Khassian felt his determination beginning to waver. His eyes could not help but stray to the great curtained bed, plumed with gilded feathers. To sleep in a soft bed again without fear of the interrogators coming in the night . . .

Don't do this to me, Ilsevir.

'There is to be a ceremony of consecration at the Fortress of Faith. I want you there, Amar. I want your music to enrich the ceremony. I want you to train the choir and musicians.'

It all seemed too golden a prospect to be possible. Khassian began to sense another's voice speaking behind Ilsevir's.

'*You* want my music? Or the Grand Maistre wants it?'

Ilsevir pointed to a pile of drawings on a marble side table.

'Have you seen the sketches for the Fortress? Look at this: the great rose window, blazing with coloured glass, the light falling on to the choir stalls. What a wonderful setting to enhance the spirituality of your music.'

Ilsevir's hand rested on the drawing. Light splintered through the petal-facets of his rose-stone ring, a red glow staining the white paper. Khassian's eye was drawn to it. Blood staining the walls of the Fortress, the blood of his fellow Sanctuarees, mixed into its cement.

'I – can't do it,' he said, each word wrung from him.

Ilsevir sighed.

'Why is it so difficult for you?'

Khassian did not, could not, reply. And it saddened him that he must play word games with the man he had once honoured as patron, protector . . . and lover.

'You have changed, Amaru. I do not recognise the man I once knew.'

'It must be the effect of the Sulien waters.'

Khassian's riposte was flippantly bitter; even as he heard himself deliver it, he knew he should have kept silent.

Ilsevir reached out and, fingers closing around the bell-rope, pulled it.

Khassian panicked.

He could still retract. There was still time –

The doors opened and the two Guerriors entered.

'The Illustre is ready to return to the Sanctuary,' Ilsevir said. His face betrayed nothing. He looked straight through Khassian as though he was not there as he turned back to the sketches of the Fortress of Faith.

Dame Jolaine Tradescar had lodged for fifty years in the same ramshackle garret over a courtyard tucked behind Millisom's Street. Behind the elegant carved façades of Sulien, many such dingy courtyards were to be found, criss-crossed with lines of washing. She had never troubled to find anywhere more spacious or elegant as she spent her days in the Museum or below ground, investigating and mapping the Undercity.

Now that she was forbidden the Undercity – and had been locked out of her own Museum – she found her rooms confining and stuffy.

Frustrated at the very moment when her researches were coming to fruition, she whiled away the days poring over her notebooks, looking at her sketches of the mosaic floor in the Hall of Whispering Reeds from every conceivable angle, and postulating, puzzling, theorising . . .

So when she heard someone tapping politely at her door, she leapt up from her chair, eager for distraction.

Theophil Philemot stood on her doorstep, a large bundle in his arms.

'Your – possessions, Dame Tradescar.' He seemed a little out of breath.

'You can bring them in,' Jolaine said stiffly, all her earlier good humour evaporating at the sight of her successor, 'and then you can be off about your business.'

But there seemed nowhere to put the bundle in her cramped parlour; every available space was piled high with books.

'Maybe on the table?' Philemot suggested, moving towards the least cluttered area.

'No!' Jolaine hurried to slam shut the open books, placing herself in front of them. Her work on the hieroglyphs. Her mosaic floor. 'Just put the bundle down. Anywhere.'

Philemot did as he was told.

'I'm sure you have much to occupy your time, Dr Philemot, I don't wish to detain you a moment longer.'

'Dame Tradescar,' he burst out, 'you must believe me – I would like to consult you on some matters of scholarship. I would truly value the benefit of your expertise which is without parallel in the field –'

'So unparalleled that I have to be pensioned off, hm? And young upstarts like you brought in?'

'It's about the hot springs.'

'Well?' At least the young man was persistent.

'You've heard that the springs have dried up?'

'I've heard that they're blaming me.'

'Which is completely ridiculous!' said Philemot hotly. 'How could meticulous scholarly excavations cause a geological phenomenon such as this?'

Meticulous? Scholarly? Jolaine Tradescar was beginning to take a reluctant liking to Dr Philemot.

'So you don't believe in this ancient evil that I have apparently awakened by desecrating the holy places with my digging?'

'Think back, Dame Tradescar. Yesterday, and two days earlier, there was distant thunder. But no storm, no rain. Most people I have spoken to agree it was coming from the mountains.'

Dame Tradescar rubbed her hands together.

'You have a theory?'

'Better. I have a map.'

Philemot produced the map from his pocket and spread it out on the table.

'No one has ever traced the source of the springs?'

'Not to my knowledge. The Temple Court discourages that kind of investigation.' Jolaine looked up at Philemot over the rim of her pince-nez spectacles. 'It's all bound up in the spirit of the place. It's hard to separate Sulien from its springs – and its springs from its tutelary Goddess.'

'But even the Goddess's gift could be abused by men. Men quarrying deep into the hills. Blasting deeper with charges of firedust. Silting up the sources of ancient springs. See here? The site of an Allegondan quarry.'

'Interesting.' Jolaine suddenly chuckled. 'Sit down, Dr Philemot.' She scooped up a pile of books from an ancient armchair and patted the upholstery. A little cloud of dust motes arose, shimmering in the sunshine.

'And there's another reason I wished to consult you. It's probably of little interest to you . . . but it's always intrigued me since I first spotted it in its case in the Antiquities Cabinet in Can Tabrien. When the Antiquarian learned I had secured a position in Sulien, he let me bring it here to ask your opinion. He has read several of your monographs on pre-Allegondan Tourmalise.'

'Has he indeed?' Jolaine was flattered, though she was damned if she was going to show it. 'So – where is this thing of little interest?'

Philemot brought from his pocket a bundle of soft cloths and carefully unwrapped the contents.

Inside lay an enamelled fragment, about half the size of a man's palm, with delicate petals, white and pink, inlaid upon verdigris. Lotos petals.

'How it came to be in Can Tabrien, I have no idea.'

'Good gracious,' Jolaine Tradescar said, staring. 'Good gracious me.'

'It *is* genuine, isn't it?'

Jolaine's fingers reached out greedily – and then stopped.

'May I?'

'Please do,' Theophil Philemot said generously.

Jolaine took up the fragment and lovingly turned it over and over in her hands.

'I think we may have something quite remarkable here.'

'Ah?' Philemot was evidently trying not to sound too excited.

'It is without doubt of Lifhendil craftmanship. Late period.'

Jolaine set it down again. Should she share her discovery with Philemot? Confound it all, why not? She went to her desk and brought over her find and laid it beside Philemot's. With trembling hands she brought the two halves together – to make a complete lotos.

241

'Extraordinary,' whispered Philemot.

'And what is more,' Jolaine said, 'I know exactly where in the Undercity these belong.' She took up her notebook and showed Philemot the sketches of the mosaic pavement.

'This should fit at the centre of the mosaic. The dragonflies can then be seen to fly into the lotos – and out of it again.'

'We must put it back in its rightful place!' Philemot said.

'The Undercity is forbidden, remember? Especially to meddling ex-Antiquarians.'

'But what is its precise significance? Decorative or ritual? What manner of rites were held in the chamber where you found it?'

Jolaine gave the young man a long, appraising look. His eagerness reminded her of a certain Jolaine Tradescar at exactly the same age: irrepressibly curious, incessantly hungry for knowledge. Perhaps she had misjudged Theophil Philemot.

'Sit down,' she said. 'Now . . . where shall we start?'

'The Priestess will not see you, Dame Tradescar.' The elderly Priest made to close the door of the Priesthouse. 'Not today or any day.'

'But I have important information.'

'We've troubles enough of our own . . . and we have only you to thank for them.'

'Then please at least give her this note – and see that she reads it. I'll be feeding the pigeons in the forecourt if she cares to speak with me.'

The Priest hesitated then put out his palsied hand to take Dame Tradescar's letter.

She went back down the steps and took a paper of bread crusts from her bag. Soon the pigeons had come fluttering down from the Temple pediment to peck at the crumbs. She sat down, humming, and centred her attention on the pigeons.

'Dame Tradescar.'

Jolaine rose to see a veiled figure beckoning to her from the colonnade. She approached.

'You used to call me Jolaine when we were at school, Elysie. Or was that in another existence?'

'These transcriptions.' The Priestess ignored the question, holding out the letter Jolaine had written. 'Are they authentic?'

'You call my scholarship into question? Of course they're authentic. Intriguing, aren't they?'

'Tell me more about this Lotos Priestess. The one you call Songspinner.'

'The role of the Songspinner, as I understand it, was to be a living channel between two worlds: this world and the next. The Lotos Priestess

– or Princess – stood at the doorway between life and death.'

'A kind of shamaness?'

'A Priestess, gifted with the ability to hear the voices of the spirit world.'

'And these spirits – Eä-Endil – they came through the Songspinner to guide the souls of the dead to the light?'

'I can only interpret this to be the origin of our present-day ceremonies. The dragonflies have become merely a symbol.'

'Don't think this information will persuade me to let you back into the Under Temple!' The Priestess wagged the folded letter at Jolaine. 'The springs are still dry. No burials can take place in the Undercity. Besides there are many amongst the Temple fellowship who will dismiss these ancient rituals you describe as primitive. We live in more enlightened times . . .'

'But *you*, Elysie? What do you think?'

The Priestess hesitated.

'The traditions are all lost, long forgotten. Even if we understand the role of the Lotos Priestess better, how can we find and train anyone to perform that role?'

'Perhaps the Lotos Priestess was not trained, she was born to shamanhood,' Jolaine said excitedly.

'I do not know.' The Priestess shook her veiled head. 'All I know is that it would be advisable for you to stay away from the Under Temple until this present crisis is over.'

'I can slip in by night. No one will see me,' pleaded Jolaine.

'No.'

'Damn.' Jolaine went slowly, desultorily, down the steps, kicking at a dried crust of bread the pigeons had ignored. 'Damn.'

'Have you taken leave of your senses?' Girim nel Ghislain rounded on Acir Korentan, pale eyes narrowed with anger. 'Countermanding my orders, *my* orders?'

Acir stood stiffly to attention before the Grand Maistre, gazing straight ahead, unblinking.

'Well? What have you got to say in your defence?'

Acir cleared his throat. What he had to say was dangerous – and could condemn him as a rebel sympathiser. But Girim had ordered him to speak, so speak he must.

'I believed the name of the Commanderie stood for honour and for justice. What I saw made me ashamed to wear the badge of the Rose. Three men hanged without fair trial.'

'Without fair trial?' Girim's voice had gone quiet.

'You sent me to the stone quarries. A day's journey. In the time I was away, those three men were tried and executed.'

Girim stared at him. Acir squared his shoulders, steadying himself for the tirade to come.

'And so you took it upon yourself to cut them down?'

'I took the action I thought fit at the time.'

'I see.' Quiet, considering words, belying the clear, cold anger Acir could see flickering like distant lightning in the Grand Maistre's face. 'And did you think your rank would help you escape punishment for this insubordination?'

'No.' Acir looked Girim full in the face, refusing to be cowed. 'But I would like it set on record that I acted in good faith to restore the good name of the Commanderie. A name that has become associated in this city – this holy city – with injustice, with cruelty, with –'

'Enough!' Girim's voice cut across his.

'Demote me. Court-martial me. But listen to what I'm saying, Maistre. If the signs, the dreams, are true and the time of His coming is drawing near . . . what will He find? A city divided. A city in fear –'

'Dreams?' interrupted Girim.

'I . . . I have dreamed of His coming. I cannot be the only one . . .'

'You saw *Him* in your dream?'

Acir hesitated. He had never spoken of his dreams before. Now it seemed as if he was breaking a sacred trust to speak of them aloud. And yet, if it would save lives, speak he must. But his throat had gone dry and tight. He swallowed, trying to find words to describe the indescribable.

'He was in a vineyard.'

'In a vineyard?' The anger seemed to leach from Girim's eyes, leaving only a blank and hungry emptiness.

'I took Him for a vineyard worker at first . . . and then when I saw His face, I knew Him.'

'Oh, Acir, Acir.' Girim's arms enfolded him. His voice had softened, the anger was dispelled . . . or cleverly disguised, Acir thought. 'This is another sign. A sign that He is near.'

'But in my dream the grape harvest was failing –'

'Your dream was a metaphor. You've seen how thin a vintage we have here in Bel'Esstar. It must be strengthened by the testament of true believers. We must increase our efforts.'

'And if that was not the true meaning of the dream?'

Girim shook his head, smiling. And Acir saw from his eyes that the Grand Maistre refused even to entertain the possibility that he might be in the wrong.

'What other possible meaning could there be?'

CHAPTER 22

The Guerriors at the Fortress had told Orial that Captain Korentan was to be found at the Sanctuary. They had given her directions.

But now she was lost. Her feet ached. She was thirsty and tired. All the broad, dusty streets of Bel'Esstar looked the same to her. If only she could find a drinking fountain.

She sat down on a doorstep to shake a little stone from her shoe.

Where were the people? She was aware that a curtain twitched at the windows of the house opposite but the street was empty. Was there a curfew? It wasn't even near twilight. She glanced around apprehensively. Maybe they thought her a woman of questionable virtue? In Sulien the thought would have made her giggle, but here she suddenly felt vulnerable and very alone.

She buttoned her shoe and, keeping to the shadowed side of the street, hurried away.

I won't give up. I'm sure to come to the Sanctuary soon.

She turned the corner.

The fire-blackened shell of a great building dominated the empty street.

A flare of pain sizzled through her hands.

'What *is* this place?' she murmured, venturing closer.

A makeshift barrier had been erected across the entrance; a few boards nailed together blocked the entrance. Behind, weeds grew in the charred ruins, the soft green of rose bay willowherb, topped with a froth of white seeds.

'Vast enough to be a temple . . .'

The remains of the fluted columns and pediment of the front façade reminded her of the Temple of the Source in Sulien.

She reached out to touch one of the columns . . . and fire gashed across her mind, bright as a sunflare. She snatched her fingers away as if they had been burned.

She gazed at the mess of blackened timbers and fallen plaster that filled the central void.

She knew this place.

The Opera House.

Tentatively she reached out again and, closing her eyes, let her finger-tips make contact with the charred stone.

Voices echoed in her head, gorgeous voices, swooping and darting like swallows. And, matching them in colour and vibrancy, she heard the sudden surge of a great body of instruments, strings, woodwind, harps . . .

An orchestra.

Dizzied by the swell of sound, she snatched her fingers away.

The echoes of the opera orchestra resonated on in her brain, a candlelit tapestry of crimson, blue and rich gold.

This was where it had all begun. This was *his* world.

'Good day to you, demselle.'

She started and, turning around, saw a streetsweeper watching her, leaning on his brush. He was ill-shaven and there was something about the way he looked at her that made her uneasy.

'The way to the Sanctuary, please, sieur?'

The man hawked and spat on the ground.

'What does a pretty girl like you want with the Sanctuary?'

'I just want to know the way.'

He gave a grunt.

'I'll set you on the right route. Follow me.'

He set off down the deserted street, Orial following a few paces behind. Soon he had slowed and was walking beside her. She drew away. He persisted. She began to glance around, hoping to see someone else whom she could ask. But the streets were empty. Maybe the people of Bel'Esstar dozed the hot afternoons away, waiting for the cooler air of evening before venturing out.

The man leaned closer to her.

'Come with me and I'll show you a much better time.'

'It's very kind of you, sieur . . .' Orial began to back away.

He made a sudden lunge at her, grabbing at her breasts. His brush fell to the pavement. Orial darted under his hands and, gathering up her skirts, began to run.

He came after her but she was fleeter-footed. Slipping into a doorway, she tried to quieten her breathing. The man loped past and stopped a few paces away, sniffing around like a hound scenting its quarry. She could hear him muttering and cursing her.

After a while, an interminable while, he gave up and went away. Still she waited, willing herself to find the courage to venture out again.

Cramoisy had warned her and she had not listened. *'Men can go where women cannot.'*

She was beginning to wish she had not come.

Although a canopy of high cloud loured over Bel'Esstar, it was not cool but oppressively warm. Orial trudged on across the heath that separated the Sanctuary from the city; the heath grasses were already parched for lack of rain and a thin, fine dust rose every time she put down her foot. Only a sulphur-leaved thistle thrived in this barren terrain: its vicious spines caught on Orial's clothes and its burgeoning thistledown seemed to give off a faintly putrid odour. She felt alone and vulnerable; the sandy hollows could easily conceal predators waiting to prey on lone women making their way to the Sanctuary to visit their loved ones.

Who would hear her cries if she was attacked and dragged off the path?

The Guerriors on duty at the gate took Orial's papers and escorted her into an ill-lit little room beside the gatehouse.

She stood waiting, listening, her heart thudding so loud she put one hand to her breast to try to still it.

Would they confiscate her papers? Would they detain her?

'Demselle Magelonne! Whatever are you doing here?'

In the shadows of the bare room, his hair looked more dull pewter than silver – but the eyes, the blue eyes, were unmistakably those of Captain Acir Korentan.

'I've come to see you, Captain.' She glanced around her, hoping he would correctly interpret what she dared not ask aloud: *Is it safe to talk here or shall we be overheard?*

'You must be tired after your journey from Sulien,' Captain Korentan said courteously. 'Can I offer you any refreshment?'

'My throat is dry. I would appreciate something to drink.'

'Please follow me.'

Nothing of any consequence had been spoken aloud between them. But he had understood. There was still, then, a spark of hope.

'I heard that you were grievously sick.' He stopped. 'Forgive me. You are evidently recovered and I am delighted to see you in good health.'

'That is why I am here. The Illustre was deported on my father's complaint. My father –' Orial hesitated. 'My father acted in haste. He regrets what has happened.'

'Then why is he not here?'

'I have come myself to prove his accusations unfounded. I am well, I am whole. There is no complaint against the Illustre.'

'No complaint in Sulien. But here –' His fingers finished the sentence with an expressive gesture.

Orial had feared such a reply. And yet she still sensed a subtle alteration in Captain Korentan's attitude. She felt she could test him a little further.

'He *is* here, isn't he?'

Korentan nodded.

'May I see him?'

'He is not allowed visitors.'

Orial took up the cup of water and drank.

'This is a terrible place,' she said softly. He nodded in reply. When she looked up, she saw that his eyes had darkened as if in pain.

'The Diva is here with me,' she said. 'Could you not make an exception in his case?'

'And will the Diva be returning straightaway to Sulien?' Captain Korentan asked. He looked her directly in the eyes, unblinking.

'Yes. He has unfinished business to attend to.' Orial held his gaze. For the second time he had understood her meaning.

'I will see what I can do. Tell me where you are lodged – and I will send word if a meeting is to be permitted.'

'The house is in the Dniera Faubourg. The Villa of Yellow Vines.'

'Thank you. I have made a note of it.'

They walked back to the gatehouse without speaking. Orial stole a glance at the Captain as they walked but his expression was guarded, giving nothing away.

Had she read more into their conversation than he had intended?

As they approached the gatehouse, the gates were dragged open and an elegant phaeton pulled into the courtyard, the horses' harnesses jingling. The coachman reined in his horses and one of the Guerriors hurried forward to open the carriage door. A woman climbed down and smoothed out the skirts of her travelling gown.

Orial felt the Captain's brisk tread falter. The woman was gazing about her, adjusting the fit of each finger of her lace gloves. Deftly, Captain Korentan positioned himself on Orial's other side and steered her into the shadows of the gatehouse door.

'Who –?' Orial whispered.

Captain Korentan hurried her to the door, out of sight of the courtyard, and unlocked it himself.

'Go. Quickly.'

He helped her up and over the high sill and thrust her papers into her hands. Beyond, the dusty wasteland menaced in the sulphureous light of late-afternoon. It seemed a very long walk back to the Dniera Faubourg.

'Wait for me at the waystone. I will escort you back to the city.'

'Captain, I –'

But even as she turned back to Captain Korentan, the door shut with a firm click and she heard the key turn in the lock.

'Captain Korentan!'

Acir turned automatically as Fiammis called his name. She stood framed in the archway to the gatehouse,

The milky pallor of her skin glimmered in the gloomy courtyard like a rare lily growing in a barren wasteland.

'Contesse.' He fought to keep his voice steady, emotionless; he must give nothing away.

'They told me you were here. I hope you find your new situation agreeable?'

Agreeable. It was her report from Sulien that had had him demoted to nel Macy's second-in-command. Had she merely come here to gloat or was there some other purpose to her visit?

'But it's not you I've come to see. I bring intelligences for the Governor. If you would be so good as to direct me, Captain . . .'

'Guerrior! Escort the Contesse to Captain nel Macy. If you will excuse me?' Acir gave Fiammis a brusque salute. 'I have affairs of my own to attend to.' If she could be oblique, then so could he. Two could play this game.

She opened her mouth as if to say something in reply – and then snapped it shut.

Had she seen Orial?

Acir leaned his forehead against the clammy stone of the gatehouse wall.

And even if she had, would she have given any indication to him?

He had the sentry unlock the door for him and hurried to find Orial.

She was sitting on the waystone, gazing towards the city. In the sultry glare she looked frail and tired . . . and yet as he came nearer, he thought he saw a pale haze of light about her. He put one hand to his eyes, thinking himself dazzled by the dry, dusty light – and at that moment, she heard him approach and rose.

'You need not trouble, Captain, I –'

'The heath is not safe, even by day. There are vagrants, cutpurses who lie in wait in the hollows. Besides . . . here we can talk without fear of being overheard.'

The narrow path led away through the gorse; soon they would be out of sight of the road. She seemed weary and yet she did not once complain; he found himself impressed by her quiet composure.

'I wrote letters, Captain, requesting an interview with the Grand Maistre to beg for clemency for Khassian. Yet not one was answered. You are the only one in Bel'Esstar to show me any courtesy.'

How he never noticed before the luminosity of her eyes, light ripples on water?

'You understand, Captain Korentan. You have heard his music. You know the power of that music . . . to move, to enoble the spirit.'

There was an affecting grace and dignity about her – yet there was also an air of other worldliness that made him fear for her safety. She had assured him she was recovered from her illness but . . .

'You are taking a grave risk, demselle. I will do all I can to aid you, but if my part in this endeavour is discovered –'

'Your risk is the greater, Captain. Believe me, I am sensible of what you are hazarding on Khassian's account.'

249

The path wound downwards towards the city gate. Orial stumbled on the loose, dry stones and Acir put out his hand to steady her. She looked up into his face and for a moment the scrubby heathland melted away and he was back in the Temple of the Source, gazing into the water-misted eyes of the tutelary spirit the Allegondans had called Elesstar . . .

'Are you all right, Captain?'

The vision faded as quickly as it had come; he put one hand to his brow and found it wet with sweat.

'I – I was remembering the Temple in Sulien. Did we ever meet there?' he heard himself asking.

'I don't think so.' She smiled at him, a small, grave smile. 'But I hope we may. In happier times. When all these troubles are resolved.'

A patrol of Guerriors was approaching along the boulevard, marching towards the Sanctuary. They saluted Acir as they passed; Orial shrank into his shadow as he returned their salute.

Their faces were dour, their eyes blank. The brisk tread of their marching feet resounded along the empty street with the harsh ring of steel-capped boots on stone.

They marched to the spectral beat of a different drum; they followed a warrior prophet conjured by Girim nel Ghislain from his fevered fantasies of fire and battle.

Acir glanced at Orial as they continued on their way to the Dniera Faubourg. Her quiet courage glowed with the same steadfast flame as the light of a lotos candle floating on the black reservoirs of the necropolis. Her calm was the water-shadowed calm of the Temple of the Source . . .

The Commanderie would interpret such a thought as heresy, the confused ramblings of an unbeliever. But in that moment of insight, Acir saw that the way forward was through the enlightenment of the Temple of the Source.

If only there was a way to bring the two faiths together . . .

Fiammis turned her back on Captain Korentan and followed the Guerrior across the Sanctuary courtyard. She snapped open her fan and began to use it furiously, trusting the swift movements would hide her face until she could compose herself.

She had felt a shiver of flame burn through her when she caught sight of him in the courtyard. And he had looked on her so sternly, so coldly; evidently he had not forgiven her for her interference in the Khassian affair.

Was she always to be torn between duty and desire?

Orial's first request on returning to the Villa of Yellow Vines was a bowl of hot water sprinkled with refreshing salts. She sat with her sore feet in the fizzing water whilst Cramoisy fussed around her, plying her with lemon tea and almond biscuits.

'Did you see him? Is he well? What happened? You were gone so long I was almost beside myself with worry. I was about to send for the watch –'

'No, I didn't see him. But I saw an acquaintance of ours.'

'In that dreadful prison?'

'Captain Korentan. And I think we can trust him. Yes, I know.' Orial saw the Diva's mouth open to protest. 'He promised me he would try to secure a meeting for you. But meetings are not normally allowed. The Sanctuary is very securely guarded.'

'Wait!' Cramoisy rose. He had adopted a dramatic pose with one hand on his breast, his eyes raised to the heavens. '*Samira – Or Virtue Assailed.*'

'Samira?' Orial echoed, wondering what role Cramoisy had slipped into now.

'In Act Four, Alkar the hero is languishing in a prison cell. Samira, the heroine – *my* part, you understand – decides to sacrifice herself for him.' Cramoisy wandered the room, already lost in memories of past triumphs. 'So she goes to bid Alkar a last farewell – and to aid his escape, exchanges clothes with him. But when the tyrant Valdaron discovers he has been duped by his rival, he kills Samira in revenge, even though he loves her.'

Orial, lost in the intricacies of the retold plot, lifted her feet out of the water and began to dry them; there were angry blisters on her heels and toes.

'Well?' Cramoisy finished, eyes shining. 'What do you think?'

'About what?'

'My plan to smuggle Amar out of the Sanctuary!'

'Wait.' Orial took the shell-shaped powder box and dusted her feet. 'You're proposing that you change clothes with the Illustre Khassian? But that means that you'll be imprisoned in his place. And when the Commanderie discovers the deception –'

'You and Amar will be across the border and safe in Sulien.'

'At the cost of your freedom – maybe even your life!'

'What else is there left for me now that I have lost my voice? What future is there for a diva who can't sing?'

'There must be another way.' A faint melody had begun to whisper in Orial's brain.

'Other than starting the revolution and leading a mob to storm the Sanctuary, I'm sure I can't think what it might be,' Cramoisy said, with a wounded sniff. 'If they turn unpleasant, I shall remind them of my intentions to convert. Publicly. I haven't any of Amar's scruples. It's my last chance to take centre-stage. Performing's in my blood, *carissa*, without an audience, I wither and die.'

Orial replaced the lid on the box of perfumed powder. The persistent melody was beginning to annoy her.

'Whatever we decide, we'll need to hire a carriage. It's a very long walk to the Sanctuary.'

'A carriage to take us all the way back to Sulien? I've spent all my money on the lodgings.'

Orial lifted the hem of her dress and began to unpick the stitching.

'Whatever are you doing, child?'

Slowly Orial eased out the string of precious pearls.

'Ahhh.' Cramoisy took them from her and held them to the light, then against his cheek. 'I *adore* pearls. So flattering to the complexion . . .'

'Will they fetch a good price? Enough to hire a private carriage?'

'Were these your mother's?' Cramoisy was gazing pensively at the pearls, threading them through his fingers.

'Yes.'

'I can't do this. Your dead mother's jewellery. Your dowry.'

'It doesn't matter.' Orial took the Diva's hand in hers, closing it around the pearls. 'She would have understood.'

'I'll not sell them. I'll see what the pawnbroker will offer me.'

Orial began to sing the melody under her breath.

'What's that?' Cramoisy said sharply.

'I don't know.' She put one hand to her head, trying to dam the flow of the music. 'Do you recognise it?'

'Sing it again.'

As Orial sang, she saw Cramoisy turn pale, clutching the pearls against his throat.

'And you don't know the name of the song?'

Orial shook her head.

'Samira's aria. Act Two. "Like a bird let me fly away". It was Iridial's favourite aria. They named her the Sulien Nightingale when she first sang it in Sulien.'

'My mother's favourite aria?' Orial swayed, dizzied and confused by Cramoisy's reaction. 'But how could I have –'

He caught hold of her and steadied her.

'I didn't mean to alarm you so, *carissa*.'

The notes of the song glittered in Orial's head, falling rain lit by the sun.

'You must have overtaxed your strength, walking so far in this heat. I think you should rest.'

Orial nodded, letting herself lean against Cramoisy.

'Lie down on the couch and I'll draw the blinds. That's right . . .'

'How could I have remembered a song I've never heard before?' Orial murmured as Cramoisy lifted her feet up on to the couch.

'You must have heard it when you were a baby. You were thinking of your mother when you took out the pearls. It triggered a memory from your past, that was all. Now rest.'

Orial lay back and closed her eyes.

Cramoisy must be right. A distant childhood memory . . .

And yet it did not feel like a memory. It felt fresh and distinct, almost as if she had 'heard' the notes telepathically . . . as if her mother had been singing to her from beyond the grave.

At night the sounds of the Sanctuary gradually stilled until the empty courtyards echoed only to the monotonous tread of the sentries on nightwatch.

Khassian lay staring at a shred of cobweb that dangled across the moonlit window-slit, counting the regular beat of the patrolling footsteps.

It was the endless, empty hour before dawn.

The darkness pressed down on him, a smothering weight. He did not know how much longer he could endure being confined in this solitary cell. He had heard of prisoners going mad . . .

A distant voice penetrated the darkness, a faint voice, ragged but true, singing from the depths of the Sanctuary

Khassian raised himself on one elbow, listening.

' "Freedom," ' he murmured.

This was no Commanderie battle psalm. He could not catch the words – but he did not need to. He knew the rise and fall of the melody better than the singer – he had composed it. He had wrestled with the notes, moulding and shaping them until he had fashioned an arching melody that aspired, that soared, to the distant stars.

He must be going mad.

Yet even as he listened, other voices joined the first, a few at a time, then more and more.

He sprang up on his bed, gazing out of the window-slit. His throat ached but he felt the music welling up inside him. He had to join the unseen singers, he had to add his voice to theirs.

' "Freedom." ' Khassian sang.

Torchlights flared in the courtyard below. The steady tread of the patrol broke up in confusion as more Guerriors came running out. A voice barked out orders – but still the singing swelled, voices issuing from all corners of the Sanctuary.

Khassian could hear the running steps coming nearer, he could hear the clank of keys. He took in a breath and sang louder; his voice split on the upper notes but he did not care.

The door crashed open and two Guerriors rushed in.

'Silence him!' shouted a voice from the corridor outside.

' "Sweeter than a lover's kiss, sweeter than –" '

They seized hold of him and flung him on to the floor. Even as he saw the booted foot lunging towards him, he tried to keep singing.

The foot caught him in the throat, cracking his chin upwards.

He tried to keep singing but only a rasping groan issued from his mouth. Another kick caught him in the diaphragm – and the last air wheezed out of him. Fire shot along his ribs as he tried to draw in a gasp of air.

' "Free—" ' he managed before another kick silenced him.

'What is the meaning of this?'

Khassian cowered into the corner, arms flung up over his head, anticipating more blows.

'Move away from the prisoner. Do as I say!'

A rush of blood fouled Khassian's mouth. When he tried to open his eyes, the cell blurred and he could not even tell how many Guerriors had come crowding in.

'But he was singing. He was inciting the others –'

'Stand to attention when you address your superiors!'

An officer, Khassian thought blearily. He coughed and retched up a mouthful of blood.

'If there's any punishment to be detailed to the Sanctuarees, *I* will give the orders. Now get out.'

There was a moment's hesitation then Khassian's assailants turned smartly, clicking their heels, and left.

A shadow loomed over Khassian. Someone gripped hold of him.

'No, no,' he whimpered. 'No more –'

'Easy, easy. I'm not going to hurt you.'

The voice, now that it had shed the harsh tones of command, was hushed, oddly gentle. Someone began to dab the blood from his split lip. Through the pain-haze, Khassian identified a blur of dark hair, grey as steel . . .

'Korentan,' he murmured. Blood and saliva came dribbling out down his chin. The first kick to the face must have driven his teeth into his tongue. 'What –'

'Don't talk,' Acir ordered. He propped Khassian up against the bed; Khassian slid drunkenly sideways. Firm hands caught him, propped him up again.

Acir Korentan's fingers moved over his face, expertly testing, feeling.

'Where does it hurt? No – don't speak. Just point.'

'Ahh.' Khassian drew in his breath as the searching fingers found another bruise. 'You're – 'sbad as your – damn – thugs.'

'Commanderie thugs,' Korentan corrected, raising Khassian's soiled tunic. 'Take in a breath. And another.'

'Whas – th'diff'rence?' Khassian shut his eyes, wincing. 'You're all – ahh – th'same.'

Korentan pulled back the tunic, all his movements brisk, efficient. He seemed not to have heard the rancour in Khassian's mumbled words.

'Cracked ribs. They need binding.'

'Don't – want – your help.' Khassian ground the words out between gritted teeth. 'Don't – want – your compassion – Guerrior.'

Korentan sat back on his heels. For the first time Khassian saw a look of puzzlement cloud the intense blue of his eyes.

'Understand?' Khassian hissed. 'Don't – interfere. Leave me – alone.'

There was a moment's silence. Then Korentan stood up.

'I'll get the surgeon.'

Khassian lay slowly back, letting the dark enfold him. His bruises throbbed but he welcomed the pain. Pain had reawakened his anger. And he needed that anger – he had begun to slip into a mire of hopelessness and self-pity.

Now he knew for sure. There were others out there who felt the same as he did. He was not alone.

Acir found nel Macy tucking into his breakfast in the dining hall; the Governor had piled his plate with spiced sausage, coddled eggs, salt pork and fried mushrooms. Acir was hungry but found his appetite fast fading as he watched the Captain busily forking in mouthfuls of food.

'Governor,' he said, saluting.

'Sit down.' Nel Macy pointed with his fork to the place beside his.

'The behaviour of your men last night was very remiss. Several of the Sanctuarees were brutally beaten.'

'My men acted swiftly and efficiently,' nel Macy said, his mouth half-full of sausage. 'The disturbance was stopped almost before it began.'

'Does singing constitute a disturbance?'

'And *what* were they singing?' Nel Macy speared another slice of sausage. 'Seditious songs. Banned songs. We can't have that, Captain Korentan. For all I know, that song could have been the signal for a mass break-out.'

'There are other ways to calm a disturbance. The surgeon's bound up three cases of cracked ribs, one broken collar bone and two smashed wrists. I want those Guerriors disciplined.'

'Are you implying that I can't control my own men?'

'Six men are out of action, that's six men fewer to work at the Fortress. What will the Grand Maistre say to that?'

Nel Macy's face darkened. When he spoke, the hairs in his sandy moustache bristled. 'Girim nel Ghislain entrusted the running of this Sanctuary to me, Captain Korentan. If you have any complaints, take them to him.'

Silence had fallen in the dining hall; Acir became aware that Guerriors and servitors alike were staring towards the officers' table.

'As I understand it, Captain, you are here in an advisory capacity. Never forget who is Governor of this Sanctuary.' The fork jabbed at Acir, emphasising each word. 'You do your job and leave me to do mine.'

Acir stayed gazing at nel Macy a moment longer. Then he turned on his heel and left him to his breakfast.

Slowly he climbed the rampart stair until he stood on the battlements, gazing out over the heath towards the city. The morning air was damp, touched with a brumy reek of mist and chimney smoke. The rose-stone shell of the half-built Fortress of Faith dominated the wasteland, encased in its cage of scaffolding and ladders.

Acir gripped the rampart rail.

Had he given away too much? Had nel Macy marked him out as a trouble-maker? There was no way he could have stayed silent – but now he knew himself to be alienated from his fellow Guerriors at the Sanctuary. And if he was to be of any help to Khassian and the other Sanctuarees, there must be no suspicion that his sympathies lay with them.

He had never felt so alone in his life before.

CHAPTER 23

The letter bore the official rose-seal of the Order of the Rosecoeur. But when Acir broke the seal, he found only the laconic instructions:

Attend on me at the Winter Palace tonight. Wistaria Apartments, West Wing, first floor.

Girim usually signed his correspondence – and there was no signature. But the seal was authentic.

Once he would have felt a genuine pleasure at being summoned to Girim's presence. Now all he felt was a dull sense of dread. What new atrocity had the Grand Maistre planned in the name of the Commanderie? Another torchlight procession to welcome more new converts to the Faith? Would he be forced to watch another unfortunate prostrate himself on Mhir's tomb and stammer out the words of contrition – words spoken in fear, not in true faith and humility?

But he had been summoned so he must go.

The night was close, sultry, and little shivers of wind stirred the trees in the Palace Gardens; Acir thought he could hear the distant rumble of thunder far out on the Dniera plain.

The West Wing was not directly connected to the royal apartments and although candles burned in the crystal chandeliers, the corridors were deserted. No one challenged Acir as he climbed the elegant winding stair, his solitary footfall echoing hollowly in the marble stairwell. Shutters rattled in the fitful wind.

He wandered the upper floor until he came to a painted door decorated with a border of wistaria; he opened it and found himself not in a private office as he had expected but a candlelit bedroom hung with wistaria-painted silks: soft green, grey and mauve.

'Good evening, Captain Korentan.'

A woman was sitting before a mirror, combing her hair with long, slow strokes; its marigold brightness glinted in the candlelight.

'Fiammis?' he said, confused.

'And you thought it was Girim who had summoned you here.'

Fiammis was smiling at her reflection, a strange smile, as if she was amused by something of which he was not yet aware.

'Have you forgotten so soon? You owe me a favour, Acir.'

'I owe you nothing.'

'Amaru Khassian?'

'Khassian? Who is even now in prison?'

'Ah, but the favour was in exchange for his life.' She set down her comb with a sudden movement that made him jump. 'Not his liberty.'

Her smile appalled him; it was as if she were playing some bizarre game with him in which only she knew the rules.

'What favour then?' he said tensely.

'Nel Macy believes you are on official Commanderie business. You are not due back on duty till dawn.' She rose and moved across to him. 'Who will ever know? Who would even care?'

Only now did he realise what she was proposing. He felt a slow flame rising through his body until his face burned. How stupid she must think him. To be so unworldly, so unimaginative, not to have understood.

She had moved closer still, one hand sliding along his collar, lifting his hair to stroke the nape of his neck.

He caught her wrist and held her at arm's length.

'Don't,' he said harshly. 'Don't do this, Fia.'

To his astonishment she began to cry. 'I had hoped you would understand.'

'What is there to understand?

'Oh, you don't have to say it aloud. I see it in your eyes. Killer. Cold, calculating killer. But I was driven to it, Acir, I had to do it – or sell myself to live.'

Still he did not believe her.

'You married the Conte. You were rich.'

'The Conte? Old and impotent.' The words came out between sobs – ugly, wrenching sobs that were not, he now saw, in the least feigned. 'When he died, his family moved in to evict me, the vultures, before he was even cold. No heir – so no estate, no money. The title I could keep.'

'I didn't know.'

Thunder rumbled closer, a long, ominous drum-roll. The storm was blowing towards Bel'Esstar.

'How could you have known? You were half a world away, fighting to preserve some ancient shrine.' She looked up at him, the perfection of her creamy skin blotched, blue eyes red with weeping. 'I was alone. And friendless. There were men who thought they could take advantage of me.' Her voice hardened. 'I proved them wrong. That was how I came to the attention of the Prince's secret service. It was pointed out to me that I could use my talents "for the good of the state". They would train me, give me authority. But if I ever chose to leave . . . then I would be fully answerable for all my crimes. A neat little piece of blackmail, yes?'

Acir listened in numbed silence.

'But killing?' He cleared his throat. 'In cold blood?'

'A woman alone has to learn to protect herself.'

'There must have been some other way –'

But she was not hearing what he was saying, she seemed snared in some private horror of her own weaving.

'Do you know what they do to convicted murderers? Don't believe Girim's talk of leniency. First they shave your head.' Her fingers moved up across her skull, touching, caressing her hair. 'Then they parade you through the streets on a cart with a noose around your neck, to be pelted with mud. Abused. Spat at.' Her voice had dropped to a monotone. 'The gallows is on Pasperdu Hill. Haven't you seen the corpses left to dangle there till they rot?'

'Oh, Fia, Fia . . .' he said, unable to hide the ache in his voice.

'Just seeing you here, just hearing you call me Fia . . .' She nestled against him. 'No one else ever called me Fia. If only we could go back – if only we could be as we were then.'

He felt the weight of her golden head against his shoulder, the warmth of her body pressed against his. If he shut his eyes, he could remember that distant summer meadow, the dazzle of sunlight, the green smell of crushed grasses as he pulled her down into his arms, the taste of her, sweet yet sharp, like early apples.

'Help me, Acir,' she said, mouth moving against the base of his throat. 'I am so very, very wretched.'

He could not bear to think that beneath this radiantly beautiful shell lay such a void of cynicism and despair.

The shutters blew inwards, gusting rain into the room.

'A storm!' Fiammis cried. She ran to the open casement and out on to the balcony, raising her face to the pouring rain. 'I love storms!'

Lightning lit the dark sky, lit her rain-streaked face, and she flung up her arms as if to welcome it.

'Are you crazy?' Acir cried. He went out on to the balcony and caught hold of her as thunder rumbled closer. 'You could get killed!'

'But what a magnificent way to die!' she cried, laughing. 'Seared by elemental fire!'

'Come back inside,' he begged her, pulling her towards him. Suddenly she was in arms and kissing him hungrily as the thunder-rain poured down, drenching them both. And a heat burned through his body like a raging fever as a host of forbidden sensations reawakened.

'No,' said Acir, gasping. Her lips were wet and cold, tainted with the bitter thunder-rain, but her tongue tasted sweet. He picked her up in his arms and lifted her back over the sill into the bedchamber.

'You're soaked to the skin,' he said hoarsely. He set her down but still she clung to him.

'So are you.' Her fingers moved to unfasten his wet jacket, his shirt.

'You should dry yourself –'

'I should?'

She gave a little shrug and the drenched gown slipped from her shoulders to the floor.

'Fia . . .' he whispered.

'Shhh.' She wound her arms around him, pressing her wet body against his burning skin. Her breasts crushed against him, slippery with rainwater.

The tempest broke outside, battering the shutters with its violence, howling about the Palace rooftops. But Acir was aware only of the raging of his senses and her subtle, sinuous movements as Fiammis entwined herself around him, drawing him inside her. And inside all was dark heat and sweetness. His veins seemed to run with honey, he could feel the golden liquid coursing through his body, coursing ever stronger until it spilled over and he felt himself melting into that dark heat –

The thunder cracked overhead and the shutters blew inwards. Out went the candle-flames and the room was filled with rainwet blackness.

Acir gave a cry and rolled away, his voice swallowed by the thunder's deafening roar that shook the whole city.

Blinded by the white glare of the flickering lightning, he rocked in silent misery, shielding his head from the storm's fury. Fiammis lay in the lightning's shadow, watching him. After a while he raised his head and gazed at her.

'Why?' It was more of a cry of pain than a word. 'Why, Fia?' First the sweetness, then the aftertaste. And the aftertaste, bitter-black as aloes, filled him with revulsion for what had first seemed so sweet.

'Because I wanted you. I always wanted you.' She stroked his cheek and he shuddered at her touch, a faint flicker of burning honey still afire in his loins. 'And you wanted me. Your need was as great, don't deny it. What point your vows of celibacy, what point all those fruitless years of self-denial and privation? Is that what Mhir asks of you?'

In one night he had broken the contract he had made with his god. All he foresaw now for himself was years of penance, of monastic desolation, shunned by his fellow Guerriors, despised as the man who betrayed his vows for one brief moment of love.

Sweat, colder than the gusting rain outside, chilled his body. He seized his clothes, tugging on his breeches, his boots, buckling on his sword.

'Where are you going?' She knelt up on the bed. 'Don't go. Don't leave me.'

'I have to go.'

'Come back, Acir!'

He heard her still calling his name as he went down the stairs and out into the night. He could not stay. If he had stayed, he would have broken his vows again.

She had revealed his weakness. He had vowed at Mhir's shrine to stay pure in mind and body, the better to serve the will of the All-Seeing. If he was unable to keep that covenant, what right had be to be a Guerrior? Heedless of the driving rain or the howling wind, he walked on through the streets of the city.

She had said she loved him . . . but was she merely playing with him? In those fleeting moments of passion, he had believed her . . . but it could all have been another deception, a cruel trap set by the Grand Maistre to test his resolve. She was Girim's agent still.

The storm seemed to be abating, rolling on across the river plain towards the sea. In the first rain-streaked light of dawn, he found he had made his way to the half-built Fortress of Faith.

He went down into the darkness of the shrine. Racked with shame and despair, he slowly bent forwards until his forehead touched the worn stone of the Prophet's tomb.

'Help me. *Help me.*'

Fiammis sat motionless in front of her mirror. Behind her, the open shutters still banged and creaked in the dying storm-wind.

She should feel triumphant. She had achieved her aim. She had made the virtuous Acir Korentan break his vow of chastity; she had proved that he was a man, like any other. Just another conquest . . .

She reached, unseeing, for her comb and began to drag it through her rain-darkened hair, still staring at her reflection.

Why then did she feel a shiver of desire when her lips framed his name? Why did her body still burn where he had touched her, held her? Why did she feel tears welling up as she remembered how he had drawn away from her, eyes bleak with betrayal.

She rose in a sudden movement, knocking over the chair on which she had been sitting.

Would he ever come back? Or would he look through her when next they met, pretending they were strangers?

The thought was unbearable.

All she wanted was to see him again, to feel his hand caress her hair. It was as if a burning wind had swept through her, searing her in its flame. She craved to be burned again, consumed to ashes in its cleansing flames.

'Acir . . .' she whispered his name aloud. 'Oh, Acir . . . come back to me.'

Sister Crespine raised her hand to knock on Dr Magelonne's door – and stopped, seeing it was ajar. Through the glass she glimpsed Magelonne

261

sitting with his head in his hands, his spectacles lying on the desk beside a pile of bills. Unpaid bills.

She hesitated. He would not want to hear the news she had brought. First his daughter . . . now the Sanatorium. Troubles, nothing but troubles. She wished she had thought to bring a tray of tea with her, to sweeten the tidings.

She tapped lightly on the engraved glass.

'Come in,' he said. There was a dragging weariness in his voice. 'Oh, it's you, Sister. Not more bills, I hope.'

'More cancellations, I'm afraid. The news has spread.'

'You've assured the patients that we can heat riverwater, we can still provide excellent treatment?'

'Yes, yes, I've made every assurance. But no one seems to want second-best. You can't blame them really, can you? We made our reputation on the healing properties of the mineral springs. Now we've no mineral water . . .'

'You've been at the Sanatorium – how many years, is it now? Fifteen, sixteen years? I don't want to have to release you but . . .' he gestured to the bills '. . . I don't know if I can pay your wages beyond this month. If you want to go elsewhere –'

'I wouldn't dream of it!' exclaimed Sister Crespine. 'I'll stand by you, Doctor. You can depend on me.'

The porter appeared in the doorway, staggering slightly.

'Message for you, Doctor.'

'Thank you.' Sister Crespine snatched the piece of paper from his hand and gave it to Doctor Magelonne. 'Doesn't that man ever knock?' she said in a loud whisper. 'And he's been at the cider again, I can smell it on his breath. Why, whatever is it, Doctor?'

Magelonne was staring at the paper.

'Not more bad news?'

'Bel'Esstar,' he muttered. '*Bel'Esstar!*' He stood up.

'News about Orial?'

'From the Diligence Company. One of their drivers says he took a young woman answering Orial's description to Bel'Esstar last week – in company with a "rather loud, theatrical person answering to the name of Cramoisy Jordelayne".'

'Bel'Esstar!' Sister Crespine was shocked. 'Whatever would make her want to go there? All those religious fanatics . . .'

Dr Magelonne suddenly walked straight past her.

'Where are you going, Doctor?'

'I'm going to get her back.'

'But the patients, Doctor – the bills!'

'Will have to wait till I return,' he called back over his shoulder.

*

Jerame sat in the antechamber to the Grand Maistre's apartments in company with many other petitioners. The hard little gilt-backed chairs that lined the walls were exceptionally uncomfortable: too low for a tall man like Jerame and too close together, so that his elbows kept colliding with the petitioners sitting on either side of him. The elegant clothes of many of the petitioners also made him feel uncomfortable in his drab doctor's suit. Was he being ignored because of his lowly dress?

This was the second day he had come to wait his turn to see the Grand Maistre – and there were still others ahead of him in the queue. How many days would he have to wait? Would he have spent his time more profitably searching the streets of Bel'Esstar, making his own enquiries?

A woman in full court dress came sweeping into the antechamber. There was a noticeable stir of admiration in the crowded room. Jerame looked up – and saw the Contesse Fiammis. Starting out of his chair, he half-raised one hand to greet her – and then, embarrassed in case she ignored him, sat down again.

'Why, Doctor Magelonne.' She had recognised him. 'Whatever are you doing here?' It was stiflingly close in the antechamber and she was fanning herself with an ivory fan.

'I'm searching for my daughter, Contesse. I have reason to believe she may be in Bel'Esstar.'

'And why is that, pray?' A seemingly innocent question . . . yet the Contesse's blue eyes suddenly glittered with curiosity.

'Amaru Khassian,' he said in a whisper.

She snapped the fan shut.

'I was just on my way in to see the Grand Maistre. You may accompany me.'

'I am grateful for this information, Dr Magelonne.' Girim nel Ghislain folded his hands upon the desk-top, as though in prayer. 'You have already been most helpful to the Cause. I would like to express my thanks to you in some appropriate way. How can the Commanderie help you?'

Jerame had vowed that he would not let himself be overawed by being granted a personal interview with the Grand Maistre himself.

'I want to find my daughter, Grand Maistre,' he said brusquely. 'That's all.'

Girim glanced up at the Contesse who had sat motionless throughout the interview. Jerame saw her nod, almost imperceptibly.

'My agents will find her, never fear, Dr Magelonne.'

'But if she has involved herself with dissidents –'

'I will endeavour to ensure she is unharmed,' the Contesse said coolly, 'although I cannot wholly guarantee it.'

'There won't be any charges, will there?' Jerame's anxiety broke through. 'She's only a young girl, she's had her head filled with idealistic claptrap, she doesn't know what she's doing –'

'There have been reports from Sulien which interest me,' Girim said. 'Is it true that the hot springs have dried up?'

'Well, yes, it appears to be so.' Jerame was flustered now; was he to be interrogated about the mineral waters – and if so, why? What possible interest could the Grand Maistre have in their domestic problems?

'I can see that this would pose a problem for healers like yourself who rely on the hot springs for their livelihood. But in a wider, more spiritual context . . .'

'I – I don't quite follow.'

' "*A time shall yet come when the sacred flame burns low in the shrines and temples.*" ' Girim's eyes were half-closed, fixed on some distant point. ' "*And the heathen shall defile the holy places, yea even the sacred name of the Prophet shall be mocked and reviled in his holy city. The healing waters shall run dry, even the hot springs that gush from the sacred womb of the earth.*" '

'The healing waters?' echoed Jerame, puzzled.

Girim's eyes were open again, staring directly into his.

'Do you not know the words of the Prophet Mhir?'

By now Jerame was feeling distinctly hot; his hand crept to his collar, trying to loosen it.

'For any believer, these words are of the utmost significance. In them, Mhir foresees His death – and His resurrection. His second coming.'

Now Jerame could see the fires burning behind the clear grey eyes. He felt suddenly afraid.

'B-but you're not saying that Sulien –'

'It is yet another fulfilment of the prophecies. First the birthplace in Enhirrë then the Prince's miraculous recovery. You bring me good tidings, Dr Magelonne. This only serves to confirm what I have known in my heart to be right. We stand on the threshold of a time of wonders. We await His return.'

Outside, in the antechamber, Jerame leant against the wall and fumbled for his handkerchief to mop his forehead. He felt ill.

There was a geological explanation for the drying of the waters, he was certain of it. Mining in the mountains could have silted up the source. Or a run of dry summers. That or – most likely of all – poorly maintained plumbing. The City Council had tried to save funds by neglecting to repair or replace worn pipes. The precious water must have been seeping away into the soil for months, maybe even years.

'Such an inspiration, our Grand Maistre,' said a voice at his elbow. He looked around to see the Grand Maistre's secretary nodding at him. 'A man of such vision. I often feel quite overcome – just like you – after our little meetings together.' He offered Jerame a glass of water. Nodding his thanks, Jerame took the glass and gulped down the water.

The doors opened again and the Contesse came out. She stopped by

Jerame and tapped him sharply on the arm with her fan. He started, spilling water down his shirt.

'Thank you for your information, Doctor. Write down your address so that I may send you any information as to your daughter's whereabouts.' She spoke without any expression.

Jerame wrote down the name of the lodging house; his hand, normally so steady, shook.

She took the paper from him and folded it.

'I cannot guarantee her safety. In the interests of state security, I will take what measures I must. Do you understand me? She has involved herself with dangerous people – and she must face the consequences.'

'Letter from the Palace for you, Captain Korentan.'

Acir glanced up from the report he was penning to see the Guerrior place a sealed paper on the table in front of him. His hand moved out automatically to pick it up – and then stayed motionless in the air above the letter. It bore the seal of the Order of the Rosecoeur, the sealing-wax rose a bright gloss-red.

Rainwet hair against his bare chest, the dark-honeyed sweetness of her kiss –
No, Fiammis was too subtle to play that trick twice.

He took up the letter and cracked open the seal:

I need to see your report on Amaru Khassian. Bring it to the shrine after even-prayer tonight.
   Girim nel Ghislain

The writing and signature were not forged; he knew Girim's firm, self-assured hand too well.

He looked down at the report. It was a fabrication, deliberately written to play for time. It spoke of a significant change in Khassian's attitude to the concept of conversion. Acir prayed that by the time Girim nel Ghislain decided to investigate that change of attitude for himself, Khassian would have crossed the border in Orial Magelonne's carriage.

As to what would become of himself when his part was discovered . . .

He put the thought from his mind. As long as Khassian was free, there was hope for the people of Bel'Esstar.

At night the unfinished walls of the Fortress of Faith towered like the sheer walls of a moonless gorge, gateway to a profound abyss.

The evening shift had worked until the end of the light. Acir passed them on the heath as they made their way back towards the Sanctuary, many stumbling with exhaustion.

The site was empty, eerily silent now that the day's clamour had ceased.

Holding aloft a lantern, he picked his way through the piles of masonry, the arched window frames, the stacked roof joists and timbers, to the concealed entrance to Mhir's shrine.

Girim knelt at prayer alone in the shrine. Alone – unguarded.

Incense smoke twirled slowly up into the gloom, spicing the air with dark and costly fumes. If he closed his eyes, Acir could think himself back in Enhirrë, standing guard at the birthplace shrine on a hot, airless night, breathing the dry and pungent scents of the desert: nard poppy, curcumine and cardamom . . .

But as his eyes closed, the cherished memories of the desert vanished and fire-streaked visions scored across his sight: the Winter Palace in flames, rebels fighting Guerriors hand-to-hand in the street, cobbles slippery with the blood of innocents –

Acir's hand crept to the hilt of his sword.

Rid Bel'Esstar of the tyrant.

The Grand Maistre suddenly senses his stealthy footfall approaching – and turns. The smile of recognition freezes on his face as he sees the assassin's steel. His hands flail wildly as he tries to fend off the frenzied blows, until he slumps forward, his blood defiling the tomb.

Acir pressed his hands to his eyes.

He could not do it. He could not kill Girim, even this changed Girim, this brutal distortion of the man he had once loved.

But neither could he stand by and let the atrocities continue.

He placed his report at the entrance to the shrine and went silently away.

Dragonflies dance over the riverwaters. They dart like arrows across the sun-warmed shallows.

Earth, air, fire and water.

Orial kneels on the bank. They flock to her, circling her head, a winged coronet.

They weave, in and out, each one threading a songline like a jewelled streamer until the air sparkles with sound.

Orial raises her hands, enchanted by the spinning singers.

The spinning circle widens. A whirlpool yawns, the cold, dark vortex opening to swallow her, to drag her down into oblivion –

Orial's eyes opened. She was lying in bed in the Villa of Yellow Vines, clutching at the coverlet, staring straight ahead of her.

The dragonflies were gone. But the melody threads had clung to her memory, sticky as spider-silk.

Somewhere in the street far below her window she could hear the clank of the water churns as the waterman delivered the Villa's supply. Sparrows were squabbling in the gutter. Ordinary sounds of an ordinary day. Yet all the sounds were distant, as though heard from the end of a far tunnel.

Orial staggered out of bed and opened the window. The slow clip-clop of the waterman's horse echoed around the empty street, the grind of the cart wheels over the cobbles.

Louder still, much louder, was the still-spinning song of her dream, the song of the winged ones. She banged the window shut. The glass shuddered in the pane – she felt its vibrations – yet the bang was a remote sound, hardly registering above the insistent web of dream-music.

She made her way back towards the bed. Each footfall resounded hollowly as though she was walking through a vast, echoing cavern. Each step was an effort as – disorientated – she seemed to have forgotten how to move in this heavy human body.

She had felt like this once before. But when was it? She had a vague memory of Papa forcing vile-tasting medicine down her throat, of this light-headedness, faces swimming above hers . . .

'Accidie,' she murmured aloud.

There was a sharp tap at the door.

'Orial, Korentan's sent us a message!' Cramoisy's voice fluttered with excitement. 'Listen to this! "A visit has been arranged for this afternoon." A visit! This is it! Start packing!'

Accidie.

Orial pressed her finger-tips to her throbbing temples.

Why? Why today, of all days, when she needed her faculties to be at their most acute? She had known the period of remission might be short – but she had never imagined it would recur so soon.

'Give me a little more time,' she pleaded silently. 'Just a little.'

'Captain Korentan?'

The youthful voice made Acir stop and turn around. The young Guerrior at the gate saluted him; beneath the guard-helm his face was brown, burned by the sun.

'Tobyn!' he said. And then, overwhelmed with gladness at the sight of a familiar face, he put his hands on the young man's shoulders and embraced him. 'But I thought you were still in Enhirrë?'

'The detachment sailed into Bel'Esstar a couple of days ago. They transferred most of us here. It's good to see you again, Captain.'

'How's the shoulder?'

'Fine, Captain.' Tobyn flashed him a broad grin. 'Though it wouldn't have been so fine with me if you hadn't beaten those Enhirran Sbarreurs off in the raid. I'll never forget what you did.'

Acir acknowledged the compliment with a smile. 'And the others?'

Tobyn leaned forward, lowering his voice.

'A mite perplexed, Captain. We didn't come back to be prison warders. Not to our own countrymen. What's been going on?'

Acir felt a brief flutter of hope in his heart. At least the members of his

Enhirran detachment were still uncorrupted.

Perhaps he was not entirely alone after all.

The closed fiacre drew up at the gate to the Sanctuary as the Guerriors on guard waved the coachman to a stop.

'What's happening?' whispered Cramoisy to Orial.

'Out. All Sanctuary visitors get out here.'

Orial and Cramoisy climbed down; as they were showing their passes, more Guerriors clambered into the fiacre, prodding the leather seats and checking the roof for concealed weapons.

'Mind where you're poking those pikes!' called the coachman, aggrieved. 'That's expensive leather. If anything's ripped, I'll take the bill direct to your Grand Maistre.'

'This isn't going to be so easy,' Cramoisy said in Orial's ear. Beneath the crimson perruque his brow was glistening with sweat.

'Think of them as a difficult audience.' Orial murmured back. 'Play them for all you're worth. You know you can do it. You're the Diva.'

Cramoisy nodded.

'Conduct the visitors to the gatehouse!' called the Guerrior who had taken their passes.

Orial darted little glances around the courtyard, hoping in vain she might catch sight of Captain Korentan. And when they were ushered into a bare, barred room and the door was instantly locked, she found herself staring apprehensively at Cramoisy, wondering if she had been deceived.

He went to the door and rattled the handle.

'There! I told you! A Commanderie trap. Pfui! What an unpleasant stink there is to this place. Next to the latrines, I shouldn't wonder.'

'Hush.' Orial raised one finger, listening. 'Someone's coming. Sit down. Keep your face in shadow.'

As she heard the key grind in the lock, Orial hurried over to Cramoisy's side. He clasped hold of her hands.

The door opened. A man, shambling and ragged, was pushed inside.

'You have a quarter of an hour.'

The door shut and the key turned again.

The man blinked in the light. He seemed unsteady on his feet. Orial went towards him.

'Orial Magelonne?' he said uncertainly. 'Orial?'

'Yes,' she said, tears starting to her eyes. 'Yes, it's me.' He looked so gaunt, so frail; the meagre light obviously hurt his eyes. 'And look who is also here to see you.'

'I don't think much of your new tailor,' Cramoisy said, venturing forwards. 'If I were you, *miu caru*, I'd take your custom elsewhere.'

'Oh, Cram,' said Khassian, extending one arm to hug him.

'God, you could do with a bath!' said Cramoisy in tones of high disgust.

But his voice wavered and Orial saw tears glistening in his eyes too. They stood rocking gently together, the three of them, locked in a triangular embrace.

'What day is it?' Khassian asked after a while. 'What time?'

Cramoisy straightened up. 'Time you were out of here.'

'They'll never agree to that.'

'Get those rags off.' After so many days languishing in self-pity, the Diva seemed suddenly charged with vitality.

'What do you mean?' Khassian looked baffled.

'You heard me. Now don't tell me you're going to make a fuss!' Cramoisy lifted the heavy perruque off his head and placed it on Khassian, tucking in escaping curls of dark hair. 'There. Not a bad fit. It hides the ear-tag rather neatly, don't you think?'

'Cram, what is all this? What've you done to your own hair? You've dyed it brown?'

'Autumn Bronze, please – not brown. Orial, watch the door. Don't turn around until I tell you.' Cramoisy had begun to unbutton his embroidered top-coat, to untie the lacy jabot. 'Strip off, Amar. She's not going to peep. Are you, Orial?'

'Exchange clothes? With you?'

'You're going on a journey. To Sulien. Here – let me.'

'Just exactly what do you think you're doing?'

'*Samira*, Act Four. Remember?'

'Cram, this isn't an opera. This is real.'

'I *know*.' Cramoisy glared at him. 'So stop wasting time and put on my clothes.'

'I can't.'

'What? Do you mean you're going to stop me giving the greatest performance of my career?'

'I won't. I won't let you do it. They'll kill you.'

'And how long will you last if you stay here?'

'I can't go and leave the other Sanctuarees behind.'

'What nonsense! How can you help the others whilst you're in here? Outside you can organise an escape far more effectively.'

Orial sensed Khassian hesitate.

'Now for Mhir's sake, give me that apology for a garment and stop delaying.'

'You'll have to help me.'

Orial heard the capitulation in his voice. But she also heard footsteps in the corridor outside.

'Someone's coming!' she cried, starting up. Only a few minutes had elapsed. Had they been betrayed?

The door opened – and Acir Korentan came in, closing the door instantly behind him. Orial saw that his face was taut, his eyes troubled.

269

'Oh, Captain,' cried Cramoisy in tones of extravagant relief, 'what a scare you gave us.'

'There's no time,' he said. 'You must go now.'

'He'll do, won't he, Captain?' Cramoisy said, stepping back to assess Khassian's transformation. 'Though I have to say he's nowhere near as devastating as me.'

'Cram—' began Khassian.

'Go!' Cramoisy gave him a push towards the door.

'Take care,' Orial whispered, pressing Cramoisy's hand in her own.

'My greatest performance,' he said.

Without the elaborate wig, fashionable clothes and exaggerated maquillage, the Diva seemed to have dwindled to a shade of his ebullient self.

Captain Korentan ushered Orial and Khassian out into the passageway and locked Cramoisy in the interview chamber.

At the entrance to the passageway, two Guerriors stood on guard.

'Take 654 back to his cell,' Captain Korentan called over his shoulder.

Khassian stumbled; Captain Korentan put out one arm to steady him. The large wig tipped awry; Orial reached up to adjust it, glancing nervously all about her to see who was watching. Wherever she looked there seemed to be grey Commanderie uniforms.

'Don't upset yourself, Diva,' she soothed. '*Keep your head down*,' she whispered as she helped Khassian up into the coach.

'Open the gates!' called Captain Korentan.

The fiacre began to move slowly, oh, so slowly, towards the gates. Orial risked a glance at Khassian who had huddled into the corner. Passing the guards at the gate was the last hurdle to be overcome. And in daylight, the exchange would be more obvious.

'Your papers.' Captain Korentan handed the papers through the window. 'May I wish you safe journey back to Sulien.'

'Thank you, Captain.' Her fingers brushed his and she was overwhelmed with a sudden premonition, clouds gathering in a lightning-gashed sky.

And then they were rattling through the gates and out on to the potholed heath road. Orial sat unmoving, clutching the papers to her, staring straight ahead.

A litle starburst of light burst on the edge of her vision. And then another. And another.

She shut her eyes; the pinpricks of light continued to form – and burst – against the darkness. She felt suddenly sick and ill. Maybe a storm was approaching . . .

The fiacre lurched suddenly, swinging to one side. Orial was almost thrown to the floor.

The driver reined the horses to a stop; Orial heard him leap up, swearing.

Opening the window, she was choked by a cloud of dust rising from the wheels of a swift phaeton, galloping past them towards the Sanctuary.

'Are you all right, demselle, Diva?'

'Yes,' gasped Orial through the dust. Khassian nodded his head.

'Cursed speedster! Almost had us in the ditch!'

'Open up! Commanderie business!'

Acir recognised Fiammis's voice. Just to hear it evoked memories, painful memories dark with anger . . . and desire.

He beckoned Tobyn over to him.

'Stall her. Give me a few minutes.'

'What's wrong, Captain?' The young man stared at him in dismay.

'Everything, Tobyn. Everything.'

He pushed the Guerrior out to greet her.

'A young Sulien woman came visiting here today. Where is she?' Fiammis's voice was sharp and keen; she was predator still, delighting in the pursuit of her prey. 'Is she still here? I need to speak with her.'

'I – I'll have to check. I've only just come on duty.'

Fiammis was on Orial's trail. It would not be long before the deception was discovered – and the alarm bell rang out across the heath.

He must warn them. Protect them. Above all, they must not fall into Commanderie hands again.

There was another way out of the Sanctuary, a side door leading from the stables – for the use of officers only. Nel Macy's roan mare was standing ready saddled and bridled in the stalls; Acir made a swift adjustment to the stirrups and led her out through the side door. Once on the heath, he climbed up into the saddle and set off in pursuit of the fiacre.

As he rode, he heard the bell began to clang.

He should have known he could not outwit Fiammis.

CHAPTER 24

The roan mare soon caught up with the fiacre as it bumped across the heath road.

Acir reined the mare to a trot, bringing her alongside the carriage window, matching her pace to the vehicle's slow progress.

The window flap opened and a head sporting an outrageously red wig appeared. Acir almost laughed aloud; the danger of the situation and the incongruity of this ludicrous perruque gave him a sudden wild surge of elation.

'What in hell's name are you doing?' demanded Khassian. Beneath the wig, his eyes burned.

'Escorting you.'

'Won't that draw attention to us?'

'There have been rumours of brigands on the heath.'

'So they're after us already?' Khassian was obviously not to be fobbed off with so lame an excuse.

'Maybe.' Acir pulled the mare's head to one side and scanned the heath. Clouds were scudding up fast, dark, boiling clouds, threatening a storm. Sunlight glittered on the towers and cupolas of Bel'Esstar, unnaturally bright.

If he was leading the pursuit, what would he do?

Simple. He would cut them off at the river.

The only way to cross the wide Dniera in a carriage was by the New Bridge. The old bridges still bristled with ramshackle houses, too narrow for a modern carriage to pass across unimpeded.

A turbulence of dust darkened the heath behind them. Horses. Skirting to the west – but also heading towards the river.

Could he get them to the bridge before their pursuers?

Orial gripped the leather strap tightly as the fiacre wheels juddered over another pothole.

Little stars of sound kept bursting in her mind, like exploding rockets on the Day of the Dead. The slightest noise, the slightest jolt, was a torment to her aching head.

'Are you all right?' Khassian was staring at her from beneath Cramoisy's wig. She so wanted to lean across and touch him to make sure

272

he was really there. 'You look as if you're going to faint.'

'I never faint,' Orial snapped back. 'I have a slight headache. That's all.'

This was no megrim or fainting fit. It was the chaos of the Accidie. Her mind was beginning to disintegrate as splinters of sound flew from the star-explosions.

She had chosen to undertake this rescue mission; she had to see it through. If it was her last conscious act before the Accidie robbed her of her reason, then at least she would have done something of merit in her brief life. She might not have been given time to compose the music she had dreamed of . . . but she would have saved Amaru Khassian to continue the fight against the tyranny of the Commanderie.

Let me just get him safely back to Sulien.

They joined other fiacres and phaetons clattering over the wide gravel avenue that led through the tree-lined Winter Gardens towards the river. Thunder growled in the distance as the sky grew darker and a few rain-spots spattered on to the plane leaves. Acir could smell the coming storm on the earthy wind; so could the mare who jittered her head nervously from side to side. But still the storm did not break and the sense of tension increased in the darkening air.

At least the new wide-arched bridge with its bronze basilisk lamps was in sight now. And traffic still seemed to be passing across.

As the fiacre slowed at the approach to the bridge, Acir rose in the saddle to try to scan the river. It was impossible to see clearly in the thunder-gloom if anyone was patrolling the opposite bank.

'The river,' Khassian said under his breath. 'We're crossing the river.'

Glancing out he could see the wide grey waters of the Dniera alive with thunderspots. For the first time he began to dare to believe that escape was possible.

'Go back,' he called out to Acir through the rain. 'You've done more than enough to help us.'

'It's too late to –'

There was a sudden flash as lightning split the sky and thunder drowned the rest of Acir's words.

Orial flinched.

'It's only a storm,' Khassian said.

She appeared not to hear him. Perhaps she was rigid with fear. He had always relished a powerful thunderstorm, the feeling of release that came when the rain had washed the humid air clean again. The thought of imminent freedom only increased his exhilaration.

And then he felt the fiacre begin to slow.

'What's up?' he called to Acir through the drumming rain.

'They're checking the carriage in front of us. Give me your papers. I'll get you through.'

Khassian held out his hand to Orial for the papers.

Can we trust him?

'We must trust him,' she said aloud, as if she had heard his question. 'There's no one else.'

Rain streamed down on Acir's head, drenching him, as he dismounted at the customs post.

'Captain!' One of the Guerriors manning the post hurried out into the rain and saluted him. 'What brings you this way on such a filthy afternoon?'

'I'm escorting these travellers back to Tourmalise.' Rain bounced off the leather folder covering the papers. 'I promised the girl's father I would protect her on the journey home.'

'All seems to be in order, Captain.' The Guerrior handed back the papers. 'I wish you better weather for your –'

There was a sudden clatter of hooves on the bridge behind them.

Acir and the Guerrior looked back. No other carriages had come across the bridge – but a troop of horsemen were riding at the gallop towards them.

'Stop that fiacre!' a voice cried through the drumming rain. Lightning split the sky apart as thunder rolled across the city.

Acir's mare shied, terrified by the noise and the oncoming horses – and bolted back across the bridge.

Acir swore.

The Guerrior, confused, seemed not to know what to do.

'Go on, man!' Acir shouted up to the driver. 'Get going!'

'Escaped Sanctuaree!'

Guerriors surrounded the fiacre and tore open the door, pulling Orial and Khassian out into the rain.

'What are you doing!' cried Acir, running forward. 'By what right do you attack innocent travellers?'

'Captain Korentan?' One of the pursuing Guerriors had recognised him; he let go of Khassian to salute. 'We have reason to believe that this is an impostor.'

A fleet phaeton was coming swiftly towards them. Its sole passenger held up a flimsy parasol, hardly any protection against the driving rain.

A parasol.

There was no time to think, hardly even time enough to react.

Acir threw himself in front of Khassian and Orial, flinging them against the side of the fiacre.

He felt the dart pierce his shoulder, a clean, pure pain, the sting of poisoned steel.

There was a stifled cry from the phaeton.

No time.

No time now.

Stumbling up, he pushed Orial and Khassian into the fiacre, clambering in after them.

'Drive!' he shouted to the driver. 'For Mhir's sake, drive!'

Lightning and thunder cracked immediately overhead. A tree on the near bank split apart in a plume of smoke and sputtering lightning fire.

The fiacre started with a jerk that flung them all to the floor.

'Keep down,' urged Acir.

The frightened horses charged on, scattering Guerriors to either side.

'They've bolted –' Orial whispered from the floor where they lay, all three tangled together.

Acir reached out with his other hand, clawing for a handhold on the leather seat to pull himself up. He could hear the driver shouting to the horses, he could feel the fiacre lurch each time he tugged on the reins.

Acir pulled open the window flap – and a cold rush of rain struck him in the face.

Behind them, their pursuers stood as though paralysed, watching. Some of the Guerriors who had been knocked over were scrambling to their feet. But even as the fiacre careered wildly from one side of the road to the other, they made no move to come after them.

Foremost amongst them he saw a woman, her gold hair windblown, darkened by the rain. She stood unmoving in the downpour beneath the dark trees. Behind her, the Dniera glistened silver with raindrops.

'Fia,' he whispered, 'farewell . . .'

A sharp shaft of pain stabbed through his shoulder.

He pressed his hand to the place and felt a sticky warmth beneath his cold fingers.

Blood.

With every movement he made, her assassin's dart would work further in, spreading its insidious poison into his bloodstream.

How long had the Sulien apothecary said before the effects of the venom began to work?

For a moment his mind went numb and blank. Then he forced himself to turn around to Orial and Khassian.

Long enough to see them safely across the border. That was all he asked.

They had huddled together in the corner, Orial clinging to Khassian. Her muslin dress was soaked, rain streaked her face. Rainbow eyes stared at him, wide with fright.

'They're slowing down,' he said, trying to sound reassuring. It was an effort to find the words; his lips and tongue seemed locked. 'Can't you feel it? And the storm's blowing away.'

Still she stared at him.

'Your shoulder,' she said. 'You're wounded.'

'A graze,' he said. 'Nothing more.'

'How far to the border?' Khassian asked.

'An hour, maybe more in this weather. The horses will be tired. It's a steep climb.'

'And if they've sent word ahead to warn the guards? A single rider travels more swiftly than a coach.'

'I'm with you.' Acir clambered clumsily on to the seat and sank back against the worn leather. 'I'll make sure – you get through – safely.'

The forest road is slowly, steadily growing darker as twilight falls. Dark cloudveils descend and a dense mist, soft as smoke, rolls through the black trees, blotting out the light.

Acir stumbles on into the night, not knowing which way to go, only that he must keep on, must keep on –

The thick mists swirl about his legs, numbing all feeling. He sinks to his knees, drowning in the chill, dark fog.

A flame sears the darkness.

Gazing upwards, he sees a sword tipped with fire cutting a path through the drowning fogs.

On his knees, he crawls towards the path.

A shadow figure moves before him through the darkness, fiery blade like a torch upheld to illumine the way.

Feathers of flame and smoke flicker in wings of fire.

The angel goes on before him and Acir follows his burning footprints into the night . . .

Someone was shaking Acir, insistently calling his name.

He regained consciousness with a start to find Khassian's eyes staring into his, dark with concern.

'S-sorry.'

'Acir, what's wrong?'

'Just – tired. Dropped off a moment.'

The ache in his shoulder had become a slow-burning fire, spreading down his arm and into his breast.

'That graze. Let Orial bind it for you. She's a doctor's daughter, after all.'

'No.' He shifted his position. He could not risk her touching the wound, for fear of contamination from the venom. Thunder still grumbled in the distance. 'How – much further now?'

'We're almost across the plain.'

'Ah.' Halfway to the border. Farther away from their pursuers – but not far enough. How long could he stay conscious this time? And when the next bout of blackness overcame him, would it be the ultimate darkness, the tumbling descent into oblivion?

Orial sat silently watching him. When he looked into her eyes, he saw the glimmer of rainwater and healing springs, mingled.

He blinked, trying to clear the rainhaze from his eyes.

Must be feverish.

Outside he glimpsed the shadows of trees. The terrain had changed. The pace of the horses slowed as the coachdriver eased them around the steep bend at the foot of the mountain road.

'Horses are all but spent, sieurs!' he called down. 'There's a coaching inn a mile or so off the road . . .'

'Keep – going,' Acir said with an effort, as much to himself as to the driver.

The light seemed to be fading from the sky. Was it already evening? Or was his sight slowly failing?

'Must – keep – going.'

Orial had fallen into a doze, her fingers twisted in the folds of her dirty gown.

And though Acir Korentan was silent, Khassian thought he detected a rattling catch in his breathing. In the growing gloom of twilight, the Guerrior's face had turned deathly pale, drawn as if with pain. The dark patch of blood crusting his grey tunic looked black in the murky light.

Just a graze.

Suppose it was not just a graze and Acir was slowly bleeding to death within? Khassian had little knowledge of wounds but he had heard of such wounds, seemingly innocuous, proving fatal. But Acir was a soldier, well-versed in wounds, surely he would know what to do?

Khassian leaned forward, trying to discern if he were asleep. He touched Acir's knee. His eyelids slowly opened. Dark bruising shadowed his eyes whose keen blue light was now glazed and dim.

'Acir,' Khassian said softly.

'I'm – glad to hear you – call me by my – soul-name.' Acir was staring fixedly into the darkness above his head; he seemed to find it hard to focus. 'Wish – had been more – time – together –'

'But you're coming to Sulien with us! You can't go back now. They'll brand you a –' He stopped, unwilling to say the word.

'Traitor.' Acir seemed to be smiling in the darkness.

The word shamed Khassian. 'I wasn't worth it.'

'You – had to be – free. You – have a – great gift.' Acir's hand moved out – fumblingly – reaching towards Khassian's face. 'Use it. Use it – to set the city – free –'

Khassian felt the caress of finger-tips that were clammily, icily, cold against his cheek. He caught hold of Acir's hand and pressed it between his own maimed hands, trying to warm it.

'What's wrong?'

But Acir's eyes had closed again. Khassian tried to feel for a pulse – but his clawed fingers were too stiff, too clumsy, to achieve such a delicate task.

What should he do? They were so far now from help.

He glanced across at Orial, curled asleep like a slender white cat in the corner. Should he wake her? He didn't want to alarm her – she had withstood too many shocks already.

Suppose word had been sent ahead to the border, suppose the Guerriors of the Commanderie had been alerted to their imminent arrival?

She had risked her life to come to his rescue. He could not bear that any more harm should come to her.

The horses laboured on upwards, the fiacre wheels grinding slower and slower over the stony mountain track.

It was so dark now, Acir could hardly see. Yet where Orial had huddled up into the corner he could distinguish a faint moonlike radiance.

Aura.

Numinous aura.

He fought to keep his leadheavy lids open. Darkness clotted his sight. A cold and terrible numbness was spreading up through his whole body. A weight seemed to press upon his ribs, stifling his breathing. Only her radiance still glimmered. He centred his concentration on her.

Lotos candles glimmer on the dark waters.

Must make it to the border.

'Hola!'

A voice hailed them from the darkness outside.

The driver reined the horses to a halt.

'Lanterns.' Khassian peered out of the window. 'The border. We've reached the border.'

Acir tried to nod his head. It felt heavier than lead cannon shot.

'Help – me – out –'

Khassian opened the door for him. Acir tried to move towards it; his legs gave way beneath him. Khassian climbed down, offering his shoulder as a support.

'N-no.' His speech slurred. 'Stay – in the – coach.'

The lantern-light swam like light ripples reflected in water. He staggered towards the dark figures looming out of the night. It was like trying to move through black waters, each step an almost insurmountable effort.

'Captain – Acir Korentan,' he said. He tried to straighten his jacket, to force his hand into some semblance of a salute. 'My friends – are travelling back to – Sulien. I – am with them – to ensure – safe passage –'

He thrust the papers towards the border guard who seemed to have a blank where a face should be.

The pain had been almost unendurable but this fast-spreading numbness was worse. Mists were slowly rising; cold, dark mists. He felt himself swaying.

Words came to him through the mist, faint, indistinct words. He struggled to keep his fading mind on the sense of what was being said. It was important. But . . . why . . .?

'All seems in order. You can cross into Tourmalise.'

Acir shakily raised his hand to return the guard's salute.

'C-cross over,' he called up to the coachdriver.

'Come on, Acir!' cried Khassian, reaching out to him.

Acir sank to his knees.

'Go – on – without – me.' He began to crawl towards the border. 'Go – on. Go.'

He was sinking slowly back down into the black waters, drowning, drowning . . .

'Go,' he whispered, falling forward.

Sliding slowly into the heart of the Rose, from black petal to black petal, soft velvet kiss of oblivion . . .

At the Rose's burning core a figure opens its arms to embrace, to enfold.

The Lotos Priestess opens the gateway to the incandescent heart of the mystery . . .

Black melds into white. The Rose is One with the Lotos.

The mud-spattered coach lurched across the border into Tourmalise.

'I can't leave him here alone!' cried Khassian. 'I can't –'

Orial let out a hoarse cry. She started up – hands raised, palms outward. Her eyes slid upwards until only the whites showed.

'Sweet Mhir, not you too,' Khassian whispered.

Words issued from her mouth. Incomprehensible words. Gibberish, maybe – but there was a coherence to them that implied a language with which he was not familiar.

'Orial,' he crooned, holding her rigid body in his arms. Tears were streaming down his cheeks unchecked. 'Orial.'

The Tourmalise border guards approached the traveller warily. Was he drunk? One of them knelt down beside him and gently turned him over.

Even in the lantern-light, they could see that he was not drunk. His lips were blue-tinged, his eyes glazed, unfocussed.

The blue lips moved a fraction. The border guard leanted near, to catch what the Captain was trying to say.

The last whispered syllable died in a hoarse rattle – and the Captain's head slipped sideways.

It was then that the phaeton arrived out of the darkness.

'Papers!' demanded the guard.

A woman came running over – and stopped, seeing the body, hands clasped over her mouth, as if to stifle a cry.

'Acir,' she said. She dropped to her knees. 'Acir!'

'You know this man?' asked the guard.

She extended one hand and tremblingly drew her fingers down over the lids, closing the sightless blue eyes.

She knelt there, head bowed. Her shoulders began to shake with suppressed sobs but she made no sound. The guards looked on, shuffling awkwardly from foot to foot.

When she raised her head, she seemed to have taken control of herself.

'Did he – did he say anything before he died?' she asked in a toneless voice.

They nodded.

'What did he say?'

'He said . . . "Elesstar".'

CHAPTER 25

Dawn was breaking over Sulien as the battered fiacre came slowly down the green mountain road into the valley of the Avenne.

Khassian opened his eyes to the clear light. Orial's head lay against his shoulder. They must both have fallen asleep, lulled by the dragging pace of the spent horses. The arm he had wrapped around her had gone numb – excruciatingly numb, threatening pins and needles – and yet he was loath to wake her.

There was a kind of trust in the way her body had moulded itself to his in sleep, born not just of exhaustion but of familiarity.

How could she trust him? He had blighted her life.

She saw him as a revolutionary hero, worthy of her self-sacrifice.

And now he knew he was no hero. He could not challenge the might of the Commanderie alone. The only man capable of such an act of heroism lay dead in the dust beside a lonely mountain road.

They had reached the bridge across the Avenne; the horses' hooves clip-clopped slowly across. No hurry now.

The river breeze stirred wisps of fine hair against his face, soft as golden silk; Orial sighed in her sleep and he felt the gentle rhythm of her breathing alter. She was drifting upwards through sleep to consciousness. He felt a pang of anxiety, remembering how the fit had gripped her last night. Once the frail thread of sanity unravelled, how possible was it to spin the separate strands back together?

'Where to?' called the driver.

'Dr Magelone's Sanatorium,' Khassian called back. 'D'you know it?'

'Pump Street? I know it well.'

The coach drew to a standstill at the entrance to Pump Street and the driver clambered down to open the door.

'Can't go any further. The street's all dug up.'

Orial stirred. Her eyes opened, misted with sleep. She looked up into Khassian's face and shrank away, as though terrified.

Did she even know him?

'Down you get, demselle.' The driver offered his hand to help her down into the street. Khassian followed slowly, stiffly, stretching his aching back.

Cramoisy's crimson wig lay abandoned on the floor of the coach.

As the coach clattered away over the cobbles, Khassian looked up at the Sanatorium. Curious. All the shutters were closed.

'Orial,' he said gently. 'You're home.'

When she did not move, he put his arm about her again and steered her slowly around the open trench in the street towards the entrance to the Sanatorium.

'That's right, my pet. Let Cook help you off with your things.'

Orial stood numb with shock whilst Cook fussed around her, tutting at the state of her clothes.

'Now you put on this clean nightgown and get into bed. Cook'll bring you up a nice hot drink later on when you've had a little sleep.'

She could hear the words Cook was saying but they seemed to make no sense.

'Milk with a grating of nutmeg . . . or cinnamon sugar, that used to be your favourite when you were young.'

Cook gathered up the travel-stained clothes and went out, still talking, 'Get tucked into bed and rest. You've had a terrible journey. Rest . . . that's what you need.'

Far above the heat of the plain, the air was cloudily cool. The red-barked trunks of the cinder pines made the winding mountain road dark, haunted by shadows. A faint scent of cinder-pine sap, aromatic yet tinged with its peculiar odour of burning, wafted into the Grand Maistre's coach. If Girim shut his eyes, he saw flames: burning timbers crashing in on the ruined Opera House, sparks of charred music flying high into the sky . . .

The coach slowed as the road levelled out. His secretary opened the window flap and looked out.

'We're here, Maistre. The border.'

'Hola!' The Tourmalise border guard emerged from his hut as they passed across the border line, and upraised. 'Your papers!'

'Don't you know who this is?' said the secretary, shocked. 'Girim nel Ghislain, spiritual adviser to His Altesse Prince Ils—'

'I need to see papers,' said the guard doggedly.

'Everything's in order.' The secretary thrust the papers in his face. 'I drew them up myself. Where's the corpse?'

Girim nel Ghislain dismounted from his coach and stood looking down at the body of Acir Korentan. Acir, the best hope of the Commanderie. Acir, his brother-in-arms.

What had become of this bright and shining star that it should have fallen so far and so fast?

Girim went down on one knee to draw back the cloak from the face. The pale skin had already taken on a blueish tinge, the lips were mauve.

He had died an agonising death.

Yet death had smoothed away any hint of that agony; the expression was remote and calm . . . almost serene.

'Why?' he whispered. 'Why did you betray me, Acir?'

Someone gave a polite cough. He turned around and saw his secretary hovering behind.

'Shall we prepare the body to take back for burial, Maistre?' asked the secretary respectfully.

'No.'

'But I had thought – given Captain Korentan's distinguished record of service – at the very least a military funeral with honours?'

'I said no, did you not hear me? The man was a traitor. No Commanderie funeral. No honours. Strip the body of the uniform and leave it here to rot. And strike his name from the records. Let all the Commanderie see how I deal with traitors.'

The Tourmalise border guard stood scratching his head, perplexed, as the coach with its fine trappings of crimson leather disappeared into Allegonde.

What was he to do with the body? The dead man must have been someone of importance for the Grand Maistre to come so far up into the mountains . . .

'Is there a cemetery in Sulien?'

The guard started. He had thought he was alone. And there the woman stood, watching him from the brown shadows of the cinder pines, pale and gaunt as a revenant.

'Wh-where did you –'

She came closer, her skirts catching on the brambles. Her white face was stained, her hair dishevelled. Reddened eyes stared at him . . . through him.

'I asked if there is a cemetery in Sulien?'

'You were here last night, weren't you? Have you been here all this time? That's against the regulations. You crossed into Tourmalise without a passport –'

'I have papers, travel permits.' she said in a dull, distant voice.

He beckoned her towards the hut. She gathered up her torn skirts and followed slowly after him, moving as if she were sleepwalking. In the hut she produced the papers.

'You'll find they're all in order. Now tell me where I may arrange for this man to be buried?'

The guard hesitated.

'He's not a citizen of Sulien.'

'I have money,' she said, her dirt-streaked face a mask. She held out a handful of coins. 'Does that cover the necessary documents?'

The guard took the money, counted it and nodded.

'I'll fill in a certificate. The Foreigners' Cemetery is down by the river. Ask for Asper, the gravedigger. He'll do what's needed. Now . . .' he said, reaching for a pen '. . . what was this man's name?'

'Korentan,' she said, her voice tightening. He saw the sudden glitter of tears in her eyes. 'Acir Korentan.'

'What you need right now, young man, is a cup of good, strong qaffë. Where did I put that qaffë filter . . .'

Khassian heard Dame Tradescar muttering to herself, the clinking of crockery – and then the delicious smell of brewing qaffë began to waft into the parlour.

The old woman at the Sanatorium had told him to go and inform Dame Tradescar of Orial's return. Now as he sat here, safe amidst the comforting clutter of books, drawings and archaeological artefacts, his hands began to shake uncontrollably.

'Sugar?' Jolaine Tradescar brought out a yellowed cane sugarloaf and chipped off granules with the edge of a spoon. 'Here.' She passed him a bowl of hot qaffë. 'Drink this.'

Khassian balanced the bowl between his shaking hands and raised it to his lips. The qaffë burned his tongue but it was strong and very sweet. He could not remember the last time he had tasted qaffë. He concentrated on savouring the taste, blanking his mind to what he knew he must do next.

As he set down the empty bowl, he saw Dame Tradescar observing him with her inquisitive blue eyes: scholar's eyes that missed nothing.

'You've been very kind.'

She shrugged the compliment aside.

'But I mustn't take up any more of your time. There's something I must attend to.'

'Ah,' said Jolaine.

'Your burial practices are very different from ours. But – with so many visitors – there must be a foreigners' cemetery in Sulien?'

'There's a sorry place, overgrown and neglected, on the other bank of the Avenne.' She was still watching him keenly.

Suddenly Khassian began to talk. All that had happened came spilling out, unchecked: the terrifying escape through the thunderstorm, Acir's dying efforts to get them safely to Sulien . . .

'I can't leave him there unburied.' Khassian turned his head away.

'I'll hire a cart.'

'You?' Khassian looked up.

'My dear young man, have you any idea how bored I've been? Fretting away the days, trying to get back down into the Undercity yet frustrated by those confounded Priests at every turn.' Jolaine thumped her fist against the table, making the qaffë pot jump. 'I'd welcome a little action to relieve the tedium. Besides, I can't have you risking recapture. Orial would never forgive me if that were to happen.'

Orial.

A black, choking sense of despair welled up within Khassian. He was free – and yet his freedom had been achieved at too dear a price.

He buried his face in his ruined hands and sobbed aloud.

Cook peeked around the door. Orial was sound asleep.

Poor mite. She looked so wan, so wasted.

And there was still no word from her father. She had sent a message to his hostelry in Bel'Esstar, but even a swift post rider took at least half a day to travel to Allegonde.

Still, a long sleep would do her good. What troubled Cook was what she should do when the girl awoke.

She had seen that lost, unfocussed look before.

She had seen Iridial the day she drowned herself.

A sombre melody wove itself into Khassian's dreams, the dark music of the slow-flowing river of oblivion, the lightless waters of the underworld.

Orial's tune.

A pale figure stands on the far shore. The music wreaths about her, caging her in a shroud of woven songthreads.

He sees her mouth open in a silent scream, sees her throw herself forward into the black waters, sees the drowning waters swallow her –

He woke, soaked in sweat, to find himself lying cramped on Dame Tradescar's couch. The sun had moved around and the long, low light of late-afternoon gilded the dusty bookshelves.

The melody still flowed on through his head – but now he heard possibilities, permutations, the beginnings of a complex contrapuntal structure.

If only he could get it down on paper.

It was late-afternoon when Jolaine Tradescar reached the border yet the sun's heat had not penetrated the thick clouds. Chill mist swathed the tops of the pines, stifling sound and light.

'Identify yourself!' The border guard's voice rang out through the trees; Jolaine thought she detected a nervous edge to the customary challenge.

'A man died here late last night,' she said.

A muscle in the guard's face twitched; he looked around, as though fearing to be overheard.

'I've come to collect the body,' she insisted.

'A relative, are you?'

'No. A friend.'

'You're too late.' The guard lowered his voice. 'He's been taken for burial already.'

'Taken back to Allegonde?' Jolaine asked.

'To Sulien. A woman came for him. I told her to ask for Asper.'

The Foreigners' Cemetery stood in a grove of trees beside the Avenne. High stone walls, built in the previous century, had begun to crumble and fall. Weeds grew in profusion amongst the neglected graves: rose bay willowherb, with its drifting white down, and red valerian.

The Contesse Fiammis counted out fifty courons in payment to the gravedigger Asper and his apprentices. Then in the hushed Sulien evening, she stood and watched as they lowered Acir's body into the grave.

No Allegondan wooden coffin could be commissioned in time; a simple white Sulien shroud had sufficed.

Fiammis found wild roses growing in profusion over the western wall of the cemetery, perfuming the twilight with a sweet fragrance.

She had pricked her hands and wrists trying to pick a spray. Now, as the first earth was thrown in, she dropped to her knees at the open grave and cast the spray of roses on to Acir's breast. The pale petals were stained with spots of her own blood.

'It won't be long now, *miu caru.*' she whispered.

She did not feel the pain of the thorns. She felt nothing. The light had been extinguished from her life. Without him, there was no point in continuing. She was weary of subterfuge, weary of killing.

There was just one thing more she must do.

Spadefuls of the soft, dark red earth fell softly on to the shrouded body. High on the broken wall, a speckled thrush began to pipe a shrill, lonely threnody into the coming night.

The garret door opened; Khassian, startled, looked up to see Dame Tradescar had just let herself in.

'Well?' he said tensely.

'The body was collected before I arrived.' She lowered herself into an armchair with a sigh; in the twilight her face looked grey with tiredness.

'Collected? By the Commanderie?'

'No, a woman. She's buried him in Sulien. I called at the Foreigners' Cemetery. Old Asper was filling in the grave.'

'A woman?' Khassian said, puzzled.

'She wouldn't leave her name ... but she paid Asper very handsomely. He was well pleased with the arrangement.' Jolaine sat forward a little, reaching for the decanter of pommerie on the table. She poured herself a glass and drank it in one gulp.

'And Orial? Is there any news?'

'I stopped by the Sanatorium. There's been no change in her condition.

She's sleeping, Cook says. Maybe that's for the best.'

Feelings of frustration and fear from the time of Fania's final illness returned to haunt him. It was happening again. If only there was some way he could stop the nightmare . . .

'Where is this Foreigners' Cemetery?'

'On the far bank of the Avenne beyond the gardens. Outside the city walls.'

Khassian reached for his – Cramoisy's – coat. He felt trapped in the garret apartment.

'It'll be dark by the time you get there,' Jolaine said, pouring another glass of apple spirit. 'Wait till morning, dear boy.'

But Khassian had already opened the door; the darkening city invited him. He had spent weeks confined in a cell; now he wanted to escape, to walk the long hours of night away . . .

'Orial . . .'

Who was calling her name?

'Orial, Orial . . .'

Many voices now, calling to her from afar, a multitude of voices, dead voices, soul-voices,

'Set us free, Orial . . .'

And she could hear them all. All at once. All jumbled, all incoherent, all in despair.

Orial slid down on to the floor, her hands clutched to her temples.

'Who are you? How can I set you free?'

The mingled voices became jagged colour, scarlet and blinding white, setting nerve endings jangling. Each collision sent sound-shards shivering into her aching head.

'Stop,' she whispered. 'Please stop.'

She curled up on the floor, arms tight-crossed, knees drawn up to her chest.

'Let me alone. Please. *Please.*'

An archaic strain seeped into the chaos, a dark trickle at first, slow-flowing.

Watermusic.

Waters of forgetfulness, waters of oblivion . . .

She stands beside Iridial in the Temple, gazing up at the statue of Elesstar. Iridial scoops some of the green spring water from the stone shell and touches her forehead and cheeks with it.

'Goddess protect you, child.'

Orial blinks as the sunlight filters on to Iridial's hair. The Goddess opens her painted eyes – and smiles at her.

Sacred springs. Healing springs.

'Springs. Must get to the springs . . .'

Down the stairs Orial went. Her feet were bare, she was clad only in the thin muslin nightgown.

A group of late-night revellers were coming along the dark street towards her. She could see their lanterns bobbing in the breeze, she could hear their drunken singing collide with the music dinning in her head.

She shrank into a doorway, hoping they would not see her. But as they drew closer, they began to point, to call and whistle, waving her to join them. She could see their mouths moving yet their voices seemed blurred, distant, voices from another dimension.

Masked faces leered at her, hands reached out for her, trying to pull her into their midst.

'Let me be!' Orial twisted free of the groping, grabbing hands. Breaking through the chain, she went running away down the street.

Cook added a dash of eau-de-vie to the hot milk and cinnamon, taking a surreptitious swig herself, wiping her mouth with the back of her hand. A nice hot posset should help restore Orial's strength.

She had left her to sleep round the clock undisturbed, hoping the rest would do her good. The Goddess only knew what the girl had been through, she had looked more like a ghost when she arrived back –

The ghost of her mother.

Cook shivered and took another swig of the eau-de-vie to stop the shivers.

'Here I come, Orial my pet.'

She walked the long corridor slowly, a little unsteadily, and climbed the stairs, trying not to spill the posset in the saucer.

'Orial?' She blinked, wondering whether the eau-de-vie had affected her sight. The bed was empty.

The cup began to judder against the saucer in Cook's trembling hand. Liquid slopped over the rim.

'Oh, no. She's gone. She's gone!'

Orial leaned on the rail, gazing down into the moonstreaked river.

Reeds whispered in the murky darkness, spirit voices, calling her . . .

'Orial . . .'

The voices were growing louder.

'Set us free . . .'

She gave a little gasp.

They were there on the far bank, she could see them now, a host of shadowforms, faintly defined by the shifting moonlight. Their pale eyes glimmered in the darkness, hungry for succour, hungry for release.

'Who are you?' she cried.

The spinning watermusic in her mind had become a gaping whirlpool. Someone placed their hands on her shoulders, holding her back.

'Now, demselle, what do you think you're doing?'

'Let me go, let me go!' She beat frantically against the restraining hands.

'No need to be alarmed, demselle. Constable Alterre of the Night Watch.'

Three short bursts on a whistle and another constable came running up.

'What is it, Alterre?'

'Attempted suicide. What's your name, demselle?'

Orial suddenly slumped, spent.

'I – have to – set them free,' she whispered. 'Into the light –'

The two constables exchanged looks.

'One for Dr Tartarus.'

'I'll get the carriage.'

'No! N-not mad.'

'Of course not, demselle,' soothed the constable. 'You need a little rest and quiet. And we're taking you to just the right place . . .'

Clouds scudded across the setting moon as Khassian slowly, wearily, made his way towards the River Avenne. He had wandered the streets and alleys of the sleeping city half the night, not knowing or caring where he was going, just walking.

Now he had come to do what he knew he must.

He found his way to the Foreigners' Cemetery, crossing the river by the bridge, stumbling over the tussocks and weeds between the overgrown graves.

The last light of the fading moon showed him the freshly dug earth of a new grave.

'Well, here I am,' he said out loud.

The only sound was the shiver of leaves in the breeze off the river. He sat down in the long grass. He would keep vigil throughout the rest of the night beside Acir's grave. It seemed the only fit thing to do in the circumstance. Tomorrow he would go and see Asper about a memorial stone; he would raise the money somehow.

But now . . . he would keep watch till morning.

In the twilight, the waters of the River Avenne glint grey.

Acir is dead.

Overcome with grief, Khassian sinks to his knees on the damp bank, weeping.

'Amaru . . .'

A voice is calling him, calling his name. He raises his tear-wet face and gazes out across the grey riverwaters. A figure stands on the far bank, a man, half-clothed in shadow.

The man moves towards the river, his hand held out in welcome. Starlight glimmers in his silver hair which falls loose about his shoulders.

'Acir?' Khassian's heart leaps within his breast. 'But I thought –'

'Amaru.' Acir's hand beckons him.

And Khassian, as though pulled by a will stronger than his own, finds himself gliding across the river, gliding towards the still-beckoning figure, passing between crumbling walls into a garden.

Acir stands, smiling at him, a warm smile, a tender smile.

Then he draws open the loose robes he wears, baring his left breast. The tattooed rose is weeping tears of blood: one by one they splash on to the ground.

And where the dark drops of blood fall, Khassian sees a green shoot pushing up through the earth, its leaves unfurling as he watches, astonished, until a crimson bud appears at the tip.

Acir plucks the Rose and hands it to Khassian. It glows, red as sunset, in his cupped hands, its perfume dark as incense.

Jerame Magelonne slept restlessly, starting awake whenever the diligence ran over a rut in the road. Cook's message had arrived as he was packing his valise, confirming the information delivered by one of Girim nel Ghislain's agents: Orial was back in Sulien.

He was only too glad to be leaving Bel'Esstar; the city was a slow-fizzing powder keg of dissent, primed and ready to explode. Though what faced him on his return was none too inviting: an empty Sanatorium; unpaid bills; creditors – the possibility of financial ruin.

But what did it matter, so long as Orial was restored to him? He could face an uncertain future with equanimity if she was at his side. There was still a reason for continuing.

He dozed off again, rocked by the steady motion of the diligence's wheels . . .

Orial floating, face down in the green waters of the Avenne. Orial dragged limp and lifeless from the river, water running from her slack mouth, her weed-trailed hair –

'Ahh!' he cried out as he awoke – to see the disapproving faces of the other passengers regarding him with suspicion.

'A – a dream,' he said, embarrassed. Yet even his embarrassment could not dispel the unpleasant taste which lingered after the dream had fled – or the growing anxiety.

The closed Constabulary carriage stopped outside the Asylum. Orial had shrunk into the corner, hugging her arms to her.

She must not let them commit her. Once committed, she would never escape Tartarus's clutches. She would never fulfil her task.

She must get away.

Constable Alterre opened the door and climbed out. The cloudy sky was streaked with the first light of dawn. Birds had begun to whistle and call in the stillness.

Beyond the stark walls of the Asylum she could just glimpse the river marshes and the faint gleam of the Avenne.

Constable Alterre had rung the bell-pull and was standing waiting for the porter to answer.

Now. While his attention was distracted.

She slipped out of the carriage and tiptoed around the back, one step at a time. The rough gravel grazed her bare feet.

'Hey!'

They had seen her.

'Come back here!'

She turned and ran towards the marshes.

'Stop! Stop!' The constables were after her.

She slipped on the dew-wet grass, forced herself back up, on towards the tall reed-beds. Her sides ached with running, her nightgown was mired and wet, yet still she stumbled on.

They would never find her in the reeds.

Khassian awoke with a groan. He was stiff, he was damp with dew . . .

And he had meant to keep vigil all night.

Now the sun was up.

He sat up, stretching his aching body.

The freshly dug earth of Acir's grave was a brown scar against the silvered grass.

A spray of green had pierced the rich earth. Fresh green.

A rose was growing in the red soil. Tender new leaves surrounded a single bud.

Where had it come from?

Khassian extended his hand – and then swiftly withdrew it. Black thorns, hooked and vicious, protected the single bloom.

His skin suddenly chilled as if the sun had been covered by fast-moving cloud. He glanced up. There were no clouds in sight.

Maybe Asper had planted it last night? Maybe he had taken a cutting from the white rose rambling over the broken wall . . . although Khassian was almost certain from the furled petals that this rose would prove to be red.

Crimson red. Red as heartblood.

'Orial at Asylum. Come at once. Tartarus.'

Jerame read the blotted note for the tenth time and scrunched it into a ball in his sweating hand. The fiacre had slowed to a crawl. The street was noisy with shouting and arguing. People were milling around, some bearing placards and banners. A rhythmic chant was building as they

291

made their way to the Temple. One or two began to thump in time on the side of the fiacre as they walked past.

'Bury our dead!'

'Respect for the dead!'

'Open the reservoirs!'

Jerame leaned out and called up to the driver, 'Hurry! I said, *hurry*!'

'The road's blocked ahead.'

'Then turn around, take another route. But be quick!'

'There she is!' Tartarus said to himself.

Moving slowly like a sleepwalker through the reed-beds, her wet feet bare, her hair drifting in the breeze, the white nightgown slipping off one shoulder, Orial looked more like a river-nymph than a madwoman.

The reeds grew in the river shallows . . . but the bank suddenly shelved steeply beyond – many drowning spans deep into black mud.

He came closer.

He must not startle her. If surprised in this precarious state, she would almost certainly throw herself into the water

And then she looked up, half-seeing him, half-seeing through him.

Her eyes.

Tartarus – who had witnessed many bizarre physical manifestations in his time as Asylum Director – shuddered.

The brilliant rainbow colours had vanished.

Dulled eyes, drowned eyes, muddied as the reflected riverwater.

'Orial,' he called lightly, coaxingly.

She seemed not to hear.

He edged a little closer to the bank.

'Orial,' He beckoned invitingly, raising the restraint-shroud he had brought. 'You must be cold. Come. I have a shawl to wrap around your shoulders.'

The whispering sigh of the reeds as they moved to the breath of the breeze was the only reply.

She turned away and began to wade further out into the reed-beds. Water lapped around her legs, staining the trailing robe with green. Beyond, the wide Avenne glistened in a brief sunslick, deceptively placid beneath the cloudy sky.

He had no choice but to go in after her.

But then, he reasoned, as he kicked off his buckle-shoes and peeled off his hose, he would have no choice now but to use his machine on her. And for that it was worth getting his feet wet.

His toes sank down into the river-ooze. It was far colder than he had anticipated and emitted a mephitic gaseous odour that almost made him choke. Decaying river-weed and a green scum of algae clung to his legs.

But in his mind he was already strapping his wayward river-nymph into the treatment chair, he was pressing the metal helmet on to her reed-bedraggled hair. She would be his triumph. The triumph of science over superstition. No more nonsense about Faer Folk or rainbow eyes.

The two constables appeared on the bank.

He waved to them to keep down, to fan out. If he could hold her attention, the other two could creep up on her unnoticed.

He lost his balance, almost falling face first into the noisome waters, grasping at the fragile reeds to steady himself.

Cursing, Tartarus tried to brush the mud-spatter from his clothes. The slender reeds had scratched his palms; the reek of the black mud filled his nostrils.

It would be necessary to administer a strong charge to the right hemisphere of the brain. At the touch of his hand, the power-spark surged into her. Her slender body convulsed, juddered . . .

Was it his imagination? Or did the noisome air suddenly smell fresh and sweet as a spring dawn?

And then his vision cleared and he was only looking at a poor, mad thing, a chit of a girl who had lost her wits and was half-naked, dirty and bedraggled.

'Set us free . . .'

Whenever Orial shut her eyes, she could still see them, the Dead, raising their shrivelled hands to her, their decaying eyes lit with the mephitic fire of marsh gas.

She lifted her hands to her throbbing head, rocking to and fro.

Dead voices filled her mind, spirit voices, soul voices . . .

'The Lotos blooms on the dark waters.'

'The Lotos Princess opens her arms to receive us.'

'The sacred springs flow again.'

The waters called to her. Beneath the cool, green Avenne lay silence – an end to the incessant clamour.

'Open the gates and let us pass through into the light.'

Walk out into the waters . . . sink slowly beneath the gently flowing river . . . seek the eternal silence of the drowning deeps.

River goddess, rock me gently to sleep . . .

Orial closed her eyes – and threw herself into the Avenne.

CHAPTER 26

As the fiacre approached the Asylum, Jerame saw the huddle of figures gathered on the riverbank.

'Dear Goddess, no. Please, no!'

The fiacre drew to a halt in front of the Asylum, the wheels sending up a spray of gravel.

'Wait here!'

He tried to run but his legs had lost their strength; he seemed to be wading through water, not air.

As he approached, one by one, they drew aside revealing the drowned girl lying on the bank.

'Orial,' he said brokenly.

Dropping to his knees beside her, he fumbled for a pulse, listened for a breath. His hands shook so much he could hardly control them.

Tartarus put one hand on his shoulder. He was drenched to the skin, trembling with cold.

'I'm sorry, Jerame. It's too late.'

'There's still a faint pulse, I can feel it –'

'I tried everything. I emptied the water from her, I breathed air into her mouth – nothing works.'

'No, no, I'm sure – look!' He cradled her limp body in his arms. 'She's just cold. Cold and wet. She'll revive. She'll be all right once I get her home. I'll make her warm and dry.'

He picked her up and went slowly back towards the waiting cab, staggering under the drowned weight of her body.

Amaru Khassian the unbeliever stared at the Rose.

In the few hours since he had first seen it, the single flower had swelled from bud to bloom. Now it trembled on the brink of unfurling its petals, petals that were crimson, dark blood-crimson.

The Rose that sprang from the breast of the dead Poet-Prophet Mhir had been red as heart's blood. And the Blood of the Rose had brought the dying Elesstar, Elesstar the Beloved, back to life.

Why was he – the cynic, the unbeliever – the one to discover this mystery?

And why here, why in Sulien?

Sulien was a place where ancient beliefs and customs persisted, where past and present mingled inextricably. A place beyond time.

Anything might happen here.

If the Rose could bring Elesstar back from the dead, could it also restore a fractured mind?

Could it heal Orial?

Khassian ran across the river towards Pump Street and the Sanatorium, tugging at the bell-pull as best he could with both hands.

Cook answered the door. Her eyes looked red and raw, her lined cheeks were wet with tears.

'Orial!' Khassian said between gasps for breath. 'I must see her.'

'You c-can't see her now, sieur.'

'Can't see her?' Something was wrong, terribly wrong, Khassian could sense it.

'Oh, sieur, she's – she's dead. Drowned.' Cook shook her head, one hand covering her mouth as though to hold back her sobs.

Dead.

The air went dark.

'Oh no, no . . .' Khassian felt as if he was falling from a great height into blackness. 'She can't be dead!'

'She's gone, sieur. There's nothing anyone can do. He's laid her in the treatment room – but now he won't let anyone near. I'm afraid – afraid he may do himself some mischief.'

Too late.

'No!' Khassian howled aloud.

A strange and aromatic fragrance drifted through the neglected cemetery; a rich, dark scent redolent of musk roses and incense.

The Rose had opened.

Its crimson petals had the velvet bloom of black grapes; as Khassian came slowly, wonderingly, closer, the scent grew stronger, potent as red wine.

And there, at the heart of the Rose, glistening in the dappled evening light, drops of dark moisture, redder than heart's blood.

He knelt beside the grave and reached out to pluck the Rose.

The Rose was not to be plucked.

The black thorns pricked his hands, tearing the burned flesh. Pain flared through his fingers, bright as fire. He gritted his teeth against the pain. He must endure this for Orial's sake.

The stem suddenly snapped and he found himself holding the precious flower head in his cupped hands.

The door to the Sanatorium was open.

Khassian, carrying the precious Rose, walked in unchallenged.

Dame Tradescar and Cook stood at the doorway to Dr Magelonne's office. When they saw Khassian, they drew aside to let him pass.

Khassian went in – and then, seeing what lay within, faltered.

Orial's body lay on the couch, riverwater still dripping on to the floor from her wet hair, her trailing fingers. Jerame Magelonne knelt at the foot of the couch, his face buried in the folds of her gown.

It was not the pallor of her skin that terrified Khassian but the absence of movement. She who had been so vibrant in life now lay still, silent.

Jerame Magelonne raised his head from the couch and stared at Khassian with eyes that burned dark with hatred.

'What are you doing here? *You have no right.*'

'Let the boy pay his respects,' said Cook.

Khassian came slowly forward. The Rose burned his bleeding fingers – but its musky perfume filled the room, darkly heady as rare Enhirran spices.

Jerame sprang up, placing himself between the couch and Khassian.

'Keep away from her! Don't touch her!'

Jolaine Tradescar went to Jerame, catching hold of him by the arm.

'Leave the boy alone. Let him do what he has come to do!'

Khassian drew closer.

Her mouth gaped slightly open.

Khassian held the soft petals until they brushed her grey lips and watched as the dark roseblood seeped between them.

A dark column of rose-red smoke swirled up, enveloping Orial and Khassian in a cloud of fragrance – and in the heart of the smoke burned a searing, cleansing shaft of flame.

Cradled in darkness, she has lain here lulled by the lapping waters. How long? Time has no meaning.

A bolt of gold suddenly penetrates the darkness, dazzling sun-splinters shiver off into the waters like firesparks.

A splinter of light pierces her eyes.

Daylight.

A splinter pierces her heart. A blaze of sun lights her breast, a pain so vivid it burns white across her darkened vision.

Awake.

Alive.

Khassian opened his eyes.

Everyone was cowering away, their eyes covered, as if to shield them against a light too bright to endure.

The Rose in his hands was burned to ashes.

And sitting up, staring dazedly around her through her strands of wet hair – was Orial Magelonne.

'Illustre?' she said, gazing questioningly into his eyes.

'Orial.' He reached out to her . . . and the rosedust fell between his fingers and drifted to the floor.

Tremblingly she raised her hands towards his – and he felt her fingers enfold his.

'Orial,' he repeated. He could find no words to express his feeling of wonder, could only repeat her name, over and over again.

She raised one hand to touch his cheek.

'Goddess save us,' Cook cried in a faint voice. 'She's alive!'

The Priestess set out from the Temple in a black sedan chair, carried by acolytes.

Passers-by stopped to watch the bizarre procession winding its way towards Dr Magelonne's Sanatorium; the curious followed in its wake and soon a small crowd had gathered in Pump Street.

The black chair meant only one thing: a death.

The Priestess descended from the chair and entered the Sanatorium. Her head was covered in black veils so that none should see her face.

News travels fast in Sulien. A journalist from the *Sulien Chronicle* sketched in a headline: 'Eminent Doctor Bereaved a Second Time in Drowning Tragedy' and, grabbing his notebook, hurried to the Sanatorium to get the details.

I must be dreaming.

Jerame pinched his arm, deliberately taking a fold of skin between finger and thumb, twisting until he winced. The pain was real enough. Unless he was dreaming he was pinching himself. What he was witnessing negated everything in his training as a student of science, a student of medicine. It could not be.

She had been dead. Her heart had ceased to beat. And now she was alive, colour tinged her pale cheeks, she moved, she spoke.

'Orial –' he faltered.

She turned to him. 'Oh, Papa.'

She knew him.

Khassian stood dazedly watching as Orial was smothered in the kisses and embraces of her family.

Jolaine Tradescar turned to him, her eyes moist with tears.

'My boy, my boy!' she cried, flung her arms about Khassian and hugged him. 'You did it! You saved her!'

'No,' said Khassian shakily. He had been seared by holy fire. Shivers of heat from the burning Rose still flickered through his body, fierce as fever

297

chills, intense as the dying pangs of ecstasy. 'It was the Rose.'

Orial gazed at the well-loved faces gathered about her bed: Papa, Cook, Jolaine, Sister Crespine.

'I have to go to the Temple,' she said. 'I know what has to be done.'

'All in good time,' said Papa, squeezing her hand. 'When you're well.'

'You don't understand. I have to go. It is not yet finished.'

'You called me here to arrange a funeral, Jerame Magelonne, to minister to the dead. What does this mean?'

The Priestess stood in the doorway, swathed in her veils, dark as thunderclouds.

There was silence as the Magelonne household looked at each other in confusion. Then Cook found her voice.

'A miracle,' she said. 'She was drowned. Dead. And the Rose brought her back to life. I never saw such a thing, not in all my born days.'

The Priestess came to Orial's bedside and, to her astonishment, knelt beside her.

'You stand between life and death. You are the one.'

'*I* am?' Orial's eyes closed, letting her mind drift back towards the far bournes of consciousness.

'You are the first since the fall of Sulien to come through the dark waters.' The Priestess took hold of her hand, pressing it.

'I hear them still,' whispered Orial.

The sombre spirit-threnody still filled her mind. But now she understood, now she knew what she must do.

Once there had been other Lifhendil to spin the intricacies of the spirit-song that would summon the Eä-Endil. Now she was the only one of her kind. Only an exceptionally gifted musician could begin to match her Lifhendil skills . . .

Orial opened her eyes.

'I can't do it alone,' she said. 'I need Khassian.'

She saw him, pale and drawn with tiredness, amongst the watchers crowding in the doorway.

'Amaru,' she said, 'we have to sing. We have to spin the song they taught me. It's the key. It will make all right again. The music will set them free.'

CHAPTER 27

At the Hall of Justice in Bel'Esstar, the castrato Cramoisy Jordelayne had been brought before the Commanderie court. The public gallery was crowded with the citizens of Bel'Esstar, curious to see what had become of the singer who had once been the idol of the city. It was generally remarked that the Diva looked a mere shadow of his former self; pale, eyes squinting against the daylight, his face darkened with several ugly bruises. It was also rumoured that the shock of his imprisonment had caused him to lose his voice – and everyone knew what that meant for a castrato. Once the voice was gone, what remained? A dreary, humdrum existence eked out by coaching or composing . . .

The three judges – all wearing the insignia of the Rose, on crimson ribbons about their necks – entered and took their places at the bench. The most senior amongst them was the Grand Maistre of the Commanderie, Girim nel Ghislain.

'Cramoisy Jordelayne – you stand accused of a capital crime; namely that you aided a convicted Sanctuaree to escape justice. How do you plead?'

The singer slowly raised his head.

'Guilty.'

'Guilty . . .' The hushed murmur echoed around the gallery.

'Are you aware of the severity of the crime you have committed? By admitting your guilt you oblige us to impose the death sentence. Perhaps you would care to reflect before your plea is set down?'

'What else can you take from me? You took my manhood to preserve the beauty of my voice.'

The court stilled. Cramoisy was still a consummate performer; he knew how to move his audience. Everything he said appeared spontaneous, yet the nuances of inflection were perfectly timed.

He knew they were listening to every word.

'I submitted to the castrating knife willingly, knowing my sacrifice was for my art. But now that my voice has gone, there's little reason for living. So take my life. I'll die happy – knowing I gave my life for the cause of freedom.'

'Treasonable talk!' cried one of the judges, rising from the bench. 'Silence him!'

'I will not be silenced!' cried Cramoisy. 'I speak on behalf of the musicians and artists you have persecuted. I speak for the people of Bel'—'

One of the Guerriors struck the singer across the face; Cramoisy staggered and fell sideways, one hand clasped to his mouth. Blood seeped between his clenched fingers.

A messenger entered the court, covered in dust.

'Not now!' cried one of the judges, waving him away.

'It's urgent, sieur.' He came forward to the Grand Maistre and handed him a folded paper.

Girim opened and scanned it swiftly. Everyone was silent now, watching him keenly.

His face flushed and then went pale.

'A miracle,' he said hoarsely. 'The Rose has bloomed again.'

'What do you mean, Grand Maistre?' asked one of the judges.

Girim got to his feet, still clutching the paper.

'This court is adjourned. Take the castrato back to work at the Fortress. Inform the Prince at once. We ride to Sulien!'

Prince Ilsevir gazed out over the massed forces of the Commanderie: row upon row of mounted Guerriors lined up in the formal gardens of the Winter Palace awaiting his signal to start for Sulien.

He turned to Girim nel Ghislain who stood at his side.

'I'm still uneasy about this, Girim.'

'I'm leaving a whole detachment behind to guard the Sanctuary. You need have no fears about Bel'Esstar, Altesse.'

'You misunderstand me,' said Ilsevir. 'This is a delicate matter. It requires diplomacy. We have no official invitation to cross into Tourmalise. It could provoke a . . . situation.'

Girim smiled. 'War?'

'An army crossing the mountains. It could be misinterpreted. It could be seen as an invasion. I wish you would wait until my ministers have communicated with the President of Tourmalise.'

'This is not a matter of diplomacy! This is a spiritual matter, Altesse. We are Mhir's chosen people. This is the sign we have been awaiting so long.'

'And have you not asked yourself why the Poet-Prophet has not chosen to manifest Himself here? In Bel'Esstar, His city?'

'It is a sign. The prophet shows us the true Way.' Girim's eyes strayed to the distant horizon, 'He calls me to convert the people of Sulien, to turn them from their pagan beliefs to His truth.'

'And if they do not wish to be converted?'

'You are full of doubts, Prince. A true believer must put his doubts aside and follow the path of his faith, wherever it leads him.'

'But to an unmarked grave in a foreign city? Suppose it's a hoax?'

'If it makes you any easier in your mind, Altesse, then I suggest you ride ahead in the royal coach – with a small detachment of the Commanderie as escort. I shall follow with the rest of my Guerriors when you have made the necessary overtures to the people of Sulien.'

Ilsevir pulled on his riding gloves; elegant gauntlets of the finest pearl-grey leather.

'To Sulien, then.'

Girim raised his arm and pointed towards the west. His eyes blazed in the sun's fire.

'To the ultimate truth of the Poet-Prophet.'

'The Poet-Prophet!' thundered back the assembled Guerriors of the Commanderie.

Amaru Khassian scoured the qaffë houses and taverns of Sulien to round up his musicians: Valentan, Azare, Astrel and Philamon.

Astrel he found busking in a shady colonnade. Valentan and Azare were entertaining fellow customers in a qaffë house with bawdy Allegondan catches. Philamon had to be dragged out of the taproom of the Moon and Sickle inn, rather the worse for Sulien cider.

By the time they reached the Temple forecourt, it was thronged with people, queuing to enter the Undercity. Widespread talk of miracles had excited the curiosity of Sulien's citizens, all eager to see the drowned girl who had been brought back from the dead.

'Why are we doing this?' Valentan whispered to Khassian. 'We're Allegondans.'

'Haven't they got their own Temple choir?' grumbled Azare. 'I feel so . . . out out of place.'

'They need us,' Khassian said. 'They need our expertise. Our aural skills. Our voices.'

'Can't we give 'em one of your choruses, Amar?'

'No.' Khassian smiled at Azare. 'Maybe another day.'

They passed through the echoing temple and made their way down into the Undercity, which was illuminated by the flames of many lotos candles.

Khassian caught sight of Orial, standing waiting, frail as a flickering lotos flame in the darkness.

'You've come.' She reached out her hands to them in greeting. 'Thank you.'

She led the musicians to the Hall of Whispering Reeds where Jolaine Tradescar and Dr Philemot were still at work, carefully brushing back the dirt of centuries to expose the rest of the mosaic floor.

Their labours had revealed new details. The carven figure of a woman could faintly be discerned on the central stone disc, a priestess with hands cupped in front of her. And the delicate tesserae of the mosaic showed a spiralling drift of winged creatures travelling from the outer rim of the mosaic towards the central figure.

The Priestess stood silently observing their work. When Khassian and Orial drew near, she looked at Orial from beneath her veils.

'A flight of dragonflies,' she said.

Khassian thought he glimpsed them exchange a secret smile.

'Are you ready, Jolaine?' Orial called softly.

'Just one thing more.'

Jolaine Tradescar leaned over the carved figure and pressed one half of an enamel disc into her cupped hands. Philemot produced the other half and slotted it into place so that the two halves became one whole: a perfect lotos.

A deep vibration shuddered through the Hall: the floor trembled beneath their feet.

'Earthquake!' someone shouted in panic.

'Earthquake be damned!' Jolaine Tradescar shouted back. 'This is Lifhendil engineering. It's a *mechanism*.'

Khassian glanced anxiously at Orial. Suppose her miraculous resurrection was but a temporary reprieve – suppose, like the dragonflies, she would be reborn for a brief while to fulfil her task, and then die?

The Priestess raised her hands for silence.

Orial began to sing in her quiet, pure treble and as the musicians matched their voices to hers, a hush fell amongst the murmuring onlookers who were gathering outside the candlelit hall.

Orial's voice faded. She was swaying on her feet.

Jerame sprang forwards, catching her as she fell.

'This must stop,' he cried. 'She's too weak. She can't sustain it. The strain on her heart –'

'No, Papa.' Orial struggled up again, 'It must work. It will work.'

'The circle,' Jolaine Tradescar called. 'Make a circle, Orial. Remember the wall-painting?'

Orial slowly, unsteadily moved forward, beckoning the musicians to join her.

'A circle!' Khassian struck his forehead with his hand, 'It doesn't work as a chant. It's a round. I can hear it. I can hear how it fits together. Watch me – I'll bring you in.'

He peered tensely at the other musicians. Then he took in a breath and began to sing. The ancient, wordless chant echoed in the darkness, each note husky but true. He caught Valentan's eye and at his signal, Valentan joined the round. The two voices wound around each other, Valentan's ringing tenor against Khassian's baritone. And now the Priests had begun to understand the musical sense of it – they added their voices. Khassian nodded to Azare and he took counter-tenor, adding a third part to the round.

Orial was watching Amaru, her whole body taut, waiting to enter with the treble.

Khassian brought her in with a movement of the hand and her voice became a filament of sound snaking its way through the others, thin, high and pure.

Each part of the round wove into the complex spiral, a growing web of music that spun upwards until the whole hall vibrated.

The complexity of the polyphony generated from the single line of chant melody astounded Khassian. Its exquisite dissonances and resolutions made him want to weep – yet he knew he must keep singing, he must not lose the thread or the whole structure would unravel.

The floor beneath their feet had begun to vibrate in sympathy with the pulsations of the music.

And suddenly Khassian sensed that their voices had been joined by . . .

Others.

Now he could hear the rustling of many voices, intricate as the tremble of breeze-rippled windchimes, the buzzing of silver-winged bees.

A softspun light seemed to shimmer in the gloom; Khassian narrowed his eyes.

Orial was surrounded.

A phosphorescent glimmer lit the darkness of the Undercity with the eldritch light of marsh-fire.

Slowly the human singers fell silent, awed.

A wreathing circle of translucent, pulsing lights filled the chamber. From time to time a firebright thread of sound would coruscate outwards from the spinning circle. Dizzied, Khassian blinked.

They had come: a host of Eä-Endil, the Winged Ones.

It seemed the vibrations of light and sound mingled until Khassian could no longer distinguish one from the other; his senses were confused; he was *hearing* the colours, *tasting* the music. Green notes, acid-sharp, pierced his brain. Then a long, low, sustained pitch, rich as a gilded shaft of autumn sunlight. Now grey, crystalline drops of sound, cold as a spatter of winter rain . . .

Stones began to shift, ancient mechanisms, older than recorded time, creaking and groaning as the circular plinth on the floor on which Orial stood, slowly swung around. High above, a crack opened in the roof as daylight pierced the darkness, a shaft lighting up the gaping hole.

Steam rose hissing from the gulf below, and with it a spray of hot spring waters.

'The springs! The springs!' cried the Priestess.

The Priests fell to their knees. Others followed.

But Khassian still stood, staring transfixed at Orial.

Her pale face was suffused with an iridescent spectrum of light: translucent violet, rose, gold, glimmered in her hair, sapphire and emerald radiated from her eyes.

Khassian had seen the statues of Elesstar in the Temple. This was nothing like those blandly smiling figures of painted plaster. A river-spirit had risen from the reeds, a vernal goddess, ancient yet eternally young. She was the green sap pulsing, the wild fluting of the birds at dawn.

Slowly she raised her arms and a host of flying shadows appeared, clustering in the darkness.

Dragonflies . . . Huge dragonflies, as long as a man's hand. Green as bottle glass, they darted around Orial's head.

Clothed in living jewels, she stood motionless, her arms upraised.

Dragonflies swarmed over her bare breasts and arms, crowned her temples. Now her eyes reflected the colours of sky and water, the intense blue and green of her living adornments.

Khassian's heart seemed to slow, to still. Time stopped.

And then the rainbow shimmer began gradually to fade from Orial's eyes, her skin, her hair.

The spinning, ever-shifting cloud of sound was diminishing, dwindling to a distant murmur. He did not want it to stop, he wanted it to go on forever, he wanted to be a part of it –

One of the dragonflies lifted off her shoulders. The daylight caught starglints of green and sapphire in its beating wings. Caught on an updraft, it began to drift upwards towards the light. Another followed, then another and another until the air was fanned with the tremulous beat of gauze wings.

Jewelled mosaics ebbed and flowed before Khassian's eyes in a dazzling kaleidoscope.

The swirling wings eddied, formed an ascending vortex, lifting upwards, upwards towards the sky.

Each darting insect trailed a line of melody, creating a glittering contrapuntal texture of interweaving translucence.

The crowd about him gasped, swaying in rhythm with the eddying flight.

'There! There they go!' cried children's voices, shrill with excitement. There was a surge of movement amongst the watchers as they strained upwards – and the host of dragonflies rose, borne on the billowing steam, floating up, up into the pale sky beyond.

One last thread of light still encircled Orial, a thread of molten gold, warm as sunlight.

Touch of a gentle hand in the dark, a voice singing softly, stilling a child's night fears, laughter trickling back on a summer breeze . . .

'Mama?' she whispered, raising her hands. Golden light trickled through her fingers – and a gilded dragonfly followed the others up into the sky. Orial blinked, blinded by the dazzling light of the sun – and when her sight cleared, all the dragonflies were gone.

CHAPTER 28

The Hall of Whispering Reeds echoed to the hiss of hot springs. All around Orial people were laughing and hugging each other. Children crept forward to plunge their hands into the fizzing steam and ran away again, squealing with delight.

Orial's mind still glittered with the final flight of dragonflies . . . she felt light, buoyant, floating on air . . .

The real world, the everyday world, began to intrude on her consciousness. The gilded vision of the otherworld began to recede, to fade . . .

Through the rising steamclouds she saw Amaru Khassian staring dazedly at her.

'Amaru,' she said, going towards him. She felt filled with warmth and affection for him.

'I – I'm a little afraid to touch you,' he stammered.

'You helped make it happen.' She stood on tiptoes and brushed his cheek with her lips. 'For that time you became Lifhendil too. I could not have spun the song without you. One voice alone was not enough.'

'Lotos Princess!' cried Jolaine Tradescar, coming forward to hug her.

'Not any more,' she said, sadly. 'It's over now.'

'Nonsense!' The Priestess stood holding out her hands to her. 'It's just beginning.' Behind her clustered the Priests and Priestesses of the Temple, all nodding and smiling.

Orial bowed her head respectfully.

'No, child.' The Priestess gently placed her hand under Orial's chin and, raising her head, kissed her on the brow. 'You are one of us. We must talk together, we must talk of your future. But only when you have rested . . .'

'One of you?' Orial stared questioningly up into the dark-veiled face.

'Your place is here in the Temple.'

'I had never thought of myself as . . . as a Priestess.'

'Come with us now to the Temple Court and take some refreshment. There are many things you will need to know before you can make your decision.'

Beyond the beaming faces in the Temple Court Orial became aware that her father was looking at her. The sadness in his eyes belied his proud smile; she could always tell when he was dissembling.

Her decision would take her along a different path from the one he had designated for her. It would lead her from his side at the Sanatorium to the mysteries of the Under Temple.

'Papa?' she said questioningly.

He came towards her through the circle of Priestesses.

'The Priestess is right; you should rest now,' he said. He put his arms around her and she rested her head against his shoulder, feeling the worn cloth of his favourite jacket against her cheek. 'The time for decisions is yet to come. Go with them, if that is what you wish.'

'But you. Will you –' The question died on her lips.

'I'll be all right.' He finished it for her. 'I have to get back to the Sanatorium. Now that you have revealed the new source, there's plenty to do: treatment pools to be cleaned, pipes to be checked . . .'

She heard the bravado in his voice; she also heard the unspoken permission to decide for herself what she must do.

'Thank you, Papa,' she said in a whisper. 'Thank you.'

He released her and walked away without a backward glance. The Priestesses closed around her.

'Illustre!'

Khassian turned around to see Jerame Magelonne approaching through the crowd. What could the doctor possibly want to say to him?

'Illustre,' he said stiffly, 'I owe you an apology. I misjudged you. I misjudged you very badly.'

Khassian, confounded, could not think what to say in reply.

'I would ask if you would shake my hand in forgiveness . . . but I know the pain that would cause you. Instead, please accept my thanks, my heartfelt thanks, for what you have done to restore my daughter. You will always be welcome at the Sanatorium.' Dr Magelonne stepped back and gave the composer a brusque little bow.

Khassian nodded his head in gratitude. He was exhausted, emotionally spent. He needed to be alone.

'Coming for a glass of pommerie?' Azare called to him.

'You go ahead,' Khassian said. 'I'll join you later.'

'Moon and Sickle tavern!'

Khassian slipped in amongst the crowd and let himself be moved slowly forward, upward, out of the Undercity.

When he emerged, he saw it was twilight. Hours must have passed below ground without his noticing.

Sulien came alight with coloured lanterns, glittering festoons of pale jewels. Spurts of fire fizzled up, punctuated by loud retorts and cries of wonder: firecrackers, rockets and candles were being let off. The city was in celebratory mood.

In the Parade Gardens families were merrily picnicking on the grass, each picnic lit by bright flares: citrus and lime green. He wandered past aimlessly, detached from the holiday mood that had infected the city.

'Amaru!' Jolaine Tradescar hailed him; she was sitting on the grass with Theophil Philemot who was busy opening up a wicker basket. 'We've got a splendid picnic hamper here. Spit-roast chicken, salads, mountain strawberries, clotted cream ... We're waiting to see the fireworks. Won't you join us?'

'We'd be honoured,' said Theophil Philemot shyly.

Khassian shook his head, smiling. He was not hungry.

He walked slowly on beside the Avenne, leaving the lanterns and the celebrations behind. On the far side of the river the walls of the Foreigners' Cemetery loomed, a shadow against the dwindling light.

He had not come here purposely ... and yet now he found himself crossing the bridge, drawn to the solitude of the silent cemetery.

The moon was rising, casting a shimmer of silver on the graves as Khassian walked through the rustling grasses. White rose petals lay scattered over the long grasses.

The last time he had seen the cemetery by night had been in a dream. Had he hoped that he might glimpse Acir Korentan once more, Acir transfigured, holding out his hand to him?

Khassian sat down in the grass beside Acir's grave and gazed up at the star-pricked sky.

A rush of memories overwhelmed him, memories from the time those strong arms had pulled him back to life from the cold drowning waters, to that final, nightmare coach-ride when he realised that Acir was slowly slipping away from him ... and there was nothing he could do to bring him back.

They had spent so much of their short acquaintance in conflict that only now did he realise how much he had come to value Acir.

Only now did he realise that he had loved him.

As dusk fell, Jerame slowly made his way back to the Sanatorium alone.

He lit a waxen lotos candle of pure white and placed it beneath Iridial's portrait.

Distant bangs and fizzes from exploding fireworks punctuated the night's silence. He felt too weary to go lighting bonfires or fireworks. Weary – and troubled. Since that transcendent moment of revelation in the Undercity, one thing alone had obsessed him.

The translucent brightness that had irradiated the Hall of Whispering Reeds, that spinning, celestial music ...

Had Iridial been a part of it?

He picked up the lock of fair, faded hair and stroked it against his cheek.

And now he was so very, very weary.

He sat down in the chair, still holding the lock of her hair. His head nodded, his eyes slowly closed . . .

The dying lotos flame flickered beneath Iridial's portrait. The image of the dead woman shimmered in its frail glow . . . then the shimmering image seemed to emerge from the portrait within the frame.

Starting up, Jerame saw a creature, transparent as molten glass. It was clothed only in long, wild strands of hair, white as hoarfrost, and strange ichors flowed in its veins: silver, rose and gold.

'Iridial?' he said uncertainly.

'Iridial . . .' The voice vibrated in his mind, brittle as silvered windchimes. Inhuman. *'That name. Dream-name. I dreamed I was called Iridial . . .'*

Slanted eyes stared curiously up at Jerame.

Rainbow eyes.

This weirdling creature of mist and air could not be his long-lost wife. And yet there was something in that iridescent gaze that awoke a frisson of memory.

He said haltingly, 'You were my wife. Your name was Iridial. We have a daughter, Orial.'

The creature writhed away from him in a whirl of glitter-mist hair.

'Don't you remember anything? This is our house, this was your room, these are your clothes.' He picked up the fragile, faded dresses from their chest, showing them to her.

'All I remember from before . . .' the bell-like voice faltered *'. . . is the dark. Then sunlight woke me. They called to me. I dragged myself from the clinging waters and let the sun dry me. They had come for me. I was part of them, and they a part of me. The spinning circle. How long I have been one with the circle I cannot tell . . .'*

'So you don't even remember me?' Jerame let the dresses drop to the floor. 'Our life together? Our – our love?' He could hardly choke the words out.

'You are part of a dream, a distant dream . . .'

He turned away from her, angrily wiping the tears from his face. How could he explain to her? How could he put it into words?

'Do not grieve, Jerame.' For the first time she used his name. *'I am always here. I am Eä-Endil.'*

'But I'm – I'm mortal.'

'Then live as a mortal. Jerame. Be free.'

'I – I don't think I can.'

'I let you go.'

'No. Don't. Iridial.'

Flowerbreath brushing his cheek, translucent lips, rose-flushed, pressed to his.

'Now let me go, Jerame.'
'I – I don't know how.'
'The lock of hair. Burn it.'
'I – I can't.'
'Burn it.'

Shaking, he took the lock of fine, fair hair from his breast and held it to the lotos candle.

It flared into pale flame . . . and a fine, grey smoke rose up in a dwindling spiral.

She seemed to fade into the flame, to merge with its soft smoke, melting into the nothingness.

With a cry he reached out to grasp her, to hold her, to bring her back – and found he was clutching empty air.

Jerame came awake with a start. The lotos candle had burned down to a faint glow within the cupped petals.

He raised his hands . . . and saw that where he had been holding her lock of hair, his hands were dusted with a powdery ash that drifted away between his fingers.

No lingering smell of burned hair tainted the room – only the faint scent of star-lilies.

CHAPTER 29

Girim nel Ghislain knelt at his private shrine in prayer. But though his lips moved, his mind had wandered far from the words of devotion.

Why had the Rose bloomed so far from Bel'Esstar? He had dedicated his life to creating a holy city fit for the Prophet, a city where sedition and blasphemy had been ruthlessly punished. He had striven to build a temple worthy of a god, the Stronghold, the Fortress of Faith. And now came the news of a miraculous rose that had blossomed not in Mhir's shrine – but in an obscure graveyard in Sulien. The news rubbed salt into a wound still raw: the rank treachery of Acir Korentan, his sword-brother. Even bringing Acir's name to mind stirred up such bitter rage that he could no longer remember the words of the prayer.

It did not matter now. Nothing mattered except the Rose. Today they would ride to Sulien and bring the Rose back to its rightful place in Mhir's shrine.

There came a discreet tap and his secretary put his head around the door.

'The Contesse Fiammis to see you, Grand Maistre.'

Girim rose from the shrine.

'Show her in. And see we are not disturbed.'

Fiammis entered. She was in full court dress: an exquisite collier of diamonds and sapphires around her slender neck, panniered taffeta skirts over a brocade underskirt, tight-laced bodice, grey, ivory and blue, the colours of winter favoured by Prince Ilsevir. Yet above this perfection of costume, her painted face was an expressionless masquerade mask of white and she moved jerkily, like an automaton.

'Contesse.' Girim extended his hand; she took it and kissed his ring. The brush of her cold lips left a chill on his skin.

'I owe you a debt of gratitude, Contesse. You took the life of a traitor. A traitor whom I had trusted as if he were my own brother.'

'A traitor,' she repeated, the words icily precise.

'But you let Khassian get away. I'm afraid I must ask you to return to Sulien with us and complete your mission. Your new weapon,' and he indicated the grey and ivory parasol which she held in one hand, 'seems remarkably effective.'

'Yes,' she said. 'It is.'

She raised the parasol until its tip was pointing at his head.

'There is no antidote to the venom,' she said, not moving. 'Though the victim can take quite a while to die. It depends on the constitution. A strong, healthy man may last several hours. A weaker one . . . an hour at most. Which are you, Grand Maistre?'

'You're teasing me.' He essayed a little laugh and turned away to the desk to pick up a travel permit. 'Now with regard to Khassian –'

'After all Acir's years of faithful service to the Cause . . .' she said. Her voice was brittle as the trembling crystal chandeliers above their heads '. . . you had his body stripped and left unburied. Don't deny it. I was there. I heard what you said.'

He had no time to argue about insignificant matters now. The Rose had bloomed. He must ride to Sulien.

He straightened up, the travel permit in his hand.

'If it had not been for you, he would still be alive.'

She was still pointing the parasol at him – directly at his eyes.

'My dear Contesse.' Girim put up one hand, backing away. His other hand reached vainly for the bell on his desk. 'Let's discuss this. Let's –'

There was a quiet click and before he could swerve away, the dart entered his eye.

Blood flooded his vision – black blood, streaming down, blotting out the light.

From somewhere far distant he thought he heard a woman's laughter, crystalline, mirthless, manic.

And then oblivion claimed him.

Girim's secretary looked up from the letter he was penning.

What was that sudden crash in the Grand Maistre's room? And, sweet Mhir, who was that laughing?

He put down his pen and crept to the door, trying to spy through the keyhole.

She was standing with her back to the door and her whole body seemed to shake with this never-ending crazed laughter.

It sent a chill through him.

He ran into the corridor and began to shout aloud, 'Help! Murder! Help!'

Flanked by Guerriors, he flung open the doors.

She turned to face him, still laughing.

And what they saw beyond the Contesse Fiammis made them stop, staring.

Girim nel Ghislain lay on the polished floor. The body still twitched a little – but one look at the ruined eye, pooling blood on to the floor, told that the Grand Maistre was dead.

'I killed him,' she said.

The Guerriors seized hold of her, wrenching the parasol from her hands.

She did not offer any resistance.

'You – you damned murderess!' said the secretary. He felt sick. He kept finding himself stealing looks at the body of his master – and wishing he hadn't. Blood trickled sluggishly from the pierced eye, from the ear and one corner of the slack mouth.

'Murderess? I am only what he made me,' she said. 'His creature. And now I am free.'

'You'll pay the highest price for this!' He shook his fist in her face; a furious, redundant gesture. 'The question. The scaffold. A long, lingering death.'

'I have already paid – the price.' Her speech sounded slurred.

'What?'

'The venom – went straight to his – brain. It may – take – a little longer – in my case –' She suddenly slumped in the Guerriors' arms.

'Poison? You've taken poison?' He slapped her face. 'Answer me, woman!'

'Too – late –' she whispered. She began to laugh again – low, husky laughter – and then the laughter turned to a retching rattle as her head jerked upwards and her body writhed in the death-spasm.

They lowered her to the floor, stepping hastily away. The doll-like face contorted – and a froth of dark liquid appeared on the lips.

'Acir . . .' She gave a soft little sigh . . . and finally lay still.

'The Grand Maistre is dead.'

At first it was only a whispered rumour passed from guard to guard, servitor to servitor, in the gilded corridors of the Winter Palace. But soon the tocsin began to clang out over the city of Bel'Esstar.

Girim nel Ghislain was dead. Assassinated.

Cramoisy Jordelayne, labouring with the other Sanctuarees at the Fortress of Faith, heard the tocsin and looked up.

'Get back to work!' shouted the foreman, cracking his whip. 'Back to work!'

A Guerrior came riding at the gallop towards the Fortress. Several of the guards left their posts to meet him.

'Ghislain is dead!' he cried. 'Assassinated!'

A look passed between the Sanctuarees. A long look.

Cramoisy cleared his throat and started to sing.

'"Freedom".' It began as a croaked whisper – but slowly gathered tone and power as the Diva found his lost voice again.

As his brilliant tone carried upwards into the shell of the unfinished building, one by one the Sanctuarees stopped their work to listen. The voice that once had ravished the hearts and souls of his listeners, soared into the air.

' "Freedom".' Other voices joined in Khassian's chorus until the walls reverberated with the fervour of their singing.

'Be silent!' cried the foreman. 'Show some respect for the dead!'

The Sanctuarees only sang louder.

'Get those men down here at once. Have them beaten for insubordination.'

The Guerriors moved towards the ladders – and stones and tiles began to hail down on them from the high platforms.

One Guerrior was hit and fell to his knees, blood streaming from his gashed head.

A ragged cheer went up from the Sanctuarees working on the ground.

The Guerriors turned on them, blades drawn. But the unsupervised Sanctuarees had been busy with their chisels and had worked off their shackles. Now they came running forward to meet their oppressors, wielding axes, tools, mallets, anything they could lay their hands on.

'Riot! Riot!' screamed the foreman, retreating before the hail of stones from above.

Guerriors went running to seize their arquebuses, positioning themselves behind stone-wagons. Metal bolts showered into the Fortress, glancing off the soft rose-red stones, pitting them with holes.

'Go to nel Macy. Get reinforcements,' the foreman ordered the rider. '*Hurry!*'

Captain nel Macy had called the Enhirran detachment into the Sanctuary courtyard. Tobyn glanced uneasily around at his confrères; there had been no sign – or word – of Acir Korentan for several days. He suspected something had gone badly amiss.

'And it is my duty, my most regrettable duty,' said nel Macy, glaring at them, 'to inform you of the death of your former commander, Acir Korentan.'

Tobyn felt the tears start to his eyes. Acir Korentan dead? He looked around him and saw the same dumbfounded expressions on his confrères' faces.

'In regrettable – most regrettable – circumstances –'

The distant hectic clang of a warning bell interrupted nel Macy's words. He faltered a moment, frowning, and then resumed.

'Circumstances which have brought shame upon the honour of your detachment.'

'Shame?' repeated Tobyn, dashing the tears from his eyes with his knuckles. Several of his confrères began to murmur angrily together.

The din of the warning bell grew louder.

'Captain Korentan was slain whilst aiding a dangerous revolutionary to

314

escape. The Grand Maistre wants me to impress upon you –'

Fists thundered on the armoured doors of the Sanctuary. A Guerrior came running in, his face streaked with blood.

'Riot!' he cried. 'Riot – at the Fortress. Girim – Girim is dead! We need reinforcements.'

'Lock the Sanctuarees in their cells!' ordered nel Macy. 'Noonwatch, fetch your arquebuses. At the double!'

No one moved.

'At once!' barked nel Macy.

'Stay where you are!' Tobyn leapt up on to the steps beside him.

'Get down, man, and do as you're ordered!' said nel Macy.

'We're Captain Korentan's men.' Tobyn folded his arms across his chest. 'And we take our orders from him.'

'Th-this is insubordination,' spluttered nel Macy. 'There'll be a riot here. A stampede. They'll massacre us all!'

The wide curve of the Crescent opened up before Khassian as he turned the corner . . . and faltered a moment. The last time he had come this way it had been night and the Constabulary had been waiting to arrest him: prelude to a nightmare, a nightmare from which he had not yet fully awoken. He saw the sunlight warming the rose-stone pillars and pediments, he saw the cedars on the broad lawns, the evidence of his eyes told him that he was in Sulien. But a part of him still cowered in the dark cells of the Sanctuary, listening in fear for the tread of the guards.

Would he ever be wholly free again?

He walked determinedly up to Mistress Permay's house.

The mistress of the house opened the door to him – and, seeing who it was, took a step backward.

'Oh! It's you.' Her expression was that of the housewife who goes for a pan of fresh milk only to find it has turned sour. 'You owe me two months' rent. I could have let that apartment ten times over! Off you go without a word, leaving all your belongings strewn about –'

'Ah, yes.' Khassian stepped forward. 'My music, Mistress Permay. What have you done with my music?'

'I don't recall any music.'

'A fir-green portfolio containing many sheets. It was left on the escritoire.'

'What? That pile of old papers left in the salon? I gave 'em to the kitchens when I cleared out. Waste not, want not. They're cheaper than buying spills to light the –'

'The kitchens!' Khassian pushed past her, making for the servants' stair beyond the elegant hall.

'Where d'you think you're going, young man?' Mistress Permay's voice rose to an outraged shriek.

Khassian hurried down the poky stair, past the pantry and into the kitchen. A scullery maid looked up in surprise from the colander of peas she was shelling; the floor at her feet was covered in empty pods.

A black cooking range was set in the chimney alcove behind her. A massive pile of papers stood beside it – mostly, it seemed, yellowing copies of the *Sulien Chronicle*.

Khassian began clumsily to sort through the pile, discarding *Chronicles* to left and to right.

'Whatever are you doing?' Mistress Permay was quivering with anger: even the frilled mob cap set atop her wig seemed to have taken on a life of its own. 'Stop at once, young man, or I shall send for the constable!'

The scullery maid was giggling behind her hand.

'Aha!' Khassian had spotted the green portfolio. He pulled it from the pile: pages of manuscript spilled out, all covered in Orial's wayward hand. He shuffled them back into the portfolio and, clasping the precious manuscript to his breast, stood up to confront Mistress Permay.

'I warn you –' she began.

'If I find one page – just one page – has been burned,' he said, trembling, '*I* shall sue.' He turned on his heel and left the kitchen. As he climbed the stairs, he heard the scullery maid explode into laughter – soon cut short by a loud slap.

Khassian went directly with his manuscript to the qaffë house where Valentan and Azare were employed.

Yet when he arrived, no strains of music drifted out into Guildhall Square. Were they still abed, recovering from last night's celebrations? He scanned the busy qaffë house, peering through the blue tobacco smoke for his friends.

'Over here, Amar!' called Valentan from the corner table.

'Welcome, Illustre.' The proprietor came out, bowing and smiling, ushering Khassian to their table. 'It's an honour to serve you. What will you have?'

Khassian looked questioningly at the musicians.

'It's on the house,' Valentan said, smiling.

'Qaffë then, I thank you . . .'

'Such music,' the proprietor said, kissing his fingers as he hurried away. 'Such heavenly music.'

Khassian sat down between the two musicians and placed the precious opera manuscript on the table.

Outside in the square a shrill voice began to shout.

'Rescued from the flames. Mistress Permay was planning to use it to light the kitchen range –'

The shouting became louder. Customers in the qaffë house crowded into the window to see what was amiss.

'What in hell's name is going on out there?' Khassian got up from his chair.

'S-s-soldiers!'

A boy, wheezing and panting for breath, his face scarlet with the exertion, collapsed on the Guildhall steps.

'Did you hear?' Khassian said to Valentan and Azaré. He went to the door; the other two followed, Valentan picking up the manuscript.

The boy was gesticulating wildly, jabbing his finger towards the foothills.

The Mayor appeared on the steps.

'S-sieur Mayor –'

'Now, lad, get your breath. What do you mean, soldiers?'

'Allegondan soldiers. Hundreds and hundreds of them. Coming d-down the mountain road.'

'The Rose,' said Khassian. 'Of course. They've come to take the Rose.'

'Send for the garrison!' shouted the Mayor in a panic.

'They're twenty leagues' ride away,' called someone.

'Then call out the Militia! The Constabulary! Get the women and children into the Undercity!'

People ran to and fro in confusion. Constables appeared clutching ancient weapons.

'I have to stop them,' Khassian said.

'Stop the Commanderie?' Azaré said with a bitter laugh. 'You might as well try to stop a thunderstorm.'

When word reached the Temple Court that Allegondan soldiers had been seen approaching the city, Orial went directly to the Priestess.

'They have come for the Rose.'

'It is not theirs to take,' the Priestess said. 'And we shall tell them so.'

Orial set out with the Temple cortège; as they approached the river, she heard someone calling her name.

She paused, then looked around.

Amaru Khassian was running towards her, weaving through the growing crowd of onlookers. She whispered to the Priestess . . . and then moved aside from the cortège to wait for him.

A dust-cloud shimmered on the brow of the hill; the soldiers were approaching.

'He was one of the Commanderie,' said Orial, 'so they have come to claim their own . . .'

'As far as the Commanderie is concerned, he was a rebel, a traitor,' said Khassian.

'I would not have them desecrate his grave,' she whispered.

'You know they are capable of perpetrating all manner of atrocities in the name of the faith.'

Orial stared up into Khassian's eyes and saw that he was afraid.

'Let me speak to them.' She was afraid too. But she would not let the Guerriors of the Commanderie intimidate her. Acir's last gift of life had restored the springs to the city. His rightful resting place was in Sulien.

A hastily mustered band of the Sulien Constabulary assembled on the bridge under the command of the Commissaire, brandishing muskets.

Khassian held one hand to his brow to shield his eyes against the hazy sunshine of late-afternoon. What he saw stirred up sick, chill feelings of fear, only half-buried since his escape from the Sanctuary.

Guerriors.

A mounted cohort of the Commanderie was coming towards the bridge. In their midst was a gilded carriage, drawn by a team of greys.

'Ilsevir,' breathed Khassian.

'What did you say, Illustre?' The Mayor came pushing through the crowd to Khassian's side. 'The Prince of Allegonde himself? Why didn't he send word ahead to us? We could have prepared a welcome ceremony.'

A liveried servitor jumped down from behind the carriage and held open the door; Ilsevir stepped out and gazed at the assembled crowds.

The Mayor came forward, bowing.

'Altesse, if we had known you were to honour us with your presence, we would have –'

'This is no state visit,' Ilsevir said, 'but a simple, personal journey of faith. A pilgrimage.'

'To Sulien?' said the Mayor, confused.

'We have heard the news of the miracle. Where is the Rose?' His voice was charged with excitement.

Khassian steeled himself; he came out of the crowd and bowed to Ilsevir.

'Altesse.'

'Amaru?' Ilsevir had obviously not expected to encounter him in Sulien; his face clouded momentarily.

'You wish to see the Rose?' Khassian extended one hand in the direction of the cemetery. 'Follow me, Altesse.'

The attendants started forward but Khassian shook his head.

'The Prince alone.'

Ilsevir hesitated – but then signalled to his attendants to wait.

The Foreigners' Cemetery drowsed in the morning sun as Khassian led the Prince past the neglected graves. Sun-silvered grasses grew knee-high. They waded through them, lulled by the drone of insects; bees and cicadas, a summer sound.

Orial rose from the grass where she had been sitting, waiting.

'Is this what you have come to see, Altesse?'

The single green spray grew out of the raw earth of Acir's grave. No fresh buds had appeared.

'Is this some Sulien hoax?' Ilsevir asked coldly. 'I see no Rose!'

'Why should we seek to deceive you?' Khassian felt his face flame, angered by the Prince's reaction. 'Look at my hands, Altesse. See the scars left by the thorns where I picked the Rose. And this girl who stands before you . . . is the girl restored to life by the Blood of the Rose.'

Ilsevir looked from Khassian to Orial and back again; he seemed confused, unable to comprehend what Khassian was saying.

'You . . . received the Blood of the Rose?'

'I did, Altesse.'

'But – but who lies buried here?'

'A simple soldier of the Commanderie.' Khassian swallowed. 'His name was Acir Korentan.'

'I don't remember the name.' Ilsevir clapped his hands. Two Guerriors appeared at the gate to the cemetery; they carried spades.

'What are you doing!' Khassian cried. 'You're not going to dig it up –'

'It belongs in Bel'Esstar. In the shrine.'

'You must not uproot it,' Orial said. Her voice was calm and clear. 'It belongs here.'

One of the Guerriors jabbed his spade deep into the earth

'No!' cried Khassian, starting forwards.

The Guerrior recoiled, yelping. His hand was torn and bleeding from the hooked thorns.

'For Mhir's sake! Give me the spade!' The Prince seized the spade and moved towards the grave.

Khassian instinctively drew closer to Orial and both placed themselves in front of the Rose. Ilsevir hesitated. And as they stared at each other the sound of galloping hooves disturbed the bee-droned stillness of the cemetery.

A messenger, caked in dust, came running into the cemetery and fell to his knees before the Prince.

'You must return, Altesse!' he gasped. 'Girim nel Ghislain is dead. The Sanctuary has fallen to the Sanctuarees. The city is in uproar. They're calling for your abdication.'

'Dead?' Ilsevir staggered. The spade dropped to the ground. 'Girim is dead?' He put out a hand shakily towards Khassian.

'Amar – help me.' He had gone very pale. 'What shall I do?'

Khassian faltered and then took Ilsevir's outstretched hand in his own, maimed hands, supporting him.

'What shall I do without him?'

'Sit down, Altesse,' Khassian said quietly.

'My own city,' Ilsevir whispered. 'Turned against me.'

'Not against you, Altesse.' Khassian knelt beside him. 'But against censorship. Against repression.'

Ilsevir turned to him, mouth twisted, working with anguish. 'I – I believe I may have made a terrible mistake –'

Khassian gazed at him.

'Is it too late, Amar?

'No!' Khassian said, impassioned. 'Free the Sanctuarees, Altesse. Send word ahead to the Sanctuary now – before the slaughter gets out of hand.'

'Come back with me, Amar. They'll listen to you. Come back – and help me restore order.'

Back to Bel'Esstar – and to the Prince's favour. Khassian could sense Orial watching him intently, waiting to hear his response.

'But I'm still a wanted man. I barely escaped Allegonde with my life.'

'I've wronged you.' Ilsevir gently touched his hands. Khassian could sense the Prince make a supreme effort of will to overcome his squeamishness and to force himself to look at, to touch, the burned skin. 'Forgive me, Amar. I treated you cruelly. Maybe I don't deserve your forgiveness. But for the city's sake, and for the sake of your fellow musicians, come back.'

Khassian glanced up and met Orial's gaze; the rainbow eyes glittered overbright, sun through rain. She nodded her head.

'Bel'Esstar is your home,' she whispered. 'You must go back.'

Beneath her words, Khassian heard Acir's dying voice whispering to him on that night of storm and thunder.

'You have a great gift . . . use it to set the city free.'

He turned back to Ilsevir. 'I will come with you.'

CHAPTER 30

The life of the Temple Court gradually drew Orial in and although she still lived with her father in the Sanatorium, she spent more and more of her time with the Priestess, learning the secrets of the rituals of the Under Temple. But in rare moments of idleness, she found her eyes straying to the heat-haze that veiled the distant mountains from sight and wondering if Khassian had forgotten her.

The *Sulien Chronicle* reported extraordinary events in distant Bel'Esstar following the assassination of Girim nel Ghislain, culminating in the freeing of all dissidents and rebels incarcerated in the prison known as the Sanctuary. Apparently the Enhirran detachment of the Commanderie had rebelled against their Commander and sided with the rebels. Then, in an unprecedented gesture, Prince Ilsevir had decreed that the Commanderie of the Rosecoeur should renounce its weapons; henceforth its members were to choose between military service in the Prince's army or a life of prayer. Priests were no longer permitted to bear arms in the service of Mhir. But there was scant mention of Amaru Khassian and the *Chronicle* soon returned to its usual listings of Sulien's eminent visitors and scandalous gossip.

Soon afterwards the first of the Allegondan pilgrims began to arrive; confrères from the disbanded Enhirran detachment came to pay their last respects at the grave of their captain. Several, led by one young Guerrior called Tobyn, requested the Temple Court that they might create a garden shrine in the cemetery where pilgrims might rest. The Temple Court was pleased to grant them permission . . . and Orial sometimes left her duties at the Temple to help them clear away the tangled weeds and plant sweet-scented herbs and plants in the borders.

Sulien in late-summer always reminded Orial of a full-blown peony: drooping and blowsily past its best. A stir of breeze at dusk was always welcome after the sleepy humidity of the long day's heat.

On one such evening, she was standing at her open window, listlessly fanning herself, wishing for a breeze.

A phaeton drew up outside the Sanatorium; Orial leaned out of the window dangerously far to try to see who the new arrivals were.

'What do you mean, who are we?' The arch tones rose vibrantly on the warm air. 'Don't you recognise the toast of Bel'Esstar, my good man?

Announce Cramoisy Jordelayne to Demselle Magelonne and be quick about it.'

'Cramoisy!' shrieked Orial. Forgetting all decorum, she came running downstairs and threw herself into the Diva's arms.

'Orial!' The Diva smothered her in a perfume-drenched embrace and then held her at arm's length to look at her. 'More radiant then ever.'

'And you – you –' Orial struggled for words to describe the Diva's new costume. 'You look gorgeous.'

'I am rather proud of this outfit.' Cramoisy turned around to display the full effect. 'See the cut of the jacket – lapels and cuffs trimmed in black and magenta to match the striped breeches.'

'But your voice –' Orial said.

'Not quite restored yet. The doctors have told me to pamper it. So I thought a little Sulien steam treatment might do the trick. But there I go, babbling on – when there's someone here who is eager to see you too.'

The Diva drew back with an elaborate gesture to reveal – Amaru Khassian standing in the doorway, watching them with a slight, wry grin.

'Amaru.' Orial could not move. Her feet seemed glued to the floor. 'I – I didn't expect –'

And then she flew across the room and into his arms.

Cramoisy insisted on taking them out to dinner at one of the most expensive restaurants in Sulien.

When they had dined and were sitting on the terrace, sipping qaffë and nibbling sugar-dusted almonds, Cramoisy drew out a tissue-wrapped package and placed it in front of Orial.

'What's this?' she said.

'Open it.' Cramoisy gave Khassian a sly wink.

Orial untied the gold ribbon and unwrapped the tissue. There lay a necklace and earrings of black and ivory pearls – her mother's pearls.

She glanced first at Cramoisy and then at Khassian.

'But how ever did you find them?'

'I have my methods,' said Cramoisy archly.

'You bought them back? You shouldn't have.'

'Put them on. I want to see you in them!'

Orial, blushing, did as Cramoisy asked.

He gave her a long, appraising look – and then clapped his hands together.

'Perfection. Isn't that so, Amar?'

'Hm?'

Orial saw Cramoisy nudge Khassian sharply.

'Yes, yes. They look very becoming.'

After they had brought her back to the Sanatorium, she stood in the hall, still fingering Iridial's pearls, listening to the phaeton wheels rolling away into the night.

The pearls felt cool and smooth against her skin. What had preoccupied Khassian tonight? Why had his attention wandered? Perhaps he had been bored, longing for the evening to end.

Perhaps he had felt it was a mistake to come back.

'Someone to see you,' Cook announced. 'I've put him in the parlour. You won't be disturbed in there.'

'Someone?' Orial came running out after her. 'Who? Who is it?'

But Cook had retreated into the kitchens.

Orial opened the parlour door – and saw Khassian standing at the window. She felt her breath catch in her throat. Why had he come?

He turned as he heard the door open.

'Demselle.'

'So formal, Illustre?' She came into the parlour and shut the door, gesturing him to a chair.

'So bemused.' He sat at the lace-covered table; she sat opposite. 'When I returned to Bel'Esstar, all that had happened here seemed like . . . like a dream. I began to wonder if I had imagined it all. And now, I come back and find you still here – and I have to believe it really happened.'

Maybe this was prelude to a proposition . . . maybe he wanted her to work with him again?

'. . . those other lesser miracles that followed in the wake of the Rose.'

'Other miracles?' She had not been paying attention to what he was saying, she had been watching his face intently, noting the tawny flecks in his eyes, the pale sickle scar on his left cheek.

'Cramoisy has found his voice again . . . and I . . .'

'You?' She could tell from the light in his eyes that he had a secret he was longing to share with her.

'Look.' He fumbled in his pocket and brought out a pencil and paper. He gripped the stub of pencil and clumsily, painstakingly, began to trace out clefs. She watched his face as he worked, saw how the muscles in his cheeks were drawn taut, how every fibre of his body strained to control the movement of his hand.

'See?' He stopped with a gasp of exertion. 'It's damnably slow – but I'm getting there, Orial, I'm getting there.'

'It's . . . very good.'

All her hopes, so swiftly raised, were dashed again.

'If I persevere, there's a chance I might get something scribbled down that Azare can transcribe.'

'So . . . you won't be needing me any more.'

'As amanuensis? It would be selfish of me to ask you to fritter your life away transcribing my music – when you have music of your own to write.'

'You're just saying that because – because you don't want me.'

He reached out across the table to touch her hands with his own.

'No. I've had time to reflect on our encounters – our musical encounters.' His hands tightened around hers and she felt a new strength in the fingers. 'The way I compose is so different from yours, Orial. Forcing you to think my way, to write my way, was wrong. You have to find your own voice, unhindered by my music. Can't you see?'

She shook her head; her eyes had filled with tears.

'Then why are you here?' she said in a whisper.

He reached into his breast pocket and drew out a card edged in gold.

'What is this?' she said in a whisper, taking it.

'Read it.'

The Demselle Orial Magelonne is cordially invited to
attend the first performance of the newly revised opera
Elesstar *by Amaru Khassian to be given at the*
Orangery in the Winter Palace.

She looked up from the smooth white invitation and saw his eyes.

'The opera – *our* opera.'

'Prince Ilsevir has requested three performances to be staged in the theatre in the Palace Orangery. All the performers will be handsomely remunerated – which may go some way towards making reparation for so many ruined lives.'

'Such a change of heart.' She tried to gulp back her tears. Selfish, really, to be thinking of herself when so many had been brought to the brink of despair.

'Ilsevir is greatly changed since Girim's death. He often asks me to tell him about Acir . . . and about you.'

'Me?' Orial said, confused.

'None of this could have taken place if it had not been for you, Orial,' he said softly. 'Your courage gave me the strength to write the opera anew. Please say you'll come and see it? Cramoisy will be mortally offended if you don't see him give the performance of his life.'

Orial broke away from him and went to the window, gazing out over the grey-green hills, the terraces and crescents of weathered rose-stone.

What had she been expecting? Cramoisy had been right all along, although she had refused to acknowledge it until now; for Amaru Khassian the music would always come first. They had shared a unique meeting of minds – and he had come to offer her the chance to share in that experience again; the music was the only way he could express his love and gratitude.

She could not refuse.

Besides, it was the first opportunity in her life to fulfil her long-cherished wish: to attend an opera.

'Very well.' She turned around to face him, smiling through her tears. 'I accept – with pleasure. But you must promise me one thing. That you will come to the Temple again before you leave for Bel'Esstar. Tomorrow.'

The young Lotos Priestess walked through the Undercity; as she passed the portal to the Hall of Whispering Reeds, a gust of steam stirred her hair, stirred the petals of the star-lilies she carried.

'And then the extraordinary genius of the Lifhendil was revealed to us when the ancient mechanism was triggered . . .'

Within, Jolaine Tradescar was explaining her discoveries to a group of visiting Antiquarians from the University of Can Tabrien. The Priestess smiled secretly to herself as she went on her way to lay star-lilies on Iridial's shrine. There she lifted out her cithara, tuned it carefully and retraced her steps.

Priests and Priestesses had gathered by the springs; she bowed her head to them and took her place. Settling the cithara against her shoulder, she took up the plectrum and struck a flurry of notes.

Orial lifted her head and sang. She sang the music she had been born to sing, the thread that linked her with the distant musicmakers of the past.

And as she sang, she scanned the assembled watchers . . . until she caught sight of a man standing aloof from the others, a man whose utter stillness told her that he was listening with rapt attention.

He had come.

Her clear voice rang out, piercing the drifting mists from the steam, darting like a dragonfly into the higher registers, lifting towards the light.